UNIVIRTUAL

UNIVIRTUAL

Charles O'Donnell

Moon Lit. Publishing
Westerville, Ohio
www.moonlitpub.com

11-19-2022

Author's website: www.charlesodonnellauthor.com

ISBN: 1-970041-11-0
ISBN-13: 978-1-970041-11-8

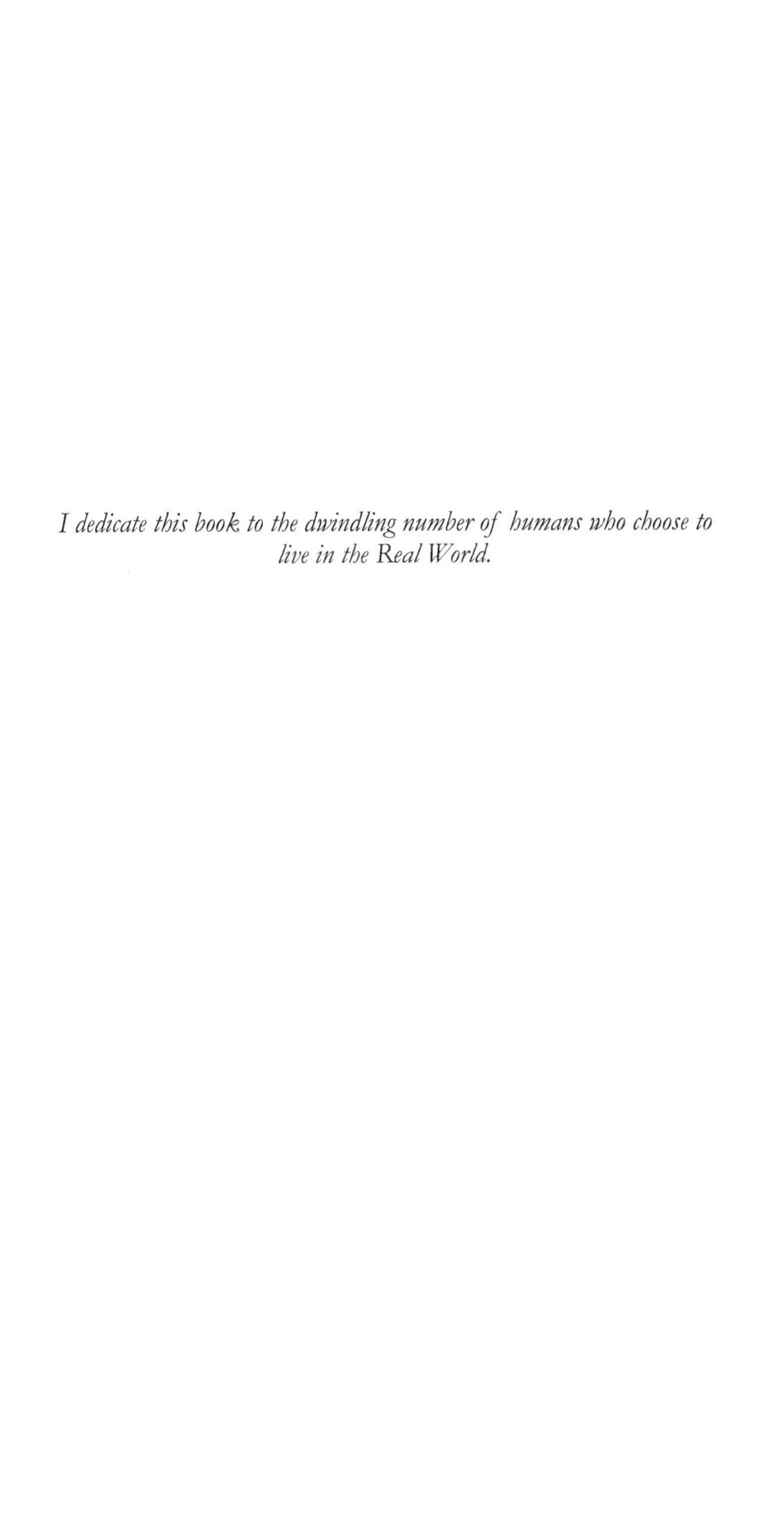

*I dedicate this book to the dwindling number of humans who choose to
live in the Real World.*

Also by Charles O'Donnell

The Girlfriend Experience (Matt Bugatti #1)
Moment of Conception (Matt Bugatti #2)
Shredded: A Dystopian Novel (Shredded #1)
Shade (Shredded #2)

Contents

Part Three—Univirtual

Part One

A Brief History of the Worldstream

1

The People's Assembly

MIRJA WAS THE first. Since then, who knows? I've lost count. Hundreds? Oh, sure.

MEER-ya. M-I-R-J-A. She didn't want it. She didn't even know about it. She was dead, for Jah's sake.

But I'm skipping ahead. Back to the massacre.

You know how we did school back then, right? We had online classes, some VR venues, but they were crappy. Most classes I climbed out of bed at some ungodly hour and dragged my tired ass to an RL classroom. A mile and a half on foot—rain, snow, sun if I was lucky, but Chicago's not a sunny clime. Jah, listen to me—I'm turning into my granddad.

Chicago was in Illinois. They teach you that in history class, right? Our fifty, nifty United States? We had to learn 'em all by name *and* their capitals. Every state had a capital, with a *state government*. We had this crazy idea that folks could govern *themselves*, you know, at the *local* level? See how that makes sense if we're not all in one homogenized Worldstream, no states, no borders, only meaningless districts? In RL, geography *matters*.

Right. The massacre.

One rare sunny day I'm walking across campus, headed to a seminar. The topic is—guess what?—the *Worldstream*. We'd heard the rumors, but nothing concrete. The Consortium had just formed, announced the new architecture, and released the spec. They'd gone on tour, hitting all the comp sci hot spots, like UC.

University of Chicago. My alma mater.

The Worldstream was all we talked about, me and Porter, a Black kid from South Chicago I'd known since forever, and the rest of the geek squad. Mirja, too, although she had *other* interests. This People's Assembly thing. You know *that* name, right? The P.A.? I thought so. Mirja was into the P.A. deep.

So, half hour before the seminar starts, I'm passing the quad—big, open space in the middle of campus—and I hear a rumble, like crashing surf only muffled, and some guy with a bullhorn talking over the noise, all garbled, but you can tell he means business. The crowd (now they say) is in the thousands, filling up the whole quad. I don't *plan* to go there, but once I'm in earshot, curiosity takes over and I detour.

From the back of the crowd, I see the bullhorn guy on the steps of the admin building. If you don't know him, you can't describe him, he's that far away and he has a bullhorn stuck in his face. But *I* know him—Chas Royce.

Yeah, *that* Chas Royce, screaming through that bullhorn, all distorted like an over-modulated voice synthesizer. He sounds clearer from inside the quad, but it doesn't matter if the crowd can't get what he's saying. He's not telling them anything they haven't heard a hundred times. He's getting them amped up, like a preacher at a tent revival.

A *tent revival.* It's like…never mind. Not important.

And amped they are. The ones in the back, where I am, aren't *too* riled up…yet. They might be curious, like me, and not really into the whole P.A. thing. But the ones up front, who got there an hour early, the kind who never shut up about the ball-less government, broken alliances, Russian aggression, and Chinese hegemony—Jah, *that* got tiresome fast—all *those* folks are waving their signs, jumping around, pushing forward like a mob on Black Friday.

Black Friday. It was the day after Thanksgiving. Biggest shopping day of the year.

Anyway, Chas yells, "What order?" and they all go, *"New order!"* "Whose assembly?" *"People's Assembly!"* On and on, yada yada, until the back-and-forth morphs into one solid roar, crowd jumping, signs flapping, until they tire out and Chas starts in again.

"Do you vote?" he asks, and the crowd goes, "No!" and he says "I don't blame you! You get to the polls, you look at the ballot, and what do you see? Self-serving bureaucrats in fossilized factions who don't give a *shit* about America! It took us 250 years to sink this low, but here we are. Patriotism? Dead! Public service? Dead! More perfect union? What a joke! Americans were the *heroes* of the world, now we're the *bums*—because petty politicians put party and power ahead of America! They get rich while *you pay!*"

That gets them going. Is there anything more vexing than being taken? Even if you've already bought the con, nobody likes being a mark.

They keep up the yelling, hoarse and red-faced. Even the looky-loos in the back get into it. One guy in a black sweater comes at me, wild-eyed, shouting, "Whose side are you on?" I think he's going to knock me down. I back away, and he keeps coming. Then he turns this way and that and goes after another slacker. That's my cue to get the hell out of there, not waiting for their enthusiasm to fizzle, and for Chas to fire up the call-and-response and boot the cycle back to main.

I circle the crowd and leave by a side path toward the comp sci building. The Guard troops are right there, helmets and shields in front, rifles behind. I don't remember seeing them, but I must have. Who could miss them?

❖ ❖ ❖

Yeah, I knew Chas. Chas thought of Mirja as his protégé. He spent a lot of time at Mirja's and my apartment—no, *really,* he did—and the two of them'd yak all night about crumbling alliances, and paralysis, and how the Earth is burning up and nothing's getting done about it because we're all a bunch of limp dicks, all over the world, but especially the U.S. It was hard to argue with them on the facts, since it was so obvious, what with another major weather-related disaster every month, saber-rattling in Europe, and China stepping up in every international crisis while America sits on her *ass*, and yet another high-ranking politician getting indicted just because he was stupider than the other crooks too smart to get caught. When they got into it, I usually checked out and let them reinforce each other's foregone conclusions while I did my own stuff—until Chas hit on his favorite subject. That's when I couldn't stay out of it anymore, when Chas went off on the "rickety, antiquated American framework."

"Corruption, impotence, abuse of power," Chas'd tick off his usual list of grievances. "Our biggest problem is, we can't solve big problems." The guy was a great debater, armed with the facts, able to counter every objection. He'd lay out his cool, calculated case for upheaval while I'd sputter, and Mirja would look at the floor.

So, I meet Porter at the seminar, which is an eye-opener. Up to then, VR had been a gaming platform, a fantasy world, where a player could be anything, look like anyone, be totally anonymous. But the Worldstream is *simulated real life*, where all the avatars look just like their owners, identities verified by a foolproof algorithm. And the architecture is genius— supports an almost *unlimited* number of avatars in the same place at the same time. Turning it into a real platform would be a vast undertaking, but for the first time, we see a path— and the endpoint is awesome: instant face-to-face interaction, massive cost and energy savings—we can feel the excitement in the hall.

Until the phones start beeping.

A hundred go off at once, all telling us the same thing: *Shooting in progress—campus lockdown—initiate active shooter protocol—all students and staff shelter in place.*

Well, I don't have to tell you that's the end of the seminar. All around me folks are calling out, trying to find out what's happening. I'd call Mirja, but I'm not quite ready to start speaking to her again, and I'm not sure she knows anything I don't know anyway. It's about the time someone in the back shouts, "There's a shooting in the quad!" that my phone buzzes again, this time with a text message from Chas.

UC trauma center—meet me—hurry.

2

A Bad Call

In Chicago, we had twenty, thirty shootings *every weekend*. We got numb to it, didn't even react unless some maniac went off and blew away a dozen or more at a time—which happened about twice a month in America.

I'm not making that up. That's why every school, church, movie theater, shopping mall, *and* college had a plan if ever an *active shooter* got loose. *Our* plan was for everyone to hunker in their classrooms and bolt the doors and stay put until the cops sorted things out.

Which is what happens next, or should, except the speaker is from Chain Corporation, one of the Consortium companies, and of course *he* has no clue about "active shooter protocols." The sponsor, a comp sci professor with no sense of organization, panics and starts for the door. Some guy in the back yells "*Lockdown!*" and points at the big, red button on the wall by the exit, but the prof is out the door in two seconds without hitting it. Five students head down the stairs for the button but the first one trips and the rest stack up behind him.

While that pile sorts itself out I tell Porter, "I'm going," but he grabs my arm and says, "Stay put." I twist out of his grip and make it to one of the back doors, opening it just as someone punches the button. The door slams shut behind me. The magnetic locks engage. Porter and the rest are sealed in for the duration.

The hospital's a mile from comp sci and I sprint the whole way, passing freaked-out folks running like from a zombie horde. I'm huffing by the time I get to the trauma center and turn the corner.

The lot is jammed, people filling in the spaces between squad cars and ambulances, and more vehicles are coming, blowing their sirens, flashing blue and red, until the crowd parts and lets them through. Some don't wait. Bodies are climbing up the hoods and rolling off the sides; people are banging on the windows of cop cars and on the sides of ambulances. One ambulance stops a good thirty yards from the entrance with no way forward, and the EMTs fling open the doors and pull out the stretcher, one of them holding an IV bottle high and the other backing through the crowd, elbowing them aside.

I check my phone.

UC trauma center—meet me—hurry. Chas's text message is ten minutes old.

I'm taller than most of the crowd. Craning my neck, I try to size up the situation near the entrance. The closer to the hospital, the crazier it looks. Another stretcher comes by, the lead guy seemingly an expert at parting crowds, so I let him run interference while I draft in his wake. I get to within twenty yards of the door when a cop almost as tall as me and half again as wide blocks my way.

"No admittance," he rumbles, like an oracle.

"I have family in there," I say, but I don't, of course. I'm crafting a convenient lie.

"You're not injured. No admittance," he repeats, like I missed it the first time.

He's in no mood to haggle, so I stand aside for the next stretcher. I tap into my phone:

Outside 50ft from door.

I'm not the only one trying to get in. The lady next to me is screaming like her baby just got snatched, I mean going *ape*, shouting, "Diedre! Diedre!" I don't know if she's hoping Diedre's in the crowd, or if Diedre's inside and she thinks she can scream loud enough for Diedre to hear. The cop is unmoved.

"Raúl!" I hear my name coming from the direction of the building. I see Chas at the door, and he looks ragged, shirt soaked through with blood, and blood on his face, too. He bullies his way through the crowd, and the police get in front of him, but all he has to say is, "I'm Chas Royce!" and they let him pass.

I'm not going anywhere in the crowd, but Chas gets to me in no time and grabs my arm, leaving bloody fingerprints on my sleeve.

"It's Mirja," he says.

He drags me through the crowd while I'm processing that. Every obstacle he comes up against he says the magic words, "Chas Royce!" and the crush parts like the sea before the chosen people.

However insane the scene is on the sidewalk, it's a thousand times crazier inside. Casualties are lined up two deep by the wall, some sitting, some standing, mostly minor injuries from the looks of them, but a few who are bleeding profusely. I'm suffocating in the heat, the sour sweat smell mixed with the iron tang of blood up in my nose starting to turn my stomach. I really don't want to retch in that crowd, so I'm holding my nose and clutching my gut. Chas is blazing a trail to the admittance window, and the six or so nurses or whatever they are behind the window are full frenetic, phones, papers, clipboards hovering between them, ignoring the babble from heads poked through the opening, and from the tiers of people squeezing in behind them. We hit a wall two yards out, with Chas still yelling, "I'm Chas Royce!" which isn't making an impression on the masses.

"Chas, what happened?" I ask him, but he's still pushing and doesn't hear me. I grab his arm and pull him back, like I'm blowing the play dead after forward progress.

That's a football term. *American* football.

"Chas, *what's going on?"* I shout in his face.

He gives up trying to get to the window. "The fucking Guard!" he yells. "They opened up on us."

You've studied it, right? So you know what went down. The feds, specifically the president, being the paranoid prick *he* was, deputized the Illinois Guard and put them in the quad to "preserve the peace." Get that? Keeping us safe from a bunch of college kids. The Commander in Chief made out the People's Assembly to be a public menace, and armed troops were his way of showing he took this dire threat seriously. So, he sent in the Guard. It was a bad call.

Chas had the audience foaming at the mouth, and those Guardsmen were a symbol of everything they and the entire P.A. movement despised. So, when Chas went on about "these fucking motherfucking lying, stealing motherfuckers," those soldiers turned into a stand-in for the hated regime and the kids closest to the line got abusive. That sentiment spread like a juicy rumor and in minutes the whole quad was screaming for blood.

"It was a nasty scene," Chas says, "and getting worse. I knew I had to calm them down, and I tried, but by then they were crowding the soldiers and the soldiers were trying to hold the line. Christ, those Guardsmen weren't much older than the students, and they were terrified. I could see it in their faces and how they gripped their rifles like they were hugging a baby blanket. The crowd kept pushing, and the front line kept pushing back with their shields, when one or two in front unholstered their nightsticks and flailed away. When the blood started flowing, that's when it turned really ugly."

And you know what happened next.

"What about Mirja?" I yell.

"Lost in the crowd," he yells back. "I can't reach her."

"Is she hurt?" I ask.

"I don't know," he says. "She was near the Guard where the stampede was when they started shooting. She might be hurt, or just out of touch. All I know is, she's not answering her phone."

I must look scared shitless, because Chas's eyes open wide, then he spins back to the window and shouts, *'I'm Chas Royce!'* over and over, but no one's letting him pass.

I watch this for about ten seconds before I shove Chas and eight or ten others aside and come through the window at the attending nurses, grab a clipboard and pinwheel it across the room. Lucky for me, the nurse sees it coming and deflects it with her arm.

As hard as it was for Chas and me to get to the window, the cops don't have any trouble at all, and they grab me from behind, get me in a very effective choke hold, and pull me out the entrance. They must have their hands full with other crises because they don't do anything else to me, like charging me with assault or disorderly, but dump me on the sidewalk, where I sit trying to sort things out in my mind while insanity rages around me.

3

Hero of the Common Man

It's natural to grab hold of a promise and attach all the world's problems to it, especially if you're young. It's a way to tidy up a messy world—makes everything *so* simple.

Virtual Reality was *my* cure-all. It doesn't have to make sense. I was a kid.

Start with climate. All the carbon we burned moving *people* to *places* would stay in the ground if instead we moved *places* to *people*—synthesized virtual experiences served up to whomever, whenever. And world peace. Seriously, we believed that. Any number of people from any number of nations meeting face-to-face at a minute's notice, everyone in the venue talking their own language—conflicts instantly addressed and resolved. But what conflicts? What would we fight over with all of human experience available to anyone at any time—the complete democratization of luxury?

That's what *I* was thinking, anyway. So was Mirja. She was in comp sci, too, and excited about VR, but not like me. She was a romantic. I loved the tech, she loved the promise. I'd have been happy coding the rest of my days, making virtual worlds out of nothing, and if I solved global warming and ended armed conflict, that'd be gravy. Mirja came at it from the other direction. She wanted to save the world and everyone in it.

"Raúl," she'd say, like she was talking to a child, "do you think all it'll take to make a utopia of the real world is to build a fake one?"

Jah, how she made me feel when she talked to me that way, like she knew all the answers and I didn't, talking down to me, yeah, but I didn't mind. Mirja was the only person in my whole life who could talk down to me without getting my back up. That includes my mother.

She had eyes that made you look twice, big, round, and as dark as a well, like she was coming from some deep place where tough questions had easy answers. Her hair was black, with waves, so thick I could bury my hands in it up to my wrist. She had a mouth that made me stare, with lips not-quite-puckered, like a mother disapproving her toddler while stifling a laugh. Her voice was low and complex, with layers like flowing water. She could tell me grass was blue and the sky was green, and I'd go outside and look for myself.

"I'm not saying it'll fix *everything*," I'd answer, but I wanted to believe that it would. "It'll *help*."

"Yes, but when?" she'd challenge me. "Ten years? Twenty? Fifty? That's too late."

If it was just me and Mirja, that was friendly banter while we smoked a blunt before going to bed and humping until we passed out. We were in a pleasant equilibrium, neither one of us pressing the controversy to the point where it interfered with our lovemaking.

Unless Chas got involved. That guy didn't know when to stop pushing.

VR was a panacea to me, just another tool in the toolbox to Mirja. So was the Popular Assembly. She and I bonded over VR, but it was Chas who got her interested in the P.A.

I don't even remember how they met. Mirja and I were both comp sci, and Chas was econ.

Economics.

He was one crazy bastard. Yeah, I know how that sounds. Name me one giant of history who wasn't borderline insane. "All mortal greatness is but disease"—isn't that the quote? I thought it was.

❖ ❖ ❖

I met Chas for the first time one night when I caught up with Mirja at The Pub, this place on campus, and he was there. That was a surprise. Mirja and I'd been living together for a couple of months and this short, stocky guy with dirty blonde hair and meaty features showed up. She'd never mentioned him. They were chatting and laughing like childhood friends, and there I was, the odd man, drinking my beer and smiling acknowledgements whenever Mirja glanced over at me.

"Mirja tells me you're in comp sci too," Chas said to me, and it caught me by surprise, because it was the first time since Mirja introduced him just as *Chas* that he even noticed me.

"Yep," I said, and took a long drink of beer.

"She says you're a genius."

"Yep."

Chas had this smile on his face like he was trying to make me feel comfortable and to like him, but it had the opposite effect.

"She says you're studying this new proposal, the *Worldstream*, they call it?"

"Yep."

"Mirja's told me a little about it, but she says *you're* the real expert. How does it work?"

His smile hadn't changed, but for some reason, the way it affected me had. With one question he turned from a condescending jerk into a guy interested in the stuff I was into.

For twenty minutes he sat there while I droned on about the Worldstream. That was before the seminar, of course, and all I knew about it was from the press releases, and Porter and me and the rest of the comp sci crowd—Mirja too—had tried to decipher the structure from whatever we could glean. But that didn't keep us from imagining a complex machine capable of emulating every sensory detail and quality of the tangible world, and extrapolating that capability to a utopian future. He never interrupted me except to ask a clarifying question, and his smile never wavered through the entire monologue, with only the occasional knit brow or knowing nod.

If you've ever wondered how leaders persuade, here's their secret: they make you feel like *you matter.*

Mirja gazed at me while I rattled on, resting her chin on curled-up fingers. I thought she had a loving look in her eyes, but her eyes darted over toward Chas every minute or so.

"It sounds like the Worldstream has great promise," he said when I stopped to take a drink.

"Raúl thinks it could mitigate climate change, even help to resolve conflicts," Mirja chimed in. "Mainly, it'll bring whole new worlds of experiences to people who never had access to them before."

"If everyone can experience everything," Chas added, "why would there be any class conflict? Is that the idea?"

"Class conflict?" I repeated.

"You seem to be saying that Virtual Reality will level the playing field," he said, "put everyone in one, big class. Anyone can do anything at any time—the elimination of envy."

"Something like that," I said, not knowing where this was going.

"I can see why you'd think of VR as a universal remedy, if your view of human existence were limited to sensory experiences only." Then he added, "But aren't you being a little naïve?"

"Naïve?" I repeated. He was losing me.

He pushed at his beer with his fingertips and said, "What you're describing is a façade, a fake world to *passivate* the masses, while the factors of production remain concentrated in the hands of a powerful few."

"What the fuck are you talking about?" I asked, as politely as I could.

Mirja put her hand on my arm. "Chas is the leader of the UC chapter of the People's Assembly," she explained.

I'd heard of the P.A. by then, but didn't know much about it. I looked at Mirja for a long time, then I looked at Chas and said, "You're a bunch of communists, right?"

Mirja looked horrified, but Chas gave me the same smile he had before, the patronizing smirk that'd turned friendly.

"That's what *some* of the bourgeois media say, but of course, they're wrong," he replied.

"Bourgeois, huh?" I said, with just a little snark. "You *talk* like a communist."

"Raúl," he said, talking down to me, which, of course, got my back up, "the Cold War ended 35 years ago. Red-baiting is a *little* out of vogue."

That got me mad, and it must have showed, because Mirja's eyes got round and she looked back and forth between Chas and me, like she was trying to think of something to say to defuse the situation, when the waiter came up to the table and asked, "Can we get you anything else, Mr. Royce?"

I just froze, and my anger turned to realization. "Chas *Royce?*" I said.

He waved off the waiter, then nodded. "Yep."

Now, you've heard of *Chas* Royce, but you might not have heard of *Derrick* Royce. Everyone in Chicago knew the name of the mayor, and that's when I made the connection. Derrick Royce wasn't just mayor of Chicago, he was *the* most powerful guy in the Democratic party. He practically hand-picked the Democratic candidate for president and almost single-handedly got him elected, much to the dismay of his son. Chas was so vocal about the corruption in the party, and of the candidate, that the mayor publicly disowned him. That didn't diminish Chas's standing among the people. He was the hero of the common man, after all. Anyone who worked for a living—cops, waiters—treated Chas extra-nice.

That revelation took all the air out of my tires and the conversation bumped to a halt. We all exchanged awkward looks until Chas smiled, took a deep breath, and said, "Well! I must be going. Pleasure meeting you, Raúl," and he stuck out his hand. I shook it numbly. He left, and Mirja and I finished our beers in silence, except we might have said something about having to buy shampoo.

❖ ❖ ❖

Over the next couple of months Mirja and I talked less about VR, and more about the P.A. That was *her* choice, not mine, and we trended like that until we found the middle ground I told you about, where each of us knew where the other stood and we'd edge up to the line but not cross it. I must not have satisfied her need to engage on the topic of the P.A., because she spent more time with Chas than with me, either inviting him to our apartment or going to the P.A. chapter meetings two or three times a week. I didn't care for the guy, but, like I said, he had this way of disarming me. When he noticed I wasn't taking part he'd ask me a question I just *had* to answer. He'd sit and listen patiently while I forgot all about what a prick he was.

I don't think I'm the jealous type, but I did have those feelings, which I pushed aside. I'm not a romantic, either, but I never could have believed that Mirja would step out on me —until she did.

She went to a P.A. meeting on a Wednesday night, like always. She usually got home by eleven, when I was still up. I'd ask, "How was the meeting?" and she'd say, "Good. You should come sometime." It'd turned into a ritual.

This one Wednesday I was up at midnight, then one a.m., and Mirja still wasn't home. I went to bed, pushing those jealous thoughts out of my mind, until I fell asleep around three. When the alarm woke me up at seven, I was still alone in bed.

I knew where the P.A. held their meetings, in a neighborhood just off campus, about a mile away. On my way to class, I decided to stroll on over and see if there was any sign of Mirja, or Chas, or anyone else who could tell me what was going on.

It doesn't have to make sense.

Of course, the whole place was deserted, nothing moving except a few leaves in the wind. I missed my 7:30 class entirely, and headed back to the apartment instead of to my ten o'clock class.

Mirja showed up at 10:30. I don't think she expected me to be there. She jumped when I said "Hello," and then she stood in the middle of the room with her big eyes cast downward and her mouth more puckery than usual.

"How was the meeting?" I asked her, like I always did.

"It was good," she replied, real soft, never lifting her eyes.

"And how's Chas?" I asked. "I haven't seen him in some time. You should invite him over."

Mirja's eyes got wet, and she wiped her face with the back of her hand.

"Do you want to tell me where you were?" I asked.

"Raúl," she said, choking a little bit, then she shook her head.

"Okay," I said. "I'll find Chas and ask him. Do you think *he'll* talk?"

She dropped into a ratty old chair, still bundled up in her coat and scarf, sniffling and wiping her face. "I didn't plan it," she whispered. "It just happened."

I suppose having my worst fears confirmed should have hit me harder, but I'd spent the last four hours beating myself up and by that time I was numb.

I stood up and headed for the bathroom. "Get out," I told her just before I closed the door.

Neither one of us starving students had much stuff. By the time I came out of the bathroom, she'd stuffed all of hers in a trash bag and was gone.

4

The Liquor Regimen

A WEEK LATER my meltdown was complete.

The morning after Mirja left, I went to class like always, not thinking about *her*, but not thinking about anything else, either. *Nothing.* Profs blathered, words and concepts sliding off me like rain off a poncho. I had two classes before lunch, and I recalled exactly zero from either one, like I'd blacked out and just woke up in time to take one bite out of a sub sandwich, dump the rest in the trash, then slide back into a walking coma. The afternoon was just like the morning.

Porter dragged me to The Pub that night, sensing that I'd undergone some life change, noticing my zombie-like demeanor but no sign of any of the usual causes, like an all-night study session, or a rare weeknight bender. He ordered us beers and a basket of pierogies, which normally would get me engaged but this time it didn't work.

"Hey, Raúl, you in there?" he asked in annoying fashion, snapping his fingers in my face like a hypnotist. "What's the matter with you?"

That move *did* have an effect, because I remember blinking and looking at Porter, and wondering how I'd gotten in The Pub and what had happened to the day.

"I kicked Mirja out last night," I told him, then gave him the rest of the story as he drained his beer.

"Oh. Rough," he said, shaking his head. He snapped his fingers again, this time at the waiter, and ordered two well bourbons and ginger ale. Now he was sipping his bourbon and ginger and I had a drink *and* a full beer in front of me.

"There's more on the Worldstream," Porter said, sliding his tablet over to me. "Check this."

It was an interview with the founder of Chain Corp., Dan Baltasar, a guy not much older than Porter and me. All us über-geeks knew him from his post-doc work on curated blockchains, but he went public in a big way when he founded Chain. He claimed to have solved the problem of validating participants in multi-person venues, a tough nut, especially for big venues like concerts. Porter and the rest of the geeks had been buzzing over it all day, mostly speculation, since the article didn't get specific. I missed out, not because I wasn't present during the discussions—I was— but none of it stuck. Even then, reading the interview, it was just words on a screen, their meaning eluding me.

"Wow, you're really out of it," Porter said to my slack face and glassy eyes. "News like this would normally stoke you."

"Yeah," I mumbled, looking back and forth between my beer and my pint jar of ginger. Porter held his lean-forward position for another minute before straightening up and finishing off the pierogies. He didn't leave me a single one.

❖ ❖ ❖

Day Two was worse than Day One, but not as bad as Day Three. I got up at one p.m., bleary-eyed, achy-headed, and sour-stomached, having kicked the last of a bottle of Crown Royal on Night Two. That left my liquor cabinet bare, which was damned inconvenient, since it was shortly after my vision cleared that I read the text on my phone: *Can we talk?*

That was the first of ten or so texts over the next 24 hours, all terse, such as *Raúl?* or *Please?* or the ultimate in minimalism: a single question mark, its meaning clear from context. By the afternoon of Day Four, thirty hours into my self-imposed hiatus from liquor therapy, Mirja took a chance, texting, *I'll be at The Pub at seven. Please come.*

So, what do you think I did? Well, of course I went.

The walk to The Pub felt like the day after Mirja left, a machine-like shamble through fog, like a self-driving transport. I got to the place and looked around for Mirja, spotting her at a corner table—only she wasn't alone.

Yep—Chas. Good guess.

The dominant theme of my few coherent thoughts over the prior four days was of Mirja and Chas together in bed— or on a table, or a kitchen counter, or bathroom sink—and the sight of them together stuck my feet to the floor. Mirja jumped up and came to me and put her arms around me like she was hugging a tree. Only a tree might've actually reacted.

"Raúl," she said with her face pressed against my chest.

"You've *got* to be fucking kidding me," I replied.

Chas had some weird radar about situations, and never missed an opportunity to gain the upper hand. He got out of his chair and headed toward us.

"Raúl," he said, like he was comforting a grieving widow. "I want to explain."

I maintained tree-like silence and let him go on.

"Neither one of us expected this thing to happen, but it did, and now it's past. We both regret it."

Mirja tightened her arms around me and said, "I'm sorry. Forgive me."

Chas put one hand on Mirja's back and his other hand on my shoulder. "We can be adults."

The most adult thing I did that whole week was to disentangle myself from Mirja and walk out of The Pub without decking that supercilious jackoff.

❖ ❖ ❖

Day Seven was the low point of the parabola. As of Day Five, I was back on the liquor regimen, upping the dosage to accelerate progress. Accelerate it did, because Day Seven (actually Afternoon Seven) was spent with my trembling hands gripping the rim of the toilet, retching until I thought my stomach lining might come up, then falling back against the wall, squeezing my head, hoping that might stop the pounding, but it didn't.

Time's the only cure for a hangover, and by Night Seven I was steady enough to call up Porter to find out what I'd missed.

"Bruh, where you been?" he asked me right off. "The profs are inquiring after you. You're in danger of flunking."

"I never flunked a course in my life," I told him, and that was true.

"Then don't start," he answered me. "Jesus, I know you're torn up, but this is your *future*." Then he added, "And I miss you, man."

I don't know why, but hearing that from Porter, at that moment, got to me and I broke down.

Yeah. Cried like a pre-teen girl at a sappy rom-com.

Rom-com. Romantic comedy. If you've never seen one, you haven't missed much.

"Hang on, Raúl," he said. "I'm on my way over. I'll bring my class notes."

❖ ❖ ❖

A night of catching up cleared my head. Porter brought me up to date on classwork and the Worldstream. The Consortium had announced a series of seminars, sending their best people to companies and colleges to sell the new standard. UC was close to the top of the list, with a session scheduled just two weeks away.

"I took the liberty of registering both of us," Porter told me. "I figured, you know…"

"Yeah, thanks," I said, then Porter pulled up the latest online traffic about the Worldstream and pointed me to the most interesting threads. Developers had coalesced around the standard, filling in gaps, proposing new mechanisms, prototyping code, arguing about how to interpret the ambiguities. It was the most excitement I'd seen in geek world since the release of the Touchstone platform, which got a whole new generation of coders working on hyper-realistic VR venues. That excitement rubbed off on me, and for the next week I immersed myself in the Worldstream, forgetting all about Mirja and Chas. It felt great.

Until I got that text message from Mirja, inviting me to a P.A. rally in the quad.

5

On the Rim of the Uncanny Valley

I IGNORED IT, of course.

But you know, it never slowed me down. I was so deep into the levers, pulleys, and gears of the Worldstream that Mirja's text didn't even register as a blip.

Okay, more than a *blip*. And it slowed me down a *little*. But not for long.

The Consortium had released a development kit and we all downloaded it. With Mirja out, I had extra room and volunteered my apartment as Worldstream Central. Porter and I were there 24/7. The headcount peaked at nine and never dropped below four.

We'd all dabbled in VR. Up to then, we'd struggled with poorly designed and even more poorly supported platforms. Coherence was okay, but not perfect for very hi-res renderings, with a lot of artifacts. Deconfliction was an issue. That's the problem of detecting when two objects collide. We generally stuck to a small number of rigid bodies for most of our apps, but the Consortium claimed perfect deconfliction even for thousands of soft, spongy bodies.

You take this stuff for granted, but I tell you, back then it was primitive and ugly.

The Consortium's tools were phenomenal. Porter mocked up a replica of Navy Pier, complete with Ferris wheel, and populated it with all nine of us and a few hundred stock avatars. The view of Lake Michigan from the top of the wheel kicked ass.

Just one small problem: we were still camped out in the Uncanny Valley.

Do you know the Uncanny Valley? *No?*

If you're gaming, it doesn't matter if the characters look like real people. They can be cartoons, or realistic, but still obviously fake, and the experience is satisfactory. Back then, rendering had progressed to the point where human avatars looked almost, but *not quite* entirely lifelike. A good game had hi-res, eye-bleeding rendering, but even the best games throttled back the realism when it came to the characters. Why? Because gamers reported that games with very realistic humans made them sick. Not *physically* ill, exactly, but they hated those games, even the bloody, non-stop action ones. They didn't even know *why* they hated them, but when they played the exact same games with cartoonier avatars, they were cool. It was a psychology thing.

That's the Uncanny Valley—the gap between a noticeably fake avatar and one that's as real as RL. *Nobody* liked the Valley, and that's where the avatars in the Worldstream squarely dwelt. Navy Pier was great, but the faces in the crowd gave us the willies.

That dampened our enthusiasm—until we saw a demo of new rendering software from Ahadi Kubwa, an outfit in *Ghana*, of all places. *Ahadi Kubwa* is Swahili for "great promise," and it was great indeed.

We all took cabs into town, to a think tank on Madison Street. We hit a traffic jam two blocks from the address and hiked rest of the way. When we got to the building there was a line around the corner. Every geek and gear-head in Chicagoland was queued up to see what Ahadi had.

We waited four hours to get inside. We were crammed into one room, not in any obvious arrangement, but everyone knew where they stood in the order. The demo room was next door. Demos lasted four minutes, like clockwork. Counting heads, we calculated another hour before any of us got our chance.

Porter went in first, and four minutes later he came out, eyes bugging like ping-pong balls, his mouth puckered up like he was going to whistle, but no sound came. I was next.

Inside the room was one guy, a short, bald, Black guy with a neck like a rhino and a big, showy grin, wearing a slightly-small suit and tie and holding what looked like a conventional VR headset.

"Welcome to Ahadi Kubwa demonstration!" he boomed in a thick west-African accent. With his free hand he gestured toward a laptop on a floor stand. "Please share your name and contact information!" I entered my info as the Ahadi guy stood by, illuminating the room with his smile. He held out the headset. "It is like any VR device!"

I put it on.

Then I took it off.

"I enjoy this every time!" the guy roared.

I rattled my head, like I was trying to bust up cobwebs, then put the headset back on.

Instead of a windowless room in downtown Chicago, I stood amid thatched dwellings, women stirring steaming kettles on wood fires, men hauling sacks of grain, and in the distance, before a landscape of scrub below a searing sun, children playing soccer in the dust. I could almost smell the goats.

The same guy stood in front of me: same ebony complexion, same toothy smile, same sparkling eyes, but instead of a suit and tie, he was wrapped in a garment, like a toga, checkered with patterns in yellow, green, red, and a dozen other colors so vivid they glowed.

"It is the *kente*, traditional garb of Ghana!" the man explained, turning from side to side, the better to admire his outfit. "What do you think of it?"

I'm sure my eyes were doing the same ping-pong thing as Porter's. I lifted the headset again, revealing the Ahadi salesman in his western suit, then replaced it, transforming him back into an African tribesman. I got up close, so close I could count the pores on his nose. Except for his clothing, the rendering and the RL man were indistinguishable. If I hadn't been wearing the headset, I would have believed in my soul that a substantial human being was in front of me, as real as any I'd ever stood with face-to-face, dressed as a Ghanaian chieftain.

I was standing on the far rim of the Uncanny Valley.

❖ ❖ ❖

Back at the apartment, Porter, me, and the rest of the geeks sat in silence as we passed around the bong, still awed by what we'd witnessed. This wasn't just better rendering. It was *qualitative*. You all are used to VR as an alternative flesh, blood, and bone world, with the same laws of physics and people as real as your mom and dad. *We* grew up in a different world, one that technology wasn't yet able to duplicate. That gave it *uniqueness*. That gave it *status*. No matter how good the rendering, when you put on that visor, you knew it was fake, just by looking. RL and VR were *different*. Ahadi had erased that difference, and that fact hit all of us like a taser. *Especially* after we were stoned.

"That's the last barrier," Porter said, exhaling a cloud of smoke.

We all nodded, still meditating on the experience.

"The doorstep to Utopia," said Ezra, a third-year undergrad with middling chops. "The Uncanny Valley has been crossed. Hallelujah."

Porter snorted another puff of smoke. "Guys, I've been thinking."

"Risky," I said. "Very risky."

Porter grinned at me, then got serious. "Have you gamed this out?"

We all looked stupid as Porter explained.

"What we saw today was a demo, a super-lifelike avatar based on physical data from the persona…right?"

We all nodded.

"Extrapolate. If we're all in the Worldstream, where does the rendering engine get the data to build our avatars?"

All the dope-addled geeks gaped before I spoke up.

"From the blockchain."

"Yeah, right," Porter said, "and where does the blockchain get it?"

We all got round-eyed, because we knew the answer: the Internet of Things, and the Cloud, the dumping ground for every byte of personal data surrendered, willingly or otherwise—what we now call the All-Seeing Eye.

"Alarmist," Ezra replied. "Folks been giving up their data for forever. So what?"

Porter sat forward, putting his elbows on his knees. "Ezra, *read the spec*. We're not talking about a bunch of social media platforms all with their own proprietary databases of purchases and porn sites. This is *every word* you say and *everything* you do, all of it catalogued and cross-referenced and verified, stored on the blockchain. Your *whole life* digitized and rendered on demand."

Well, *that* was a sobering thought, put that way, and we all pondered it gravely, until I broke the silence.

"Porter, we've been talking about the potential of VR for years, if we could only overcome the technical hurdles. Now, with the Worldstream and Ahadi, we're almost there. Are you giving up on the promise?"

Porter wiped his face with his hand. "I don't know," he said. "Maybe I just never thought about the cost as long as the endpoint was unattainable."

That made sense, seeing as how for the last twenty years, the endpoint had always been five years in the future.

Anyhow, that's how I spent those three weeks, from the day Mirja left to the day of the massacre.

6

Martyr to the Cause

Shortly after the cops dump me on the pavement the news crews show up with their microwave trucks, portable cameras, and on-air talent. They talk with anyone who'll stand still long enough for them to stick a microphone in their faces. One of them, a short, busty blonde, spots me, 'cause I'm towering over everyone else, or because I have this terrified, confused look on my face, and she heads my way.

"Sir, sir!" she shouts. "Where were you?"

"Where?" I repeat dumbly.

"When the shooting started?"

I turn away, but she won't be denied.

"Were you in the quad?" She's waving her microphone like she's sprinkling me with holy water. I turn back.

"How many hurt?" I ask her. She pulls her head back like she's surprised to get a question instead of an answer.

"We don't know," she says, "five, at least, maybe more. Were you there?"

"I was in class," I answer. "Five? Men or women?"

She rolls her eyes and goes off looking for other victims, cameraman jogging behind.

I take out my phone and tap a message to a number I haven't texted in two weeks: *M it's R where r u?*

I stare at the screen for two minutes, then text again: *At UC trauma. Chas is here.*

Another two minutes. Nothing.

By that time I'm walking in circles, searching the crowd for Mirja's face, slapping my phone against my thigh, people bouncing off me from all directions. I look for a reply from Mirja every three seconds, but nothing comes.

Then a man's voice distracts me.

"Raúl!"

I see Porter muscling his way toward me, as though he's swimming upstream in a mudslide, one arm raised like he's hailing a cab. He's not far, but it takes another two minutes to reach me. His face is sweaty and he's out of breath, bent over with a hand on my arm, huffing.

"Ran here when they lifted the lockdown," he chokes. "Whole town's insane."

"What have you heard?" I ask.

He gulps, his breath coming easier now, and shakes his head. "Not much. Happened in the quad. Ran into a guy I know, back of the crowd. Heard shots, then a stampede. Said he heard ten dead. Overheard someone else on the way saying twenty. Sniper? Do you know?"

"Not a sniper," I correct him.

I tell him the story Chas told me, about the Guard flipping out, and the scene inside trauma. Porter looks at me like he's about to throw up.

"Mirja?" he asks.

I look at my phone. "No word."

Another ambulance turns into the lot, siren whining and the driver leaning on the horn. It gets almost to where I am, then they give up on getting closer to the entrance. The rear door opens and EMTs drag the stretcher out.

It's a woman, wearing a respirator mask, but I recognize her—thick, wavy black hair, matted with blood.

"Oh, Jesus, oh sweet Jesus," I rasp as the stretcher rolls by, the EMT clearing the way. "God, Mirja—it's *Mirja!*" I go after her but Porter pulls me back.

"Raúl—*Raúl!* It's not her! It's not Mirja!"

"She is—she's…" The woman on the stretcher morphs before my eyes, from raven-maned Mirja, to a plump girl with brown hair. Porter squeezes my arm, saying, "She's okay," over and over, trying to convince me, but I'm not convinced.

I check my phone—still no reply. I show Porter.

"It was a crazy scene, man—crazy, okay?" he says. "Here's what happened: Things went to hell, Mirja took out her phone to text you, then got knocked around in the stampede and the phone hit the ground. Five hundred feet trampled it into the turf."

I check the phone again.

"Look," Porter says, "we're not going to accomplish anything hanging out in the mob." He pulls my arm. "Let's get out of here."

I know he's right. If Mirja's okay, I'll hear from her soon enough, and if not, there's nothing I can do.

"You go," I tell him. "I'm staying here."

He loosens his grip on me and puts his hands in his pockets. "I'm not going anywhere."

About that time the insanity plateaus, with no new arrivals since the brown-haired woman, and the crowd thinning out. There's an occasional primal scream as some next-of-kin gets notification. More news crews arrive, and more cops.

Porter and I huddle as night falls and the temperature drops. I can tell Porter's getting antsy, but he doesn't say a word unless I talk first.

"Raúl," I hear, not a shout, but a normal speaking voice from behind me, then I feel a hand on my back. I turn around and it's Chas.

"What?" I ask, but I already know what he's going to say.

"Mirja didn't make it," he mumbles.

I'm just staring, like the words aren't registering. Porter takes hold of my arm.

"She's been in the OR for hours," Chas continues. "She got here before we did. I talked to one of the victims, one of the P.A. He knew Mirja. They were at the edge of the crowd, right in front of the Guard. When the nightsticks came out, they turned to run but there was nowhere to go. Mirja took a bullet in the back, lost a lot of blood."

Porter's grip gets tighter. I turn to him and he hugs me, and I press my face against the top of his head as the tears come.

Chas grabs my arm, tugging like he's trying to pull me and Porter apart. We break the clinch, and Chas moves in like he wants a hug, too. I step back.

Chas looks disappointed I won't accept his warm embrace, then he puts his hand on my arm.

"This massacre won't be for nothing," he says fiercely, like he's gearing up for another rally. "When the people hear what happened, they'll see this regime for what it is: violent and corrupt. You'll see. The people will come to our side in numbers. The tide will finally crest, and we will remake America." He gives my arm a squeeze. "Mirja won't have died in vain. She's a martyr to the cause."

He's looking at me real serious, then his face goes soft, and he smiles that same smug smile, the one that screams *I know what's best for you.*

Chas's hand falls away as I drop my arm. I pull my fist back, then come around and hit him so hard he goes down like a dead deer and I fracture a knuckle.

The crowd reacts with a gasp as Chas hits the pavement. A cop materializes beside me, and he and Porter pull me back. Good thing, too, because I would have pummeled that fucker senseless.

7

Payback With Interest

TEN DEAD, EIGHT wounded—that was the final tally.

They didn't bust me for punching out Chas, my second lucky break of the day. Chas waved off the cop, saying, "He's distraught, Officer," and "I'm Chas Royce," one last condescending dig. It was the last time I ever saw him in person.

But I have to give Chas props—he called it. The reaction *was* extreme. Chas went national, showing up on every talk show on every news outlet. Hell, he even went to Congress, the front for the rickety antiquated American framework— the belly of the beast.

The P.A. ramped up demonstrations on campuses and in cities across the country and overseas, especially in Europe, where anti-American sentiments were running high. Chas was in big demand, going from city to city, rallying the resistance. His gimmick: the shirt from the day of the shooting. He had a canned speech, which he delivered with minor variations, but at its climax, he'd shout, "We know what kind of people lead us, if you can call it *leadership*." Then he'd hoist that bloody shirt like a banner and the crowd would go nuts.

The time was ripe for a mass movement, with all that was going down at the time—Russia invading the Baltic states, Europe threatening to lob nukes at Moscow, and China playing the peacemaker while America sat on the sidelines.

Chas used that.

He had this idea that America couldn't succeed in the new geopolitics so long as we hamstrung our leadership with the rusty machinery of democracy. China didn't mess with such outdated institutions as *elections, representation, checks and balances.* That gave China an advantage in the clutch, and that's why they rocketed to the number one spot. That rankled the average American. The situation gave Chas leverage.

So he called in the strikes.

Rallies and demonstrations got great airplay, but the president could ignore them if they weren't *too* disruptive, especially after the shootings. All that changed when Chas, the proletariat superman, urged the working class to make themselves heard in a very practical way. They started by shutting down Washington D.C.

Every subway crew, cab driver, fireman, policeman, and a good many others called in sick for a week. The havoc got worldwide coverage, inspiring strikes in New York, Atlanta, Houston, and in Chicago, my hometown. Whole regions shut down. But when a fire in Dallas burned down an apartment building, killing fourteen, with the Dallas fire department lifting not so much as a finger, the president couldn't ignore the situation any longer.

So, what do you suppose he did? Of course—he declared martial law. Curfews, summary arrests, *habeas corpus* out the window, the whole routine.

The results were predictable—confrontations, crackdowns, casualties, rinse and repeat. While Europe balanced on the brink of nuclear war, and China gripped the levers of global domination, America floundered. It was a bad scene.

Sympathy for the People's Assembly grew to the point where the P.A.'s call for a constitutional convention took root, and one state legislature after another passed resolutions. When the number of states passed the halfway mark, the Commander in Chief capitulated and lifted martial law, but by then it was too late. Momentum was with the P.A., in no small part because every state and every political persuasion saw an opportunity to inject their pet issues into the New Order. Two-thirds of the states passed resolutions —the deciding votes coming in special sessions of the

Wyoming and Rhode Island legislatures on Christmas Eve—and the convention was scheduled for the following year. The parade through the streets of Chicago lasted more than eight hours, with Chas leading the way—when he wasn't being carried on the shoulders of his acolytes.

❖ ❖ ❖

I know all this now, but at the time I wasn't paying close attention. After Mirja died, I dropped out, just like I did when we split. If it wasn't for Porter, I'd have never recovered, but he kept after me, doing double-time with his own studies and tutoring me, even when I didn't want him to, and, frankly speaking, he didn't either. But in Porter's mind, it was payback.

He and I grew up together on the south side, in different neighborhoods, though not far apart. I grew tall early, and I was good at basketball, so I was always looking for a pickup game, and if I, a big white kid, had to go into a Black neighborhood to find a game, I did. Word spread about the white guy with skills, so I didn't stay a stranger for long.

Porter Wilkes was a nerdy little Black kid, a foot and a half shorter than me, but scrappy as hell. He was an easy target, and he would've attracted a lot of bullying if it wasn't for his big brother Omar. I must confess, I took a few cheap shots at the little guy, but others nearby overheard and warned me about Omar. I stopped the teasing, not only because I didn't want Porter's gangbanger brother coming after me, but also because he was such a determined kid and I respected that.

Gangbanger. It means Omar belonged to a gang. Remember I told you about the shootings? Mostly gangs.

Porter and I played a lot of one-on-one. He was short, but fast, with good hands. He never beat me, but he was always in the game. When we discovered our common interest in computers, we started spending time off the court.

I'd known Porter for three years—we were sixteen—by the time Omar died, shot, of course, a gang-related homicide, just another tick in the tally. We never knew the reason. Porter was ready to join Omar's gang (and they were eager to have him) just to get his revenge. It would've ruined him, if I hadn't talked him out of it.

"Talked" really doesn't describe what we went through. Porter disappeared, left home without so much as saying goodbye, with nothing but a backpack full of clothes, his laptop, and a charger. I kept in touch via his online presence, but he wouldn't tell me where he was. He posted a lot of scary stuff, like gang-related videos, and text posts in some emoji-heavy lingo I couldn't decipher. He was hanging with the gang, but from what I could find out, he hadn't yet joined up. I had to get to him, and time was not my friend.

I planted a Trojan horse in his laptop, which forwarded his IP address, traceable to a hot dog place near Western and Columbus. Porter's mom and I, and a few sympathetic friends, confronted him and took him home. We practically kidnapped him. We were lucky his would-be gang brothers weren't with him. Or maybe they were nearby but weren't so depraved that they'd take us out with Mom right there.

When word got out that Porter was back home, the house became a target, the rival gang staging drive-by shootings every other night. We stayed with Porter in shifts, like prison guards, never letting him out of our sight. It freaked out my own mother that I was camped out in that neighborhood, and she came close to sending a rescue party for *me*.

It all ended a week later, when the ones who shot Omar got shot themselves at the hands of Omar's gang. They still wanted Porter, and he was ready to take the pledge, which involved surviving a knife fight—Omar had over 150 stitches from *his* initiation. Even though Porter was majorly pissed at me, I hung with him another week until he cooled down, while I helped his mom with fixing up the house. He wouldn't play B-ball with me for another month. A year later we were back where we were, but with one difference: Porter owed me. We never talked about it, and I never thought of it like that, but *he* did.

Ten years later he paid me back, with interest. I was a terrible student, but Porter never let up. Good thing—if he had, I might have fallen so far behind I'd have never caught up.

Developments in the Worldstream came at us fast. The forums exploded with chatter and links to mocked-up venues using the Worldstream platform and the Ahadi Kubwa rendering engine. Everyone was trying to outdo everyone else, with stunning results.

Even with all that happening, exciting as it was, I couldn't focus. And as for the global crisis and upheavals in the U.S., I couldn't have cared less.

My attitude changed dramatically when those federal agents showed up at *my* place.

8

Two Stooges

Two humorless guys in black suits banging on my door and flashing DHS badges snapped me out of my funk like nothing else.

DHS. Department of Homeland Security. They were like the Jedi Knights of the Old Republic.

Jedi Knights. Never mind. Not important.

They came in the morning, around nine. I was still in shorts and a hoodie, standing in the doorway looking like I'd just woken up, which I had. I let 'em in. I didn't ask why they were there. I even offered them coffee, which they refused. I poured myself a large mug.

One of them was bald. The other had black hair that needed cutting. For a minute or two they sat in silence, stone-like, as if they were studying my reactions to a stressful situation.

"So…what?" I asked.

The bald one produced a tablet as if from nowhere and handed it to me. On it was a beautifully composed shot of Chas in full rally mode, a bullhorn in one hand and his other hand raised in a fist.

"Do you know this man?" he asked.

"Chas Royce," I said. "Everyone knows who he is."

"Do you know him *personally?*" he clarified.

"I met him a few times."

He tapped the tablet. "Do you know this woman?" he asked, mechanically, like a synthesized voice.

It was a picture of Mirja, or rather, a series of pictures flipping by, one after the other: Mirja at a rally, holding a protest sign, Mirja with Chas Royce at the head of a march, Mirja in a classroom, at The Pub, strolling across campus, alone or with others. Some of them were with me.

One of them was me, Mirja, and Chas in our apartment. That made me lean forward, trying to figure out from where it was taken but it flipped by too fast.

"Where did that come from?" I asked.

He took the tablet back and made it disappear as easily as he'd conjured it.

"Mirja Przestworczak. How do you know her?" He pronounced *Przestworczak* perfectly, a name that took me a week to master.

"Why are you asking me this?" I protested, the coffee having cleared my head.

"Are you refusing to answer my question?" he asked in a tone that scared me.

"We lived together," I answered, "but we don't anymore. She's dead."

"What is your association with this terrorist organization, the People's Assembly?" he went on, expression never changing.

"Terrorists?" I blurted. "What makes them *terrorists?*"

"What is your association?" he repeated.

I got up for another cup of coffee, but what I was thinking was, *I'd really like a glass of bourbon.*

"There's no association," I answered. "That was Mirja's thing, not mine."

"You were cohabitating with this woman, correct?" he asked.

"*Cohabitating?*" I repeated, since that wasn't a word I'd heard too often. "Yeah, I just told you that. What's this about?"

The two exchanged a look, then the hairy one continued where the bald one left off.

"We believe you have detailed knowledge of the leadership and organization of the People's Assembly. Your president expects you to do your duty and to help us bring this criminal enterprise to justice."

About that time I stopped being intimidated and started being pissed.

"Okay, listen Moe and Curly," I said, trying to sound as tough as I could, "the P.A. was *Mirja*, not me. Ask *her*. Oh, but you can't, because my president *killed her.*"

Moe and Curly. The Three Stooges. *Stooges.* Jah, don't they teach you kids the classics anymore?

The suits either didn't get the reference or they ignored it.

"Let's be clear," said Curly, the bald one, "we're not ignorant of your associations."

In the twenty minutes that followed Moe went through an account of Mirja's, Chas's, and my time together, almost minute-by-minute, starting with the first meeting with Chas in The Pub, while Curly flashed photos of me and Mirja, me and Chas, Mirja and Chas, all hi-res shots taken from every angle. They showed me online posts, videos, *and* text messages. They traced our movements through multiple days without a break. They even played audio clips of what I was sure were private conversations.

They gave me a detailed chronology of the day of the massacre, placing me in the quad, then tracing my movements to the comp sci building and then to the trauma center, the encounter with the cop, clocking Chas on the chin, and Chas's charitable dismissal.

They saved the best for last, spending five full minutes on the night Mirja slept with Chas, starting with the P.A. meeting, Chas and Mirja alone in his apartment afterward, reciting their short conversation word-for-word, ending with, "The two subjects retired to the bedroom for conjugal relations."

"How'd you get this?" I demanded, but they didn't look like they were accepting of demands.

Curly said, "Sir, we recommend that you cooperate *voluntarily.*"

The way he said *voluntarily* gave me goosebumps. That caused me to pause and think about what to say next, but ultimately I said what was already on my mind.

"I want to see your warrant."

"You're not under arrest," Moe said, "and you're not wanted for questioning—*yet*."

"Not that kind of warrant," I said. "I want to see the warrant you used to gather all this info, the one that you got to put us under surveillance."

For the first time since they'd arrived unannounced, Moe and Curly broke a smile, not a big one, but a smirky, creepy one. Moe looked at Curly, who mouthed the word *warrant*, then pinched his face like he was stifling a laugh.

Curly held out a card as they stood up.

"If you decide to talk, call this number." He slipped the tablet into a holster inside his jacket, the secret pocket from which he could produce it or conceal it as needed. "If not," he continued, "we'll find *you*."

9

Loyalty Points

I TEXTED PORTER: *Two feds stopped by this morning to harass me. How's *your* day going?*

The reply came in seconds: *Come over. Don't text me.*

Porter lived far enough away that I summoned a driver—*driverless*, actually. They were trending in those days, driverless cabs. The procedure was simple: I tapped in the destination, then relaxed in the apartment until the app chimed the two-minute warning, just enough time to make it to the curb. A touch of the smartphone to a panel and the door sprang open, I got in, and the robo-car took me to Porter's place in safety and comfort.

Easy and cheap, just ten bucks, plus my identity, point of origin, destination, times of departure and arrival, and means of payment, all absorbed into the Cloud. I don't know what happened to all that info once it got there.

Porter was acting as weird as I'd ever seen him. He cracked the door, peeking through the slit before opening it just far enough to let me in.

"Bruh, what's with the routine?" I asked him. "Do you think I was followed?"

He put his finger to his lip and shook his head *no*. I followed him down the hall to his living room. I'd been there hundreds of times, but that day he had something I'd never seen in his place before: a box the size of a suitcase, made of dull orange metal, sitting on his coffee table.

Porter opened the box. It was filled with gear: a laptop, two smartphones, an eBook reader, a tablet—all his computers, but also a coffeemaker, blender, toaster, and a few other appliances I couldn't identify for sure. He stood with his hand on the lid and tilted his head.

I got the message. I took out my phone, ready to toss it on the pile, but Porter pointed at it, then drew a finger across his throat. I turned off the phone and dropped it in. He closed the lid, locked it, and rolled the combination to a random number.

"We're safe now," he said softly. "You can talk, but keep it low."

"Why do you have a whole fucking appliance store in a suitcase?" I asked.

"A precaution," he answered mysteriously. "The box is made of copper. It cuts off those devices from the Internet. Everything in that box is connected."

"But they're turned off," I said.

"They're never off, not completely."

I sat down on the couch, that big copper box on the table in front of me.

"Porter, I've been over here a hundred times," I said. "Why have I never seen this ridiculous thing before?"

He picked it up and lugged it to the closet, sticking it in and closing the door.

"We never talked about this subject before," he answered, still sounding like a spy.

"About the government? Sure we have, right here in your apartment. We talk all the time."

"*No*, not about the government. About the All-Seeing Eye."

Now he was scaring me, talking in code like that.

"What kind of paranoid shit are you into?" I asked.

He sat on the edge of the coffee table, close enough that I could smell the pizza on his breath. "Tell me what happened," he said.

I gave him the unabridged version, word-for-word as best I could remember it, right down to the looks on the feds' faces. He never interrupted, not even to ask a question. He just sat there, nodding.

When I was done, he pressed his hands to his face and sighed through his fingers.

"How do you suppose those shots of you, Mirja, and Chas got into their file?" he asked.

"I've been puzzling over that," I answered, "and about the ones from The Pub." I tapped my fingers against my chin. "Mostly I'm obsessing over the whole thing with Mirja and Chas in his apartment, you know, the—"

"Yeah," he interrupted, like he knew I didn't want to repeat the details. "The feds had the whole scene, like the place was bugged. How'd that happen?"

I wasn't sure where Porter was coming from. "Answered your own question, didn't you? They bugged the place. They had Chas in their sights, so they bugged him."

"And the other things? From The Pub, and your apartment? Did they bug those, too?"

I must have looked confused.

"You said you asked if they had a warrant for surveillance, right?" he asked. "And they laughed?"

"More like snickered," I corrected. "But they thought that was funny for some reason."

Porter leaned closer, reeking of pepperoni. "Raúl, they didn't need a *warrant*. All that stuff they found on you, Mirja, and Chas? It's all in the Cloud."

Right away, I thought this was Porter being paranoid again, like after the Ahadi demo. "Naw," I said with a sneer. "This stuff was *detailed*, I mean *every move*. They had to've had ten feds tailing us—me—them."

"You think?" he whispered. He moved off the table to the couch, next to me. "Do you keep your phone with you?" he asked. "Did Mirja?"

"Sure, of course," I said. "Doesn't everyone?"

Porter closed his eyes and nodded, like he was the Zen master and I was his grasshopper.

Then I heard the sound of one hand clapping.

"Jesus," I said.

"The phone goes with you everywhere. The phone has a camera. The phone has a microphone. It's *better* than a bug. It's the wire you wear to tell on *yourself.*"

I ran through the whole sequence again in my mind, correlating every item Moe and Curly had on the three of us with what they could've gleaned from my phone records. It still didn't make sense.

"I hear you, but I'm not convinced. The day Mirja…the shooting…they knew everything—no breaks. *Everything.* Sure, we all had our phones, but those records are private, right? They can't get my records without a *warrant.*"

Porter turned his shoulders so he was facing me. "Two months ago, I texted you. I asked if you wanted to meet, you and Mirja. Remember?"

"Jeez, Porter," I answered, "you must've done that a thousand times. I'm supposed to remember one time out of a thousand?"

He had a look halfway between a grimace and a smile. "This time I texted you, I said I'll meet you at The Pub."

He seemed to put a lot of significance on that, but I didn't see it. "We *always* meet there."

"Yeah, but this time, I already knew you were there."

Then it dawned on me. It was an app I'd loaded, turned on and forgot about: *Find Me.*

Porter grabbed my arm. "You broadcast your location 24/7, you and whoever you're with."

"*Companion,*" I blurted out. It was another app—whenever I was with Mirja, Chas, or anyone else I knew with a smartphone, their blips would show up next to mine.

I stood up to pace. "That's still private data, isn't it? Only shared with friends?"

"If that's what you chose," he said, "but the default is to make the info public. Your personal data only has value if they can sell it. Unless you opt out, potentially every person with an Internet connection can find you, any time, any place."

It was starting to make sense. I put my hands on my head, pressing my palms against my temples. "The pictures in my apartment…what happened at Chas's…"

"That'd be Chas's phone is my best guess," Porter interrupted. "Could be he wanted a memento."

I wished he hadn't said that. The image of Chas and Mirja together had stuck with me for weeks, like an annoying song on an endless loop. To think that Chas got it on tape made me nauseous.

Tape. Primitive twentieth-century technology. It's how we used to record stuff.

I dropped into the couch and fell forward, head in hands.

"No warrant needed," Porter said. "You, me, and the whole world, we've already opened the kimono. Every time we link our profile to an app, every time we accept the terms and conditions, we give up another piece of ourselves, expose another facet of our private lives to the world. And for what?"

I picked up my head from my hands and looked at him, asking the same question with my face.

"This is the way our freedom ends," he answered, "not with a coup, but with loyalty points."

For the first time since I'd known him, Porter's paranoia seemed justified. He might even have underplayed it before.

He kept talking, like he was revealing the rites of some secret society, laying out a plot worthy of the most crazed conspiracy nut. And that's what I felt like, a lunatic, all my reason suspended, taking in Porter's Byzantine theories, and every peculiar puzzle piece—the players, connections, motives, the step-by-scary-step progression—it all made sense.

"I never heard you talk like this before," I said, when Porter stopped to take a breath.

"Sure I have," he objected. "I've *always* worried about the erosion of privacy, especially since they released the Worldstream spec."

"But not like this," I came back, "with all the Big Data and AI cabal talk. The *All-Seeing Eye?*"

He grinned, which seemed out of place in this grave discussion. "This stealing of our lives, it's all been ad hoc and opportunistic up to now." His smile disappeared. "The Worldstream is a *machine*, taking in all our personal info and outputting a one-to-one scale digital map of reality. And everything—*everything*—that makes each of us unique will be catalogued and codified."

He had a way of putting things.

"What do we do?" I asked.

He leaned in real close and whispered, "*Vita Occulta.*"

10

Novus Ordo

PORTER'S ODD HABIT of only riding in one of the dwindling number of old-style taxis with actual human drivers (and always paying cash) now made sense.

We took the cab to an apartment on the North Side, a top-end unit in a high-rise. Porter wore an oversized hoodie, and made me wear one, too.

"They won't let us in otherwise," was his only explanation.

We took the elevator to the fiftieth floor. Porter kept his hood forward so his face didn't show, turning away from the surveillance camera. His paranoia filled the elevator like bad body odor.

"We're going to attract more attention with the hoodies than without them in this neighborhood," I warned.

"Can't be helped," he mumbled.

The only time Porter showed his face was for the peephole at the apartment door. He pushed the doorbell, pulled back his hood to light up his face, and the door opened.

That was a damn fine apartment: a living room bigger than my whole place, full-height windows with a million-dollar view. The woman at the door was older than Porter and me, in her thirties, I'd guess, with short brown hair and glasses, attractive but not quite beautiful, in a very expensive sweater, fashion jeans, and shoes that just screamed money. Of the fifteen or so people in her place, all holding drinks and food, she was the only one not wearing a hoodie.

I waited for someone to say something but she and Porter kept their mouths shut tight—really, their lips pressed together like they were holding their breath, and everyone else in the room shut up, too. On a table in the front hall was a big, copper suitcase like the one Porter had, and she opened it to reveal a pile of phones and tablets. Porter patted himself to show that he wasn't holding a phone, then tilted his head at me and I tossed mine in. She shut it and locked it with the same ritual as Porter's. As soon as the case was closed and the tumblers spun, the conversations resumed and the party picked back up again.

"Porter," she said, kissing him on the cheek. She looked at me with a squint and asked, "Who's this?"

"Chloe, this is Raúl," Porter introduced me. "You can trust him. We've known each other since we were kids."

Chloe stuck out her hand and gave me a cold shake that felt like she was still skeptical. "Welcome to *Vita Occulta*," she said.

❖ ❖ ❖

I helped myself to a drink from Chloe's impressive bar, and noshed on a plate of cold cuts. The crowd reminded me of a comp sci seminar, same seedy outfits (except for Chloe), same pasty, undernourished faces, including one I recognized. It was Ezra, the guy who called Porter an alarmist over his privacy concerns. His eye caught mine.

"Raúl!" he yelled, heading my way. "What're *you* doing here?"

"I was going to ask you the same thing," I answered. "I never expected to find you here among these paranoids."

Ezra rolled his eyes. "My profile got hacked. Personal details, private messages, pics, videos, all my contacts. My whole address book got bombed with scam messages, all designed to look like they came from me."

"Whoa," I said. "I sympathize."

"Yeah, took me weeks to sort it out and apologize," he explained.

"And now you're here, in paranoia town."

That made him smile. "Porter got a scam email from my address," he went on, "and he got in touch."

48

"Let me guess," I said, "he texted you to meet him at a place you were already at."

Ezra nodded vigorously. "*Yeah*," he said, very excited. "You know—we're all out in the digital frontier, totally exposed." He sipped his drink, got close to me and whispered, "So now I'm with *Vita Occulta*."

"I don't think you have to whisper in here," I pointed out. "These folks are already *of the body* and all our devices are in the can."

We heard a clap from the corner, where the two windowed walls met. It was Chloe.

"Okay, let's get started!" she shouted. "I know we have some newcomers tonight, so we'll start with introductions."

It was like a damn AA meeting. One by one, each person raised a hand and said their first name and how long they've been a member, like "Hi, I'm Penny, and I've been hidden for two weeks." That's how they put it—*hidden*, like instead of abstaining from alcohol, they'd gone off-world. When they got to me I said, "I'm Raúl. I just got here."

Chloe wouldn't let that pass. "Raúl," she said, "Porter was telling me what happened with you. Please share."

I didn't feel like *sharing*, but every eye was on me, and Porter nodded, so I told the whole story, not with the same level of detail I told Porter (more like a highlight reel), but I got the point across.

The room went dead quiet, and Chloe had a look on her face like I'd just told her my dog died.

That got things rolling. The newcomers, and a few of the long-hidden, told their stories: Rachael, harassed online, feared for her children's safety. Carly, whose identity was hijacked, was still untangling the string of unauthorized purchases a year later. Justin, convinced that his car was ratting him out to his phone, which was in cahoots with his computer, all of them sharing information overheard by his voice responder, which seemed to be in charge. Linus, spooked by advertisements popping up everywhere (including street kiosks), featuring products and services he'd merely thought of, not even saying them out loud. If I hadn't been freaked out when they started, I sure as hell was by the time they got through.

What caught my ear was this: they all used the same phrase, the one I'd first heard from Porter—the *All-Seeing Eye*.

The rest of the meeting was all about sharing pro tips on how to keep a low profile in the Cloud. Everyone was encrypting their comms. Many had opted out of any social media whatsoever. A hot topic was how to search the Internet for personal data and erase it, but no one had figured that out. They all were resigned to the fact that once something got into the Cloud, it was there for good, as the saying goes, like pee in a pool.

❖ ❖ ❖

After the formal part of the agenda, I got with Porter and Chloe. She was less standoffish than she'd been when we got there.

"Raúl, are you convinced?" she asked.

"Yeah," I said, "but after what I went through, I didn't need a lot of convincing."

She touched my arm. "You've got friends here, folks who'll help you manage your footprint."

I scanned the room. The crowd had separated into smaller groups, most of them chatting in animated fashion. "So it's all about shrinking your online presence?"

"That's what we focus on, mostly," Porter said. "Other chapters do it differently."

Chloe nodded. "The San Francisco chapter tries to *manage* their profiles, without minimizing them. They're careful about what they put out there, to shape their presence. They selectively shade their movements, use encrypted channels for sensitive communication, and clear channels for everything benign. They'll even expose false, but positive, material to enhance their image."

"Then there's the New York chapter," Porter added.

Chloe winced. "That's overkill."

"What?" I asked.

She rolled her eyes. "A small number of V.O. members won't go outside unless they're wearing a cloak and a hood, like a *burka*. They won't talk to anyone when they're cloaked, either."

"That sounds extreme," I agreed, then added, "But the hoodies…"

Chloe sniffed. "That's a reasonable precaution. I don't think we'll get to the point of hiding ourselves in public. On the other hand, New York *does* have a very high concentration of surveillance cameras, smart phones—all the billions of sensors that make up the All-Seeing Eye."

"About that," I said, and I asked her about the *All-Seeing Eye*.

She pulled a dollar bill out of her pocket and showed me the back of it.

Dollar bill. Paper money. It's how we paid for stuff.

"See this?" she said, pointing to a drawing of a pyramid, topped by a lurid eyeball in a triangle, radiating fire. "It's an occult symbol of Freemasonry, the Eye of Providence, also called the All-Seeing Eye of God."

I studied the symbol. I'd never taken a close look at it before, but in the context of the moment, it looked really creepy. Around it were the words: *ANNUIT CŒPTIS, NOVUS ORDO SECLORUM.*

"What do the words mean?" I asked.

"*Novus ordo seclorum* means *A new order of the ages,*" she explained. "With the explosion of the Internet of Things, with everything connected and communicating, we feel we're on the verge of a new order—but not a good one."

"And the other?" I asked.

"*Annuit cœptis.* It means *I approve what you're doing.*" She glanced sideways at Porter, then up at me. "*I* take it to mean that the All-Seeing Eye isn't just watching us—it's passing judgment."

11

Incognito

I KEPT GOING to the meetings, and every meeting was bigger than the last. The V.O. was catching on.

My experience with Moe and Curly was not unique. I must have heard a dozen stories like mine during Sharing Time, all of them with a common theme: The feds had detailed accounts of their whereabouts over days or weeks at a time, including pics, videos, and audio clips. One woman (a girl, really) named Pammie told her story, her voice softening to a whisper as she described explicit photos she'd shared with an ex, thinking them personal and private, until a fed whipped out his tablet and showed the startled girl the uncensored images. The photos had nothing to do with their line of questioning—they went after her, like they went after me, because her ex was involved with the P.A.—but the personal porn was pure intimidation. She felt like a bug under a microscope. All of us in the meeting were close to tears when she shared.

Pammie's story and others were gut-twisting, but they shocked me past Mirja and back into my work.

Me, Porter, Ezra, and the rest of the group dived back into the Worldstream, but it was Porter and me who were masters of the spec. We were the go-to guys for anything Worldstream, local celebrities, in fact, masters of the intricate details of the future Utopia. We felt like old men in a cave, gurus whom the tyros sought out for wisdom. That notoriety attracted another kind, the type who attended the V.O., like Pammie, looking for some way to scrub their online persona.

Jah, it was *so* simple back then. The data in the Cloud was like a damp lawn compared with the ocean of data in the Worldstream. But we were just getting started, dissecting the tangled web of social media, personal communications, sales and purchases, official records, not to mention all the stuff inadvertently picked up by smart phones, surveillance cams, and personal digital assistants. As limited as the Cloud was, it still seemed an impenetrable mess. How the feds managed to stitch together long narratives, like mine and Pammie's, from that jumble of disconnected factoids eluded us. It was like restoring a medieval fresco from a pile of fragments.

The only way we knew to solve the mystery of that feat was to duplicate it. And the first step was to sweep all the fragments into a pile.

Ezra had been working on the problem of combing the Cloud for life data weeks before Porter and I started, but his skills were lame. Porter was better, but if I'm allowed to say it, I was king of *that* hill. I'd delved into AI apps as an undergrad, and that kind of machine learning came in handy when searching for disconnected images and all the other references related to a person that get caught up, intentionally or not, in the all-consuming Cloud. Within a month, I'd catalogued terabytes of Raúl-related data, scattered across thousands of sites, the raw material for the mosaic of my life.

The thing was, despite having accumulated that trove, I couldn't replicate Moe and Curly's whole sequence. Major gaps still remained, with nothing to fill them. I'd worked on Pammie's profile and hers came up short, too.

"There's more out there," Porter said at three a.m. one morning, near the end of a marathon hacking session. He and Ezra and I had bounced ideas back and forth, tracking leads, hitting one wall after another, until tired and bleary-eyed, we were close to calling it quits.

"Yeah, you think?" I cast my laptop display to the TV to show the feds' timeline I'd reconstructed from memory, with hours-long gaps shown in red. The gaps showed up in almost every day of the timeline, in private locations—my apartment, or Chas's place, for example—or in public spots, like the time Mirja and I drove to Wisconsin and spent the weekend sailing on Lake Geneva. Curly detailed the entire trip, down to the make and model of the sailboat and what kind of liquor we drank. He even had video. Every gap was a hole we couldn't fill with data from the Cloud, no matter how diligently we searched.

"We need to hook in the rootkits," Porter proposed.

That was a place I didn't want to go.

You know rootkits, right? Like a tool for hacking into computers? Oh, of course you do.

We'd used rootkits before—what hacker hasn't?—but rarely, mostly out of curiosity, and never maliciously. What Porter suggested was plugging our collection of rootkits into our search algorithms to break security and collect data on a massive scale. The chance of detection from a single use was small, but multiplied across thousands of systems, it added up.

"I don't get how that'd work," I objected. "You still have to gain access system by system."

"I know," Porter continued. "That's why I'm working with Incognito."

That prospect made our eyebrows prickle.

Never heard of Incognito? I'm not surprised. They were a long time ago.

They called themselves *hacktivists*, geeks with a grudge who used their computer skills to wreak havoc on the Man— governments, corporations, individuals—*anyone* they took a dislike to. They had skills, but what really made them a force to deal with was their scale. No one knew how many Incogs there were, but there must have been tens of thousands, judging from results. Whatever target they aimed for, they blew away.

One time Incognito came down on a kiddie porn ring, invisible to normal, non-sick human beings who stuck to the Internet and never ventured into the Dark Web. It took them two days to hack the site and track down more than a hundred perverts, catalogue their contact info, and post it on the website of a Baptist church in Lynchburg, Virginia, whose pastor just happened to be the most prolific porn trafficker on the list. That turned the Incogs into folk heroes, even though it was child's play for them. When they busted the security of the British Ministry of Defense and left their calling card on 10,000 computers, we all knew for sure they were a primal force. They pulled that prank just for laughs.

Ezra and I were impressed, but also scared.

"They're criminals," Ezra pointed out.

"More like outlaws," Porter countered.

"Porter," I added, "the whole country's under curfew, the feds are crawling around the Internet, mocking up entire life stories from Cloud data. Scrutiny is intense. Do we really want to get involved with *Incognito?*"

Porter leaned back and pointed at the broken timeline on the TV, shaking his finger with each syllable. "We've wrung every last byte out of the Cloud and we still can't complete this picture." He picked at a loose thread on the arm of the chair. "How serious are we about this?"

That was a good question.

We were hobby hackers, not criminals. We didn't bust firewalls, exploit security holes, or plant malware in order to steal credit card numbers and porn site passwords. We were in it for the *challenge*. It was our way of honing chops, of showing our guns. A good hack won bragging rights, not stolen identities. We'd already strayed way beyond our usual boundaries gleaning data from the Cloud to reconstruct the Raúl biopic. What Porter was doing crossed a line—the point of no return.

I got up to pace. I think better when I'm pacing.

You know, this might happen to you some day, when you have to make a decision you can't take back. You'll dig down and figure out what you really want, and how much you want it, and how much you're willing to give up for it.

I wasn't over Mirja. I never had been. *She* mattered, and what happened to her—and why—mattered almost as much. Moe and Curly's ugly power play still irked me. I blamed the same people for both those things, even though I didn't know who they were.

I really, *really* wanted to find out.

Ezra and Porter watched me pace, working this all out in my mind, Porter with a *shit or get off the pot* expression and Ezra just looking spooked. I think they could tell which way I was leaning, and Ezra did this thing with his eyebrows that told me he'd go along with whatever Porter and I decided.

"Why would Incognito even want to help us?" I asked. "What's in it for them?"

"They know about your run-in with the feds, and Pammie's and the others. I told them. In fact, they'd already heard similar stories from their own members. When I told them what we had, they wanted it. They're not helping *us*, *we're* helping *them*."

"Okay," I said, "tell us what to do."

A week later our hacking engine and turbo-charged data sucker was ready to launch to a hundred thousand systems, courtesy of Incognito.

12

The Sweater Was Yellow

WE ALL WAITED on edge for any reaction, some mention in the forums of unusual activity, or security alarms, but nothing came. Our carpet-bombing campaign went undetected. Incognito was *good*.

And the data poured in, terabytes of personal stuff on thousands of folks the Moes and Curlys of the world had harassed, and the Incog legions got to work piecing together timelines just like mine and Pammie's.

Funny thing—our timelines, mine and Pammie's, never got any more complete. Oh, there were a few more bits sprinkled among the gaps, and lots of duplicates of what we already had, but the gaps persisted.

Somehow, Moe and Curly had filled them in, with data neither we nor the unnumbered members of Incognito could find.

❖ ❖ ❖

"*Think*, Raúl," Porter said to me over and over, until it pissed me off.

"Stop it!" I snapped. "I've thought it through 'til my head hurts." He was fixated on the trip to Lake Geneva and the weekend on the boat. They'd had videos of Mirja and me, lounging on deck, as if they'd shot us through a telephoto lens, real hi-res, and every word we said like it was recorded in a studio. I know *we* didn't take that video, in fact, we *couldn't* have. It was physically impossible. But I saw it, and Incognito's data-scrounging operation *hadn't* found it.

Porter wouldn't let up. "What was Mirja wearing?"

"Hell, I don't remember. A sweater of some kind."

57

"What color?"

That question annoyed me, because Mirja was always needling me about not noticing when she'd bought something new. There was this one time she bought a sweater, and she was excited to show me, turning around in our apartment like a model, asking, "Notice anything?" and me looking stupid until she pointed out her new yellow sweater, my favorite color, even, and I hadn't noticed. That yellow sweater was a sticking point between us for months.

And that's when I got it.

"The sweater," I whispered. "It was blue—navy blue."

"In the video?" he asked.

"No," I answered, "the sweater in the video was yellow, but the sweater she wore on the boat was blue."

And then Porter got it, too.

That video of Mirja and me on the boat wasn't real.

❖ ❖ ❖

"I think you guys are missing the point," is how I led off my turn at Sharing Time. Chloe didn't appreciate that.

"And just how are we missing the point?" she asked icily.

Porter jumped in. "This stream of Raúl's is manufactured. Parts of it are real, but there are gaps in the data where the feds interpolated."

"Interpolated?" Chloe asked.

I answered, "Filled in with synthesized data—photos, audio, video—even if there's no record of it. And it looks *real*, because it's all based on real data already in the Cloud."

Chloe gave us a little bit of a sneer. "You're talking about a deep fake," she huffed, with a theatrical roll of her eyes.

Deep fake. You've probably never heard of a deep fake before. We'd get a video of someone, like an actor, or a president, and morph another face onto it, or dub another voice over it and make the lips synch up. We could make the subject say anything we wanted. Quaint, right? It was so simple, any tyro could figure out how to do it in a few hours. Thing is, even if it wasn't an obvious fake, it didn't take much analysis to show the artifacts. A deep fake never fooled anyone for very long.

"No," I said, "we know what a deep fake looks like. This wasn't an *altered* video. It was synthesized from raw data. And it was slick—totally real, no artifacts."

"I don't see how that's possible," Chloe objected. I think she felt like she was losing control of the meeting, because everyone else was riveted.

"It's true," Pammie said. "They showed me stuff that I'm sure was private. After I talked to Raúl, I remembered some differences. And I remember now where those differences came from."

"Like the yellow sweater Mirja wore on the boat, only it wasn't yellow, it was blue," I said. "When Mirja bought it, she left a record behind, something like *sweater, women's, size six, yellow.* The algorithm must have made a connection between that record and our time on the boat."

Chloe laughed, kind of nervous. "I know a *little* about data manipulation, and what you're saying is—"

"I admit it's not easy," Porter conceded, "but it's not impossible. It *does* take massive resources, more than an amateur deep faker would have."

Chloe closed her eyes and sniffed. "Porter, really, you're not saying—"

"Here's what I'm saying," he interrupted. "Our American government, supposedly the protector of our rights, has built a massive AI engine designed to weave together all the little separate bits of data in the Cloud and recreate the life of anyone they want to intimidate."

"That's why the V.O. is missing the point," I added. "It's not enough to keep a low profile. Any missing pieces, they'll fabricate, and you won't be able to tell truth from fiction."

"But it's impossible!" Chloe shouted, loud enough to startle all of us into silence, until Porter said, real low, "Tell them, Raúl."

"This AI the government has," I began, "it's heavy-duty. Only a state actor…"

"Like America," Porter interjected.

"…has the resources to do this on a massive scale. But I've been working on this…"

"Wait 'til you hear this," Porter said over me.

"...and I can duplicate some of the same effects for individuals. What's more..."

"Here's the good part," Porter interrupted, bouncing on his toes.

"...I think I can put the synthesized material back into the Cloud."

That got their attention.

Pammie was the first to talk. "Then I could change my data?"

"That's the theory," I answered.

Well, the whole room started jabbering, but Chloe killed the buzz.

"Really, *Raúl*, is that *practical?*"

She was talking down. You know how that gets to me.

"Really, *Chloe*, I don't *know*. I'm *working* on it," I said, a little too over-the-top for the situation. The snark was not wasted on her.

"I don't appreciate that tone," she replied, sounding uncannily like my mother.

"Fine," I said, knowing it'd be better to keep my mouth shut, but not really caring. "You and your V.O.s can keep up your passive resistance, and your data will continue to seep into the Cloud no matter how hard you try to keep it out."

Porter was bouncing even harder, not because he was excited, but anxious, looking back and forth between me and Chloe.

"I *think* we know what we're doing," she said.

"And I *think* you lack vision," I countered, knowing that if I didn't end this it would blow up. I went to the big copper case and tapped on it. "Can you open this? I need my stuff."

"Leaving?" she asked in real oily fashion. "Good idea."

"C'mon, guys," Porter pleaded, "we're all here for the same thing, right?"

The room got very quiet. Porter waited for an answer, and I gave it.

"I don't think so, Bruh."

I left and I never went back.

13

Breaking the Rules

THAT'S WHEN WE kicked it into overdrive.

Overdrive. It's a car-related term. It means we went really fast.

We knew that if Uncle Sam could synthesize real events, they could invent fake ones that nobody could tell from real. If the feds wanted something from a target, and the target couldn't be intimidated, maybe they could be framed. I'd hoped that'd be a line they weren't willing to cross, actually fabricating stuff that never happened, but that line didn't seem all that bright, and they were toeing it already. Also, we knew that as hard as it was to make stuff up from Cloud data, it'd be a snap in the Worldstream. I told you that weaving a lifestream from the Cloud was like reassembling a shattered fresco, right? In the Worldstream, it's paint-by-numbers.

And that's why we had to hurry.

In the few weeks since martial law was lifted, and the goons in army olive drab went back to their barracks, and freedom of speech was in vogue again, the number of demonstrations multiplied. Porter and I took a cab (human driver paid in cash) to Grant Park one night, scene of a rare Incognito march. They were doing them all over the country, a sort of victory celebration for having hacked into the Department of Homeland Security computers and committing acts of mayhem, most notably posting a video on the DHS website apologizing for the government crackdown. We didn't know it at the time, but we learned later that the DHS hack was a diversionary tactic, a benign act of domestic terrorism, a red herring to throw the government dogs off the scent of Incognito's massive computer infiltration. The marches were more of the same, keeping the hack in the public eye, to keep security specialists worldwide from looking elsewhere. It worked really well.

An Incog march was nothing like a P.A. rally. There were no bullhorns or chanting crowds. It was kind of spooky, really, the Incogs milling around holding signs, saying nothing at all behind their masks.

Did I mention that? Oh, yeah. Incogs all wore Edward Snowden masks to hide their faces, like the V.O. in New York wearing hoods, but instead they wore dopey masks of some dork with glasses. Honestly, I don't even remember now who Edward Snowden was.

We took a position by the big fountain north of the march. We waited almost an hour in the freezing rain and the wind coming off the lake until the march broke up and the Incogs wandered away.

"Where's your guy?" I asked Porter once the last of the Snowdens disappeared. Porter nodded toward a dark figure heading toward us, wearing a parka, his face hidden inside a fur-trimmed hood.

He got to within ten feet of us then stopped and said in a thin voice I could barely hear over the wind, "Porter?"

"Yeah," Porter answered, and added, "This is Raúl."

The mysterious stranger came closer, pulling back the parka hood.

It was a woman, Asian, with a round face and her hair in cornrows.

"Case?" Porter asked, obviously surprised.

"My name's Molly," she said. "Can we go someplace warm?"

❖ ❖ ❖

We hiked across Michigan Avenue to Buddy Guy's and got a table a ways back from the stage about an hour before showtime. Porter ordered beers for the table and he and I ordered sandwiches. Molly, a.k.a. "Case," stuck with her beer.

Buddy Guy. I only caught the tail end of his career. You missed out. *I* missed out.

"I hope my coming down here all the way from Madison in this weather proves that I'm serious," Molly began.

"I never doubted you," Porter answered.

"How 'bout you fill me in," I said, not having been briefed, other than Porter telling me *We're meeting my Incog contact.* "Porter's been all cloak and dagger with me."

Molly didn't smile, just sipped her beer, smacked her lips, and said, "I'm breaking all kinds of rules meeting in person. We're *Incognito* for chrissakes." She lowered her voice when she said that, just as the waiter showed up with our sandwiches.

I took a bite. "So how do *we* rate?" I asked around a mouthful of po' boy.

"I found Case on a Dark Web hacker site," Porter said, real quiet, like he was violating *omertà*. "Wait," he said suddenly, "where's your smart phone?"

"I left it at home, like you told me," I answered, wiping tartar sauce from my chin.

"Good." He checked his watch. "We've got twenty minutes before they start live-streaming the show."

"That's another rule I'm breaking," Molly added, "being in public as an Incog without my Snowden."

"So, I'll ask again: how do we rate?" I pressed.

"This project," Molly replied, "what we're talking about—it's new, not like anything we've done. Requires different coordination. Very risky."

"I'm not following," I said. "How's this different from the DHS hack, or busting the child porn ring?"

She pushed her beer aside and leaned toward me. "Those were all crowdsourced," she said, "the way we normally operate. We post a target and let the Incogs go to work. Shit happens, like magic. We don't know who's involved and we don't need to know. Fuck, we don't *want* to know. There're thousands and thousands of Incogs and I know less than a hundred by name. I've only ever met six or seven face to face." She picked up her beer like she was going to take a drink, but held it in mid-air. *"This* thing, a toolkit for manipulating Cloud data—that's a *product."* She finally drank. "I've done product development. It takes a team. I'll need to make contacts, assign tasks, follow up. It's a totally different paradigm. A lot of Incogs will have to come out from behind their Snowdens. It's *risky."*

She looked genuinely concerned, to the point where it worried me, too.

"If it's that big a risk, why are we talking?" I asked.

Molly drained the last of her beer, which was most of it. "Porter told me about your run-in with the Man," she said. "The same fucking thing happened to me."

14

Shredded

By the time two-thirds of state legislatures had ratified a resolution calling for a constitutional convention, we had our prototype crawler.

Molly and Porter were machines, pulling together the resources we needed to craft the crawlers, hack security, and set up the repositories for any given individual's lifestream. My part was the AI to morph the data cache into a made-to-order Cloud presence. I liked that just fine, what I considered the creative element, compared with the drudgery of scavenging the Internet for data.

We tried it out on my own footprint, building a cache of my Cloud data about the time the convention convened. It went on for three months, the proceedings broadcast non-stop, with 24/7 commentary, about as long as it took Porter, Molly and her team to perfect the crawler and build caches for Molly and Pammie.

It didn't take long for the states to ratify the new constitution, no longer than it took me to craft new personas for Molly, Pammie, and me. We were born anew in the Cloud.

We advertised our new service via the Dark Web, and in no time had more business than we could handle, burnishing the Cloud footprints of ne'er-do-wells and unfortunates caught up in the federal dragnet. We had to turn folks away, even after we raised our prices. We talked about franchising but decided against it. We didn't want the hassle, and we weren't in it for the money anyway. The cryptocurrency income was more than enough to support us lavishly.

We took a break, as did the entire nation, to celebrate the founding of the Millennium Republic of the Americas. It was a week-long bacchanal, as much a requiem for the failed American experiment as it was for the dawning of the New Order.

After we sobered up, we got to work on another concept we'd been kicking around: If it was possible to collect all the data for a target and reshape it, we reasoned, it must be possible (in some ways easier) to simply delete it, as if that person never existed.

Yeah, that's right—the shredder, a machine to obliterate a life.

It took us two more months before we were ready to try it out. And I had a target in mind, a life lived with abandon, devoted to all the passion I lacked, passion I sought but which had always eluded me—a life that needn't be vulnerable to prying government eyes, that deserved a memorial in the hearts of those who loved her and nowhere else.

Uh-huh. Mirja. She didn't want it. She didn't even know about it. She was dead, for Jah's sake.

❖ ❖ ❖

You all studied history. So, you know what happened next.

Chas and the P.A. got prime seats at the convention, and they pushed hard for their parliamentary plan. In theory it might have worked out, but Madison, Jefferson, and Hamilton were absent, and the product wasn't a well-framed foundation for a republic. Instead we got a slide show, mashed up by feuding factions with hundreds of provisions intending to please everyone, but mostly avoiding pissing off any one person to the point of blowing up the proceedings. It was the lowest common denominator. Instead of a modern, efficient, globally competitive government, everyone working to the same ends, we escalated squabbling to a new level. I suppose you could say we were just being honest with ourselves, that infighting is a fact of human nature, and the way to deal with it was simply to vest one person, the First Minister, with supreme power. I think that's what Chas wanted most of all, and he might have made it, if he hadn't been gunned down, one of the last high-profile assassinations before the gun ban.

Yeah, the mass shootings stopped, not only because we drained the ocean of firearms, but because of the miraculous birth of Jahbulon. We harnessed the fine mesh of electronic eyes and ears to a single intelligence, a pervasive, omnipotent voice responder, who would dispatch his army of angels in black to the aid of any who would call on his mighty name. The old gods were dead. We didn't even need them to curse anymore.

Over time the states lost their significance. For the purposes of governance, we citizens were all partitioned into equal-sized districts, and our minds got reconciled to that structure. State boundaries faded away. And anyway, we weren't the *United States* any longer, we were one *Millennium Republic*. The idea of sovereign states came to be regarded as subversive.

World peace didn't work out like we planned. Sure, the Baltic conflict was the last shooting war, not counting a dozen or so regional dust-ups. VR gave every nation the ability to meet in a safe venue without language barriers, the better to resolve our differences, but we couldn't give them the desire to do so. Old tribal urges die hard. What kept the peace wasn't reasoning at the bargaining table, or universal love and understanding, but the same thing that's always kept it: a global cop with overwhelming destructive power, one which wasn't afraid to use it. America? Hardly.

No one doubted that the Chinese would launch a missile just to make a point.

That didn't mean the end of conflict, of course. Rivalries simply moved from the battlefield to cyberspace, where no nation had a monopoly on virtual armaments.

Luxury was never democratized like we'd imagined. VR gear got cheap, but not free, and no matter how good the experience, how perfect the simulation of RL, there was always some new thing for only a few thousand credits promising a nuance that'd been missing up to then. When

Stimulus Rex invented the Belt, we thought it was the last word in authentic VR—how could it get any better? Now we're up to Gen 5. I'm sure there's some subtlety in my virtual life that I'll desperately crave as soon as some seller of VR gear points it out to me.

And the venues turned into lucrative revenue streams, siphoning credits from the masses to the monopolies. Accumulation of wealth, whether from real or virtual commerce, seems programmed into human DNA.

Which explains the diversion of all industry and innovation from the creation of lasting works to the coding of fleeting digitized assets, and from the upkeep of the physical world to the care and feeding of the Worldstream. We kept just enough of the infrastructure to move food and raw materials around.

Yes, people *did* stay put, crammed into urban centers where bandwidth was plentiful and cheap, letting the world come to them, but all the energy we saved not moving people around we burned in hyperscale computing farms where every last word, image, thought, desire, hope, and dream was stored, and the universe was replicated in perfect detail and endless repetition. Nobody worried about global warming anymore—why would they? We never left our homes, and the Earth's ugly decay stayed comfortably hidden on the RL side of our visors. We lived in the flawless reproduction of Real Life, bought at the cost of a perfect, complete, and indelible record of every move and every word—the extinction of privacy.

And we learned too late the potential for the mass distribution of faux reality to manipulate minds on an epic scale.

Porter? He's still around. Molly, too.

Anyway, that all happened fifty years ago.

What else do you want to know?

PART TWO
ORWELL 2075

15

Ogallala

Mom's stories *almost* got our minds off the storm.

Ogallala in the winter was lo-res. That wasn't even a term I used anymore, *lo-res*, not since Hammad and I busted confinement in Nodaway, but I don't have a better word. It was minus twenty outside, we were buried under a meter of snow, and the wind hadn't stopped howling for three days. The wind turbines were spinning, so at least we had power, although the heat wasn't great in our little three-room cabin. But Hammad had built a fire in the fireplace, and with the cracks, pops, and smoke smell, and the flames making weird patterns, it was all very real.

I had a stack of books from the library because I like to read when I'm alone, but I was never alone in that place when more than one person was in it, especially in winter. Those nights Hammad, Mom, and I huddled around the fire to keep warm, Hammad's dark skin glowing in the firelight, and Mom's pale face blazing, hair redder than usual, her brown eyes reflecting tiny flickering flames. She looked younger than she did in daytime, and seeing her then was like looking in a mirror.

We talked about our lives back in the world, catching up on all the time me and Mom were apart. She filled me in on her life with the Shade, and the background of her crew members Bjorg and Elisha who came with her to Orwell (their real names were Celeste and Thomas). She told us about Adrian, whose Shade name was Nemesio, how they'd had a relationship, and how he'd been nabbed in a Kliegl raid. Adrian had some scheme, called the *persona*, to let Shade re-enter the Worldstream without triggering an alarm. She'd told us the whole story before, but that was okay, because every time she told it, she remembered something new, and besides, we didn't have anything else to do. Hammad listened patiently, though he didn't have the same stake in the story that I did. It kept us from going nuts for a couple days until she had told us everything she could remember. After that we played cards.

Just to illustrate how lo-res it was, the pipes froze night before last. No washing, no cleaning, not even water to drink until we figured out how to unfreeze the pipes. I finally did it by using the clothes iron, an old antique thing the first Orwellians brought from the world. It took forever, even at the high setting (cotton), tied to the pipe with a rope, and for some reason the iron kept shutting itself off. I had to untie it and shake it 'til the light came on and tie it back on again, but at least we had water. Mom suggested letting the faucet drip overnight so the pipes wouldn't freeze again, which Hammad thought was a good idea. I didn't have an opinion. We tried it, and it worked.

If this had been a VR venue, I'd have suspended it— flipped a switch and made the storm, the cabin, the fire, and the sour smell of bodies unwashed for three days all fade away and raster out to the pure white staging venue.

But then what would I do? Go off to Australia and chase wombats? Climb old Incan ruins in Peru? I'd probably ask my voice responder to recommend an ultra-hi-res venue, picked out just for me based on my VR history and psych profile. Fake—all fake.

Or else jack into some sleazy lifestream, the Belt mainlining my amygdala, jamming my brain like some IO peripheral made of muscle and blood, twitching me like a frog. It's two-way—did you know that? It can keep track of responses. Mom told me. The Belt doesn't just give you the full immersive experience, it also monitors you—takes your pulse at the neuron level. It's how Madeleine did *her* thing, how she got data on thousands of stream riders, so she could work her evil on millions the way she'd fucked over my mom.

Winter in Ogallala may've been lo-res, but it was *real.* And you know, if it's real, I guess it can't *really* be lo-res, can it?

But I don't want to give the impression that just because it was freezing and we were up to our chest in snow that life stopped. Jackson made the rounds once a week at least. The last time was before the blizzard hit when he handed out work assignments.

"Muhammad, storm's a-comin', so you have snow duty," Jackson said.

Hammad's face turned glum, his eyes downcast and mouth tightening, but he knows better than to complain out loud in front of Jackson. Clearing snow from the streets of Orwell sounds worse than it is, because Orwell has a tractor with a snowplow on it, but it's still pretty bad. Hammad is definitely not a cold-weather person, and our hand-made coats, mittens, and boots aren't the best at keeping a body warm.

"Grace—Making and maintenance," Jackson continued, handing Mom her hours for the week on a printed-out schedule. Mom likes Making. It's how everyone in Orwell gets their furniture, tools, and things, whether printed or fabbed out of wood or metal, or clothing cut and sewn. Even though Mom's not our best maker, she's enthusiastic and her output is high. Maintenance she *doesn't* care for, but everyone takes turns at the drudge jobs.

"Dylan, it's your lucky day," Jackson said. "You're foreman on the maintenance shift with Grace."

Mom smiled and put her hand on my shoulder and squeezed, like she was proud of her little man. The foreman's responsible for everything that happens on the shift, including keeping everyone on task, so if something goes wrong, Jackson goes after the foreman, not the crew. But he knows Mom's not the most compliant of workers. She just doesn't like to be told what to do. Jackson regularly puts me and Mom on the same shift, because she takes orders better from me than anyone else.

A lot of maintenance is outdoors, and with nasty weather on the way, the only thing that could make it worse is a bad crew.

"Who else is on my shift?" I asked.

I cringed when Jackson answered, "Tomorrow, Frank and Grace. Tuesday, Frank and Max." Mom squeezed my shoulder a little harder. Max is okay to work with. Frank is *not*. Jackson gave us his steeliest stare—his signal not to complain. *Shoulder-to-shoulder, arm-in-arm, hearts and minds*, as Jackson is fond of saying.

And everyone takes turns.

❖ ❖ ❖

The Monday shift came just before the blizzard. It was fifteen outside, unseasonably warm for January. That also meant we were in for a nasty storm when the front came through. Mom and I met Frank at town hall, or, more like it, we went to town hall and waited for Frank to show up late for the shift—without a tool belt.

"Frank," I said, trying not to sound overly bossy, "where's your belt?"

He looked at us kind of dumb with his hands on his waist, feeling around for the missing belt, as though he'd find it there.

"I figured we'd be inside today," he explained, which made no sense, because even if we were working inside we'd have toolboxes, and he didn't have one of those, either.

I got close and spoke in a low, steady voice, not threatening, but firm, like Jackson would do. "Look at the sky, Frank. There's a storm on its way, and we need to get the outside jobs done before the storm. So head on back to the tool locker and *get your belt*."

Frank looked like he was going to spit.

"Yes, sir," he muttered and shuffled off to the tool locker. I could smell the moonshine on his breath.

"Frobnitz," I grumbled, which is what Frank is—totally useless. I looked at Mom. "He's been drinking. Not even nine in the morning, and he's *already* drinking. I could smell it."

Mom put her hand behind my head and ran her fingers through my hair. We were right out on the main street, and people were already out for the morning. I pulled her hand away.

"Could you please *not* do that, Mom? Not while we're working."

She took her hand back. She was hurt, I could tell, and I probably didn't need to say what I said. But when we're working together, she's not my Mom. She's my crew.

16

Hearts and Minds

OBVIOUSLY, I DON'T like Frank. It's not because he's lax in his habits, or because he drinks corn liquor for breakfast, although those things offend me. He's slovenly in his clothes and in his personal grooming, but it would be fake of me to judge him on that, though it does say something about a man if he doesn't at least *try* to present himself. I suppose a man can be loose in his morals, or weak when it comes to keeping himself fit, and not be lazy otherwise, as long as he works hard and keeps his promises to his friends (if he has them), you know? Those things—virtues—seem to come naturally to those who like other people and themselves. But if a man thinks everyone owes him and they haven't paid up, it's hard for him to like anyone, except maybe his fellow loafers. Frank's like that. He seems to hate everything and everyone.

Our first work ticket was a roof repair on Ms. Ubuntu's house. She's 89 years old, nearly blind and mostly deaf. Anyone in Orwell can order a repair, though some folks work on their own houses when they're not on a shift. Jackson makes his rounds and inspects the senior citizens' houses for needed repairs, opening tickets for folks like Ms. Ubuntu, because he knows they can't fend for themselves, and may not even know they have a problem.

Our first stop after Frank fetched his tool belt was the equipment shed.

"Extension ladder," I said to Benny, the maintenance manager. He was bent over the engine of a beat-up tractor, checking the fluid levels. I held up the ticket for Ms. Ubuntu's.

"Checked out," Benny yelled, sounding upset.

"Something eating at you, Benny?" I asked, because he's an easy-going guy who rarely raises his voice.

Benny wiped the dipstick with an oily rag and stuck it back in the engine. "Been checked out for a week." He pointed at Frank. "To that guy right there. Never brought it back. Who needs a ladder for a whole week?"

Frank's eyes narrowed and his mouth pinched. He always acts righteous when he's called out for something that we all know is true. The act never fooled anyone.

"I'm still using it," Frank said.

"For what?" Benny yelled, louder than before. "'I need to nail up some soffit' is what you said. How long did that take you? Ten minutes? Five?" He tossed the rag on a bench and spat on the floor, angrier than I'd ever seen him.

"I'll get to it," Frank mumbled.

I realized that Frank had checked out the ladder and never even used it. That's no different from stealing in my judgment. Still, Benny was overreacting.

"Benny, ease off," I said, one friend to another. "We'll stop off at Frank's for the ladder. No problems."

Benny pushed his mouth to one side, as if chewing the inside of his cheek. "While you're there," he said, spitting again, "pick up the chainsaw, *and* the trencher, *and* the log-splitter. Hey Frank—how long you had that log-splitter? A month, now? Hold on, don't tax your brain too much." He unhooked a clipboard from the wall and paged through it. "Did I say a month? I'm being too damned charitable. *Seven weeks!*" He pitched the clipboard onto the bench. "Splitting a lot of logs, Frank? Your woodpile good for the winter?"

Frank got red-faced and splotchy. His hands were clenched as if he wanted to deck Benny. He might have, too, if Mom and I hadn't been there. He's done it before.

"I got a downed tree," Frank said through gritted teeth.

Benny's shoulders drooped, his anger used up, and he picked up the clipboard, hanging it back on the wall. He grabbed the rag and pulled the dipstick on the next tractor without a word.

I couldn't let it drop. Benny had calmed down for now, but Frank wasn't going to be any more conscientious about returning the tools. The longer Frank dragged this out, the more Benny would stew over it.

Mom must've been thinking the same thing, because she jumped in. "Benny," she said softly, "we'll get all those things back to you, the ladder, the chainsaw, and…what else?"

"Trencher. Log-splitter." Benny looked back at the clipboard. "And power washer. He's had that since November."

Frank turned three more shades of red, almost purple, and I braced for the backlash.

"Nobody else *wanted* 'em," Frank hissed. "You'd've come to me if anyone else wanted 'em."

It was Benny who lashed out. "That's not the *fucking point!*" he yelled, and threw the rag against the window, leaving a big, greasy spot. "That's not *your* equipment. It belongs to everyone in Orwell. You treat it like it's yours, and it's an insult to *all* of us!"

I decided it was time to get some distance between Frank and Benny.

Mom had other ideas.

"Oh, we'll make sure everything gets back to the shed, okay?" she said, in a motherly way. "And everything will be back to normal."

That didn't sit well with Benny *or* Frank.

"Nothin'll be normal as long as that *avatar* keeps hoarding equipment," Benny growled, using just about the worst insult you can throw at anybody in Orwell. That signaled to me that things were spiraling out of control, which didn't register with Mom at all, since she just frowned with mom eyes, which might have infuriated Benny even more if he wasn't glaring at Frank.

"That's enough!" I said, short of yelling. It'd gotten scarily quiet in the shed, like two animals facing off with menacing, almost sub-sonic growling.

I put my hand on Frank's shoulder and turned him away, which he was only too happy to do. I tried the same with

Mom but she gave me a surprised, pained look, like I was interfering instead of taking charge and running my crew. I didn't have time to deal with her objections at that exact moment. I kept pressure on her shoulder and she got the message and followed Frank out of the shed.

"Equipment'll be back before sundown, Benny," I said.

Benny gave me a cold stare, then turned away, like he was ashamed of having acted out. I felt for him, because Benny is a gentle soul, and it doesn't come easy to him to stand his ground when his job calls for it. I could see he was embarrassed over the whole scene, and the best way I could honor him was to let him be and get his equipment back to him as quickly as I could.

❖ ❖ ❖

At Frank's we picked up the ladder, which he'd leaned up against the side of his house a week ago under the loose soffit. It seemed like a quick, easy job. And I was right, because I climbed the ladder myself and nailed the soffit in place. It took me two minutes.

❖ ❖ ❖

By the time we got to Ms. Ubuntu's house it was almost noon, nearly two hours behind schedule. We'd have to hurry to take care of all the tickets we had on hand. Believe it or not, Frank suggested we stop for lunch.

"After Ms. Ubuntu," I told him, not quite holding my temper in check. "We're already behind schedule, we don't have a lot of daylight left, and we've got a stack of work tickets we'll be lucky to finish by sunset." I stopped before adding *thanks to you*, since that wouldn't have made Frank work any faster.

Ms. Ubuntu is a short little Black lady who looks like a toy, with very thick glasses and a sweet smile. Mom really likes her, and she spent time with her while Frank and I got up on the roof. Mom's 100% capable of working up top, after training and practice on repairs and new construction. But Frank and I could do the repairs while Mom visited, since the work crews will often give comfort to the older Orwellians, and Mom's experience taking care of old folks living IRL for years made her the obvious choice. And there's no way Frank could do it.

The repair was a leak where the roof met the chimney. I saw the problem right away: water pooling at the angle between the chimney and the roof, and the flashing was inadequate. I told Frank to fetch a can of roofing cement and a roll of flashing.

"Can't you get it?" he protested. He was sweating even though it was cool outside, and out of breath just from climbing the ladder. It was sad to see a man like him so unfit, maybe twice my age yet not *really* old, but I couldn't let that be an excuse for him not doing his job.

"No, I told *you* to get it. It'll take you ten minutes. While you're getting the stuff, I'll be pulling back the shingles so we can lay down the flashing."

"I can pull back the shingles," he said, gulping for air between sentences. "You're the young buck who can run up and down ladders all day, while Mommy sits inside drinking tea."

It crossed my mind that I should just get the damn materials myself, to avoid an argument, and besides, I could get to the supply shed and back way faster. We were short on time anyway. But that *Mommy* comment went too far, and I wasn't going to let it pass.

"Frank, you can get the fucking materials, or you can go home, and I'll let Jackson know that you're available for trash collection," I said calmly and evenly, but swearing to let him know I meant it.

And it worked, or I thought it did, because Frank climbed down without another word and headed off in the direction of the supply shed.

Ten minutes was all it took to pull up the shingles. An hour later, Frank was still gone.

I found him in a chair leaning back against the wall in the Taproom, drinking a beer. How about that—one o'clock in the afternoon and he was drinking a beer after walking off the job. And that was *after* he'd showed up late with alcohol on his breath.

It was just him and me.

"What's this about, Frank?" I asked him as calmly as I could manage. He stuck his mug in his face and refused to make eye contact.

"Are you going to answer me?" I felt like I was talking to a little kid.

"You told me to go home, remember?" he muttered, flicking little bits of foam down his front.

"This is the *Taproom*, Frank," I shot back, then I realized that was a stupid comeback. Better to stick to business, as Jackson would. "We have a job to do. Let's get it done."

"Oh no," he said. He stood up a little unsteadily, like that last beer wasn't his first, and got himself another. "Sent me home, that's what you did. You and Mommy can finish the job. Go tell Jackson you sent me home."

How a man could be so hateful to the world, and to himself, just overloaded my mind. I started thrashing, unable to think of how to resolve the situation. I'm not a hateful person but at that moment I hated Frank, and I hated myself for letting him get to me. I could have kicked him.

❖ ❖ ❖

I found Jackson in the maker space working on a chair and filled him in. It would've been just like Jackson to say, "It's your crew. Deal with it," but he didn't, maybe because he knew what a frobnitz Frank could be, but more likely because he thought I couldn't handle it. And that made me hate Frank all the more.

"You and Grace finish what you can and report back. I'll take care of Frank," he said. I mentioned the equipment Frank had checked out, and Jackson gave me his master key if I needed it to get into Frank's shed and retrieve the tools. That impressed me, because Jackson almost *never* parts with that key.

❖ ❖ ❖

Mom and I finished the repair on Ms. Ubuntu's house and cleared two other tickets, leaving three undone. We kept our promise to Benny and returned everything to the equipment shed, though it was past sunset by the time we did. I had to use the master key to get in, since it was way past Benny's work hours.

Frank spent the next four weeks on trash pickup.

That night the blizzard hit, and nobody left their houses for three days.

17

Frankendrone

It was a month after the blizzard and snow still sat in piles at both ends of the street, though it had warmed up by the time the drone came.

There were no drones in Orwell; the only bugs were back in the world. So, when I heard it, I perked up. I hadn't heard that sound in almost a year, not since Nodaway, but I knew it. I hurried out of the library to find the street lined with folks who'd reacted the same way, astounded to see a black six-rotor drone fifteen meters overhead, moving slowly down the street.

The drones from confinement had a camera and two taser magazines—standard configuration for security bugs—but this one had two additional cameras, three in all, and no tasers. This bug was purely for surveillance. All us *Vitreous Orb* townspeople, staring up at that damn thing…well, that was just about the dumbest thing we could've done.

We all followed it with our eyes until we flinched at the sound of a gunshot. The bug pitched forward with a grinding noise, losing altitude, until it hit the sidewalk, spitting sparks all the way down. It barely missed a woman, who ducked at the last second. Three or four rotors were still spinning, and the thing bounced along the walls of buildings, like a giant wounded insect, then ran off the end of the walk, partially burying itself in a snow pile. Another shot rang out and the bug exploded into pieces, sending shards of debris and a spray of dirty snow flying ten meters or more.

The shooter strolled over to the dead bug, loosely holding his 9mm rifle. It was Max, an important man in Orwell and a really good guy, who runs a number of operations, including the grain elevator and processing plant. Max is also the best shot in Orwell. He can hit a deer at a hundred meters almost every time, but putting a bullet through a moving drone? Still massively impressive, even at close range.

I ran to where the bug lay. It had stopped sparking, the rotors dead—fully crumped. The snow melted around it, sizzling on its metal skin, sending up a little plume of steam. Max pointed his gun as if to shoot it again point-blank, which would've vaporized it, but Jackson caught up to him. He put his hand on Max's gun arm and pushed it down, then tossed his jacket over the drone.

"I don't think we want to destroy it completely, Max," Jackson said softly, as though he thought the bug had ears. "Not yet."

Max understood, and so did I—a drone in Orwell was inexplicable, and Jackson wanted an explanation.

Jackson looked at me. "Dylan, take this thing to the maker space. Lay it out on one of the workbenches. Keep the jacket on it. And whatever you do, *don't* let it get a look at anything."

The drone was big, a meter across, ungainly though not very heavy. I also had to gather up all the bits of debris. Jackson's jacket didn't cover a lot of it, just the cameras, one of which was already destroyed. I thought it unlikely that the drone was still communicating with base, if it ever was, being out here in the wilderness. But Jackson clearly didn't want to take chances, and neither did I.

❖ ❖ ❖

We were gathered around the bug: me, Jackson, Max, and Naia, another one of the town leaders, and the one who busted Hammad and me out of confinement. She had pulled off that operation like an RL ninja, dressed in camo and wielding a plasma torch like a samurai sword to cut through the perimeter fence like a spider web. She's beautiful, too, but fierce, with intense eyes, an angular mouth, dark skin, long black hair, and a body like an ultimate fighter.

"Is that a standard configuration?" Jackson asked, squinting at the drone, arms crossed. "I don't think it is."

"No tasers," Naia replied. "Two magazines are standard, here and here, where these cameras are." She'd scanned the bug and verified it was dead, but she unscrewed the lenses anyway, just to be safe. Naia also saves *everything*. I'm sure she already had plans for those lenses.

"How'd it get here?" Jackson asked.

"No clue. The power cell is good for five hours, max, and with a top speed of 60 kph, that's not even enough juice to make it the 800 klicks from Omaha, let alone the return trip."

"And if they didn't plan for a round trip?"

Naia scratched the back of her neck and puckered her lips. "We already know it didn't come all the way from Omaha, so round trip or no, it had to come from someplace closer, 150 klicks or less if whoever sent this bug wanted it back, 300 klicks if they didn't. But that's not the only open question." Naia was always gaming out all possible scenarios, looking for the one that made the most sense. I saw where she was going.

"How does it talk?" I asked. "There're no comms out here."

Naia smiled in her severe way. "Right. Either this bug was recording, and our unknown friends expected to get it back, or it was communicating with them somehow."

"But they couldn't count on getting it back," I pointed out, waving my hand over the savagely crumped bug, "for obvious reasons."

"Right. Which means…"

"This thing was in contact."

Jackson looked around the circle before settling on Naia. "Can you do a scan?"

She shook her head. "I've already scanned what I could with the gear I've got. Nothing. But…"

"But what?" Jackson asked.

"When's our next supply run?" she said.

"Not for another week," Max answered.

Naia rapped her knuckles on the table. "Maybe we should pull that in."

❖ ❖ ❖

Max made the drive the next day, leaving before sunrise with the usual list of key items we couldn't make ourselves, and with a couple of additional items Naia requested: a spectrum analyzer, DC to 60 gigahertz, and a broadband antenna. They weren't cheap—more than we normally spend on tech gear in a year—but we were sufficiently spooked that we were ready to spend a significant fraction of the Orwell treasury on a piece of sophisticated equipment we had almost no use for. That was especially true once we heard from Laputa and Burgess, two other V.O. towns, that they'd spotted bugs, and Laputa had also shot one out of the sky.

A supply run usually takes three or four days—one day out, a day or two to fulfill the shopping list, and a day back. Max left on a Thursday and didn't return until the following Tuesday. Naia was anxious about not having her gear with so many unanswered questions concerning the bug, and I was worried something might have gone wrong, but Jackson kept calm, saying, "It'll take him time to track down that analyzer." And he was right—according to Max, there was nothing at all like it in Omaha, like *nowhere*, and he had to make a trip via hypertube to Chicago to fetch one, and the antenna to go with it. In the world, getting an item like that would've been as simple as ordering dim sum via drone, but we were doing this all outside the Worldstream.

Our time wasn't *totally* wasted. We retrieved the other bug from Laputa, which the folks there were only too happy for us to take off their hands. There were enough parts from the two bugs for Naia to reconstruct a complete, functioning drone, minus the cameras. The Frankendrone sat in the maker space for a day, powered down, waiting for Max's return.

18

Conspiracy Theories

"THEY COME OUT around midnight, groups of five or ten, dressed all in white except for a red sash across their chests, and a ridiculous red cap, like a squat upside-down flowerpot, with the Kliegl searchlight symbol on it. They carry wicked collapsible batons they can whip out in one move and beat the snot out of anyone who gets in their way. But nobody does. The streets are deserted after dark, except for the Kliegl gangs."

That was Max talking, the day after the supply run. We were all in the Taproom: Max, Jackson, Naia, and the regular pre-dinner group, which gathers earlier in the day in winter than summer, daylight being in short supply and not much work to complete. I don't go to the Taproom often, but lately that's where most of the important decisions get made, casually, instead of at town meetings, or leader council. That seems loose to me, as if Orwell lacks a formal process, but at least at the Taproom I can listen in.

"And that's in Omaha?" Jackson asked.

"Chicago's where I saw the worst of it," Max answered. "It's just now hitting Omaha. There's not much Shade in Omaha, so I guess it's not a priority. Chicago, New York, Atlanta, Denver, L.A., from what I heard, it's panic in the streets."

"But in Omaha—there're Kliegls there?"

"Mostly Civils," Max replied, referring to Civil Authorities, the law in the world: black-shirted, taser-toting agents of Jahbulon. "But, yeah, there's a few." He took a swig. "Chicago's overrun with Kliegls. They're on every corner from dusk until dawn. What the fuck does it take to be a Kliegl? I don't know. Just show up, I guess. Anyway, there's thousands of 'em, and they're orchestrating a freaking reign of terror."

"What do you mean?"

"Now that all the unaffiliated Shade crews are in confinement, Kliegls have a lot of free time. They fancy themselves a vigilante army, the hand of Jahbulon. Civils don't lift a finger to stop 'em. Less work for them."

"The unaffiliated crews? What's that about?"

Max scrunched up his face and nodded. "Yeah. Rounded them all up. Raided their dorms and ran 'em in. But just the independents. That's the thing—the affiliated crews, the *Vita Occulta,* they're all intact."

"How do you know?"

"My supplier. He contracts with V.O. for services. Not only has the workforce *not* dried up, the lead time's gone down."

"That doesn't make sense," Naia said. "Why would the V.O. crews be faster? You'd think that with the crackdown, there'd be a shortage of labor." She paused and drank. "Unless…"

"Unless the independents aren't all going into confinement," I jumped in, even though I wasn't supposed to be eavesdropping.

"Right!" Naia agreed, as if I'd read her mind. "Meaning…" She trailed off and held her hand out, inviting me to finish the sentence.

"Some of those independent Shade are going to the V.O., maybe even most," I said.

Everyone stared at me in silence.

"When Naia and Raúl broke me and Hammad out of confinement," I continued, "Raúl told us most of the confinees he busted out went to work for the V.O. They paid him for the new head, he shredded 'em, and the warden of the confinement facility got a piece of it. They were all in it together."

Jackson narrowed his eyes and shook his head. "So, you're saying that the Kliegl campaign to round up the evil Shade is just an excuse for the *Vita Occulta* to wipe out their competition," he said sarcastically.

"I don't know," I mumbled, wishing I could take it back. I thought that's exactly what was happening, but I hate it when Jackson does that, makes me feel like I said something dumb.

Everyone looked down awkwardly, until Naia broke the silence.

"Hold on, Jackson, I think the kid's onto something."

Jackson set down his mug and crossed his arms, the way he does when someone challenges him, which doesn't happen often. "The Kliegl party is about getting rid of the outlaw Shade," he said. "It's their whole reason for being. It's what put them in power. And now you're saying it's a *ploy?* Just a phony issue to get them elected?"

"Shocking, isn't it?" Naia replied, unperturbed. I loved the way she could turn a person's argument around on them with only a few words. I wish I could do that.

And it worked. Jackson bit his lip and reached for his beer. "I'm not buying it," he said into the mug, blowing foam over the rim, but he was starting to *think* about it.

"The whole regime depends on the Worldstream, right?" Naia continued.

"Right!" I agreed.

"And the Worldstream depends on the Shade for everything—coding, maintenance, support. If the Shade go away, then the Worldstream grinds to a halt. So—"

"So, you're making my point for me," Jackson interrupted.

"No, she's not," I said, feeling a little more confident knowing Naia was on my side. "Max said the V.O.'s getting faster, which means they're getting bigger."

"But then why the big campaign?" Jackson argued. "Why the crackdown? Why the vigilante gangs?"

"You answered that question yourself," I shot back. "It got them elected."

Jackson glared at me before breaking eye contact and draining his beer. "Hmph," he grunted.

"Doesn't really matter," Max said. "We're outside the Worldstream, so if the damn thing collapses from lack of bodies, what do we care? That's not *our* problem. It's certainly not our *main* problem."

"Well, what is?" Jackson snapped.

"Finding goods outside the Worldstream is getting harder and harder. With all the Cloak and Shade driven underground, all the RL shops that catered to them are shut down. If they didn't go under from lack of customers, the Kliegls harassed them out of business. They're cracking down on any commerce outside the 'stream, and on crypto transactions."

"But why?" Jackson asked. "What's their beef with RL commerce?"

"You got me," Max answered, "but it's not just commerce they're down on. Even State Live Services is cutting back. It's harder than ever for someone living IRL to get pay vouchers, documents, medical attention—anything, really. They're all being driven straight into the Worldstream."

"It's Madeleine," I said, referring to the woman who had almost ruined Mom's life. Madeleine was Mom's counselor, and Mom really came to depend on her and trust her, but it turned out Madeleine (her Cloak name is "The Eye of Providence") was using her. The Eye wove Mom's lifestream. It went viral. And it almost killed her.

Jackson grimaced. "You and your conspiracy theories. I thought we dropped all that nonsense months ago."

That aggravated me, because I truly believed that Madeleine was out to force everyone in the world into VR—why, I don't know—but Jackson and the rest of the leader council never took me seriously. It got so frustrating that I'd stopped talking about it. I didn't even mention it to Mom. Now, Jackson was treating me like a dope again for bringing it up, and I wasn't going to let it pass, even if it *was* Jackson.

"You can call it a fake conspiracy if you want, Jackson, but it seems a little more plausible now than it did a week ago, doesn't it?"

"And just what in the hell are you talking about?" Jackson spat.

I waited a beat before answering. "The bug."

The look that came over Jackson's face told me that I'd scored a Naia-like comeback. It stopped him cold.

"Yeah," Naia agreed. "The bug. Maybe that damn thing can give us some answers."

19

The Method of Socrates

"Dylan, get over here!" Naia yelled to me, though I stood only ten feet away. She had the antenna on a pole and the spectrum analyzer on a table next to it. The whole setup was massively real. The antenna looked like a cooking utensil, the kind you'd use to whip up eggs, only much bigger. The analyzer was tiny, no larger than a VR console, which surprised me, given how much we'd paid for it.

"Pay attention and learn something," she said, a line that was practically her motto. She pointed first at a grid of jagged lines on the analyzer display, then to a cluster of peaks, looking like a narrow comb with its teeth pointing up, jittering up and down. "That's the Orwell muni band. Each peak is one channel. When you connect, your radio will jump from channel to channel and synch up with the far endpoint."

I nodded like I understood how it worked, and I did, at a high level, but not the details. I decided now wasn't the time to get into it. Naia wasn't there to tutor me in spread-spectrum comms, but she was always using these opportunities to teach me.

"The muni band is good for about three klicks from town center," she went on, "so it's not likely that this bug homed in on our comms. What does that tell you?"

I was expecting this. Naia never tells me stuff straight out. She always asks questions instead. She calls it the *Method of Socrates*, and the first time I heard that, I went to the library for a book about Socrates, a philosopher from Ancient Greece.

"There're no other peaks," I answered. "Just that one cluster."

"Right. So how did this thing talk to the mother ship?"

"I guess that's what we're here to find out."

She smiled and nodded. "Uh-huh." We went to the bug on the table, and she pointed to a switch she'd kluged into it. "When I give you the word, turn it on." She went back to the analyzer, pointed at me, and said, "Okay, Dylan, now."

Well, I flipped that switch, and Naia had waited about five seconds when she screamed, "Off! Off! Turn it *off!*" She was so frantic that I smacked the switch without actually turning it off, and she kept yelling "*Off!*" It took me two more tries before I powered it down.

Naia was staring at the display, eyes wide and mouth clenched, a rare sight since she's always in charge of her emotions. I ran to see what had spooked her.

The display had gone crazy. Even with the bug powered down, whole new clusters of peaks popped up, not as strong as the muni band, but a lot more. They looked like grass waving in the wind.

"What's that?" I asked.

"Something that shouldn't be there," she answered. "Something that hasn't existed for thirty years."

❖ ❖ ❖

I'd never seen Naia so worked up. She searched the whole maker space for Jackson, then sent me out to hunt for him.

I headed for the power plant. Even if Jackson wasn't there, it was jacked into the muni band and I could hail him. The downside was, it was outside of town, a good two klicks from the maker space, and it was still freezing cold. I was wrapped up in a parka Mom made for me, but the seams were a little loose, letting the cold through.

It took me fifteen minutes jogging against the wind. By the time I got there my face was almost frozen and I couldn't feel my toes or fingers. The inside of the power plant was warm as always, but it took stamping my feet and slapping my hands against my chest for the feeling to come back.

"What the hell?" I heard from the control room, which made me forget about my numb hands and feet, because I recognized Frank's voice.

He came through the door with one hand on the jamb. When he caught sight of me he snorted, rolled his eyes, turned around, and went back without a word.

"Frank!" I yelled as I followed.

The control room was a cluttered mess. Frank's coat and mittens were tossed on the console, and his boots were in the middle of the floor, at the end of a trail of big, wet footprints. He had his back to me, bent over, like he was hiding something under the console.

"Have you seen Jackson?" I asked. He turned around and dropped into his chair, rolling it in front of the console where he'd just before leaned under it.

"Jackson's not here," he answered. He sounded tired and his eyes looked glassy, which is not a good state to be in when it's your shift at the power plant.

I glanced up at the display, a big, curved screen going from floor to ceiling. A turbine was in alarm.

"Frank, look," I said, pointing. "What's going on with that turbine?"

"Huh? What?" He looked up at the screen with his mouth slack like he'd never seen that display before, even though the first thing they teach you in power plant training is to check the display regularly. "Oh. Silla…"

"Silla!" I cut him off, calling to the power plant voice responder. "Let Jackson know that turbine 22 is in alarm."

"Yes, Dylan," Silla answered in her silky voice.

Frank was stewing in his chair. "I was going to report it, *Dylan*," he snarked.

"Yeah? When?" I came back at him with even more snark, which only provoked him.

He got out of his chair and came at me until he was close enough that I could smell the liquor. He kept coming but stopped a ways from my nose, and the alcohol fumes filled my whole head. And when he came off his chair, I saw the jar under the console, half-full.

"You're drunk on the job, Frank," I told him, and that caused him to take a step back. He'd just come off a month of trash collection, and another incident could send him straight to sewer maintenance.

"I'm not drunk, *Dylan*. Just a nip to keep warm. What, you never had a little drink to warm you up?"

"Dylan, I've informed Jackson of the alarm condition, and he's acknowledged the report," Silla the voice responder said. "He also asks why you are reporting the alarm, and not Frank. What is your reply?"

"Silla, tell Jackson that Naia and I are looking for him, and ask him to please meet us in the maker space."

"Yes, Dylan. Shall I tell Jackson that you will attend to the alarm?"

I looked Frank right in his rheumy eyes and said, "No, Frank will take care of the alarm. I'm going straight to the maker space."

"Yes, Dylan."

As I buttoned up my coat, Frank asked, "Are you going to report me?"

He looked so miserable and pathetic that the thought of reporting him felt like kicking a stray dog, something I didn't think I could do, even if the dog had just bit me.

I pulled on my mittens. "Fix the turbine, Frank," I answered, and I headed back to the maker space.

❖ ❖ ❖

"Is that what I think it is?" Jackson asked.

Jackson was finally with me, Max, and Naia in front of the spectrum analyzer. Naia had recorded the peaks and was playing them back.

"Yeah, if you think it's a satellite beacon," Naia replied. "I've never seen one myself, but it's exactly how I'd expect a satellite to look."

"Me too," Jackson agreed. "And that's how the drone communicates?"

"Pretty sure. As soon as we powered up the bug, the bird woke up and this happened," she said, waving her hand at the display.

"That answers *that* question," Max said, sticking his hands in his pockets and leaning back on his heels. "So, why's this so urgent?"

"Because there *aren't* any satellites anymore," Jackson answered. "No comms satellites, anyway, none that function. The whole world's hooked up via fiber and terrestrial wireless broadband. Nobody uses satellites for communication."

The conversation wasn't really registering with me. I didn't know anything about comms infrastructure. I only knew that when I jacked into a venue, everything worked. Back in the world, I'd hacked the Worldstream data structures, but the physical layer, how comms got done, was a mystery.

"Why's that?" I asked. "Not enough bandwidth?"

"That's part of it," Naia explained, "but not the real reason. You can run a fat pipe through a satellite, if you're willing to pay for it, and that's what they did before the Worldstream. The move to VR put a strain on the satellite infrastructure, but bandwidth limitations didn't kill it." She squinted at me. "Can you guess what did?"

"Latency?" I answered hesitantly.

"Correct," Jackson said. "The round-trip time through a geosynchronous satellite is more than a half-second. Imagine what a venue would be like if the server had to deal with that kind of lag."

He was right. I'd been in cheap hacker venues on overloaded servers, where avatars bled and pixelated and rastered in and out, usually because the server is underpowered and slammed, or the hackers are tunneling through another protocol to avoid detection—that always cuts down the data rate. But sometimes I'd get in a venue, one that avoided the Worldstream entirely by tapping into some ancient legacy comms channel between stealth gateways. I'd make a move with my hands or feet, and my avatar couldn't keep up with me, or I'd say something to someone and they'd take forever to answer. That had to be latency, and it drove me crazy. If every venue was like that, I'd *never* jack in.

"If nobody had used or maintained these old satellites for thirty years, they couldn't possibly still be working," I pointed out. "Is this a *new* satellite?"

"Who knows?" Naia replied. "It's possible it's an old bird —there're thousands of 'em up there—or something new. I suppose I could try to compare this signature with known satellite protocols, but…" She tugged on her lip. "I'd need access to the Worldstream to find *that* information."

"And that's not even the important question," Jackson jumped in. "I'm much less interested in *how* than I am in *why*."

"And *who*," Naia added.

The conversation died right there as we stood staring at that bug.

Then the lights went out.

20

This Predator Thing

"He'll make it," Kruse told us.

Kruse is the only doctor in Orwell, and he's kept somewhat busy with injuries like Frank's, mostly, though not as severe. We'd found Frank slumped against a bulkhead in the wind turbine nacelle, 130 meters in the air, semi-conscious and half-frozen. From the looks of things, he'd gone up the tower by himself chasing the fault. Even *climbing* the tower alone is a violation of safety protocols, one of the first things they teach us in power plant training, but to crawl *inside* the nacelle and dig around in the electrical panel without someone else present? That's strictly prohibited. Judging from the scorch marks on the alternator housing, Frank had poked around in the panel (I don't think he had a clue as to what he was looking for) and managed to trigger an arc flash, which flung him against the alternator and gave him second- and third-degree burns over a quarter of his body. At least he was wearing his face shield and coveralls. He'd be dead or permanently maimed otherwise. It took three of us an hour to lower him from the top of the tower.

"He's sedated," Kruse continued. "He'll be in some serious pain when he comes to, and he'll be laid up for a month or more before he can return to light duties."

"Fuckin' idiot," Jackson muttered. We were gathered in the kitchen of Frank's house, Jackson, Naia, Kruse, and me, the only light coming from oil lamps set around the room, since the power was still out after several failed attempts to re-energize the main—it was the fault in the turbine that tripped the main breaker and plunged Orwell into darkness. "He knows better than to try a repair up in the turbine by himself. What the fuck's got into him?"

We were all silent. I thought about keeping my mouth shut and letting Jackson believe that Frank was an idiot who couldn't follow simple instructions (that was true, anyway), but it was more complicated than that. I had a duty to tell him what I knew.

"Jackson," I said quietly, "I was at the power plant before the outage."

He raised his eyebrows. "Yes, that's right. You were." He scrutinized me, and I think he figured out from my face that I knew something I wasn't telling. "What do you want to say to me?"

I looked at the floor, avoiding his eyes. "He'd been drinking. I could smell it on him, and he hid one of his moonshine jars under the console."

Jackson's eyes narrowed. "And you didn't report it?" he said through clenched teeth.

"Huh-uh," I mumbled. "I was trying to find you, to get you to the maker space. The bug, you know?"

"That's an *excuse*, Dylan." Not owning your actions is one thing that makes Jackson crazy. I've seen him go off on others for it (Frank, for example) and it's very ugly when he does, but when he comes down on me, he's more restrained. I don't know why that is, but sometimes I wish he'd just explode and rant instead.

"I apologize, sir," I said, but that was a mistake, too.

"Don't *sir* me," he growled. He *hated* being called "sir."

Jackson jammed his hands in his pockets and looked at me with a mix of disgust and disappointment. That hurt.

"Naia," he said, "take young Dylan here and get the power back on. Then the two of you go see just how much damage that drunken dumbass in the next room caused."

After another three tries we finally restored power, once we islanded the entire sub-grid of the failed turbine. The biofuel generators were running flat out to compensate, which left us with no peak reserve. Orwell was lit again, but we were close to the limit. Some Orwellian could turn on an electric oven and put us in the red zone. Naia and I were working against the clock.

Next stop was back up the turbine tower to inspect the carnage. Naia and I squeezed past the gearbox between the alternator and the electrical panel, near the spot where we'd found Frank.

The door to the panel was blackened and bent, and the side of the panel had a hole melted through it the size of my hand. If Frank had been in the path of that arc, he'd have had a hole through him, too. As it was, he'd only suffered some burns, though severe, and what little sense he had was knocked out of him.

"Dylan, do a zero-energy check," Naia ordered. We'd locked out the main at the base of the tower, but standard procedure is to verify that the panel is completely de-energized before working on it. The panel was a bitch to get off, as bent up as it was, and I was in full protective gear, which didn't make it any easier. Still, I got to the bus and checked all conductors with my meter. They were cold.

I pulled off my gloves and balaclava. "What now?" I asked.

Naia reached in the field pack and pulled out an analyzer the size of a small book. It hung from a strap with a magnet, which she stuck to the panel, then plugged the instrument into the diagnostic port. "Let's see what this thing can tell us."

While we waited for the diagnostic to run, Naia and I looked at each other uncertainly, like we were trying to read each other's minds. I spoke first.

"What does Jackson think of me?"

She smiled thinly and shook her head.

"He likes you. You're his *boy*."

"Huh?"

"Jackson thinks you have *possibilities*, or some damn thing," she answered in a way that told me she disagreed.

"What do *you* think?" I asked.

"Oh, I think you have potential." She checked the progress bar on the diagnostic. It was less than half done. Then she looked at me with her eyes raised, me being taller. "Look, Dylan, you're a smart kid, way smarter than I was at your age."

"But…?"

"But you have a lot of growing-up ahead of you, more than you think you do."

"What makes you say that?" I asked, a little irritated. Sure, I wasn't yet eighteen and yeah, I knew I had a lot to learn, but I'd still been through a *lot* for my age, so Naia passing judgment on me? That wasn't fair.

She checked the diagnostic—another minute or so to go. Then she lowered her head and looked at me sideways, from the corners of her eyes.

"You don't think you have more to learn?"

The way she said that—*You don't think you have more to learn?*—was different from the way she said *you have a lot of growing up ahead of you*. She said it like, if I *did* have more to learn, *she* had it in mind to teach me.

I told you Naia's pretty in her face, and her body is very fit, but I never came on to her like I had to other women in Orwell. That's not something I did a lot, and I'm not proud of the times I did.

Mom had warned me that I shared some tendencies of hers. *She'd* gone after men, and sometimes women, a lot more than I had. For her it was all about power—predator and prey. It wrecked her life. She was worried that I'd ruin *my* life, too, though I thought she was overreacting. Still, I'd slipped up a few times, when my inner predator spotted prey, and I moved on her. It's one thing to do that in VR, with some random girl god knows where IRL, but in that little RL town I earned a rep. All the Orwell women avoided me, all except Naia and Mom—Naia because I'd never moved on her, I guess, and Mom because she's Mom.

That night in the nacelle, squeezed into the space between the panel and the alternator, not even a meter wide, with only the work light to see by—well, at that moment Naia looked cool and hard-edged and exceptionally *real*. I could smell the sweat on her, mixed with the grease and oil, and the sooty residue from the arc flash, and you wouldn't think that was an odor that could turn on that feeling you get when you want someone, but it did. I don't know if it was because of the smell or in spite of it, but Naia, the way she looked—eyes sideways, leaning against the alternator housing with her arms loose—seemed very pliable, an easy mark.

I got close to her, maybe twenty centimeters or so, and said to her in a low voice, "Sometimes I feel like I don't know anything—nothing at all." That sort of thing works surprisingly well. It gets a girl wondering if maybe I'm torn up inside, needing a woman's sympathetic hand to cure all my troubles. Most girls are pushovers for a lost, disturbed boy they think they can salvage.

And I was right—or I thought I was. Naia moved off the alternator and brought her face just centimeters from mine. Her dark skin, sharp nose, and chiseled cheeks filled up my field of view, her breath mixed with the industrial-strength wind turbine aromas, and I felt that thing, you know, the thing when the person you're going for drops her shields and you can go in for the kill.

She put her hand on my chest and got closer still, her lips not more than three centimeters from mine. Her eyes were locked on mine and I knew then, like I'd known dozens of times before, that I had her.

Until she pressed her finger into my chest so hard that her finger bent back and I stumbled. I'd have fallen if I hadn't caught myself against the alternator housing. I was back on one foot, my left hand on the lip of an access panel, when she came at me and wrapped her fingers around my throat.

"What the *fuck?*" she growled, and jammed her finger against my chest again, so hard that it hurt. "What did you think was going to happen? That I'd fall for your *troubled teen* act? That you'd notch another kill on your trophy stick?"

She squeezed harder until I had trouble breathing. I closed my eyes and choked. She let go and I fell back onto the catwalk, gasping for air.

I looked up, her image swimming in my eyes as I caught my breath. She calmly checked the diagnostic again. "We'll need to replace two breakers. That's not what's faulting the sub-grid, though. There's an induced fault in turbine 24. Shouldn't take us long to find it."

I was still recovering from being almost strangled, choking, gasping, and spitting, when Naia held out her hand. I grabbed it and she helped me up.

"You're a good kid, Dylan, and I like you. But you have to deal with this predator thing of yours."

She looked at me like a mother might look at her kid who's acting up, and I couldn't return her gaze, feeling the way I did. For the rest of the night I followed Naia's lead without a word. We found the fault in turbine 24 and fixed it, then brought the sub-grid back online and Orwell was at full capacity.

It was never the same between me and Naia after that night. Mom's warning about addiction to sex and conquest made sense, she having the same problem; but the fact that Naia nailed it without having the same insight just rastered me out of my mind.

21

A Hundred and Fifty Crises

IT DIDN'T TAKE long for folks to forget about the drone. But I couldn't get it out of my mind.

Two weeks after we discovered the bug was talking to a satellite, I was in the dinner line with Mom and Hammad, as usual, when I saw Jackson, Naia, and Max together at a table with one open chair.

"Go get a table," I told them. "I need to talk with Jackson."

Mom gave me a pained look, like she does when she thinks I'm not paying enough attention to her. "Dylan, do you think it's a good time to bring it up?" she asked. She knew what I wanted to talk about—that bug. It was almost all I talked about in the cabin.

"Never a good time," I replied. Mom frowned. Hammad tipped his head with a *good luck* look in his eyes. They went to their table, and I headed for Jackson's.

He saw me coming and looked at me with more pain than Mom did. Naia and Max did too, because they *all* knew what I was going to say.

"Hey, Dylan," Max said as I approached. He was the only one who acknowledged me with words. Jackson was tired of me hounding him, and Naia and I had been awkward ever since that night in the wind turbine, so neither of them had said much to me lately except to be polite.

"Hey, Max," I answered, nodding to the others.

I set down my tray and didn't even pick up a fork before leaning into Max on my right. "Max, I've been thinking about what you said about Live Services. Tell me again what you heard."

Jackson closed his eyes and sighed. Naia blinked at me slowly.

"I don't know what else I can tell you that I haven't already," Max answered. "Everything I know I learned second-hand."

"Yeah," I replied, "that's my point. We need some first-hand intel on what's happening with Live Services and why."

Jackson slammed his knife on the table. "How many times are we going to have this conversation?"

"Jackson, I'm just thinking, when Max makes his next supply run, why can't he do some looking around?" I said it as calmly as possible, since Jackson looked like he was near his trigger point. "He's still in the Worldstream, not tagged or anything. If he gets spotted, no alarms. I'm just suggesting…"

"What do *we* care about Live Services?" Jackson interrupted. "That's the world we left, not the world we're in. It *doesn't matter.*"

"But the drone…" I began.

"Dylan, *drop it!*" he barked. If I hadn't already crossed the line, I could tell I was right at it. "Live services, Kliegls, Madeleine…what've they got to do with the drone? For all we know that drone was sent here by a hacker."

"A *hacker?*" I said sarcastically. "Like, some guy spent a whole bunch of credits on three long-range drones, tapped into a satellite link that hasn't been used since the late forties so he can do…what? *Spy* on us Orwellians? And what for? *Dirty thrills?*"

I shouldn't have said that. Jackson picked up his knife and fork but he wasn't eating with them—he was gripping them so hard they squeaked. Naia leaned away from him, like she expected him to flail around with his eating utensils or blow up and spew brains all over. But he did neither.

Instead, he closed his eyes and took a couple of deep breaths, which is what Jackson does when he's ready to erupt but catches himself. The color came back into his fingers.

"Dylan," he said, "we *are* dealing with it. *We* are. The leaders." He scooped up a forkful of roasted potatoes and shoved them in his mouth, chewing really hard. "I know you're concerned," he went on, his mouth full, "and I know you want to help, but…" He swallowed. "…have some faith in us." He pointed to Naia, Max, and then himself, adding, "Thirty-five, fifty, forty-five." Then he pointed at me. "Seventeen. That's *130* years of experience to your *seventeen*. Don't overstep!"

Max was staring at his plate, and Naia shifted her eyes from me to Jackson and back. I got the hint, took my tray and untouched meal, and went back to Hammad and Mom.

Mom had her head down, taking her time slicing meat off a chicken thigh. Hammad raised eyebrows at me: *So?*

I shook my head: *Nope.*

I pushed food around the plate, head down, mulling over the situation, when Mom said, "What's your work detail tomorrow, dear?"

I looked at her sideways, then dropped my fork and put my hand to my face. "My work detail?" I repeated into my palm.

"I'm Making. Jackson says there'll be a lot of Making between now and the planting."

"Mom, do you know what's coming?" I asked.

"The drone." She kept poking at her chicken without looking up. "I don't want to think about it."

Hammad looked as frustrated as I felt. I shoved my plate away.

"Not the *drone*. The drone is just the beginning. *Madeleine*. She's coming for us whether you think about it or not."

Finally, she looked up, her hands frozen in mid-slice. *"I don't want to think about it,"* she said, slowly, one word at a time. Her mouth was pinched and her eyes locked on mine. I fell back in my chair.

"Fine. Let Madeleine come round us up and throw us in confinement. Let her run experiments on all of us Orwellians. In no time we'll all be jacked into a world of fake wonders, no worry, no want. Oh, joy."

Mom held her expression for another moment, then looked back down and carved a slice of dark meat.

I went back to my dinner, but with zero appetite. A push, a poke, and I'd had enough.

"You'll just let things happen?" I said, loud enough to quiet conversations two tables away. "After all you've gone through?"

Mom raised her head, looking startled. She stood and threw sharp looks at the eavesdroppers, then grabbed my arm and pulled me up.

"Come," she said, and dragged me outside.

She pulled me away from the door into the dark, with only the light of the waxing moon to see by. She was looking up at me, her face pale in the moonlight, but fierce nonetheless.

"You *don't know* what I've been through," she said, as intense as I'd ever heard her. It scared me.

"Mom—"

"You *can't* know. You, a *boy?* You could *never* know."

"But, Mom, you *told* me *everything*. The lifestream, the shredding, the Shade—"

"That's not what I'm talking about!"

That shocked me into silence. Even in the dim light, I could see the pain in her face.

"Only a mother could understand," she continued, not angry anymore, but sad and tired. "Since I lost you to your Aunt Donna, when the court ruled that I was…" She choked and stamped her foot. *"…unfit."*

"Mom…"

She shook her head. "But I was—unfit. I was a *horrible* mother. I was a terrible *person."* She poked my chest—*hard.* "But *you didn't need to know that."*

We stood without talking for a minute, then she hugged me.

"I worked so hard—*so hard*—to get you back. Then Madeleine wove all my mistakes into that viral lifestream," she said, her cheek against my chest. "Every bad decision, every self-destructive impulse I surrendered to, strung together in full-immersion hi-res fidelity, waiting in the Worldstream for *you* to find it."

She pulled back. Her face wasn't as hard as it was a minute before. "I shredded my life to protect *you*. I went back into the Worldstream to find *you*. Everything I did, all of it, I did for *you*."

"But, Mom—"

"I know. You think I'm not worried about Madeleine, but I am. But there's nothing *I* can do about it—nothing *you* can do. Jackson will handle it. Meanwhile…" She patted my chest. "I have you back. We're together, and that's all I ever wanted." Her face hardened. "And *I don't want to lose you again!*"

She took my hand. "C'mon. Let's eat."

❖ ❖ ❖

I was dropping off my plates and scraping the leavings of my meal into the compost can when I felt a nudge on my elbow. It was Naia, who I'd said barely ten words to in the last week. She must've notice how startled I looked, and still a little ashamed, because she shook her head and halfway smiled. "What?" I asked.

"Dylan," she replied, "Jackson gets it. He's as worried about the drone as you are." She raised her eyes, then continued. "Maybe not *quite* as much as you are, but he's worried."

"Then why is he busting my ass?" I asked.

"Dylan, remember what I told you? That you're one of Jackson's favorites?"

"Yeah," I said. She hadn't used that exact word—*favorite*—that night in the nacelle, but I got the gist.

"Well, you're more than that. He feels threatened."

"Huh?"

Others were pushing past us to drop off their plates, so Naia pulled me aside. "He's our leader. He takes that seriously. And he doesn't need *you* to set priorities for him."

That sort of made sense to me, but I still didn't get why he'd be upset with me pointing out the urgency of a situation that he himself thought was urgent. "So, he's just as worked up over the bug as I am?"

"Like I said, not quite. And I'll tell you something—*I'm* worried. *More* than you."

I dropped the last of my plates, cups, and utensils in the bin, a little more forcefully than usual. "Then why didn't you stand up for me?"

"Because you were out of line."

"Out of line how?"

She sighed. "Leave him be, is what I'm saying. He'll do the right thing, just like he'll do the other hundred and fifty right things for the hundred and fifty crises he's dealing with, and he'll do them in the right order—more or less." Then she smiled all the way. "You want to know where that drone came from and why, right? Right. So do I. And so does Jackson. But pushing him, with everything he has on his plate, isn't the way to get him to reprioritize. Sometimes it's better to recognize that Jackson gets it and let him deal with it in his own time." She wrapped her fingers around my arm, the first real physical contact between us since the nacelle. "He's a smart guy, Dylan, smarter than you, if you want to know the truth. He gets it. And he'll deal with it."

I didn't doubt that Jackson knew a lot more than me, and that he was really smart, but I wasn't ready to admit that he was smarter than *me*, and it wasn't necessary for Naia to say so. I saw her point, though, and understood that pushing on Jackson would just provoke him, and *that* wouldn't get me any closer to *my* goal.

"I understand," I said.

She squeezed my arm. "I know," she replied, and at that moment I had this weird mental situation in which Naia and Mom overlapped in a way that made it hard for me to tell them apart. With the memory of the night in the nacelle still fresh in my mind, it weirded me out. I pulled away and left the hall without a word, rubbing the spot where Naia had squeezed me all the way home.

❖ ❖ ❖

I didn't share Mom's and Naia's faith in Jackson's leadership skills.

I'd done my best to impress upon him the looming threat of incursion from the world, including my knowledge that Madeleine was coming for us. And he wasn't doing anything about it, despite Naia's claims to the contrary. The situation became even more intolerable when Jackson kept up his lax attitude, even after more drones appeared in Orwell and Laputa, this time with tasers.

22

Too Much Thinking

MAX'S BUSIEST TIME of year is the harvest, when we bring in corn, soybeans, sorghum, and wheat. He needs to put it up in the grain elevators (which is not as simple as it sounds), ensure the grain is dry enough that it won't rot, and plan the processing.

Max spends most of the rest of the year turning field crops into food, fuel, and materials, particularly corn, which we use for alcohol to run the engines, plastic to make things, and edibles like cornmeal and syrup. And that's where I found him, in the corn processing plant, the day after the new drones appeared.

The scene was much the same as it'd been with the first drone: a tell-tale buzz overhead, and people coming outside to watch, though not as many. Folks were more hesitant than before to show their faces to a camera on a strange bug. I peeked out the window and saw right away that this one was different: instead of three cameras, like drone number one, this bug looked more like a stock configuration, with a camera and two taser magazines.

The bug moved down the street like before, panning its camera back and forth, keeping the same pattern, up the main street and back, then reversed course and swept the street again.

Until Max got his deer rifle and tried to take it out like the first one.

He was drawing a bead on the bug when its camera swept past him where he stood. It stopped panning, fixed on Max for a split-second, then its rotors spun up and the thing gained altitude, fast enough that Max's first shot went underneath it.

He cocked the gun and took aim, but this bug clearly had an evasive flight pattern programmed into it, swerving erratically. Max swung his rifle crazily, trying to keep it in his sights, when it did a wide loop behind the library building, out of his firing line. It emerged at low altitude, coming up fast behind him. He spun and aimed, pulling the trigger simultaneously with the sound like sharp pops of compressed gas propelling four taser rounds. The rifle bullet missed, and so did two of the tasers. The other two struck Max in the chest and thigh. He seized, going down like a 50-kilo sack of sorghum. The bug veered off, then shot straight up until we lost it in the clouds.

When I got to the processing plant, Max was just starting a fresh batch of mash, dumping cracked corn into the slurry tank. He was moving a little slow, understandable after having been shocked into semi-consciousness the day before. I have to hand it to him—he didn't let his taser experience keep him off the job. I saw Max and thought of Frank, and what different kinds of men they were.

"Max!" I shouted over the noise of the grinder.

He hobbled over to shut down the machine, then started toward me. I held up my hand and trotted to him instead.

"You doing okay?" I asked.

"Yep," he replied with a half-hearted smile. He pulled up his sweater to show me two ugly welts where the electrodes penetrated. "Swelling's coming down. Still hurts like a bastard, though." He pulled down his sweater. "Drones have a self-defense algorithm. Shoot at 'em, they shoot back. If you don't kill a bug with the first shot, you're gonna get a taser in the ass. Shoulda remembered that. Whassup?"

"When's your next supply run?" I asked.

He scratched his chin, looking at me sideways. "Two weeks. Do you need something? 'Cause if you do, you can go and add it to the list at the community hall, just like always. You don't have to come to me personally."

"I know that," I answered. "I was just thinking about the bug that tased you."

"Yeah, what a surprise," he said. "I guess after we swatted the first one, they put stingers on 'em." He rubbed the sore spot on his thigh. "What's that got to do with the supply run?"

"Here's my thinking," I began, shifting on my feet. "With this latest bug having self-defense capability, it's pretty clear that whoever sent it expected to get it back. I mean, after it tased you, it took off like it had somewhere to go."

"Home base?" he asked. "Or maybe Laputa or Burgess or one of the other V.O. towns?"

"Good point," I conceded. I hadn't thought that the owners *didn't* want the drone back, but only wanted to maximize mission time. "But...there's still the question of *who* sent it and *why*."

Max dumped the partially-filled tub of cracked corn into the tank, then shoved the empty tub under the grinder and opened the chute to refill the bin. He stood with his hand on the switch, looking down, then looked at me. "The supply run?"

I took a breath. "Can you nose around when you're in Omaha? See what developments there've been, you know, with the Kliegls?"

Max gave me a look that said I was wasting his time. He switched on the grinder. "I always nose around!" he shouted. "That's partly why we do the supply runs!"

"Okay, yeah," I shouted back, "but can you also make a side trip?"

Max grimaced as he shut off the grinder. "I assume you're asking me this because you need some more special equipment, and *not* because you want me to gather intel on your nemesis."

He was referring to Madeleine. Some of the leaders, Jackson especially, had taken to calling her my *nemesis* to make light of my concerns. I tried not to act insulted.

"What I'm suggesting is to take the tube down to Chicago and meet with Raúl."

"Uh-huh. And what exactly would that accomplish?"

I didn't want to push Max too hard because he was already skeptical. "Like you said, you get intel whenever you make a run, but if you could spend time with Raúl—well, he's plugged in still, and he could really catch you up on the latest developments."

He hung his head. "Ask Jackson. If he okays it, I'll make the trip."

Max knew that wasn't practical. Jackson would 100% say no, just to make the point that he was in charge. And that was odd, because he never used to be so uncompromising. It'd only been since the drones showed up and I kept asking questions that he'd become a hardass.

"Max," I pleaded, "as a personal favor?"

He looked like he was thinking it over. "How would I find him?"

"I'll talk to Mom. She knows," I replied. "I'll give you directions from the tube terminal."

I left him alone in the plant with the sound of the corn grinder echoing off the rafters.

❖ ❖ ❖

I had never seen Jackson as angry as he was when he came to the cabin that night. It was right after dinner at the dining hall. Max must have told him about my request at dinner.

He pounded on the door so hard we all jumped. Mom let him in. He came straight for me and stuck his finger in my face without even saying hello.

"Did I tell you to *drop this?*" he asked in a low, menacing tone.

"Max," I said.

"Yes, Max, who doesn't take orders from *you.*" Jackson's face was red and the veins in his temple bulged. I thought he was going to blow a blood vessel.

"Jackson, I just thought—"

"You're doing *way* too much thinking for someone your age, you know that?" He wagged his finger just a centimeter from my nose. "You will *not* go off on your own like this again, not on this topic or any other."

He stood still for a second, finger still shaking and veins throbbing, then he straightened up and ran his fingers through his hair.

"Look, Dylan," he said, his voice closer to normal but still loud, "if you think we need to take action on an issue, bring it to the council and make your case. That's how it's done. We can't have you or anyone else freelancing. Got it?"

I nodded, which must have been good enough for him, because he turned to Mom and Hammad, saying, "Grace… Muhammad…have a pleasant evening." And then he left.

It got really quiet in the cabin and stayed that way for the rest of the night. Mom shot me a look that stung, then went back to her knitting. Hammad shrugged. Words weren't necessary—Jackson had said enough.

As angry as Jackson was that night, it was nothing compared with how he came at me the next day after I went to Benny to requisition a vehicle to drive to Chicago. That was chancy, I know, with me being tagged, but I figured if I traveled at night and met Raúl at the Cloakroom, where the All-Seeing Eye is blind, I stood a good chance of making it in and out without triggering an alert. Looking back, I realized it was a stupid plan. So it was a good thing, in the end, that Benny went to Jackson and Jackson came and reamed me for overstepping again, even if I did spend a month on trash pickup.

23

The Junk Room

"OH," HAMMAD SAID when he saw it, "this is massively hi-res."

We were in what Naia called the "Salvage Depot," but everyone else called it the junk room. Naia kept it locked most of the time, but when she was in and out of it a lot, she left the door open, and others in the maker space could sneak a peek.

Technically, I wasn't peeking, because Hammad and I were on Maker duty that day (my reward for sticking out a whole month collecting garbage without complaining), and Naia had sent us into the junk room to fetch a radio module for a muni band range extender she was building. She needed it right away, but it was Hammad's first junk room visit, and we couldn't help but linger. I think she even expected us to, because she'd sent both of us, though there was no reason for Hammad to go.

Shelves covered all four walls from floor to ceiling, crammed with every kind of cast-off, from high-tech to ancient relics. Free-standing cabinets stood in rows, either open shelves with more salvaged goods, or grids of drawers ranging from motor-sized to microcircuit. The cabinets surrounded an open space big enough for a bench, covered with tools, small parts, and newly acquired junk which Naia hadn't yet catalogued and shelved. The lenses she'd removed from the drone lay there, greenish-tinted glass reflecting the overhead lights like huge animal eyes, and the remains of the bug itself leaned against one of the legs. The junk room was like a geek toy store, or a candy shop, but didn't smell like either. Instead, it had a heady tech smell, like oil, plastic, and that burnt dust odor that old electronics gets from years of running hot.

"Where'd all this stuff come from?" Hammad asked.

"Naia's been collecting it for years. Some she brought from the world when she and Jackson and the rest founded Orwell, some was already here, and some they salvaged from other towns."

Both Hammad and I knew the history of Orwell. Jackson told us the story one night in the Taproom, about how the original Orwellians from Omaha packed up vans full of supplies and headed out to parts unknown, like a desert caravan to a disconnected oasis. They kept driving until they couldn't detect any broadband at all, then they drove another two hundred klicks, until they came upon what they judged to be a suitable long-abandoned town. He told us the name of the town, Custer, I think it was, but they renamed it Orwell. The history lesson had lasted well into the night, as Jackson, Naia, Max, and Benny told one tale after another. In the dim light from the lamp, and my mind fogged over from three or four mugs of beer, I'd imagined them as tribal elders, passing on sacred oral lore.

"C'mon," I said, pointing to the far corner at a stack of silvery, palm-sized packages, "the modules are over there." Hammad hung back, looking over the contents of the shelves like he was in some VR tech store, while I got the module.

"Looky," he said when I came back. He held up a VR visor and headset. It looked old, definitely not the latest gen, but still very serviceable. Hammad pointed at a box on the shelf. "And this."

It was a VR console, again, not recent vintage, but also perfectly usable. Naia had salvaged a reasonably complete VR setup.

"Let's go," I said. Hammad put the visor back on the shelf and followed me out.

"I wonder," he said, "what in hell good is a VR console in Orwell?"

❖ ❖ ❖

There wasn't much for me and Hammad to do while Naia assembled the range extender, at least until it was ready to power up and test. "Dylan, get me the spectrum scanner," she said.

"That one?" I asked, pointing to the spectrum analyzer we'd gotten from Chicago. It sat on a table near the wall, right where she'd left it after we scanned the bug, still connected to the biconical antenna.

"No!" she yelled. "The muni band scanner." She pointed to a small instrument about the size of a pocket screen, lying on the table next to the spectrum analyzer. "That little thing."

I fetched it and handed it to her. "Did you mean to leave the spectrum analyzer on?" I asked.

She tapped the screen of the scanner, then checked the spectrum envelope of the range extender. Smiling with satisfaction, she powered down the extender.

"What?" she asked.

"The analyzer. It's on."

"Oh! Yeah, let me show you this." Naia led me and Hammad to the analyzer and punched the screen with her finger. "I've had this on continuously since the first bug, recording everything out of normal activity. Good thing, too, because when that second drone showed up, I captured the whole conversation."

She pulled up a saved file showing the spectrum for the entire time that the drone was in sight, and for hours before and after.

"Wow, Naia," I said, "it looks like you knew the drone was on its way. Why didn't you warn us?" She gave me a pained look, and I immediately regretted asking, but it *was* a legitimate question after all.

"I've been kicking myself for weeks. Yeah, you're right, we could've seen it coming, *if* I'd been monitoring it. My fault—I glitched that task. But no more—now the analyzer is linked to the muni band, and if another outburst happens, we'll know about it."

"And this?" Hammad asked, pointing to a sleek steel box with a cable jack and a big, orange button.

"Jamming device. My last resort. If we get a heads up, I push this. Wipes out all comms within a two-klick radius. It'll drown out the drone, but everything else, too, including the muni band."

She went into some detail about the recording, and the mechanism by which the satellite detects a drone and sets up a comm link. I didn't follow it completely, but Hammad kept nodding and saying "Mm-hmm," and even asking what sounded like intelligent questions. That kept Naia going for almost an hour. At the end of it, I had a vague idea of what was going on between the birds and the bugs, but what Hammad got out of it, I didn't know until later.

❖ ❖ ❖

"I have an idea," Hammad said on our walk back to the cabin, just before sunset.

"Tell me," I replied, a little anxiously, not knowing if this was another of his hare-brained schemes, like the one he had to bust out of confinement on our own. That stunt got me another ten years in confinement and life for Hammad, just two more reasons why it had been so important for us to escape.

"You need some intel from the world, Raúl's your obvious source for it, and Jackson absolutely forbids contact."

"Uh-huh," I said, in a way that let Hammad know he wasn't giving me new information.

"So, if you can't go to Raúl, and Raúl can't come here, why not meet him in VR?"

I stopped walking and stared at him in the dim light. His eyes were wide, catching the light of the setting sun, the reddish tinge making his dark skin glow. He smiled, closed-mouth, but when he saw that I understood, he grinned his big, toothy grin and his eyes crinkled.

"You're thinking of tunneling through the satellite," I said, having picked up enough from Naia's explanation to see the possibilities.

"Uh-huh. And with that VR gear in the junk room, we could meet him face-to-face."

He seemed so excited about the prospect that I felt bad about bringing up flaws in his idea. "How well would that work, you know, with the limited bandwidth and the latency?"

That question didn't seem to dampen his enthusiasm one bit. "How well does it have to work?"

He had a point. Even if it was glitchy and slow, we'd have our mole in the world. "Okay, let's assume we make this work. What venue do we use? And how do we make contact with Raúl?"

Hammad grabbed my arm and started walking again. "Details!" he said, and we talked through the plan on our way to the cabin.

❖ ❖ ❖

We skipped dinner at the dining hall (Mom went alone) and brainstormed the steps until after midnight, writing them all out and putting them in order. A lot had to go right for it to work, but we generated our own anti-reality field, and it all seemed doable. By one a.m. we were dragging, and I told Hammad I was turning in.

"I'm wired," he said, and looked it. I'm sure my eyes were drooping but he was still wide awake.

"We have Making duty again tomorrow," I yawned. "I need sleep."

I left him at the table, still scrawling on our list. I was asleep in minutes but woke up briefly when Hammad came to bed and slipped his arms around me and put his face in my hair, and I fell asleep again with his breath warm on my head.

24

The 70,000 Kilometer Kluge

THE NEXT DAY we put our plan into action.

Hammad and I were on Making duty for the rest of the week. Naia gave me the job of locking up the junk room at night, which was perfect: as long as we were on Making, we had free access.

The first step was to gather materials, the number-one item being the drone's radio, the only device we knew for sure could talk to the satellite.

I covered for Hammad when he snuck in to check out the bug, figure out just what parts we needed, and how hard it would be to get them out. We needed the radio, antenna, and battery at a minimum, plus any other parts that were either necessary to the operation of the radio, or that we couldn't disconnect without disabling it.

"I'll need an hour, just to be safe," he whispered to me as I set up a 3D print of a pair of shoes. "The housing is almost obliterated, so I'll only need tools to remove the modules— no breaking into the thing."

I nodded. "What about the VR gear?" I whispered back.

"The connection to the console will be the tricky part. I have no idea what the interface to that radio looks like, and even if I did, I didn't see anything in the junk room that we could use to build it."

"You'll figure it out," I assured him.

By day three, we'd rigged up the radio and hooked up the VR console. Our cabin bedroom looked like a kluged-up command center. We'd smoke-tested the rig (no smoke) and were ready to go live, but we had one more thing to do, something if we didn't do would kill the whole program. I was the one who thought of it.

"Naia's alarm," I told Hammad.

His eyes got wide. "Oh, yeah. Good thing you remembered. The second we fire up that radio, her analyzer's going to wig out and she'll get pinged via the muni band."

"And our line to Raúl will get cut before we make our first call," I added, "and we'll both be back on trash pickup for the rest of our lives."

The next day Hammad covered for me while I fiddled with the analyzer programming and found the command to disconnect it from the muni band. We couldn't shut down the analyzer entirely (Naia's routine was to check it morning and evening). We knew the analyzer would record every stray radio transmission, but we gambled that it would go unnoticed if no alarm had been raised. By the end of our shift we were massively nervous, because we had only one step left: turn on the rig and see if the satellite would talk to us.

❖ ❖ ❖

It was past eleven when Mom headed for bed. As she went to her room, she squinted at us and asked, "Are you boys up to something?"

We looked as innocent as we could and said "No" at the same time.

She pressed her lips together like she doubted our honesty but said no more. We'd kept the room locked but wondered if Mom had gone in anyway (the locks are not the most secure) or if she'd at least tried the door. That would be unusual for Mom though, so we figured she was suspicious because we *looked* suspicious.

We waited ten minutes before we went in and locked the door behind us.

The rig was laid out on a table, spilling over the edges to a chair and then to the floor, a waterfall of cables, connectors, and haywired circuit modules. The interface between the VR console and the drone radio was an ugly tangle. It had no display, just an array of status lights, which only Hammad could decipher. On a second chair was the VR headgear.

Hammad powered up the console and interface, then ran through some checks. He gave one quick nod, then slumped back in his chair and sighed.

"Everything okay?" I asked.

"Just one more switch to throw."

"The radio."

"Yep." His finger hovered over the power switch. He pressed.

The only change was to the indicator lights on the interface. Hammad stared at them intently as they flashed in a mysterious sequence. He was sitting statue-still, holding his breath, when the lights went solid and he exhaled.

"We got a lock," he said.

The radio was talking to the satellite.

He picked up the VR gear and held it out. "You first."

I shook my head. "It was your idea. You take the honors."

He didn't look honored. He looked scared. But he put on the visor.

"Mia, staging venue," Hammad said. We'd named the VR console voice responder *Mia* after a girl I knew back in the world.

I couldn't see what Hammad was seeing, but I got the feeling that it wasn't what he expected.

"What?" I asked.

"I'm not getting a thing…it's…wait…wait…there! *There!* We're in!" He pulled off the visor and stuck it on my head.

It was like most staging venues, all white, with a scrolling menu, but the scroll was slow and jerky.

"Why's it doing that?"

"Latency, I think. It's making a 70,000-kilometer round trip. Also, we're tunneling through the maintenance protocol to avoid detection. The peak throughput can't be more than twenty or thirty megabits per second."

"Wow," I said, "smoke signals would be faster."

The staging venue ran locally on the console, but would only come up if it had established a connection to a gateway.

In our case, we pointed the venue to a stealth gateway, outside the Worldstream. Our plan was to test the rig by going into a hacker venue, which was relatively safe from detection. If that worked, we'd move on to the next step: making contact with Raúl.

For that I had an idea.

Back when I was in the world, I got nabbed for unlawful hacking and put on probation. Every move I made, VR or IRL, was tracked, recorded, and scrutinized. During that period Raúl got in touch with me and set up a venue shielded from the Worldstream and its prying eyes. I could summon him any time I wanted by going to a particular kind of venue: a re-creation of some violent military battle from the past. Hammad and I planned to use the same tactic to contact Raúl on the chance that he hadn't disabled the alert. The only catch was, I had to enter the venue in the clear. And that was the risk: being an escaped confinee, I was tagged. The millisecond I showed up in the Worldstream, sirens would sound.

But first, the hacker venue.

"Mia, Cap'n Crunch."

The venue darkened and morphed into a blur of blocky forms, like an animated abstract painting, or simulations I'd seen of primitive twentieth-century video games. Who or what was in the venue I could only guess, though some odd shapes moved like crude low-poly avatars. I heard muffled pops, grunts, growls, and what sounded like a laugh coming from a different room through thick walls. The overall effect was grotesque. My stomach knotted and my throat tightened like I was going to vomit, in part because of the eerie surroundings, but mostly because I was still suffering the after-effects of my time in confinement.

You see, I hadn't been in a VR venue in almost a year, not since we broke confinement, where the Civils put us through VR torture sessions every day. They called it "therapy." The scars from months of therapy still smarted. I had fears that there might be some residual effects, even under the lowest of lo-res circumstances, in a hacker venue on a slammed server through a skinny pipe with massive latency, but the old feelings hit me like a taser.

I tore off the visor and doubled over. Hammad put his hand on my shoulder. He knew exactly what was happening to me.

"Dylan, breathe."

After a minute, with my breathing under control, I sat up and swallowed the sour taste. I looked into Hammad's eyes. He nodded, and I put the gear back on.

The console had trained up and reset its optimization parameters, increasing the static resolution of the rendering at the expense of realistic motion. Avatars now remotely resembled human beings, though their movements were coarse and jerky. The sound had optimized as well, and I could make out conversations among the avatars.

"*…bootleg lifestreams, eight of 'em, one-fifty per…*"

"*…grabbed this key from a concert venue. Wanna be a rock star?*"

"*…it's a Belt hack, guaranteed to rewire your head…*"

My metabolism had adjusted to being back in VR, as lo-res as it was, and I wandered through the venue eavesdropping on various groups, discreetly as I could.

"Dylan!"

My gut clenched again at the sound of my name. A morphing mass of shapes came at me like storm clouds, stopping a meter away, and resolved into the avatar of a man with a long beard and close-cropped hair, pixelated and diffuse, but recognizable. It looked like a hacker I knew from years ago.

"Micah?" I asked. A couple seconds passed before he answered.

"Holy shit, partner! It *is* you!" He stuck out his hand to shake, and I put out my hand, but with no tactile gloves my hands were only clumsily rendered in the venue, and of course I couldn't feel Micah's hand when he shook.

"Brother, I heard you went in confinement. I was real sad to hear it. Done your time, have ya?"

"Not exactly," I answered. "Long story, and complicated." Another second passed, the consequence of two round trips to a satellite in distant space and a data pipe not much wider than a drinking straw.

"Well, good to see ya, so to speak, 'cause *damn* your avatar looks shitty. Where you jackin' in from?"

"Again, complicated." I was dying to tell Micah about the rig Hammad and I came up with, it being about as hi-res a hack as I'd ever seen, but I didn't want to reveal too much, and besides, the lag was exhausting. From inside the venue, it was easy to see why the rural population had migrated to the cities, where bandwidth was abundant, but mostly because no latency.

"Might as well be on the fuckin' moon, judging from the lag," he said. I fought the urge to tell him how close to right he was.

"Hey, Micah, I can't stay. But it's great to see you again after all this time."

"And you, partner. Can't say I'm puzzled over why I ain't seen you lately, what with things the way they are."

As eager as I was to jack out, that got my attention. "How things are? How are they?"

"Lean times for hackers, my friend. Big crackdowns." At that point I wished the resolution was higher so I could read Micah's expression, but his face was only vague blobs of pink and yellow and brown. It was only my knowledge that it *was* a human face that distinguished it from splatters of paint on a wall.

"Kliegls are busting everyone," he went on. "Look around: How many avatars do you see?"

I didn't know how to answer, because anything in the venue more than five meters away looked like background noise.

"Uh…not many?"

"Almost none, partner. Nobody comes to the hacks anymore. Too risky. Kliegls have eyes in every corner of the Worldstream and beyond. All the tyros have been nabbed, and the dabblers won't chance it." His avatar shivered and oozed. "If you're still coming to the hacker venues, either you've got some hi-res skills or you're lucky."

"Why?" I asked.

"Why what? Why are they cracking down?" he said, after a second or two delay. "Some bullshit about the integrity of the Worldstream. Like it's our fault that they can't keep their technology secure. Hell, if there's flaws in their defenses, it's our fucking *duty* to exploit 'em."

"They're zeroing in on hackers?"

"Yeah, but not just us. The Shade—they're the real targets."

❖ ❖ ❖

I exited the venue still queasy.

"You made contact," Hammad said. He had no monitor, so he only heard my half of the conversation.

"Hacker I used to know—Micah. He's the one who sold me the hack that got me busted."

"Nice guy."

"Aw, he's okay. It's my own damn fault I ended up in confinement."

"But it worked. The link, I mean. You made it in."

I rubbed my eyes. "Somewhat. We can make contact, but the rendering is horrible, and the latency is a killer."

"So, what do you think? Raúl next?"

"The way I see it, it's a tunneled connection, so the chances the Worldstream will know where we are physically are slim. I'll still raise an alarm, but that could work in our favor—a red alert with my name on it will probably go straight to the top of Raúl's stack."

That's what I said. In fact, I had no idea. Hammad wasn't buying it either, but after a couple beats, he swallowed hard and said, "Let's go."

I put on the VR gear. "Mia," I said, "Iwo Jima."

I flinched at the sound, like thunder, only louder and non-stop, with low-frequency components that rattled my head, and muffled *pop, pop, pop, pop* in rapid succession, coming from all directions. The scene in the visor was indistinct. It was daytime, I think, and looking around I saw a wall of black in front of me and blue stretching to infinity behind. Blurred forms, looking vaguely like men, moved quickly past me and through me, scrambling every which way, some falling, some exploding in a hazy patch of red. A crappily rendered voice droned in my ears: "Shortly after ten a.m., Japanese forces, under the command of General Kuribayashi, let loose a barrage of machine gun fire, mortar, and artillery on the American forces, stranding them on the beach, inflicting…"

The voice stopped, the bedlam ceased, and the blurry landscape melted into a wash of gray, fading to pure white.

"Well, fuck me," a familiar voice said, through a thin, narrowband audio channel. "Look who it is."

I instantly recognized the figure that rastered in, lo-res and skewed as it was, like an impressionist painting: a tall man, with long, silver hair.

"Hello, Raúl," I said. "Been awhile."

25

Letters from the Worldstream

"Is it safe here?"

In previous sessions, Raúl had used blocking technology to keep us hidden from the Worldstream, but this was a new situation.

"Sophie, chair," Raúl ordered his voice responder. A flat, wobbly image of something that resembled a chair appeared and he sat down. "Safe? Hell if I know. We're not being observed by the All-Seeing Eye, if that's what you mean. The venue is locked down. But safe? If I knew how you were doing this, I might could say for sure."

"Am I still in the Worldstream? Or did you duplicate me in your venue?"

"Oh." He raised an arm, a smear of color as it moved to his face. I guessed that he was scratching his chin, the way I'd seen him do a hundred times. "Yeah, I plucked you from the 'stream. I figured it was prudent. Do you have any idea of the commotion caused by your sudden re-entry? The klaxon almost ruptured my eardrums."

Our plan had worked—Raúl hadn't deactivated his alert, and the fact that I was a fugitive from the Civil Authorities meant that the All-Seeing Eye amped up the alarm.

"Then we're safe," I said.

"Probably. But no guarantees. Your rendering is pathetic, and the lag is making me nauseous. I'm guessing you're tunneling through some stealth pipe into the world—you're still in Orwell, right?—and whether The Eye can figure out how you managed that, I can't say. Wanna fill me in?"

I told him the whole story, about the drone, how it communicated, and how we patched the console through the satellite. He gave me what looked like a nod.

"Impressive," he said. "I always knew you were a smart kid."

"It was Hammad, mostly. He figured out how to interface the VR console to the drone radio. That was the hard part."

"No doubt. To answer your question, I still can't say if you're in the clear. For all I know, whoever sent that bug to Orwell is scratching his head over why his drone is talking without saying anything. Might make him curious."

"We thought of that," I admitted, "but it was a chance we had to take."

"Yeah, a *big* chance, bigger than I would've advised. What was so fucking urgent that you thought you had to risk exposure, not to mention wake me up in the middle of the night?"

"Madeleine," I replied. "She has a plan to pull us all back into the Worldstream."

"So you say. I'm not convinced. But that doesn't answer my question."

"I think she has something to do with the drones."

"Still not an answer."

It was so much like Raúl to push back, like Naia in some ways, forcing me to be precise. I respected him for that, but it was still frustrating. "It's a *theory*, Raúl. If Madeleine really wants the whole world in VR, wouldn't she want to get some remote intel on the *Vitreous Orb* towns? We're the biggest community outside the Worldstream, and we're getting bigger."

"Maybe, but why so urgent?"

Now he sounded like Jackson.

"Damn it, Raúl, I don't *know* how urgent! I only know that if I'm right, it could get urgent real quick. And no one in Orwell other than *me* seems to give a shit."

"Fair point. What do you want from me?"

"What's happening in Chicago? What's going on in the world?"

"Oh. Long story, old chum." His avatar pixelated as he stood. "Sophie, chair," he said, and it vanished. "Seeing as how we still don't know if your connection is secure, and given the lateness of the hour, let me suggest an alternate venue, where you don't have to wake up the entire surveillance regime of the All-Seeing Eye to get my attention. Sophie…" He paused. "Dylan, what's the name of your voice responder?"

"Mia," I said.

"Mia, meet Sophie—Sophie, Mia. Sophie, give Mia the locator for the Fortress of Solitude."

"Yes, Raúl—done," a female voice said, distorted but comprehensible.

"From now on, we meet in the Fortress," Raúl explained. "No more battle zones. The guns give me a headache."

"Fine," I answered. "Can we go there now?"

"No, we can *not*. I'm an old man. I value my sleeping hours."

"Tomorrow night, then?"

"Does it have to be at night?"

"It's the only time we can jack in undetected."

"Sure. Fine. Same time tomorrow night. Sophie, suspend the venue."

The surroundings blinked out with a static crackle, leaving me in the local staging venue. I peeled off the gear to see Hammad grinning.

"It worked," he said.

"Yep. And we have an appointment with Raúl tomorrow night."

❖ ❖ ❖

The next day we were tired, but jacked over our success. We'd made it back to the maker space early enough to re-enable Naia's alert before she found out. We left the VR gear in the cabin, since it was such a pain to disconnect it from our kluged-up rig, and we didn't have access to the junk room anyway. We could only hope that it wouldn't be noticed. And it wasn't, as far as we knew.

It was our last day Making. The next day Hammad would work a shift at the power station, and I'd be prepping to harvest the winter wheat, inspecting the fields, and doing maintenance on the combines and wagons. Harvest was still a few weeks away, but Jackson doesn't let things go until the last minute. When Max decides the wheat is ripe, we'll be ready to reap. But the fact that we'd be switching roles meant that next day we'd have to find some excuse to go into the maker space to mung with Naia's alert in the evening and morning, or else sneak in and out when no one was watching.

❖ ❖ ❖

Just before 11:30 that night we fired up the rig. I was the one geared up.

"Mia, Fortress of Solitude."

The change was subtle at first, with the white staging venue faintly scintillating in polychromatic sparks, like I'd held my breath a long time and then stood up really fast. Then I saw blocky forms emerge, like silvery columns of metal. With the crappy rendering, I thought they were random at first, until I saw a pattern, the criss-crossed columns forming arched hallways radiating to infinity in all directions, and overhead a shifting abstract design, multicolored, like a kaleidoscope. Even in lo-res, the effect was massively impressive. I craned my neck to take it all in

I heard Hammad ask, "What do you see?"

I was about to answer when Raúl rastered in. Though his avatar was blocky and pixelated, it was obvious that he wasn't dressed in his usual 20th-century style, but wore a stylized futuristic outfit, blue, like a summer sky only more intense, with some indistinct pattern on his chest.

"Greetings from Krypton," he said, raising his hand and forming a V with his fingers. "Live long and prosper."

"Hey," was all I could think to say. It was out of character for Raúl to wear anything other than retro clothes, and he wasn't one to babble in code words, either.

"Sophie, chair," he said, and a chair—more like a throne—rastered in, made of smooth crystal, which caught the rainbow colors overhead and reflected them in weird liquid patterns. "I have an update for you, young Dylan. I analyzed the logs from our meeting last night."

"And?"

"Good thing we're here in my Fortress. You hung your ass out last night. The All-Seeing Eye could easily have found you."

"But…"

"But you dodged the taser—I think. I'm pretty sure. Anyway, we're safe in here. And another thing—you're not maximizing the capacity of your tunnel." He waved his hands at the columns and ceiling. "This could be a much more impactful experience with a few changes to your protocol."

"Changes? What? Can you tell me?"

"Don't get me wrong, son, I respect your game, but you don't have the chops to pull it off."

I hate it when he does that, I thought, *minimizes my skills*. He'd done it before.

"How would you know?" I snapped.

Raúl shook his head, his features smearing as he moved. "Settle down, Dylan. I didn't mean to rile you. But it's complicated—for *you*. Fortunately, not so complicated for *me*. Sophie, compression."

"Yes, Raúl."

The effect was instantaneous, and so dramatic it made me dizzy. The steely columns sharpened, each one reflecting the overhead colors, Raúl and me, and images from other columns, all the reflections from the round columns stretched and narrow, like a nest of sharp spindles jutting from an icy floor. The light from each column was concentrated in the hallways the further back they went, until each passage disappeared in the distance in a point of light so intense it hurt my eyes. It was as if I was at the focal point of a hundred searchlights. The kaleidoscope overhead resolved into a mosaic of forms, some geometrical, some organic, all saturated with colors that had only been hinted at when rendered in lo-res. Raúl's costume also came into focus, an elegant blue tunic which went to the floor, on his chest a red *S* on a yellow background. The familiar features of his face returned: deep-set eyes, sharp nose, bronze, leathery skin, and his long, silver hair. He was smiling.

"Oh. Oh, god," I said, almost overcome. *This* was the VR I remembered, so vivid it tricked my mind into believing I was somewhere I wasn't, a place which didn't even exist—an unreality.

Raúl chuckled at my reaction. "I thought that might impress you," he said. "This compression algorithm is optimized for your tunnel through the satellite. The quality is almost as good as full bandwidth. I can't reproduce all the sensations, and motion artifacts are still a problem, but it's not bad. Unfortunately, there's nothing I can do about the latency. That's physics."

Words still eluded me as I turned my head in all directions. Hammad nudged my arm, asking, "What? What do you see?"

"Raúl fixed the resolution. It's massively hi-res," I answered, which wasn't really true, but after a year IRL with no VR at all, and after the previous night's session, glitchy and lo-res, it rewired my head.

"What about the world?" Hammad asked.

"Hammad's asking about the world," I said to Raúl.

"I know, I can hear him." He stood up and paced. "The world. Sure. That's why you kluged this whole thing in the first place."

"So, what can you tell us?"

"Tell you? I'm not telling you *nothing*."

"You're not?"

His smile got wider. "Why *tell* you when I can *show* you?"

26

Nasty Buggers

"Sᴏᴘʜɪᴇ, Lᴏᴏᴘ."

The kaleidoscopic patterns and sharp shards of metal melted away, morphing into a lonely late night urban scene, the only light coming from the few functional streetlights. It was the first time in more than a year that I'd been free of the boundaries of Real Life, in a venue from the Worldstream.

It creeped me out.

I grew up in Chicago. I knew where the Loop was in a general sense, but I'd never been there, being raised in a VR world. My aunt Donna, who took me in at the age of ten, never let me go out IRL by myself, but when Mom visited, she and I would sometimes venture forth. I loved those times, when we could take off the VR gear and see what the world was like, even if the choice of RL venues was scanty, like run-down, overgrown local parks. We *never* went down to the Loop.

Raúl and I stood on a street which a century ago might have been clogged with people, bumping shoulders in their rush to get someplace—a store, a job, a home. Chicago was a big city, filled with massive crowds all squirting themselves through narrow pipes of city streets to get from where they were to where they weren't. But not this night, in this venue. The street was deserted.

"What is this?" I asked.

"Downtown Chicago, present day," Raúl answered. "This is a live shot, rendered from surveillance cameras." He stood next to me, no longer dressed in his Krypton garb, but in the usual drab retro clothes. "It's still early."

"Early for what?"

He raised a finger. A timestamp appeared in glowing green digits, reading *11:55 PM.*

"Five minutes, that's when they'll come. Every midnight, like roaches after lights out."

"Who?"

"Kliegls."

Those were the guys Max told us about after his last supply run, and which Raúl had described right after we first came to Orwell. Mom had told me about how Civils and Kliegls raided her Shade dorm and put her out on the streets.

"Who are they exactly?" I asked.

"The ruling party, more or less," he replied. He flicked a finger and the timestamp dissolved. "Don't you follow politics?"

"Not really," I admitted, and I hadn't, not even when I was in the world, and neither did anyone else I knew. We all figured things would happen whether we were in it or not, and nothing we did would change that.

"Kliegls—first outright majority party in the history of the Millennium Republic," Raúl explained. "That's something the founders never anticipated, one party with absolute power, no need to compromise. We were born in an age of factions, each cult-like community organized around some core issue, each one finding their fellow fanatics in the untamed ocean of social media."

"Then, how?"

"How'd they do it? I'm not sure—nobody is, nobody *I* know, anyway. Their leader, Dax, focused on the Shade as some imminent threat, blaming an uptick in RL crime on them, but that was all bullshit. No, something else was going on, almost like folks' minds were being manipulated directly." He pointed. "Look there."

A group of eight or so people came around a corner, easily visible in the dim streetlights, all of them dressed in white with a wide red sash across their chests, and a red cap, like a cylinder (I think they're called *fez*), with a symbol like two searchlights with crossed beams.

"Kliegls?" I asked.

"That's them. Nasty buggers."

They were strolling casually, chatting and laughing. They didn't look so menacing   until someone else appeared on the scene, an older-looking man in a dark jacket who came out of a door at street level. He was around the corner from the Kliegl gang, and though he looked both ways before leaving the door, he couldn't see them. He turned to his right, heading for the corner, the Kliegls coming from the other direction.

"Can they see us?" I asked Raúl.

"This isn't VR, Dylan. This shit's happening," he said. "And we're invisible."

The man in the jacket hobbled to the corner slowly, as if it pained him to walk, then stopped, peeking around the edge of the building. By that time the Kliegls were close enough that he should have heard them, since they weren't making any effort to keep quiet. Maybe the old man was deaf.

They saw him at about the same time he saw them. He turned and ran, or tried to, but the gang got to the corner and around it before he could take two steps.

"Old man!" one of them shouted.

The old guy tried to run faster but tripped and fell. He curled up in a ball as the gang surrounded him. A short, fat Kliegl, who might have been the leader, shouted, "He thinks he's real!" which made them all laugh.

The fat one tugged at a rod stuck to his belt, maybe twenty centimeters long. Then he flicked it, and it expanded to about half a meter, with a *hiss-click-click*. When the rest of them flicked their own batons, *hissing* and *clicking* in rapid sequence, it became obvious that this would not end well.

"What are those things?" I asked.

"They call 'em *ASPs*."

"They're not going to…"

"Yes. They're going to," Raúl answered.

The fat one took the first shot, swinging the baton with one hand, first from one direction, then the other, *bam, bam,* while the old man curled up tighter and covered his head. He didn't cry out, only whimpered like a wounded animal. The others joined in, batons rising and falling, the Kliegls crowding closer, like hyenas around a kill. It was only the occasional mis-placed blow landing on a fellow Kliegl that kept them at some distance, forcing a little restraint.

"What, what, *what?*" I sputtered.

Without thinking, I went toward them. Raúl put out a hand to stop me, but it was ineffective; the satellite pipe couldn't sustain any kind of deconfliction algorithm, even with Raúl's compression, and his hand passed right through my arm like a phantom.

"Don't go there, Dylan!" he shouted, but I was already by them, grabbing at them, trying to pull them off the old man. Of course, I couldn't get a grip on them any more than Raúl could get hold of me. I ended up in the center of the ring of Kliegls, my feet passing ghost-like through the old man where he lay, batons whizzing through my body, the heavy metal tips landing on the man, sounding like *thwack, thwack, thwack,* his body twitching with every blow, until he stopped twitching and rolled over, and his hands fell away from his face.

"That'll do," the fat one said. A few more batons bashed the man and Fatty yelled "Enough!" like *he* was the voice of restraint.

Blood ran from the man's nose and from cuts on his head. His hands were bruised and bloody too, his only movement a tiny shudder of his fingers.

I turned around where I stood, looking at each face. Fatso wore a scowl, the only face with anything on it that resembled displeasure. To his right was a heavier, taller woman with a half-smile like a sneer, then a still taller, emaciated man with an open smile, missing teeth in front. Then another fat man, his red sash stretched across a bloated belly that sagged over his belt, and two men who might've been twins, plump faces with identical smirks, smooth, oily skin and long, greasy hair sticking out from under their fezzes. And one more, maybe the creepiest of all: a kid, younger than me, eyes wide, leering at the motionless body at my feet, tapping his baton against his leg like a nervous tic, leaving bloody stripes on white pants.

"*Uh-uh uh*," I groaned. I felt Hammad squeezing my arm and I heard him ask, "What do you see?"

"I'm showing him the world, Hammad," Raúl said. "You know, the world you bailed from, so you could live your idyllic life in Orwell."

"He says he's showing me what the world's like since we left," I repeated, "and it's making me sick."

27

Ham Radio and Pork Belly

The gang of leering Kliegls and their unconscious victim flattened and rastered out, dissolving into another scene, just as dark and ugly, though not as lonely—a street, like the last one, but even seedier. We stood across from a façade made of the same fake wood clapboard as the houses in Orwell, covered in graffiti, like it was painted layer on layer, so thick the color of the clapboard only showed through in random spots no bigger than my hand. Along the top of the façade was a sign, hand-painted directly on the wall: HOPE HOUSE.

The people crowded around the door were seedy, too, much worse off than the old guy on the Loop the Kliegls had bludgeoned to death. There were fifteen at least, or twenty, in clothes likely salvaged from refuse bins at the city disposal plants. All of them were in the middle of a big argument.

"What is this?" I asked.

"Homeless shelter," Raúl answered.

"What're they fighting about?"

"Sophie," he said, "eavesdrop."

A dozen voices crowded into my headset—men and women, some shouting, others pleading, and while they all sounded different, together the effect was pure desperation, like each person's life depended on winning the argument.

"*…I been stay here before…*"

"*…full, all full—can't take any more. It's the law…*"

"*…gotta take us in, man, thass the law…*"

"Only if it's freezing. Forecast is four above. That's *the law."*

"I have a child…Jah, have some pity."

"God, shut it off!" I yelled, and Raúl didn't even have to tell Sophie before the voices muted, leaving only the barely audible metallic sidetone, an artifact of Raúl's compression algorithm.

"Why?" I asked. I'd never seen a homeless shelter before.

"They're turning people away, the shelters are—every one of them."

"I didn't know there were that many people on the streets. Is this normal?"

"There didn't used to be," Raúl explained, "not until lately. Dax cut funds for live services, so folks who'd normally keep themselves afloat on their basic income, pensions, or whatever, living in the material world, can't get the help they need."

"My mom used to work at live services," I said.

"And kept damn busy at it," he added. "Not anymore. If these poor souls aren't lined up during the day at one of the few live service offices still open, they're trying to beg a spot in a homeless shelter at night."

While we were talking a gang of Kliegls marched up to the crowd and started taunting them. One of them, a woman, eyes narrowed, her hair pulled back and rolled up in a bun behind her fez, unholstered her baton, went *hiss-click-click* and started poking the homeless folks. Most of them turned their bodies sideways to shield themselves, but one slapped the baton aside and got in her face. That was the sign for the rest of the Kliegls, six in all, to whip out their collapsible cudgels and start swinging. They landed a couple of hard blows in the few seconds it took for five good-sized guys in green shirts and pants to pop out of the shelter and get between the Kliegls and the street people, arms folded and impenetrable. The Kliegls stepped back, holding their batons in the air. They shouted, waving their arms, but the shelter guards stood firm, not saying a thing. The Kliegls kept up the taunts for another minute before stowing their clubs and leaving.

That was all it took for these bullies to slink away: five guys who wouldn't back down.

"It's a war on reality," Raúl explained after the Kliegls were gone and the guys in the greens started passing out food, bottled water, and blankets. "Kliegl policy: everything goes to VR."

A few homeless in the crowd drifted off once they got water and a bite, and some sat down on the sidewalk in front of the shelter, curling up and pulling blankets over themselves, settling in for the night. Some bunched up together, so they could double up on blankets and share body heat.

"Can we get out of here?" I asked.

"Sophie, exit venue."

We were back in the white staging venue, just me and Raúl. Hammad was still poking my arm, asking again, "What's happening?"

"Boys, since you left, things have changed," Raúl answered. "*Anyone* caught out at night, the Kliegls harass."

Hammad couldn't hear Raúl, so I repeated what he said, then turned back to Raúl. "Because they're IRL and not in VR?" I asked.

"Thus spake Dax: go VR or you're on your own," he replied.

"And you don't know why?"

"Not for sure. The official reasons are greater efficiency, lower cost for services, the usual horseshit."

"But you're not buying it."

"I don't have a better explanation, but I do find it odd that Dax almost never brings it up. Whenever the Kliegls announce new policies to bring folks into VR, Dax never announces it himself. Instead, he sends out a surrogate— someone you know."

That's what I was waiting to hear: some sign that my theory was right, and I could convince others that it was right, too.

"Madeleine?"

Raúl nodded. "You're still a smart kid, Dylan."

❖ ❖ ❖

That was the final proof in my mind, and Hammad's too. Now we were faced with the problem of how to convince Jackson and the rest of the leaders that Madeleine was coming for us—without giving away our kluge. We had no choice but to keep Raúl on deep background.

"What was Madeleine up to?" I asked Mom one night after we came home from the dining hall. She sat in a chair by the fireplace, knitting socks.

"I've told you ten times already," she replied evenly, not missing a stitch.

"You told us *what* she did," Hammad said, "but not *why*."

She set down her knitting and looked up at the ceiling. "Because I don't know *why*. She said she wanted to study me, something about virtual reality being 'the greatest advancement in psychological therapy in the last fifty years.' I never knew what that had to do with me."

"So, no idea?" I prompted.

"No," she answered, shaking her head, and took up her knitting again.

Hammad tipped his head toward Mom with a *keep talking* look. I was a little fidgety, not getting the answers I was looking for, not wanting to push too hard, and *really* not wanting to give away what we'd found out from Raúl. I was about to suggest to her that maybe Madeleine had some broader scheme in mind, when she spoke again without looking up from her knitting.

"Boys, what's that thing in your room?"

Hammad and I had hidden the VR gear in a corner of the closet, that being the most suspicious-looking gear in our rig, but the rest—the drone radio and interface to the console— was too complicated to break down after every session. We threw a sheet over it, but one look and Mom had to know that it didn't belong in the cabin.

Hammad jumped in before I could get out a word. "It's a ham radio. Do you know what ham radio is?"

She looked at Hammad with narrowed eyes. "Ham?" It's a good thing she wasn't looking at me, because that *ham* thing came out of nowhere. All I could think of was a big smoked pig butt. One look at my face and Mom could tell that I didn't know ham radio from pork belly.

"Oh, yeah," Hammad continued. "It's a way to communicate over long distance without going through the Worldstream. I heard that some folks still communicate via radio, all IRL, like us."

"Oh," she said, knitting away. "And the VR gear in the closet?"

I figured at that point we were totally tagged, but Hammad never even flinched. "Yeah, some hams work virtual mode, but it's pretty lo-res. Not like I'd know firsthand, though. We haven't got it working yet—Mom."

Hammad called her *Mom* whenever he felt like he was about to get in trouble with her. He'd come to think of her as his mom.

"So, that chattering I overhear at night, that's not to your...*hams*, is it?"

Hammad sputtered a bit, but I knew the game was over, and we needed to own up. Any more lying would only have made Mom feel that we thought she was stupid.

"No," I said. "We were talking to Raúl."

❖ ❖ ❖

We told her everything. Well, *I* told her, and Hammad just stared at the floor. Mom didn't say much, just an occasional *"Uh-huh"* and *"I see,"* keeping her jaw clenched the whole time. When I was done, she stared at me, then Hammad, then me again, before picking up her socks and knitting on them.

"You disobeyed me," she said.

"No, I didn't," I replied. "You never—"

"Dylan!" she interrupted. *"Jackson* will handle this."

I bit my lip and glanced at Hammad from under my eyebrows, though he didn't see. He was looking at his feet.

"But Raúl...the Kliegls!" I sputtered.

"You heard what Jackson said. That's not our world anymore."

"Mom!" I said, standing. *"Madeleine!"*

"Enough! You put us all in danger. You put *yourself* in danger. *And I don't want to lose you again!*"

She held up the sock to examine it, then went back to knitting. "Tomorrow, first thing, you're going to take all those things back to the junk room. And we won't talk about this again."

We did exactly as she asked. And for a week, I really didn't think about Madeleine much, or the old man at the Loop, or the homeless crowds freezing in the streets on the South Side. I put all that out of my mind, staying focused on Making, maintenance, and planting.

Then the invasion happened, and *everyone* stopped working.

28

A Plague of Bugs

PLANTING TIME IN Orwell is a month-long festival. Everyone pitches in. We've got more than two thousand hectares of cropland, and although a third goes fallow each year, the rest is planted in corn, beans, sorghum, and wheat. Even with every able Orwellian at it, planting can take more than a month, if the weather holds, and providing we don't get overrun by killer drones.

Hammad and I were planting the land east of Orwell, in the hundred-hectare section set aside for soybeans. It was our first time planting, and normally we wouldn't be trusted to plant without supervision, but after a few hectares, Benny decided that we were competent and wouldn't mangle ourselves in the planter. He'd left us alone and gone back to the equipment shed to work on a broken-down tractor.

By eleven a.m. we'd planted fifteen hectares, and we were running low on fuel. We unhitched the planter and headed back to the shed, Hammad driving the tractor, which, for some reason, he *loved* to do, me sitting on the fender, gripping the top of the cab. We'd been up since before sunrise, and though we ate a big breakfast (every planting day starts and ends with meals in the community dining hall, but we take our lunch in the field) we were famished, and the biodiesel exhaust, which smells like fried potatoes, only made us hungrier.

"Fill 'er up?" Benny yelled as we approached. He was standing next to the fuel tank, smiling and holding the hose.

"Are you talking about the tractor or my grumbling belly?" I shouted back, and Benny's smile grew wider. We halted the tractor by the tank, Benny unscrewed the fuel cap, and began refilling.

"How far?" he asked.

"Fifteen," I answered.

He nodded as if he was satisfied with that. When the tank was full, he put the cap back and stowed the hose before eyeing us and scratching his chin.

"Fifteen," he said. "Not bad for a couple of planting virgins. I guess you've earned some food."

There was a long table under a tree outside the shed where we spread out lunch. Though it was earlier than our usual lunchtime, we saw about a dozen others breaking from work and heading to the shed to join us.

Then they stopped walking, and we stopped eating.

What caught our attention was a hum, like an electric buzz, far off but powerful. I thought it might have been another malfunction from the wind farm, but it wasn't a sound I'd heard before, and it was coming from the wrong direction. Hammad, Benny, and I stood up for a better look. As ominous as the sound was, what we saw was way worse.

It was like a flock of birds, except that birds fly in chaotic patterns, and these birds didn't. They formed a wall, like low, dark clouds. As they got closer the solid mass became a bunch of evenly-spaced groups, then the groups became dots in a grid. The hum got louder, now with familiar high-frequency overtones—*drones*. I'd heard drones before, but never so many at once. There were hundreds. And they were coming fast.

Each group looked like thirty or so bugs in formation, with one bigger bug in the lead. The groups split up, some heading out toward the fields where workers were still planting, and some into town. One group headed straight for us.

All the workers stood still, eyes locked on the approaching swarm. Benny trotted out into the open and shouted, "Into the shed! C'mon! *Run!*"

Even then they hesitated, until the first tasers launched— six rounds, six hits. Half of the crew went down, and the other half sprinted for the shed, but too late. Another volley took down the rest, and the bugs kept coming.

"Jesus!" Benny yelled, then he turned and ran for the shed, with Hammad and me on his heels. Benny held the door and slammed it behind us, just as two taser rounds slammed into it.

We stood staring at each other, breathing hard, mouths hanging open, the sound of thirty drones in the sky so loud it penetrated the roof and walls and vibrated in my chest. Benny went to the window to size up the situation. As soon as he looked out, a taser round crashed through the window, missing Benny by a hair and burying itself in the floor. Broken glass flew everywhere, but mostly at Benny. He lifted his arm in time to shield his face, but shards hit him in the arm and chest, tearing his clothes and cutting him. He put his hand up under his T-shirt and pulled it out, dripping blood.

"Shit," he said, more pissed off than in pain. Then he got on one knee, sucking air, and his face turned pasty white.

"Hammad, check him," I said.

Hammad had already completed the last of his emergency training, and I still had two modules to go. He grabbed the first aid kit hanging on the wall, then went to Benny's side and lowered him to the floor.

I propped a sheet of fiberglass over the window, leaving just a crack to peek through. I half expected a taser in the eye when I looked through the crack, but nothing came.

Five drones hovered perfectly still outside the shed, aiming their taser arsenals at the window and door. Another twenty-five bugs hung over the field where twelve of our fellow Orwellians lay disabled. I puzzled over the drones' appearance—they *looked* like regular bugs, but something was missing. Then I noticed one drone, bigger than the rest, high above the formation. It had no tasers, only an array of cameras, like the first surveillance drone in February, only bigger. Then it hit me: It was the only bug that could see. The rest of the drones, the thirty or so hovering stock-still above the killing field, had no cameras. They were taser gunships, all sting, no eyes.

"How's Benny?" I asked.

Benny was paler and struggling to breathe. Hammad had taped a thick wad of gauze to Benny's chest. "Pneumothorax," he replied. "He's in pain, but not life-threatening—yet. Gotta get to Kruse stat. What's it like out there?"

"Ugly," I said, "and also weird."

"Weird how?"

I turned away from the window and moved the fiberglass to close the peephole. "Did you see what those bugs did? With their tasers, I mean?"

"Yeah, they crumped all our friends. How are they?"

"Still down. But that's not what I'm talking about."

"What, then?"

"Twelve rounds, twelve hits," I answered, and then Hammad got it. Bugs have terrible aim. When they attack, they shoot large numbers in a spread pattern. Most of the rounds miss, but it only takes one.

"Jeez, that's not right," he said.

"It's even weirder," I added. "They don't have cameras."

"Firing blind? How does that work?"

I cracked open the peephole again and peered out. The drones hadn't moved, but the big bug was panning its cameras, looking for movement.

"There's one bug with eyes. I think it's calling the shots for the others."

"Then…take out the sentry, and the bugs will scatter."

"The shotgun," Benny rasped, "by the supply cabinet, and the shells inside, top shelf."

I went to the cabinet and grabbed the gun, an ancient single-shot model, and got the box of shells—three left.

"Can you shoot a shotgun?" Hammad asked, as he applied another layer of tape to Benny's chest.

I'd seen Benny shoot before, though I couldn't say I was paying close attention.

"How hard can it be?" I asked.

I broke open the gun and loaded a shell. Very slowly, I slid the fiberglass sheet to one side, just wide enough to get the barrel through and aim. As I stuck the barrel out, an arsenal bug fired two taser rounds, one of them glancing off the gun barrel and burrowing into the window frame, and the other crashing into the fiberglass, causing it to fly across the room. With the window unblocked, and all of us exposed, I aimed and fired before they could get off another volley.

A shotgun makes a big noise, much worse when it's in an enclosed space. My ears were ringing, and the recoil threw me back, a good thing, because four taser rounds rocketed through the open window and missed me by centimeters. From where I was on the floor, I could see the sentry drone weaving from side to side, either damaged or trying to evade another shot. Six more rounds slammed into the shed, only one of which made it through the window and missed me by a meter.

"That was a spread pattern," Hammad said. He was right —without the queen drone, the bugs reverted to their default firing mode.

I broke the gun, loaded another shell, snapped it shut, aimed, and fired again.

This time I was prepared for the kickback. The big drone pitched backward, and bits of it fell away, but it was still airborne. It revved its blades and flew straight up, disappearing into the sky.

"Now's our chance," I said, and ran out the door to try and bring as many Orwellians as I could into the relative safety of the equipment shed. Hammad followed right behind me.

The drones had taken up a new formation, spread out in a grid covering the entire field where the others lay. As we neared them, they started firing single rounds in a random pattern, protecting their kill like hyenas.

Hammad and I pulled first one, then another into the shed, dodging tasers fired from eyeless bugs. We were feeling more confident, because the pattern didn't seem so random after all, and we were able to avoid getting hit almost by instinct.

Until the replacement arrived.

We saw another sentry drone in the distance speeding toward us. The swarm broke their grid formation and got back to their places, and as the sentry got into position, the drones locked onto us and fired.

I was the lucky one. The round tore my shirt and ripped a gash in my side, giving me a jolt as it passed. It felt like getting hit by a brick. I went to my knees, but I was still conscious. Hammad got his in the thigh and went down.

"Hammad!" I shouted. I didn't know if the bugs could hear me, but with the sentry in place, they sure as hell could *see* me, and a couple of them pivoted in my direction.

Then the shotgun fired.

The sentry shattered, turning into a cloud of debris, raining down in smoking trails. The bugs went back to the grid. I dragged Hammad to the shed, dodging tasers as I went.

Benny was at the window, holding the shotgun, breathing hard. His face was the color of an overcast sky. In all, we'd pulled four others from the field. I'd pulled out the taser rounds and they were starting to come to.

"What in hell?" Benny wheezed. "This makes no damn sense, taking down folks out here. We're *going* to recover. Is someone just trying to scare us?"

We didn't wait long for an answer. The drones assumed a new arrangement, then spun up and flew off in the direction they came from. We saw the other swarms, the ones from the town, flying off after them.

Then we saw the trucks.

29

Heading Overland

WE COUNTED SIX vehicles, like large autobuses, with dull steel bodies and streamlined windshields that reflected the sun into our eyes. They were 150 meters away and silent, most likely electric. I was so used to the grumbling bio-diesels we drove in Orwell that I'd forgotten transports could be silent.

When the fleet came within 100 meters, they split into two groups, and then we realized that the six vehicles we saw were only the first row—two came on toward us, and ten more turned toward town.

Benny and I stared out the window.

"What the hell?" I muttered, hands clammy and heart pounding in double-time.

"Truck out back," Benny said, his voice shakier than it was even a minute ago.

The back wall of the shed was a wide door that rolled up overhead. I heaved it open. Just outside the door, facing away from me, was a flatbed truck for hauling equipment, covered with dirt clods and dried mud.

"C'mon," I said to Benny, pulling his arm around my shoulder to lift him. I got him into the cab. He was rasping and holding onto his side.

By that time a couple of the ones we'd pulled in from the field had come around, and they pulled Hammad and the others onto the back of the truck, sweeping dirt and debris from the bed with their hands.

I checked the situation outside.

Three men dressed in the black uniform of the Civils went to work collecting the disabled Orwellians, moving as if they'd done it a hundred times. A compartment on the side of the vehicle popped open, and inside was a stack of stretchers. Two Civils took positions at either end of a downed Orwellian, grabbing his feet and arms, while the third whipped a stretcher from the compartment and slid it underneath. The two Civils strapped the body down, then slid it into the back of the transport. The whole operation took less than ten seconds. And there was no confusion about in which order they collected the fallen, because there was one person directing the action, not in the black Civil uniform, but in white, with a red sash across his chest.

"What's that about?" asked one of those who'd recovered. She was a sturdy woman with tan cheeks and dark blond hair tied up under a blue bandana, like most of the women who worked the fields. I recognized her—Abby, more than twice my age, but she can still outwork me. She'd hauled the unconscious and semi-conscious Orwellians onto the truck single-handedly.

"That's a Kliegl," I replied. "Not nice people."

After collecting the last tasered worker, the Civils closed the door to the stretcher compartment, and climbed inside the vehicles.

I grabbed Abby's arm and pulled her toward the back.

"I'll drive," I said, "you keep them on the truck. Could get bumpy."

She climbed on and I got into the cab. I pushed the button to start the engine. It turned over, chugging like it always does when it's starting cold, which never causes me concern any other time, but at that precise moment it sounded like death. I pushed it again, then again, harder, until my thumb turned white, and it chugged, caught and sputtered, then chugged again, until after an eternity it coughed and growled to life.

What now? I thought, but only for a second, before I shifted into gear and stood on the accelerator.

We headed down a slope, to a side road into town. It got bumpy right away. I looked in the mirror and saw Abby scrambling to pull folks from the edge, but a few of the others had recovered to where they could take care of themselves, and even Hammad was sitting up. The motion wasn't doing Benny any good, and he heaved a thick, liquid cough with every bump.

But I also saw the first transport in the mirror, coming over the hill, followed by the other, not more than a hundred meters back. My plan to go into town would leave us out in the open the whole way, and those transports looked *much* faster than the diesel I was driving.

"Woods," Benny croaked.

"Got it," I replied, and veered to the left toward a stand of trees, to an access road we used when harvesting maple sap. It was a curvy road I knew well.

As we turned into the trees, the road took a sharp right, and I rounded it as fast as I thought was safe for my passengers. They were all up by then, some still groggy, but hanging on. I pushed harder. The road wasn't built for speed, and we didn't do a lot of maintenance on it, which made for a hell of a bumpy ride. I could only hope it was as hard on those meat wagons behind us.

The next curve we weren't so lucky. I braked, then accelerated through the turn, which caused the tires to lose traction. The truck swerved into a tree. I heard a shout and I looked in the mirror to see Hammad over the side, Abby holding his hand, and two others holding Abby.

"Oh, Jesus!" I yelled and made the mistake of slamming on the brakes.

Abby lost her grip, sending Hammad into the trees. Everyone else on the bed tumbled forward, slamming into the cab or each other. Benny hit the dashboard, his eyes rolling back in his head and his mouth open, screaming silent agony.

Hammad leaned against a tree trunk, sitting up without moving. I jumped out of the cab and got to him a step ahead of Abby.

"Hammad!" I yelled, patting his cheek, but he didn't respond.

Abby got under one arm and lifted him up. I was about to get his other arm when Abby said, "Dylan, get back in the cab."

"When we get Hammad to the truck."

"Dylan, *look!*" she said, tilting her head toward the trees.

I caught a glimpse of the lead transport on another fork of the road. It would take them a few minutes to backtrack and get on our road, but if *we* could see *them*, *they* could see *us*.

I sprinted to the cab, shifting into gear just as Abby hauled Hammad onto the bed and jumped on herself. Everyone in the back had found a handhold, thankfully, because the ride got even rougher. I'm sure I hit every wheel rut and fallen branch. Crossing the creek bed I thought we'd busted an axle. Benny had passed out, still breathing with a horrifying rattle.

We stayed in the woods another twenty minutes or so. One road led to a pasture just outside of Orwell, on the other side of a rise. I took it, and the grass was a much smoother ride than the road. There was no sign of the transports, so I headed to the top of the hill.

From where we were, we could see the whole town. The population of Orwell is just under 2,000. The town is laid out on a grid of streets a little more than a couple square kilometers in size, now patrolled by transports, with a line of Civils in riot gear toting taser rifles in the lead. There were no bodies on the ground; they'd already been collected, like bundles left by the streets on trash day. The Civils were going door to door, rousting out anyone who'd escaped the drone onslaught. And on every corner, directing the action, was a white-shirted Kliegl.

"Oh, Lord," Abby said.

Two Civils came at our cabin near the outskirts. One stood back while the other pounded the door before kicking it open. They'd just entered when I saw Mom run out the back. She'd only made it about twenty meters when a Civil dropped her with a taser.

"Mom!" I shouted, and I lunged forward, but Abby and two others held me back.

"What're you going to do?" Abby said close to my ear. "You go down there, they'll take you, too."

"It's my mom!"

"*Look* at them," she said. "We can't help her. We can't help any of them. And we've got injured. *Those* are the people we can help."

She was right. It was an army of black and white, and the whole town was theirs. But in that moment, her words weren't registering with me. The only thing going through my mind, the one thought that overloaded all rational thinking was that my mom, for whom I gave up everything I had to find, was being taken away from me again. Hell, I'd even forgotten about Hammad.

"Get him on the truck," Abby ordered the two men holding me. "We're heading overland. And *I'm* driving."

30

The Last of the Laputans

THE ROAD WE took was barely a road, or maybe it never was. It was two overgrown ruts not quite the same distance apart as the wheels of the truck, and the wheels kept jumping out of one, then the other. Each time it jumped a rut, everyone on the bed took a jolt. By the time we were ten or twenty klicks from Orwell, even the ruts had disappeared and we were bouncing over open ground. In the back, we hung on by our fingernails, the flatbed spanking our butts with every bump. It couldn't have been good for Benny.

But we'd lost the transports, and not even the drones had followed us. An hour after we'd seen the last of the Civils and Kliegls, Abby was still driving like a maniac until I banged on the back window. She turned and craned her neck to look, then slowed down and came to a stop.

She jumped down from the cab and came around. "How's folks?" she asked, looking us over.

"Okay, fine," some replied. The tased Orwellians were awake, tired and achy, and *all* of us were ragged, but we were all intact.

"How's Benny?" I asked.

Abby spit on the ground, then looked up at the cab. "Rough. He's out. He sounds like a leaky window in a windstorm."

Kruse was the only doctor in Orwell, and he wasn't on the truck. My best guess was that he was strapped to a board in a Kliegl transport.

"Hammad, anything you can do for Benny?" I asked.

Hammad was rubbing his thigh where he'd been hit, still looking half-crumped.

"He needs a chest tube," Hammad answered. "I could try, but it'd be half guesswork. I'd probably do more damage."

"And how would we drain it?" Abby added.

I had no idea what either of them was talking about. Some of the others spoke up with ideas, none of them any good, according to Abby. The conversation around how to keep Benny from dying got kind of heated, until Hammad pointed to the horizon and said, "Look there."

It was another vehicle coming over a rise just ahead. That quieted everyone down. Abby jumped in the cab, and the rest of us gripped the sides of the truck, expecting her to tear out across the prairie to parts unknown. Then I noticed that the oncoming vehicle was making noise.

"Abby, wait!" I shouted.

"What?" she yelled over the sound of the engine cranking. She looked again at the vehicle, then let up on the starter, opened the door, and stepped up on the running board to get a better view.

"It's a truck," I said. In fact it was a flatbed, beat-up and running rough, like the one we were on, though I didn't recognize it as one of Orwell's. By then we were all standing on the bed peering at it, now close enough to make out three people in the cab and three more on the bed. It pulled up next to us and shut down, the engine coughing and rattling to a stop. The driver, an old, skinny Black guy with gray whiskers leaned out his window. He wore a soft cap with a bill, which he picked up off his head, then ran his fingers over his wiry hair as he looked us over.

"Orwell?" he asked wearily as he put the cap back on.

"Yeah," Abby answered. "Laputa?"

The old man nodded. "How many of you did they get?" he asked.

"We're all that's left, as far as we know," Abby replied.

"Same. Might be a couple others lit out to Burgess. There was another truck in the north fields. Don't know for sure, though." He craned his neck to see past Abby. "You got a man hurt," he said, referring to Benny.

"Collapsed lung," Abby said.

"Casey!" the man yelled. "You got your bag, right? They's a man in need here."

A short, heavy woman clutching an oversized backpack climbed off the truck bed. Hammad and I scrambled to the passenger door and opened it. We gasped when we saw Benny. His skin was gray and he was dead still. The woman, Casey, came around and stepped up on the running board. She reached out and put her finger on Benny's throat.

"He's got a pulse," she said. "You two, get him out of there and back on the truck bed."

We were careful, but Casey said, "Faster, boys, time's short for this man."

Casey knelt next to Benny (who looked as much like a corpse as any living person could), undid his shirt and pulled back the bloody gauze to scrutinize the wound. She put her ear next to his nose.

"Respiration is shallow," she said. "The wound is aspirating." She cut off his shirt, wadded it up, and put it under his head. Then she pulled a big foil packet out of the backpack, tore it open, and scrubbed the area around the wound with some greenish stuff, until his whole chest and side was green.

"You," she said, pointing to Hammad. "I'm going to need your help." Why she pointed to Hammad instead of me I don't know, unless it was because my face was about as green as Benny's chest. Hammad climbed up next to Casey. She handed him a massive syringe, as big as a grease cartridge.

"I'm going to make an incision here to open the wound," Casey explained calmly.

Hammad looked on like he was watching someone clean a fuel injector. My stomach was turning itself inside-out. Casey tore open a plastic bag and pulled out a clear tube, then handed one end to Hammad.

"Attach the tube to the syringe while I insert my end in the incision," she said. "When I tell you, pull back on the plunger. Take it slow. I'll let you know if you're doing it right."

She and Hammad continued with the procedure, and some of the others on the truck watched over their shoulders, but when Hammad pulled on that syringe and the tube filled up with blood and yellowish fluid, I turned away and tried not to retch. Then, when the onlookers gasped and murmured in a good way, I looked back. Benny was breathing easier, and his color was coming back. He grimaced as he came to, but didn't look like a corpse anymore.

"Keep going, son, you're doing great," Casey said to Hammad. "A little more. There. Hold it." She clamped off the tube and plastered the wound with tape. "He's out of danger. We'll need to keep the tube in place for a while, and suction from time to time."

Folks around them patted Hammad on the back, and he grinned like he'd raised the dead, which he practically had.

The old man came around to check on the situation. "Well done, Casey. Another miracle worked. Who's your nurse?"

Hammad's grin got wider, if that was possible. "I'm Muhammad," he replied.

"I'm Heath," the old man said, and stuck out his hand. "You got skills, Muhammad."

By that time Abby was out of the cab and standing next to Heath.

"We barely made it out," Abby said. "We got nothing—no food, no supplies. The truck's almost empty, too."

Heath scratched his chin. "We managed to grab a few things. Some rations, some water. No fuel, though. We've got half a tank, but that's it. And the medical kit. We were damn lucky on that account."

"Thanks for that," Abby said, while she patted Benny on the arm. "You gonna make it, Benny?"

Benny forced a little bit of a smile and stuck up his thumb.

I'd already counted heads: eight Orwellians, including me, and six Laputans. Their truck had a few boxes, and a couple metal cans of maybe 20 liters each, which I assumed were filled with water. If the boxes were full of food, I figured maybe it'd last a week; more, if we ate light.

"What now?" I asked.

Abby and Heath looked at me like I'd asked a dumb question, but in my mind, it was the *only* question worth asking, even if we didn't have a good answer.

"What about Burgess?" I asked. That took the *What a dumb question* look off their faces.

"It's worth a shot," Abby agreed. "But I couldn't even guess which direction they are from here."

Heath pointed to what I guessed was south, judging by the location of the sun in late afternoon. "That way," he said. "We should come on the creek before too far, then follow it into Burgess."

"Why would Burgess be any safer?" Hammad asked. "They came for Orwell and Laputa at the same time. Don't you think they'd've gone for Burgess, too?"

That sparked another discussion, which went nowhere, since none of us knew anything. After about ten minutes, it was obvious that we were all going on pure gut feelings, with no one in charge to break the deadlock.

The conversation stopped when we heard another sound, a low grumble like another truck at a distance. Abby and Heath jumped in their trucks and cranked the engines, while the rest of us grabbed hold. The engines caught just as the vehicle came over the rise from the direction of Orwell. I recognized it right away. It was one of the rolling houses that a few of the Orwellians had kluged together, and some lived in them full time. It was rolling along right behind another vehicle I knew: Naia's buggy, with Naia in the driver's seat and Jackson by her side.

"Abby, wait!" I yelled. "It's Jackson and Naia!"

Abby and Heath shut down their engines. We watched the buggy come faster, the mobile house lagging behind. Naia pulled up beside the truck, right next to me. I grinned and waved, but Naia didn't wave back. Instead, she jumped out of the buggy and came at me, Jackson close on her heels. I thought he was going to tackle her, but she got to me first, pulled me off the truck bed and threw me on the ground. I hit butt first, then came down on a rock with my elbow. The pain shot up my arm, and I cried out, but the pain wasn't as intense as the shock of Naia coming at me. Naia had a temper, but she didn't usually act out unless she had reason. This came out of nowhere.

"Naia, take it easy," Jackson said, in the voice he used to cool off a hot situation.

"What was that for?" I asked, rubbing my elbow, which hurt like a bitch.

"*They were the only ones who knew*," she growled. "*Him* and *Hammad*. It couldn't have been anyone else."

"Knew what?" I asked.

"The scanner. When the attack came, I ran to the maker space. The scanner was going crazy."

I still didn't catch on, but Hammad did.

"The muni band link," he said, and then I got it. I had disconnected the scanner from the Orwell muni band so Naia wouldn't know about our satellite link. And I forgot to hook it back up.

31

Signs of Life

"Get Benny in the mobile," Jackson said to Hammad, but I took him to mean me, too. Naia was shooting tasers at me with her eyes, and Jackson saw the need to dial down the situation. Ordering us into the mobile house seemed an obvious way to separate me and Naia and allow some cooling off time. If I'd known what was waiting for me inside the mobile though, I might've taken my chances with Naia.

Benny looked more comfortable by then, though he was unconscious, and he didn't wake up as Hammad and I lifted him off the truck bed to lay him out on the lower bunk of the mobile.

Max was in the mobile, and three others from Orwell, all of whom we knew well. They must have overheard what had happened outside, because they all looked grim, glancing at Hammad and me before looking away.

All except one.

Frank was staring at me with pure hatred, but also with a little bit of a smile. He was as sloppy as ever, and his eyes were glassy like he'd been sucking moonshine straight from the fuel tank. When our eyes met, it was me who looked away.

"Little Dylan fucked up," he said. Normally, when Frank says something nasty like that, others will admonish him. Not this time. Everyone was probably thinking the same thing.

We got underway. Jackson and Heath agreed to head toward Burgess, keeping an eye out for bugs or transports. If there were any Burgessers who had escaped they'd probably be heading our way and we'd run into them. Once we were all together, we'd figure out what to do next. We didn't really have a plan beyond that.

The going was rough, all of us hanging on as the big mobile bounced along the prairie. Hammad kept an eye on Benny's chest tube, suctioning it now and again. I forced myself to watch, though it made me queasy, just so I wouldn't have to look at Frank.

But of course, Frank wouldn't leave me be. He got next to me, and hovered. I kept my eyes on that gory wound like Benny's life depended on it.

"*Little Dylan* got us all *tased*. *Little Dylan* got us all kicked out of *Orwell*." He was over-pronouncing his words, like he almost always does when he's drunk, which he almost always is.

"Shut up, Frank," Hammad said. I was hoping someone else would say it, too, but no one did, not even Max. It was me and Hammad versus Frank, with the others looking on and Benny fast asleep.

"Oh, *look. Little Dylan's sweetheart* is sticking up for him. Isn't that *precious?*"

Finally Max did speak up. "That's *enough*, Frank. Sit down before you fall down."

Frank slowly turned toward Max. "How's Lois, Max? Seen her lately?"

Lois is Max's wife. I assumed that she had been swept up by the Kliegls, and Frank was using that fact to set Max against me. I also assumed that it worked, because Max glared at Frank, then at me, then at the floor.

"Max," I said, "did Lois…"

He nodded without looking up. "I guess. I didn't see it myself. I was out at the processing plant when they came. Lois was at the maker space. I started toward town when I ran into Jackson and Naia in the buggy and the mobile right behind. They told me to get in the mobile, I think…I wasn't really hearing them. I kept running toward town when Naia got me by the arm and dragged me to the door."

Max choked up a bit, and I felt like choking too. "I saw them take my mom," I said, and that was enough for Max to lose it. He put his hands to his face and heaved a couple sobs. My eyes got watery, but I never cried.

"You two want a little *pity party* together?" Frank sneered. "Max, are you *forgetting* something? Didn't you hear what *little Dylan* did? *He* pulled the plug on the alarm." He swung around unsteadily, the result of the rough terrain and the corn liquor. "If it wasn't for *little Dylan,* we'd've *seen it coming.* We'd've had a *head start.*" He bent low enough for me to smell his breath, adding harshly, "For all we know, Lois is *dead*. For all we know, little Dylan *killed her.*"

At that moment I was feeling very down on myself, guilt-ridden about forgetting to turn the alarm back on, but I never even considered that anyone *died* because of my screw up. Frank's saying that, and *how* he said it, on top of my own self-loathing, and how it affected Max, all came together at once, and I acted out.

I stood up fast, swinging my elbow and catching Frank square in the nose. He fell back against Max, putting his hand to his face. In another second the blood came through his fingers—lots of blood, more than Benny ever shed, but for some reason seeing Frank's blood didn't make me nauseous. He was sprawled with his back against Max, stunned, but when he looked at his hand, now dripping red, he bellowed like a bull elk and came at me.

He was clumsy and slow. I felt tight as a spring, my senses sharp and hi-res. I sidestepped Frank in the cramped space and brought a fist into his gut with force. He doubled over, throwing up on the floor and my shoes. For some reason, Frank puking on me was like a trigger, and all the anger and hatred I'd felt toward him for months collected in my stomach like a bad meal, and I dropped on him and got him in a choke hold.

Max was pulling at Frank, and Hammad was pulling at me, but I kept the hold on, tightening it until Frank dug his fingernails into my arm while making gurgling noises, spitting flecks of puke all over both of us. Hammad and Max were shouting and pulling, trying to separate us, and the rest jumped in, too. I'm sure I'd have strangled him to death if the mobile hadn't come to a sudden stop, throwing all of us forward. I let go the choke hold and grabbed for the edge of a seat to keep from sliding all the way up to the driver. Frank rolled over, face down in the aisle.

The door opened and Jackson poked his head in. There was blood everywhere, on me, on Frank, and smeared across the floor The air stank of vomit. Jackson gave the scene a once-over with a *What the fuck?* look on his face, then growled, "Get out here—*all* of you."

We were on a hill overlooking Burgess. The sun was low by that time, glinting red off the windows of the buildings below. All of us stood silent, hoping to see some sign of life, but the town was dead, like Laputa and Orwell.

"What do you think, Naia?" Jackson asked.

"They've come and gone," she answered. She craned her neck to scan the sky, for bugs, I assumed. "Do you think they're still watching?"

Jackson shook his head. "Who can say? If I knew what they were after and why, maybe I'd have an opinion." He scratched the back of his neck and turned to Heath. "How 'bout you, Heath? What d'ya say?"

Heath readjusted his cap. "I say we got a bunch of tired 'n' hungry folks here, and the sun goin' down. Maybe we go down there and find 'em shelter for the night."

Jackson nodded. "All right. Naia and I will take the lead. Abby, you follow, then Heath, then the mobile. Any one of us sees anything the least bit hinky, lay on the horn and reverse course." He looked over the ragged bunch, settling his eyes on me. "Dylan, on the flatbed. Max, Frank, the rest of you, in the mobile. You too, Muhammad. Keep an eye on Benny."

I got up on the back of the truck and settled in against the cab. I watched the rest of the Orwell crew climb onto the mobile. Frank was the last to get on. He lingered by the door for a second, staring straight at me, before climbing the steps.

In all the time I'd known Frank, I never gave him much thought, and I didn't suppose that he thought much about me. But from the look on his face, I understood that he'd thought about me a *lot*, and would still.

I had my first real enemy.

32

Naia to the Rescue

We were in a house near the outskirts of Burgess. The Orwell-Laputa caravan was camped a half-klick from the edge of town. Jackson had sent out search parties to do recon, sending Hammad and me to the far end. Our orders were to snoop around our sector for any sign of life, friendly or not, and report back in an hour.

There was no problem getting into the house—the door was lying in the front room, two taser rounds sticking straight up, knocked off its hinges so hard the door frame was splintered. Anyone running from the drones would've barely made it inside before the bugs fired, followed shortly by Civils with a battering ram.

We looked at each other. Hammad's eyes told me he was reliving our ordeal in the shed the same as I was.

Inside was dark, not the least bit inviting. We tried the lights, but the power was out. All the window shades were lowered, flapping loosely in the evening breeze, but even after Hammad raised them, we couldn't see null until our eyes adjusted and even then not much.

But we could hear—a scratching sound, coming from under the floor, almost exactly where we stood in the middle of the room.

"Did you hear that?" Hammad whispered.

"Uh-huh," I whispered back.

We kept still, waiting to see if we'd hear it again, and after a minute we did, like fingernails on a wooden table.

"Drone?" I whispered.

Hammad gave me a *Wait, what?* look. "Under the floor? Not likely."

We listened a bit longer, and we heard it again.

"Rats, maybe," I suggested.

"Big ones," Hammad replied. He stomped on the floor. The scratching stopped, and we heard a whimper instead, like a person in pain.

"Hey!" Hammad called, a little louder than a normal voice, and way louder than I felt comfortable with. The person under the floor whimpered again.

Hammad went for the door. I followed him around to the side of the house, where he crouched by a vent on the foundation.

"Someone there?" he shouted.

"Shh," I said, still antsy about the possibility of drones or other menaces lingering in town.

He waved his hand at me and put his ear to the vent. More whimpering.

"Someone's in the crawl space," he said. He looked both ways. "There has to be an access door somewhere." He ran off toward the rear of the house, with me right behind. The access door was open a crack. Hammad pushed it open the rest of the way.

"Someone there?" he yelled.

Silence. He looked at me, then he leaned into the opening like he was going in.

I grabbed him by the waist of his pants. "Hammad, wait! You don't know what's in there."

"Dylan, it's *someone*. They're hurt. Tased, maybe, or clubbed."

He was right, but I still felt anxious. "Careful," I said. He pushed in another half meter before I heard another whimper, then a growl.

"Holy shit!" Hammad shouted, then pulled out, hitting his head on the frame and digging deep scratches in his arm. He scrambled sideways on hands and knees, crab-like.

"What—" I began, then stumbled toward Hammad when I saw it: a dog, I thought at first, like a small German shepherd, but once it was out from under the house I realized it was like no dog I'd ever seen.

The scrawny animal lowered its head and let out a long, low growl, then turned and sprinted for the prairie.

I helped Hammad to his feet. "Do you think that thing is the last living resident of Burgess?" I asked.

"It might be," Hammad replied, brushing the dirt from his knees. "Let's go see what the others found."

❖ ❖ ❖

We were late to the rendezvous. The other search parties had returned, all standing in a circle around Jackson, Heath, and Naia. I let Hammad take the lead, since Naia's wrath seemed to be directed mostly at me, and I couldn't take much more of her glaring.

"Report," Jackson said.

"One skinny coyote," Hammad replied. "Otherwise, deserted."

"What about provisions?" Naia asked. She seemed to have cooled down a bit, but she was talking to Hammad, not me.

"They only nabbed the people," Hammad replied. "All the food, clothes, household stuff—all untouched."

The folks in the circle nodded and murmured.

"Okay then," Jackson said. "We can salvage food, water, fuel, whatever else we need."

"If they've come and gone, then why don't we just move in?" I asked. "Or why not go back to Orwell? Or Laputa?"

"We talked about that," Naia snapped, "which you'd've *known* if you'd been back on time."

"*And?*" I shot back. Naia flared up again and came toward me, before Jackson got in her way.

"Naia, c'mon," he said, then turned to me. "We think it's better to keep moving, at least for a while. We don't know what they're up to, which means we don't know if they'll be back."

"Don't we?" I asked.

Jackson tipped his head back and looked down his nose at me. "Don't we *what?*"

170

I was a little tenuous about bringing up such a touchy subject again, but in my mind, it all made sense. "It's Madeleine. *This* was the next step in her plan to get us all back in the Worldstream."

Jackson rolled his eyes as only Jackson can. "Oh, for chrissake—*this* again?" He spat on the ground. Naia was eyeing me as well. The only thing to do was brazen it out.

"I have proof," I said. A few people perked up, but Jackson was even more dismissive. He turned away from me like he hadn't heard and started ordering the crews from Orwell and Laputa to go into Burgess to forage. What happened next surprised the hell out of me.

Naia put her hand on Jackson's arm and said, "Hear him out."

Why she did that, I still can't say. Maybe she just wanted all the info available, so we could make an informed decision. Or maybe she felt like she'd been hard on me and wanted to show we still had *some* kind of relationship, even if it was broken. In any case, I was grateful.

Jackson paused, hung his head, and held out his hand like he was inviting me to speak.

"I know what Madeleine's been up to in the world." I gulped hard. "I've been there. I've seen it."

❖ ❖ ❖

Hammad and I told them everything—the VR rig we kluged from the drone radio, the satellite link, Raúl's Fortress of Solitude, the South Side, the Loop—the whole saga. Over the half-hour it took to tell the tale, Jackson kept quiet, but the more we talked, the more fearful I was (others, too, judging from appearances) that Jackson was headed for a meltdown. His jaw muscles flexed, and his face reddened like he was reacting to the heat, though the temperature had dropped after sunset. When I finished the account, ending with the campaign by Kliegls to get everyone in the Worldstream, and Mom's command to dismantle the rig, the group got quiet, waiting for Jackson's recoil.

It was bad.

"If I'm hearing you right," he began in a low, edgy voice, "you not only disabled Naia's alarm, but you also *gave away our location*."

Hammad and I were puzzled. That had *never* occurred to us.

"Um, what?" I said, and that was enough to set Jackson off. He came at me and grabbed my shirt, pushing me back so hard I stumbled and fell.

Jackson bent over me, holding me just off the ground by my shirt, still tangled up in his fingers.

"You *gave us up!*" he growled, spit flicking off his lips. He pulled me up higher and shook me. "You might as well have sent up signal flares!" With one final jerk, he let me drop.

Folks had backed off a bit. I wanted to say something in my own defense, but nothing came to mind. Instead, I balled up to protect myself. I was sure Jackson was going to rear back and kick me. But he didn't.

"Jackson," Naia said softly, putting her hand on his shoulder. "They *already* knew where we were."

"What?" Jackson sputtered. "What are you saying?"

She leaned close to him and spoke quietly, but everyone heard her clearly.

"They found us *long* before the kids built their rig, remember? There were the drones in February, and the others in April. They'd *already* found us—Laputa and Burgess, too."

Naia had come to our rescue again. I could've kissed her, if she'd've let me.

Jackson stood simmering, his eyes locked on me, then broke his stare and shot a look at Hammad before turning to Naia.

"They disabled the alarm," Jackson mumbled, like he wanted to keep the rant going, but had lost all his steam.

"Yeah," Naia said, "they did. There'd be a lot more of us out here in the wilderness instead of in the custody of Kliegls if they hadn't, but you can't blame them for bringing on the invasion. That was going to come anyway."

Jackson looked deflated at that moment. The rest of us unclenched as well.

"So…what now?" Heath asked. It was the question we all had on our minds.

"We have to get our people back," Naia answered. "Step one is to find out where they are. Let's get back to Orwell so Hammad can rebuild his rig." She put her hand out. I grabbed it and she helped me to my feet. "Dylan, we need you to go back into the Worldstream."

33

A Previous Job

NAIA HAD GEAR we didn't know about.

The VR console and headset we'd found in the junk room were only the demonstrators. Hammad and I were in the kitchen of Naia's house, where she'd brought out two more consoles, two sets of headgear, several pairs of tactile gloves, and one more thing I hadn't seen since confinement: a Belt, gen 3.

"Why do you even *have* a Belt?" I asked her. "This is like the complete *opposite* of what the *Vitreous Orb* stands for."

"Yeah. Ironic, isn't it?" she replied. She turned the Belt over in her hands and ran her fingers over the shiny fabric. "I should've trashed it—hell, *burned* it—when we left Omaha." She laid it on the kitchen table. "Dylan, what's it like to be an addict?"

My face got red, because we'd already had this conversation, and I wasn't completely over it.

"Never mind," she said. "You know what it's like. So do I. *This* was *my* addiction. Not just hanging in VR—*everyone's* in VR." She pushed at the Belt with her fingers as if trying to wake up a sleeping cat. "Lifestreams, that's what I did. Hooked, totally." She got quiet, poking at the Belt, with a weird, un-Naia-like vacant stare.

"Yeah?" Hammad said, breaking the awkward silence.

"You wake up, hope you don't give in, hope, wish, *pray*, if the hoping and wishing don't work, which they never do," she continued, as though she was talking to herself. "*One ride,* you tell yourself—a lie, but you believe it—a short one before you jack in for work. Then a short one turns into

174

another short one, or a long one, then you're late and you haven't even eaten breakfast. You shake your head trying to focus, and you do, for a while. Never for long."

She looked like I'd never seen her, like she was unsure of herself, which she never is.

"Why'd you keep this stuff?" I asked.

"It's a reminder, to me, to others in Orwell like me. We all got to a point where our lives were being eaten up with nothing to show for it. Certainly *we* weren't any better for all the time we wasted. We upped and left the Worldstream for a reason." She picked up the Belt and shook it, like she was shaking out a dirty towel. "*This* is the reason."

"Seems to me like you wouldn't *want* to be reminded," Hammad said.

"But I do. There're a thousand ways to waste a life." She glanced at me sideways. "Right, Dylan?"

That only embarrassed me more, and I didn't say anything.

"I look at this stuff every morning, and swear that I'll never let another day, not even another *hour* pass without making my life or someone else's better."

"But this stuff," Hammad said, picking up the headset, "it's a temptation, like having alcohol around a drunk."

Naia laughed softly. "No, it's not. We're in Orwell, remember? Ogallala—the wilderness where the Worldstream can't reach. We all came here—Jackson, Max, Benny, me—because the only life worth living is a *real* life. We're not tempted because we cut the cord." She dropped the Belt, and her mouth turned grim. Her eyes bore straight into me. "Until *you* jacked us in again."

❖ ❖ ❖

We loaded all the VR gear into Naia's buggy, including the drone radio and Hammad's rig, like smugglers hauling a cargo of contraband. We headed back to where the group was camped, about two klicks from town in an open field. In fact, it was the same field Hammad and I were planting when the bugs swarmed—the shed where we made our stand looked the same, with the shattered window, and two taser rounds still stuck in the door. There was even drone debris scattered everywhere.

Jackson and Heath thought it was better to stay away from town, so we could pick up and move in any direction if we should be invaded again. We'd already salvaged food and fuel from Orwell, plus tents and blankets, and those supplies along with what we'd picked up in Burgess should've been enough to keep us alive and mobile for a couple of weeks. Our planning horizon didn't extend much beyond that.

"Let's see what you got here," Jackson said, digging through the pile in the back of the buggy. He pulled out two of the consoles. "This looks familiar. I think one of these was mine."

"That one," Naia said, pointing to the smaller, sleeker one, a later model, well-maintained. "Brings back memories, doesn't it?"

"Yeah. Not good ones." Jackson kept digging until he pulled out the Belt. "I didn't know you brought this," he said.

"A trophy for my lodgepole," Naia replied. "Strong medicine."

"*Very* strong. I have a hard time even looking at it." He held it at a distance for a minute like it was a bloody pelt before dropping it back into the buggy. He wiped his hands on his pants, then turned to Hammad. "What now, boy genius?"

❖ ❖ ❖

We set up in the shed. It took an hour for Hammad to haywire the rig, and another twenty minutes to check it out. He'd hooked up two consoles instead of just the one. We didn't know how the link would handle two streams, but we could always disconnect one if it overloaded. Naia insisted on jacking in with me, though Jackson was a little hesitant to allow it, given her history. But she said she could handle it.

Hammad studied the flashing lights on the interface like a fortune teller scrutinizing the entrails of a chicken.

"Okay, ready?" he asked. Naia and I nodded and strapped in.

"Here goes." He pressed the last switch.

Naia and I were transported to the staging venue. Her rendering wasn't too bad, being local, but she was flashing artifacts and her motion was stop-and-go. Even with the substandard resolution, she looked like she might be sick.

"You all right?" I asked.

She nodded, and I heard her gulp. It felt weird seeing Naia that way, worse than she'd been earlier in her kitchen. It was the difference between just talking about her greatest fear and facing it head-on. I wanted to take her hand, but I didn't have to. She took mine.

"Mia, Fortress of Solitude."

The white venue gave way to Raúl's fortress, kaleidoscope ceiling and polished chrome column-lined hallways radiating outward like the spokes of a wheel, with me and Naia seated at the hub. Naia squeezed my hand harder. "Oh, lord," she said.

My first thought was to tell her, "Hi-res, huh?" but I didn't say it. I don't think she was as impressed as I was by Raúl's compression algorithm. She was feeling something other than awe.

A smear of blue shimmered into view in front of us, then sharpened into Raúl's avatar in his alien tunic. He paused a few seconds, looking back and forth between Naia and me.

"Greetings, friend Dylan. And is that…Naia?"

"Hello, Raúl," she said.

"Well, spank me hard and send me to bed. Been a while, hasn't it, Naia? Welcome to the Fortress." He narrowed his eyes at me. "Dylan, you should call before dropping in."

"Sorry. Did I wake you?"

"Sophie, chair." Raúl's throne materialized under him. "Fortunately, I was working late. But you did interrupt me— for something *important*, I hope."

"Yeah, kind of important."

I gave him the long version of the raid, our escape, and current state with the last survivors of Orwell and Laputa living like nomads in western Ogallala. Raúl sat king-like through the whole saga without moving a muscle.

When I finished, he paused for a long time before saying, "Tragic."

I waited to see if he was going to say anything else, but it appeared he wasn't.

"Yeah, tragic," I repeated.

"So, why are we having this conversation?" he asked.

Naia gave my hand a squeeze, then let go. I got the vibe from her that she thought this was a big waste of time, and she had subjected herself to her hated VR addiction for nothing. Having dealt with Raúl on previous occasions, I knew otherwise.

"We want you to help us find our friends and bring them back," I said.

Raúl stood up and the throne vanished. "You interrupted a paying gig. This little confab is costing me money. See where I'm going?"

"This is about more than money," Naia said. It was true, but it's not where I would've gone.

"Whatever it is to you, Naia, it's *definitely* something different to me," Raúl said. "They're not *my* people. Why should I care?"

Naia was about to jump up when I put my hand on her shoulder.

"But you know them," I said, "and you care about *one* of them, at least."

Raúl stared at me and I stared back. The corner of his mouth twitched up.

"Sophie, chair." The throne reappeared and he sat down.

"The Kliegls aren't subtle, as you've observed," he said. "The raid that made you homeless sent a tsunami through the Worldstream. Every person they rounded up, in Orwell, Laputa, Burgess, and a dozen other RL outposts was either long absent from the 'Stream, tagged, or a non-person."

"Shredded, you mean," I said.

"Yep."

"You knew all along."

"Well, *yeah*. Keeping my ear to the virtual ground is my thing. Nothing happens without I get a report—especially not something *this* big."

Naia looked surprised, but I wasn't. I knew we'd get to this point. I just didn't think Raúl would drag it out so long.

"Can you help?" I asked.

He rolled his eyes and sighed. "In all the cacophony of alerts that clogged my queue, one stood out. It was a signature of broken links undetectable by anyone but me."

"Why's that?" I asked.

"Because it was from one of my previous jobs, a shredding. A lady named Grace."

34

Old Friends

"THE SATELLITE LINK isn't bulletproof," Raúl began as he paced, "but unless the Worldstream stumbles across you, you're safe. Don't make yourselves easy to find."

"Like how?" I asked.

"Your tunnel through the maintenance protocol is easy to detect, but no one's looking for it. As long as you only go to off-world venues via stealth pipes, you can fly under the radar and no one'll be the wiser. Jah, you can even hang—*briefly*—in a legit venue without raising alarms, if you're not tagged or otherwise suspicious." He stopped pacing and shook a finger at me. "You don't know how close you came to blowing your cover."

"When I first jacked in, you mean."

"Yep. Do it again and you'll bring the whole Kliegl army down on you. Stick to the Fortress and stay mobile. Then even if you raise some eyebrows, by the time they get a fix on you and lower the hammer, you'll pop up elsewhere, like Whac-A-Mole."

"Like what?"

"*Whac-A-Mole*. Ancient game of skill and cunning."

Neither Naia nor I understood Raúl's obscure reference, but we didn't push it further. After the raid in Orwell, we took all of his warnings seriously.

"Do you know where they are?" Naia asked.

"No, I do *not*. First, I haven't been looking for them. Second, finding them in the Worldstream is one thing, finding them in the *world* is something completely different."

"But you have an idea," I said.

"A *vague* idea. The raid came from the east, right?"

We nodded.

"Then Omaha is likely where they started from. That doesn't mean they went *back* to Omaha. For all we know, they could've kept going to Denver or Provo. Doesn't matter, anyway. With all the population centers connected by hypertubes, Kliegls could've trucked them to Provo or Omaha, then tubed them anywhere in the country within hours. You'll have to search the whole Millennium Republic."

He made it seem hopeless, but I saw a way.

"Why did they come for us in the first place?" I asked.

"Good question," Naia said. "It doesn't make sense."

To *me*, it *did* make sense, and the possibility that the Civils and Kliegls would come get us had lingered in my mind since I first came to Orwell. But that was a touchy subject with Naia, and also with Jackson, who, I was keenly aware, was listening in on our side of the conversation as we sat in that shed outside of Orwell, jacked into Raúl's Fortress of Solitude.

"Kliegl policy—everything goes to VR. Right, Raúl?"

"That's the word on the street. But what's that got to do with Orwell?"

"Raúl—*everything*."

"In the *cities*, Dylan," Raúl said, "where the people are. What do they care about your pitiful little band of rebel scum?"

"I don't know why, exactly," I replied, and I didn't, but I was certain that Madeleine was maniacally focused on getting *everyone* in VR, regardless of where they were. "But I'm sure of it."

Naia looked at me the way she has before, like I'm involved in some conspiracy cult and ripe for an intervention. I thought I heard Jackson groan through my earphones.

"Sounds like your fellow renegades are not backing your theory," Raúl said.

"I know." My face was burning. I wondered if the VR console could detect my frustration, and whether the satellite link had the bandwidth to render it. If Raúl could see me this way, the way I was IRL, would he understand that I believed down to my chromosomes that Madeleine was behind the abductions? And if someone—*anyone*—believed a thing that intensely, then that person at least deserved a fair hearing!

Jackson, Naia, Benny, Max—*Mom*—I lived with the knowledge that they all thought I was…if not crazy, at least misguided. Hammad was the only one who never made me feel that way, but at that moment, with Raúl smirking at me, Naia holding her head in her hands, and Jackson snorting in the background, I felt like the world's biggest frobnitz. I wanted to exit the venue, peel off the VR gear, and live the rest of my life wandering the prairies of Ogallala like the plains tribes, all thoughts of VR, Kliegls, Dax, Madeleine, and the All-Seeing Eye crowded out by the single thought of killing something and eating it.

Then I thought of Mom back in Madeleine's hands.

"Okay, forget about Madeleine. Forget about what she did to my mom, and all the lives she hijacked to make her lifestreams. Forget all that. But here's why I brought it up: If I'm right, they're all *going* to show up in the Worldstream. Because getting them all back in VR is Madeleine's ultimate goal."

"*If* you're right," Naia said.

"*But they did show up!*" I shouted. "Raúl, you said that you saw a *tsunami* in the Worldstream. And you found Mom!"

That quieted everyone down, including Jackson.

"I did indeed," Raúl replied. "Not *physically*, mind you. But she's out there, somewhere. She touched the Worldstream for sure."

"Then *find her*."

"That sounds like a commission. A commission generally involves a fee."

"Fuck it," I mumbled. "I'll find her myself."

Raúl laughed out loud. I think it was the only time I'd ever heard him laugh.

"How're you going to do that? Jack in through the satellite and snoop around? You're a *fugitive*, Dylan. The second you show your youthful avatar in the Worldstream, the *fucking metaverse* will implode. You spend more than five seconds in the clear, the drones will fly and the trucks will roll."

"What if I'm not in the clear?"

That shut him up. He got it.

"You're talking about the persona, aren't you?" he asked.

The persona was a way for disconnected people, Shade, mostly, to re-enter the Worldstream without triggering an alarm. Mom had used it to find me, showing up in teen venues in the avatar of a little brown man. I told Raúl about it once, but I didn't know if he'd ever followed up.

But he had.

"I've checked into it. It's not practical, kid."

"Mom used it."

"Sophie, chair." The throne reappeared and Raúl dropped into it.

"First, the persona is based on a flaw in the Worldstream code. Flaws don't stay flawed forever, and word in the hacker venues is that the Consortium is working feverishly to heal the breach. Second, we'd have to cobble together an avatar. Not a simple procedure, *and*, it's not in my core skill set— yours either. Third, *so what* if you can stealth around in the Worldstream? How're you going to find your buddies in the real world?"

"The Consortium's been working on it for two years," I began. "No one, especially the entire Consortium, works on *anything* that long without coming up with a fix, unless the fix is really, *really* hard. They're not going to figure this out any time soon."

Raúl's lips twitched a bit, but he kept quiet.

"Once you get me in—"

"Get *you* in?" he interrupted. "*You're* going in?"

"Yeah. Me. I know a guy who knows how to find someone IRL if I can find them in the Worldstream."

Now his lips more than twitched. He outright sneered.

"You want to steal a key. You want to steal *thousands* of keys."

Raúl and I both knew that a *key*, a person's unique identifier, really *was* a key—to *everything*. If I could get someone's key, I could find out where they were in the physical world.

"Do you remember the last time you stole a key?" he asked.

Of course I remembered. I'd stolen the key to the fake avatar Mom was inhabiting to find me. The Worldstream went nuclear and I got nabbed and sent to confinement. I'd still be locked up if Hammad and I hadn't busted out.

"I'll be more careful this time."

I knew what I was proposing had its sketchy aspects, and the risk was high. Everyone else knew it, too. Raúl was grim, Naia was shaking her head, and I felt a hand on my shoulder —Jackson meant to reel me in before I blew our cover. I shook him off, but he grabbed me harder and pulled me off my chair. I ended up on the floor of the Fortress, grabbing my gear to keep it on my head and to stay in the venue.

"I can see that Jackson doesn't like your plan either," Raúl said.

"Hold on a second." I pulled off the gear to see Jackson standing over me, and the rest of the Orwellian and Laputan refugees standing around, a ring of faces lit up by oil lamps.

"Let me finish," I said.

"You'll get us *all* tased and taken," Jackson snarled. "I don't know why I ever agreed to this." He reached for my gear but I twisted away from him. He'd have ripped it away and torn up the rig if Naia hadn't stepped out of the venue and into the shed. She put her hand on Jackson's arm.

"Let him finish, Jackson," she said. "We've already taken the risk. If we pull out now we'll have nothing to show for it. Once we have all the options, then we can make a decision. And we'll *all* buy in."

Once again Naia had softened Jackson's heart, and he let go of me.

"Wrap it up, goddamn it."

Naia and I strapped in again. Raúl was still perched on his throne.

"Just to recap," he said, "you want to recreate the persona based on sketchy information before the fucking Worldstream Consortium slams the door shut, cook up an avatar to go with it, jack into the Worldstream in the clear—*you*, a fugitive with about a hundred tags on you—use a buggy hack to steal a thousand keys, then hunt down every one of your friends IRL and bring them home to Ogallala. How was that? Did I get it right?"

"Yeah, more or less. Step by step. Can we do it?"

"No, *we* can't. Not the two of us." That twitch of his returned, not a sneer, but the way he gets when the gears are turning. "But I know some people. Old friends. Porter and Molly."

35

Baby We Gotta

"WHAT ELSE DO you want to know?"

Naia, Hammad, and I sat cross-legged around a fire pit in the center of an Aboriginal dwelling, another stealth venue of Raúl's creation. Raúl was in the avatar of a native storyteller, looking very authentic, and the three of us were in buckskin garb. Naia and Hammad fit right in, with their dark skin, black hair, and firelight flickering in their dark eyes, but me, the red-headed paleface, glowed like a peeled potato. Raúl, resplendent in a white headband and red shirt, his long, silver hair falling around his shoulders, neck draped with turquoise necklaces and wearing a belt of silver that looked like it weighed ten kilos, had just wound up his oral history of the Worldstream and the Millennium Republic. All we'd asked was, "How'd you become a shredder?" and he said, "Sophie, tepee." We were whisked from the ice-and-steel Fortress of Solitude to a tent made of painted hides, complete with weird flute music and a crackling fire. I could almost smell the smoke.

He went on for hours about his ex-girlfriend Mirja, who was killed in the Chicago massacre of 2025, and who later was the first person Raúl—or anyone else—had shredded. I knew that's what Raúl did, shredding, but until he told the story, I didn't know that he was the *first* shredder. I also had no idea he was as close as he was to people like Chas Royce, who we'd all studied in history venues. It was weird hearing about those times from someone who'd seen it first-hand, and with the fire, flutes, and wigwam, it had a satisfying quality of realness to it, even if we were in a lo-res VR venue.

"Where's Porter now?" Hammad asked as Raúl wound down the history lesson.

"He's still around. Molly, too."

"Are they willing to help us?" I asked.

"Let's ask 'em. Sophie, Fortress."

We transported out of the tepee back to the Fortress of Solitude. Raúl had quick-changed out of his Navajo costume into his alien outfit, and the three of us were rendered in retro clothes, the kind Raúl might wear IRL, except Naia was in a black dress. I had never seen her in a dress before, and she looked amazing. She must've sensed I thought so, because she looked straight at me, radiating annoyance. I turned away from her, and that's when I noticed that instead of one throne, there were three: Raúl in the center, on his right an old Black guy with a long, white beard, wearing a purple robe, looking like some mythical wizard, and on his left a younger Asian woman, hair in tight braids with bangles on the ends, dressed in Ninja clothes, right down to the samurai swords sticking up from behind her back.

The Black guy picked at his robe, then leaned forward to get a look at the woman. "Funny, Raúl," he said. "Ha, ha."

The woman grabbed the hilt of a sword. She whipped it out and brandished it in a highly practiced move. It gave off a low, threatening buzz, and its edge glowed like fire. "I like it. Very savage. Porter, don't you have a magic wand or something?"

The Black guy, Porter, raised his hand and a wand appeared, a gnarled wooden thing radiating a silver aura. "Good golly, Miss Molly," he said as the wand gushed glitter rainbows like water from a hose.

"Molly, Porter, so good of you to come," Raúl said. "You can stow your weapons, now." Porter flipped the wand in the air and it disappeared with a *pop* and a puff of smoke. Molly slipped the sword in its scabbard with the same smooth move she'd used to draw it.

"Naia…Hammad…Dylan," Raúl said, "I've already given Porter and Molly the brief on your situation."

"A situation that has *nothing* to do with us," Porter grumbled.

"Don't, old man. We haven't even started yet," Molly scolded.

Porter spread his arms, the loose sleeves of his robe flapping like sheets in the wind. "We *started*. We talked about it," he shot back. "And I'm out. I like my life. Why would I invite violent disruption? For people I don't even know? We've kept our heads down for fifty years, three respectable shredders living inconspicuous lives. Now you wanna mung with the Worldstream gears and draw the ire of the Consortium, the Civils, the *Kliegls?*" He dug his fingers into his beard and scratched his cheeks. "Why is the high likelihood and monumental magnitude of the shitstorm from this scheme obvious to me and not to you?"

Molly rolled her eyes. "Where's your sense of adventure? Did your balls shrink over the years?"

"I don't need no adventures. I'm an old man." He grabbed his crotch, the bunched-up robe sticking out between his fingers. "Ain't nothing wrong with my balls, either."

"Don't embarrass me," Molly said with a sniff.

Porter lifted his handful of robe. "This embarrasses you? This?"

"No. I get embarrassed by sissy fraidy cats."

Porter gripped the robe harder, then he let go and fell back in his throne.

"He was always paranoid," Molly said to us in a very loud whisper, "but he hasn't always been a pussy."

None of us knew where to look. It might've been funny if the stakes weren't so high.

There was a period of awkward silence before Raúl spoke up.

"You were gung ho for this mission, Porter. What changed?"

Porter shifted in his chair. "It's a cool concept, I'll grant you—exploit a flaw in the encryption algorithm, a piece of code so deeply embedded in the Worldstream that any fix will break something else. The tech grabbed me. So did the anti-authoritarian aspects."

"What flaw?" Hammad asked.

Porter sat forward. He flashed a smile from deep inside of his generous beard. "How much do you know about Worldstream validation?"

"A little," Hammad replied, and I nodded, too.

"What happens when you enter a venue?" he asked.

"The venue validates my key."

"Right—sort of. The venue server submits the key to the Worldstream, and the Worldstream either accepts it or rejects it." He stroked his beard. "How long does that take?"

"I don't know. A few seconds?"

Porter stuck his thumb up, as if he was saying *higher*.

"Minutes?"

"Sometimes *many* minutes. The key has to propagate through the network and be validated by a minimum number of nodes. And what are you doing while that's going on?"

Hammad and I looked at each other, but it was Naia who answered.

"I'm already in the venue."

"Right! No one wants to wait ten minutes for the Worldstream to bless a key before enjoying their venue. The venue server lets you in, you have a powerful VR experience, and when the Worldstream calls back, the server either lets you stay or kicks you out."

"Then what's the flaw?"

"The flaw is, if the Worldstream doesn't respond, the venue server lets you stay. And that's the genius of the hack: the key's designed so that it looks legit, but it puts the Worldstream in an endless recursive verification loop. *It never calls back!*"

"That's stupid," I said. "Why doesn't the venue time out?"

"Some of them are adding a timeout, that's true," Porter answered, "but not many. Hardly any venue coders even know about the problem—the Consortium doesn't want this flaw widely advertised. Besides, most venues have bigger problems than this. The average administrator is four or five security updates behind. But the biggest reason is, there's no theoretical upper limit on how long it takes the Worldstream to validate a key. If the venue puts a timer on it, legitimate keys will get kicked for no reason."

Raúl jumped in at that point. "Porter, listen to yourself. You're totally stoked over this tech. You're *itching* to dig in. Why are you holding back now?"

Porter, who'd been getting more excited the more he talked, suddenly deflated. "I'm tired, Raúl. Fifty years we've been fighting the Man, and where's it got us? Not a move by *nobody* that doesn't get picked up by the All-Seeing Eye and recorded in the bottomless pit of the Worldstream. There's no place to hide anymore."

"That's the point," Raúl said. "Our *Vitreous Orb* friends can't even hide in the wilderness. They're coming to get 'em."

"I'm tired."

"The fight's not over," Molly said.

"I'm *tired!*"

"Then you better wake up," I said. Porter was starting to irritate me. "Don't you care at *all* about our people?"

"*Your* people. Not *my* people."

"Okay. I get it now. It's about *you.*"

"Yeah." Porter lifted himself up on the arms of his throne, looking wobbly as he stood. "*Me.* You got a problem with that?"

I was gritting my teeth in contempt for that old man, even though in Raúl's stories of the old days about him, Porter, and Molly taking on the All-Seeing Eye, he seemed more like a hero than a worn-out old hacker. Now he and I were facing off, and everyone else was staring at us like we were two sumos ready to collide.

"A *little* problem—just a little one," I answered. "We *are* taking on the Kliegls and the Civils. We have a better chance if you help, but we're doing it with or without you."

"Without."

"Fine, then. But think about this: Madeleine's plan is to get *everyone* in VR, *everyone* accounted for. She wants it so much that she's willing to send squads into the territories to round up the stragglers."

"Got a point, kid?"

"My *point* is, don't you think they'll come for the shredders? You know, the ones whose job is to take people *out* of the Worldstream?"

Porter snorted. "They've been watching us for years. They can't pin anything on us."

"So what? Homeless people are being bludgeoned on the streets. Folks just living their lives in the countryside are being clubbed and hauled off in meat transports. None of them got *pinned*. They just got tased. Haven't you been paying attention?"

"You wanted a point, Porter? There's the boy's point," Raúl said. "The old rules don't apply anymore."

"They're already after us," Molly added. "You know it."

"Not for sure," Porter said.

"Have you heard from Ezra lately?" Raúl asked, referring to one of the hackers he'd told us about, from the old days.

"Ezra never stayed in touch," Porter mumbled, sounding every bit as worn out as he looked.

"Yes, he did, with his circle if not with us. None of them's heard a thing from him in weeks."

"I'm *tired*," Porter repeated.

I'm sure that Porter felt ganged-up-on, and my upset with him faded a little. When he slumped, sighed, and let his head fall to his shoulder, I even felt sorry for him.

Molly dematerialized and teleported next to Porter's throne. She took his arm and squeezed it. "Baby, we gotta do this," she whispered close to his ear, but loud enough for us to hear. Porter raised his head from his shoulder, his eyes old and damp, and he kissed Molly full on the lips.

"I'm tired."

"I know."

He looked at me, and Naia, and Hammad. Then he looked at Molly and nodded.

"Same time tomorrow, troops," Raúl said. "Get some sleep. We have a world to destroy."

36

Klicks to the Liter

WE HAD NO idea how to pull it off.

Actually, we had *kind of* an idea. First, recreate the persona. That was a two-part task. Molly took the lead on the Worldstream hack, with Porter's and Hammad's help. That was the risky part. I'd work with Raúl on the avatar, since both of us had experience digging through the worldstream for stray data. Once we had the persona, one of us would tunnel into the Worldstream with a fake ID and nose around for any of the kidnapped *Vitreous Orb*. Assuming we could get a lead on all the locations, we would then steal enough keys to find them. If they weren't scattered across the country, we stood a slim chance at locating most if not all of them. Laid out like that, an overly simplified bullet list, it looked doable, but the trapdoors were many.

Hammad and I were jacked in to the Fortress from our rig in Ogallala, with Raúl, Porter, and Molly from wherever *they* were IRL. We held sessions almost daily, while Jackson, Naia, Heath and the rest took care of the business of staying alive and mobile. The Orwellians had relocated from the previous night, leaving the others at the last campsite until they'd finished foraging in Laputa. Naia's part was to keep Jackson informed of our progress. He recognized the value of having a plan, which is why he indulged us, but until we could show some results, he was skeptical.

"Get me something concrete, or I'll call it off and we'll go to Plan B," he said about three times a day. But he didn't have a Plan B. He was antsy because he was in charge with no way forward. Calming down Jackson was Naia's full-time job.

❖ ❖ ❖

"I don't like it," Porter said. "Too many unknowns."

We had replicated a complete development environment in the Fortress, with virtual screens, VR simulators, 3D visualization, almost as good as if we were doing RL coding. Porter, Molly, and Hammad sat at one set of consoles, while Raúl and I were in a parallel venue, out of sight of the others, but we could still hear them.

"Look at this," Porter said, though I couldn't see what he was talking about. "I get how to spoof the validation algorithm, but the key generation—how does that work?"

"Once it's through the gate, the Worldstream will chew on it forever," Hammad answered. "It only has to satisfy the initial check."

"Yeah, I *get* that, kid. That's exactly what the key generation algorithm is designed to *prevent*."

"Uh-huh. Yeah." I recognized that tone from Hammad. It's when he doesn't know a thing but he doesn't want me (or anyone else) to *know* he doesn't know.

"Can I make a suggestion?" I broke in, knowing that not only could Raúl hear me in our venue, but the others in their venue could, too.

"Is it a new suggestion, or the same old one?" Porter asked, because I'd suggested it many times before, and they'd always considered it too risky.

"Nemesio," I replied. That was the Shade name of Adrian, the man my mom had lived with in the Summerland, the dorm where she spent her years in the Shade. Nemesio was the one who came up with the hack in the first place. What *we* were trying to build, Nemesio had figured out years ago.

"Right. Same old suggestion," Porter said. "Can we get back to work now?"

"Sophie, conference," I commanded. The two parallel venues merged, and we were now all in the same Fortress of Solitude. "If we get the hack from Nemesio it'll save us months."

"It won't take us *months*," Porter objected.

"Oh. Sure. You're on the verge. Any minute now."

"Don't you have a persona to build?" Porter asked. My face got so red it showed up in my avatar.

"Porter, it's not just about time, it's about *risk*," I replied. "Nemesio has a working hack. It's tested. And he's had the last two years to patch it."

"That's a valid argument," Molly said.

Porter pulled on his beard. "No, it's not. He's not even on the street anymore. He was nabbed in the Summerland raid, remember?"

He was talking about the Kliegl raid on Mom's dorm, the one that took most of her crew, including Nemesio.

"Raúl, you told us that the Shade picked up in the raids didn't all go into confinement," I said.

"Not even most," Raúl replied. "Only a few, in fact, just enough to make it look good."

"And the rest?"

"All went to *Vita Occulta* crews."

Porter snorted. "If he went to another crew, then he's still Shade. He sticks to stealth venues, never shows up in the Worldstream. We'll *never* find him." He waved his arms. "And *we've covered all this before!* Why are we *still* talking about it?"

"Because you're behind on the hack," I answered.

"Goddamn it, get out of my venue," Porter growled.

I was afraid the conversation was over at that point, and I was about to instruct Sophie to split the venue again, but Raúl spoke up.

"One thing has changed," he said. We all turned to him.

"I found the Aletheia dorm."

That news quieted us all down. The Aletheia was The Eye of Providence's—Madeleine's—crew. We suspected that a lot of the Summerland Shade went to the Aletheia after the raid, and what Raúl had been hearing on the street tended to confirm it.

"So what?" Porter asked. "What're we gonna do? Raid the Aletheia and kidnap Nemesio?"

"Yeah," I replied. "That's exactly what we're gonna do."

"*We* aren't gonna do anything of the kind," Porter said.

"What about it, Raúl? Can it be done?" I asked.

"Kidnap a Shade from the most powerful *Vita Occulta* crew in the Millenium Republic? It's not something *I* can do. Let me put that differently: It's not something I'm *willing* to do."

"But I am," I said.

That actually made all of them laugh—all except Hammad.

"You won't be two seconds inside the perimeter before Jahbulon and all his black angels swoop down on you," Porter said. "Can we get back to work now?"

"Sophie, parallel venue," I commanded. I wasn't going to win the argument.

Not that day.

❖ ❖ ❖

"What if we drive?" I asked Naia. To get to Nemesio, we'd have to go to Chicago, but riding the tube from Omaha was obviously not an option. Overland seemed the only way.

"Twenty-three hours over rough territory," Naia answered, "then sneaking around inside the perimeter while tagged for apprehension."

"We could wear cloaks."

"And get beaten up on the street by Kliegls."

"Damn it, Naia, there's no other way."

"There's another way. You all are working on another way."

"Naia, there's no *time*."

"Time? We're wandering the prairie like nomads. We've got nothing *but* time."

"Not *us. Them*."

She knew who I meant—all our friends from Orwell, and the rest from the other towns. The longer we took to find them, the more spread out and deeper in they'd be. We might never get them out. That made her stop and think. But she shook her head. "No. Too risky."

I gave her a grim look. She put her hand on my shoulder. "Dylan, I know where you're coming from. I feel it, too, like *we're* the ones who got away, so we owe it to *them* to get them out."

"Don't we?"

She smiled a sad, tired smile, like she didn't know how to answer me. "Yeah." She took her hand off my shoulder. "But I'm not going to lose another one. Stay put."

It was the second argument I'd lost that day. I was getting used to it.

❖❖❖

We stood around outside the mobile in late afternoon and the Laputans still hadn't caught up with us.

"Should've been here two hours ago," Jackson said. "Naia, go check it out while there's still daylight."

She trotted off to the buggy and I ran up behind.

"Want some company?" I asked.

"Sure," she said like she didn't care one way or the other. "Just don't bring up that subject."

Shit, I thought, because that's exactly why I wanted to tag along. But I got in the buggy anyway, hoping I could work it into the conversation somehow.

The ride to the last campsite was about forty klicks, thirty minutes or so over rough ground. Naia was quiet the whole time, and I was afraid to say anything for the first ten klicks.

"How many klicks to the liter does this buggy get?" I asked casually.

"What did I tell you?" Naia answered, keeping her eyes straight ahead.

"What?"

"Don't start."

"Start what?"

She turned and gave me her flintiest look. "That subject."

"I'm just asking about the buggy. God."

"Your round trip to Chicago will consume about 300 liters of ethanol. That's 240, maybe 250 kilos. In other words, a lot. Are you going to stow it in the cargo space, or drag it behind?"

Naia was peeved. It's not like her to be so sarcastic.

"Jesus, forget I asked."

We both shut up, the only sound being the whining engine and the wind in our ears. I was thinking of what to say next, when we came over a hill near where the Laputans were camped, and Naia stood on the brake, killing the engine and almost pitching me out of the buggy.

The camp site was deserted—fuel cans, food hampers, water containers all knocked off the flatbed in piles or scattered. The grass was flattened, not like it was trampled by foot, but like it was driven over by heavy vehicles. That wasn't the first thing that caught our attention. It was the smoking remains of a drone in the middle of a scorched patch, with a few flames still flickering at the edges.

"Oh, fuck," Naia said. We scanned the skies for other drones but saw none. We listened but heard only the breeze.

She started the engine and eased the buggy forward. The closer we came the more ominous it looked. The flatbed had taser rounds buried in the wood, and the rear window of the cab was shattered. A shotgun lay by the truck, broken open, and four or five empty shells beside it.

"They put up a fight," Naia said. She got out of the buggy and went to the cab. The door was open, and she reached inside. When she pulled her hand out, it was red with blood. All I could think of, with the blood and the shattered window, was Benny in the shed, dying of a collapsed lung.

She walked over to the drone and stamped on the flames. "Help me with this," she said, and I did.

"Let's get these supplies on the truck," Naia said quietly, like she was out of energy from dealing with bugs, Kliegls, and Civils—and me.

After we'd loaded everything, Naia got back in the buggy. "You drive the truck," she said. "Follow me back to camp. Then we'll talk about that trip to Chicago."

37

Call Me Sir

"HOW THE *FUCK* did this happen?"

I'd seen Jackson worked up before, but when Naia and I made our report, he short-circuited. He didn't even scold us in private, which was his usual policy. He reamed us (me and Hammad, and to some extent Naia, but mostly me), face red, eyes bulging, and spraying spit, while the last remaining survivors of the West Ogallala *Vitreous Orb*—Benny, Abby, Max, Frank, and the others—stood around not knowing where to look or what to do with their hands.

"Well, *I* don't know," Naia answered. "*Nobody* knows. How *could* we know?"

"Bullshit," he grumbled. "You know *exactly* how this happened." He got in my face, spraying me with little flecks of saliva. I turned my face away. "You will end that science project *now*. You will *never* fire up that kluge again. It's a fucking homing beacon."

"Sir, I don't…" I began, then I remembered Jackson's pet peeve and I stopped.

"No, go ahead," Jackson said, straightening up and wiping his mouth on his sleeve. "Call me *sir*. From now on you will *always* call me *sir*. Maybe it'll remind you who's in charge, and maybe you'll respect the people who actually have a *responsibility*—"

"Jackson," Naia interrupted, "it could've been another recon drone, part of a mop-up operation. Could've happened to Laputa, could've happened to us."

Jackson glared at Naia, like he was going to make *her* call him *sir*. "I don't buy it. That thing is broadcasting our location, and—"

"But it's not," I said.

Jackson got in my face again. *"What do you call me?"*

"Sir?" I answered softly.

He looked away like he was ashamed of himself for going too far. But he recovered.

"Where's the rig?"

"It's in the mobile," I replied, "—sir."

Jackson straightened up. "Dylan, Hammad, do *not* go in the mobile. It's off-limits." He turned away. "And, Dylan…"

"Yes, sir?"

"Don't call me *sir*," he said, and walked away.

❖ ❖ ❖

"He doesn't have a plan," Naia told me.

I'd asked her how we were going to rescue the Orwellians without the persona, hoping that Jackson had figured out an alternative. We were leaning against the wheels of the flatbed, a few meters from the fire. It was just me and Naia, since all the others were either in the mobile or had already sacked out in tents or in the open.

"Then, what?" I asked.

She pinched her face. "He doesn't know."

"Damn it," I said. "Why's he like this?"

She gave me a look like she did in the buggy, when I'd pestered her over the Chicago trip. "He's in charge, Dylan. Do you know what it means? To be the boss and to fail at it? He's a failure, in his mind, at least."

"This isn't his fault," I said, but I was thinking that if we couldn't go with our plan, then Jackson should at least have a Plan B.

Naia turned to me, looking like she had in the wigwam venue, only better, because the firelight flickering in her eyes was real. "I've known Jackson for…oh, God…*forever*, it seems. I worked for him, then I worked *with* him. We were side-by-side for most of my career. There's not a better man, not anywhere. You know what makes him great?"

I shook my head.

"He takes his job seriously. When things go wrong, it's personal. He's a leader. A leader gives away the credit and hogs the blame."

"He was handing out the blame today," I said.

Naia looked back at the fire. "He'll hand out the blame if he thinks it's deserved. He thinks you deserve it."

"Is that what *you* think?" I asked.

"I don't know." She looked back at me, her eyes serious. "I've never seen him like this. He's faced challenges, sure, and he's been responsible for lives before, but this..." She squeezed her eyes shut and ran her fingers over her forehead. "He lost a whole town, folks he's known for years. He takes it very personally. That rant of his? Maybe that wasn't aimed at you. Maybe he was taking it out on himself."

"And I just happened to be in the blast radius."

Naia snickered. "One way to put it."

I stood up and brushed the dirt from my pants. "How do *you* think the Kliegls found us?"

"Hell if I know. Could've been pure chance, like I said."

"But that's not likely, is it? They've already got most of us in confinement. Why would they send out a mission to collect the last few of us unless they had solid intel?"

"From the rig, you mean," she added. "But we've always tunneled in through the maintenance protocol, and Raúl's venue is off-stream. How'd they spot us?"

There was so much we didn't know about the satellite link. It could've been detected any number of ways. But Raúl was sure—well, *almost* sure—that we were safe. The only risk, he said, was if we jacked into the Worldstream in the clear.

"Naia, I need to get to the console."

"No access for you or Hammad. Jackson's orders."

"I only need a minute or two."

"Nope, sorry. Not gonna do it. You thought Jackson was pissed? Wait'll he finds out you violated a direct order."

"But he didn't say *you* couldn't."

"Couldn't what?"

I sat down again, leaning very close and whispering. "Just check on a couple things."

❖ ❖ ❖

The next day we were striking camp to relocate. Jackson had picked a spot forty klicks to the north, a longer distance than usual, but he figured that if Kliegls were following us, he was going to put as much distance as possible between us and them.

Hammad and I worked extra-quick, so that we'd have some time when the last of the gear was stowed. Naia did too, and while the group was going over the last of the checklist, she snuck into the mobile while we stood guard at the door.

"What're you doing here?" Jackson asked suspiciously. He was making his final rounds before we bugged out. I was leaning against the mobile like I was resting, and Hammad was sitting on the ground.

"Finished my tasks. Just waiting for the order to move out," I answered.

He squinted at me sideways and looked over the campsite, like he was counting heads.

"Where's Naia?"

I looked around the same way Jackson did. "Can't say. What duty did she have?"

His lips were pressed tight, but even with his mouth closed, I saw he was gritting his teeth. He went to the flatbed and rummaged in a gear bag, then pulled out a shotgun.

I tensed up, of course. Hammad stood, and we both got directly in front of the door as Jackson came at us. He'd already broken the gun and jammed a shell into it. He closed the gun, got within a half-meter of me and pressed the barrel against my chest.

"You disobeyed," he snarled.

"Jackson, what?" I asked, trying to look calm. That in itself was probably a giveaway.

"Step aside."

"What? Hey, I'm just hanging here until we bug out. Why're you pointing that at me?"

He reached across me and grabbed my shoulder, pushing me aside, then banged on the door with the butt of the gun.

"Naia! Get out here!" he yelled.

Naia came to the door after a second or two. Jackson pointed the gun skyward.

"Are you going to shoot me, Jackson?" she asked.

"Just give me a fucking explanation."

"We were following a hunch," I answered, and turned to Naia. "What'd you find?"

"I found out how we got spotted," she replied.

Jackson lowered the gun. "Go on."

"I checked the console log—that was Dylan's idea. Someone's been sneaking time on the rig, riding lifestreams. Not tunneling, either—in the clear."

"Can you tell who it was?"

"Yeah," she answered. "I verified the key."

38

The Corridor

THE DRIVE TO Chicago was rougher than I thought it would be. Naia and I started out before sunrise, heading southeast to Omaha on highways and roads last travelled in the sixties, if then. Where the roads were too rough to travel, washed out or turned to rubble, we drove overland, on prairie, or cropland ridged with furrows recently planted. The time we made wasn't as good as we were used to, with the terrain and the giant tank of ethanol mounted on the rear. Naia had beefed up the suspension to handle the weight, but we still took it slow. We had to. We were a bomb on wheels.

Once we found out that it was Frank who had given us away, Jackson turned his wrath from me to him. He couldn't sentence Frank to a month of trash collection out in the wild, but he did ban him from the mobile as long as the rig was there. When he issued the ban he did so with a shotgun pointed at Frank's crotch, just for emphasis. Nobody believed that Jackson would actually neuter Frank with buckshot, but it was effective anyway.

"Frank was as bad as I was," Naia yelled over the engine noise about fifty clicks from the Omaha perimeter. "Maybe worse, although I was pretty bad myself, so I won't say that for sure."

"Addicted to lifestreams, you mean?" I yelled back.

She nodded. "Frank was in supply chain management for our Make-On-Demand operation. It was a job so simple even Frank could handle it, keeping our micro-factories stocked with raw materials. Twelve, fifteen items he had to manage—planning, buying, receiving, like that."

"Did he fuck it up?"

"Yeah, from time to time. Whenever I got an alarm on a stockout at an MOD it was almost always one of Frank's."

"Why didn't you fire him?"

"The network of MODs was pretty robust. If one went down for a few hours, the others could take up the slack. Frank wasn't great, but he was good enough." Her mouth tightened up as though she had more to say, but wasn't sure if she wanted to say it.

"What?" I asked.

"Frank was a screw-up because he was riding lifestreams on company time instead of doing his job."

"And you couldn't fire him because you were doing the same thing."

She shrugged. "Yeah."

We didn't say another thing to each other until Omaha.

❖ ❖ ❖

We headed south, skirting the Omaha perimeter. Though we had no connected articles with us (the satellite rig was shut down and packed in a copper-lined Faraday box), we stayed on the safe side of the fringe of the municipal wideband network. The last thing we needed was to make waves in the Worldstream ether.

We'd circled Omaha from west to east until just after sunset, when we ran up against the hypertube corridor. The tube was a pair of pressure vessels, side by side, six meters high, solid steel without windows of any kind, meaning that the chance of being spotted by human eyes was zero. An access road ran between them, gravel-covered and fairly well-maintained, though not perfectly smooth, but compared with our trek over the prairie we could double our forward progress. The corridor cut through Nodaway, Sagamon, and Gary, a straight shot all the way to Chicago. We drove in shifts, six hours on, six hours off. I went first.

A full moon rose between the tubes directly ahead, edging up over the horizon as big as I'd ever seen. An hour into my shift the road was washed in moonlight, like a gray ribbon on the black plain. The curved sides of the tubes reflected the moon in a pair of silver streaks, the road and tubes stretching out to infinity, coming together at the horizon. While Naia slept beside me, I imagined I was flying, the road and streaks like a heads-up display defining a corridor, like a game venue of interstellar travel I'd once played. Though the moon glowed like a beacon, the sky was dark enough for the stars to come out, adding to the illusion that I was piloting a spacecraft instead of an overloaded buggy. The buzzing engine was a rocket motor, straining to turn the earth under me, pushing the moon higher and higher, until the light on the road darkened, and the streaks disappeared from the tubes. I was down on the ground again, racing to Chicago.

Naia took her shift when the moon was straight overhead. I wondered if could sleep with the noise of the engine and the wind, but it took me two minutes at most to nod off. By the time I woke up, the rising sun was full in my face. Naia was holding her hand up to block the light, but even so she was squinting against the brightness.

"How close?" I asked.

She didn't answer right away, instead slowing down and shutting off the engine. My ears kept ringing, then quieted down until there was only the wind. The tubes and the road went to the horizon with no other signs of civilization.

"I make it about fifty klicks from the perimeter," Naia answered. "A hundred from the periphery." She pulled the Faraday crate from the cargo space. "Time to jack in and see if anybody's home."

That was my cue to fire up the rig and make contact with Raúl. I'd gotten good at setup, just ten minutes from crate open to lights on. I got a lock almost instantly. We only brought one set of VR gear to save space. I slipped it on.

"Mia, Fortress of Solitude."

Raúl was waiting for me in the Fortress, wearing his blues. It was just him and me.

"You're late," he said.

"Not *that* late. We've been driving for twenty-four hours, for god's sake."

"Where are you?"

"On the tube corridor from Omaha, just outside the perimeter, twenty-five klicks, maybe."

"My guy should be there in an hour or less. Don't go anywhere. And look out for the drones."

"Drones?"

"Yep. Drones patrol the whole length of the corridor for damage, incursions…whatever. Anything out of the ordinary, really. I'd get off the corridor if I were you. Don't show yourself until your ride gets there."

I was seriously concerned. "What…what if they spot us?"

"They won't see you. They're only interested in what's happening near the tube. Get off the corridor and you'll be fine."

"But what'll happen if they do?"

"Probably nothing. Maybe. Jah, you're a worry wart."

Even with the narrow pipe to the venue, the look on my face must've told Raúl that I found his assurances unsatisfying.

"Calm down," he said. "If you're still there when the bug goes by, it'll raise an alarm, but only to the tube authorities. The AI will figure you for a trespasser and send another drone to shoo you away. But you'll be long gone by then."

That relaxed me a little, until Raúl kept talking.

"Just don't let them see your face."

I exited the venue and jacked out.

"Drones—what's that about?" Naia asked.

"We need to move," I said.

"Move where?"

"Outside of the tubes. Away."

"Because—drones?" She looked puzzled, but only for a few seconds. "Okay. I get it. Pack up the rig. There's an access tunnel a couple klicks back."

I tossed it all in the crate in a tangle. The lid didn't quite close, but I got it stowed just as we heard it, both of us at the same time—a high, thin buzz, far off, but we knew what it was.

"Shit," Naia said. "Get in."

She did a three-point turn, almost hitting a pylon, then sped back the way we came. "How close?" she yelled.

I looked back. It took a few seconds to find the drone, what with the buggy bouncing over the gravel road and kicking up dust. It was a ways back but gaining.

"Getting closer!" I yelled. "Punch it!"

She stood on the gas pedal and the buggy lurched forward. I could see the access tunnel up ahead, just a dug-out spot under the tubes, where vehicles could get in and out.

"Hang on!" Naia yelled. She yanked the steering wheel to the left, heading for the access tunnel at an angle. The ground fell away and we were airborne for a second, then the fuel tank hit the tube with a *clang* and the front wheels made contact. Naia and I were thrown forward against our harnesses, and the front wheels twisted under the carriage. The buggy popped out the other side, getting air again, turning 180 by the time we crashed, throwing dirt clods in the air. We were shook up but no permanent damage. I couldn't say the same for the buggy.

The drone passed us, blowing up swirls of dust. It went by without slowing down, but one of its cameras panned our way, pointing toward us as it sped on.

And I was looking straight at it.

39

Hue and Cry

THAT BUGGY WAS messed up.

Everything from the steering wheel back seemed okay, but the front suspension was busted beyond repair. The left front wheel was hanging by a shard. The lower control arm was cracked and torn from its bushings. The ball joint was separated and the tie rod was in two pieces.

Naia stood staring at the wreckage, hands on hips. "Raúl's guy better get here quick," was all she said.

What *I* said was, "What's that smell?"

Naia wrinkled her nose, then her eyes went wide. "Oh, geez."

Then I recognized the smell of ethanol and saw a trickle running from a crack in the tank.

"C'mon," Naia said, and she started running, with me close behind. We put about fifty meters between us and the buggy.

"Do you think it'll go up?" I asked.

She shook her head. "I doubt it. The engine is hot, but probably not hot enough to ignite the fuel. There's no other ignition source—"

The flash came an instant before we were knocked down by the shock wave. What parts of the buggy that were previously undamaged now flew in six directions.

Naia rolled to one side and got up on her elbow.

"Guess I was wrong," she said. She stood and slapped the dirt from her jeans and jacket. She stared at the black column of smoke rising from the flaming wreck for a minute, then grabbed my hand and pulled me up.

"There goes our ride home."

"Not to mention the rig—our link to Raúl," I added.

Naia looked at me. "The battery."

She was referring to the battery for the satellite rig. I hung my head.

"Must've sparked." I punched my thigh. "I didn't close the lid. I should've, but I didn't." I stamped my foot and kept punching my thigh, until Naia touched my shoulder.

"We were in a hurry, both of us. You left the lid open; I wrecked the buggy. We can't change any of that now."

She was right. Her touch on my shoulder and her sympathy was enough to stop me from punching myself.

"What now?" I asked.

She sat cross-legged on the ground and tilted her head up at me like she wanted me to sit, too, which I did.

"Wait for Raúl," she answered, "and hope another drone doesn't come by."

Raúl had said that the ride would come in less than an hour, but it was actually a *lot* less. I don't think it was 20 minutes before we saw it coming, first as a cloud of dust, then, when it came into view, a black, boxy vehicle almost as big as a flatbed. It was bouncing along at 100 kph minimum, catching air off the knolls and coming down hard, throwing up grass and dirt in a rooster tail. We stood up as it skidded to a stop in front of us. The window came down and a severe-looking woman with tight braids poked her head out. It was Molly.

"Jesus Hussein Christ, get the fuck in here!" she yelled, and we obeyed instantly, scrambling into the back seat. She looked over her shoulder at us. "No gear?"

"It went up with the buggy," Naia explained, pointing at the smoldering ruin, still billowing smoke.

"Oh, yeah," Molly said. She cranked the wheel and turned around, then got back up to speed, bouncing us off the seat until we managed to fasten our belts.

"Could you be any more fucking conspicuous?" she yelled, not sounding at all like the old woman in the venue. There's something about an RL voice, a quality that sets it apart from a VR analog, no matter how good the rendering is. But she also sounded angry and anxious at the same time. I'd never heard her so keyed up.

"The smoke?" I said.

"Yeah, the smoke, sure. That doesn't help. That's also not what I'm talking about."

"Then what?"

She pointed at the screen in the console. In yellow letters on a red background it read:

HUE AND CRY
ALL CITIZENS ARE OBLIGED TO AID IN THE
APPREHENSION OF THIS FUGITIVE
FAILURE TO DO SO WILL RESULT IN
PROSECUTION AND CONFINEMENT

Next to the alert was my name, my personal stats, and my picture.

"How in hell did that happen?" Naia asked.

"The same damn question occurred to me," Molly replied. "Dylan, any thoughts?"

"The drone," I said, just barely loud enough to be heard in that noisy vehicle. I looked sideways at Naia, who was clenching her jaw. "I think it got a good look at me."

Once again I felt like I'd let down Naia, and now Molly, not only because of the drone, but because I knew and I didn't warn them.

"Damn bad break," Molly said. "Puts a kink in our plans." She pointed. "Witness."

We bent low to peer out the windshield. A squadron of drones was headed straight for us.

"Oh, shit, what now?" Naia asked, like she'd read my mind

"Evasive maneuvers," Molly answered. She cranked the steering wheel, nearly tipping over the truck, and headed away from the tube corridor at an insane rate of speed. She was barreling over a pasture that looked like it'd been fallow for decades, with grass as high as the grill on the truck. The drones changed course and kept closing.

"We can't outrun those bugs," I said.

"Oh, thanks for clearing that up," Molly shot back. "What else can you tell me that I already know?"

I got the message and kept my mouth shut, though it was hard because it wasn't clear to me that Molly had any kind of plan. I shouldn't have doubted her though.

"Reach in the back," Molly ordered, jabbing her thumb toward the rear. "Behind the seats. There should be three. Get 'em all."

Three what? I wondered, but not for long. Naia and I turned and felt around. Our hands came down on a stash of firearms.

"Two shotguns and a long gun," Molly shouted. "Did you find them?"

"Got 'em," we said.

"You know how to use one of those things?" Molly asked.

"Yeah," Naia answered, and I added, "The shotguns, yeah."

"Of course the shotguns," Molly yelled. "Leave the rifle for me. You could be Annie Oakley for all I know, but *I* get the rifle."

We still weren't sure what the plan was, but just holding that shotgun made me feel better.

Molly sped up, coming off one mound and clearing two more before landing hard. We were traveling uphill, coming to the crest when the ground fell away entirely.

"Brace for impact!" Molly shouted, and we did, but it still felt like getting nailed with a hammer when we hit the ground. Our forward vision was blocked by a spray of dirt and sand, but the truck was still mobile and Molly drove through it.

We were by what I guessed was a river, but it was the biggest river I'd ever seen, VR or IRL, maybe five or six hundred meters wide. Molly turned the wheel and skidded to a stop just as the drones came over the crest.

"Out of the vehicle! Ready arms!" Molly ordered, and as soon as we did, the drones took up positions surrounding us.

There were five, all with the standard issue of cams and magazines.

"Aim first. Don't waste ammo, but don't waste time," Molly said.

Molly raised her rifle and fired, winging one of the bugs. It wavered, then steadied itself and flew off. Naia blew one away with her first shot. Then the three remaining bugs unleashed a barrage.

I got one shot off, but I don't know if I hit anything. I felt a jolt to my back and stiffened up, like my whole body got a cramp.

Then I blacked out.

40

A Pitiful Footprint

I woke up in someone else's bed.

It was big enough to sleep three people, or four, if they were intimate. I rolled to my right, and as soon as I did a pain jolted me, like being punched in a place I'd been punched hard before. My fingers tested the painful spot, in my lower back, and found where the taser round zapped me. Though the welts were the most tender, my whole body hurt, like I'd done two shifts of harvesting without a break and woken up the next day sore all over.

So that's what a taser feels like, I thought. *Nope. I don't like it.*

I took my time sitting up, dropping my legs over the side. The effort was enough to bend my head down to my hands. The veins in my temples were pulsing. I was nauseous. I stayed still until the feeling passed, or at least tapered off enough that I could raise my head.

The room was dark, but enough light came through the curtains that I could see. It had been lived in—a dresser with drawers half-open, clothes on the floor, a towel draped on a chair. The bed itself was a tangle of sheets and covers. One pillow was on the bed, three on the floor.

I've been kidnapped by slobs.

When my pounding head settled down to a throb, I heard voices from the next room. I stood up and shambled zombie-like toward the sound. A hallway out the door went straight, then left, into a large room with a high ceiling. It wasn't easy to move around in, crammed as it was with screens, consoles, and VR gear of every description. Amid the clutter sat Naia and Molly, and one other person, a Black man with a long, gray-and-white-streaked beard, the hair from the sides of his balding head pulled back into a braid, lolling in a stuffed chair, resting his chin in his hand. I recognized him from his avatar.

"Boy's up," Porter said. Naia and Molly turned to look, then Naia got up and came to me.

"Let me see," she said.

I pulled up my shirt and turned my back to her.

"Oh, yes, those are nasty," Naia said. "The close-range ones are the worst."

"You ever been tased?" I asked.

"Huh-uh. I hope I never am."

"Not fun." I lowered my shirt, lightly rubbing the spot, when a flicker behind Naia caught my eye. It was a screen, one of twenty or so mounted on a metal framework bolted to a circular desk. Some had lines of computer code, others looked like scoreboards, with numbers ticking up like digital clocks. But most had scenes of what looked like VR venues, some as if they were from a lifestream, through the eyes of the avatar. The one that attracted my attention did so for a reason: It was *me*.

The screen showed me and a friend named Wayne in a VR venue, a dance club crowded with teens, a retro metal band hovering over the floor. We were with two girls we knew, Mia and Kiera. It was so hi-res it was chilling. Then I checked another screen—Hammad and me in confinement, crammed into the commissary during common time. It was the first time I'd seen myself from the outside while in confinement. I looked like an old man.

The next screen had me, no more than nine years old, in a VR baseball game. Another in a birthday party. A VR class outing to Huayna Picchu. I craned my neck at all the screens. They were a gallery of my life, from toddler to tween to present day. My head, already woozy from the tasing, went muddy and my vision faded around the edges, like I was looking through a tube. My eyes flicked from one screen to another, settling on one scene I knew well, the day the courts took me away from Mom and made me live with Aunt

Donna. I saw my miserable self, sitting at the table, looking down, arms crossed and pissed as hell. And across from me, where Mom was on that day, a black void—a scar from Mom's shredded life.

"What…what…" I stammered. My stomach churned like I was going to be sick. I put my hand on Porter's chair to steady myself.

"Better sit," Molly said, offering me her chair. "I'll fill you in."

I plopped down, giving up my last erg of energy, the end result of being tased into unconsciousness, followed by my life on display in hi-res.

Molly sat across from me. She lowered her head so she could see into my eyes. And she smiled. For some weird reason, that smile, at that time, hit me like another taser shot (but in a good way) and I broke down.

She patted my knee. "First off, you took out one of those bugs. Naia got the one that tased you. The last one buzzed off before I could kill it."

"Where am I?" I asked.

"You are a guest at Chez Wilkes," Porter replied. "Molly and Porter welcome you."

Molly smiled, leaned over, and kissed Porter on the cheek. "Forty years under the same management," she said, and turned back to me. "We made it across the Mississippi on the old Centennial Bridge. That meant penetrating the Quad Cities perimeter, but we had no choice—we couldn't risk crossing in the corridor, and we knew the drones could come back any time. And we were right. We made another stand about a half-hour later, four drones, four shots, four kills. Naia turned out to be Annie Oakley after all. We didn't encounter any more after that."

I waved my hands at all the screens passing my life before my eyes. "This…"

"Oh. Yeah. That's gotta be a shock."

Another scene popped up, of my Aunt Donna scolding me the day the Civils raided our apartment and put me on restriction.

"Why?" I asked.

A chime sounded before she could answer. An image flashed on a screen near the middle of the array—a tall man with long, silver hair, not in a glowing blue tunic, but wearing familiar retro jeans, shirt, and vest.

"Frodo, let him in," Molly said.

I heard the latch click on the door, and a second later Raúl strode in. It'd been more than two years since I'd seen him IRL. He was still Raúl, but not quite. The old Raúl didn't look as mean and worn out as this one did.

"How's our boy?" he said, not even looking at me. Instead, he was looking at the screens.

"Looser," Molly answered. "He was pretty stiff for a while."

Raúl scratched his chin, still looking at the screens and not at me. "How's the crawl?"

Porter twisted in his chair to the screens and squinted. "Not quite 400 terabytes."

"That all?" Raúl *tsked, tsked* and looked at me for the first time. "What a pitiful footprint."

"I don't know what that means," I said.

He leaned against the desk. "Your Worldstream footprint, young Dylan. Pathetic. Not even half a petabyte. Your mom's lifestream was almost five petabytes when I shredded her. Biggest one I ever did. Took days to crawl it, and an hour to shred. But Grace had The Eye of Providence and the Aletheia crew on her case, weaving her data into the longest, most detailed, most mind-wrecking lifestream ever—up to then, that is."

My confusion was clearing up. I waved a hand at the screens. "So, all this—"

Porter interrupted. "See that?" He pointed at a screen in the corner: yellow lettering, red background, and my full dossier—a duplicate of the display in Molly's truck. "You got a hue and cry tagged on you, Dylan. You know what that means?"

I shook my head.

"It means Civils, Jahbulon, the Worldstream, *everyone*—including regular folks—are hunting your ass. Every spare compute cycle, every live asset, every AI algorithm is devoted to locating you and bringing you in. If they don't know where you are now, they will soon. As long as you're in the Worldstream, you're a danger to everyone around you. At this moment, that's us."

"What's more," Raúl added, "Jahbulon doesn't raise a hue and cry for no reason. I've only ever seen it happen during a shredding. You? A tag of apprehension is about as hot as I'd expect."

"Then, why?" I asked.

"Can't say for sure. Best guess is, somebody wants you—somebody important." He turned to Porter. "How much longer?"

"A few more minutes. Ten, tops."

I had another question but I never got to ask it. A klaxon sounded and a screen flashed a feed of two Civils in full riot gear standing on Porter's and Molly's front stoop with a battering ram. They pounded the door loud enough to be heard over the horn.

"Shut that fucking thing off," Raúl said.

"Frodo, mute!" Molly shouted.

The ear-splitting sound ceased, replaced by a voice from the other side of the door.

"Citizen! You are harboring a fugitive from the Civil Authorities. Open, or we *will* enter forcibly!"

41

Nobody Can Catch You If You Don't Exist

"Frodo, time remaining!"

"The crawl is complete, Molly," the gruff-sounding voice responder answered. "Indexing is in progress. I estimate eight minutes to completion."

"I don't want 'em busting in our door again," Porter said.

Molly gave Porter a *Not now* look. "Frodo, tell those guys we're on our way."

Porter did a slow walk to the door to the sound of *"Open or we will enter forcibly!"*

"Coming!" Porter yelled.

"What do *we* do?" Naia asked. I was too freaked out to say anything.

"*We'll* stall 'em. *You* stay cool. Dylan, come with me."

Molly took me downstairs to a cramped cellar, cluttered with musty old clothes, furniture in all states of disrepair, and gear—mountains of computers, computer parts, consoles, VR headsets, tactile gloves—on shelves and piled on the floor. It was like Naia's junk room, except it was more like a junk dump.

"Hang here until it blows over," she whispered. "If it gets too hot, go through the side exit—*and run!*" She pointed to some steps under a slanted door.

"Then what?"

"Come back when it's over."

"When it's *over?* When will it be over?"

She put her finger to her lips. "You'll know." She went upstairs two steps at a time. When she slammed the door shut I sat there in the dark, more alone and scared than at any time since I was in confinement.

It was quiet for about half a minute, then it got *really* noisy, starting with shouting, then a sound like someone being thrown to the floor, then another body hitting the deck. The words were muffled and I couldn't make out what the topic was, but I could guess. When a noise came from the top of the stairs, like someone trying the door, I got frantic and made for the escape hatch.

But it wouldn't budge. I doubted it had been opened in the last decade.

I sailed past *frantic* to *panic*. I looked around for something in that trash pile I could use to open the door. It was a sure bet that computer stuff was worthless for my immediate needs, unless I could find something heavy enough to throw. I needed a lever, a pry bar, or something shaped like it.

What I settled on was a part of a bicycle, the *fork* I think they called it. At least that's what I thought it was, never having ridden a bicycle IRL. I pulled it off a pile of rusting metal and ran toward the door. But I stopped when I saw something else.

It was a baseball bat, a real one, made of wood, not the VR version I'd used as a kid. I held it, curling my fingers around the narrow part. It felt heavy and powerful. That got me out of my panicky state for some reason I still don't understand. I took the bat and the fork to the door.

The fork barely fit between the two halves of the door, but it fit well enough to get some leverage. I pushed into it with all my strength and the door gave way just as the upstairs door opened, and footsteps tromped down the stairs.

Sunlight blinded me for a second, but I was thinking well enough to grab the bat as I went through. Good thing, too, because I came face-to-face with a fully-armed drone. The bug pivoted and let fly a round, which missed me by a centimeter at most. The anxiety that had built up over the last hour, the Civils in the basement coming after me, and the memory of being tased that morning all came together like cosmic forces, concentrating in my hands and the bat, and as fast as the drone fired its taser round, I swung, connected, and sent that fucking bug over the backyard fence.

Then Molly's warning came to me—*run!* I dropped the bat and sprinted like I was beating the throw to first base.

Molly's and Porter's house was one of a row of little houses each about a meter apart with all their yards connected. I ran from backyard to backyard, but the same sound came from each house as I passed, a piercing shriek, and an urgent warning: *Hue and cry, hue and cry, all citizens are obliged to aid in the apprehension of this fugitive.* Faces appeared in windows and doors; some of them pointed at me as I ran by.

Some pointed behind me.

"Citizen, halt!" The voices were way too close. I kicked harder, hoping to stay ahead of them until—what? Molly said I'd know, but I didn't know. What I *did* know was, there were two or more Civils behind me, and ahead of me folks were coming out of their houses to aid in my apprehension.

And over all of that came a buzz from above. In spite of me still being in recovery from a taser attack, or maybe because of it, I ran faster, maybe as fast as I'd ever run.

Four people, three men and a woman, formed a wall in front of me. With Civils and drones behind and citizens hueing and crying ahead I didn't have time to think and acted on instinct. I faked right with my head and pivoted left, keeping just out of reach of the guy on the end. I headed for the gap between two houses, while from behind me came sounds I'd come to know well: a *pop* of compressed gas, a *thunk* of a taser round embedding itself in human flesh, a strangled *gluck* of a person stiffening and passing out. Those sounds made my skin prickle and my gut churn, knowing now what getting tased felt like. It was especially hurtful, because even though I was executing out of ROM and running on fumes, the faces of those folks got burned into my memory as if I'd studied them. They weren't angry with me. They were sad and worn, like they were doing something they really didn't want to do, but knew that *not* doing it would be worse for them. They didn't need to get tased because of me.

I came out from between the houses onto the street, the shrieking and warning coming from all directions. More folks came out of their houses toward me, like a zombie horde, and two more drones appeared overhead. I made a right and kept running, though my legs were rubbery and my lungs were burning. My mind was all in on running, but my body was out of juice. I started to slow just as the drones caught up.

Tasers fired as I ducked between two houses, one round ricocheting off a gutter and the other smashing a window. The backyard wasn't any safer, with a dozen more citizens crowding around, drones above, and the warning siren sounding from all directions. The last gram of strength gave out and I dropped to my knees, putting my hands over my head, hoping the taser would hit me somewhere that wouldn't hurt too bad.

Then…nothing. The siren stopped shrieking, and the *hue and cry* stopped barking. The bugs halted, hovered, then flew away. The posse around me said nothing, just looked at each other and walked off. Some of them shrugged.

I caught my breath and my legs got some of their strength back. I stood up slowly. The row of backyards, filled with citizens a minute ago, was now deserted. I heard a bird chirp, then the sound of an engine from the street.

I walked between the houses and peeked out. Molly's big, black truck crawled down the street, and I saw her in the driver's seat. She pulled up and stopped as soon as she spotted me.

The door swung open. Molly tipped her head and said, "In."

"What happened?" I asked once inside.

"The Civils roughed us up a bit, but they didn't have anything on us, so they let us go—me, Porter, and Raúl, that is. One of the perks of being a shredder—no fingerprints."

"Naia?"

She pinched her face. "They took Naia. They didn't give a reason, just hauled her away."

Any stamina I'd recovered drained out of me and I slumped in the seat.

"The Civils, the bugs, the hue and cry…they all stopped," I said.

"The shred finished," Molly explained. "You're shredded. Nobody can catch you if you don't exist."

42

Pulled Up by the Roots

"Am I Shade?" I asked.

Molly, Porter, and Raúl sat in a row, and I sat facing them, like a defendant facing a jury.

"Technically, no," Raúl answered. "While all Shade are shredded, not all shredded are Shade."

"So…not Shade, not *Vitreous Orb*. Am I even a person?"

"As far as the Worldstream is concerned, you're not," Molly answered. "Does that matter?"

"What matters is getting Mom and the others back."

Raúl sneered. "This here's what you call a *setback*."

"Can we still get to Nemesio? He's the key."

"Better think of a new key, young Dylan. Nemesio is out of reach."

My chest felt tight. My hands were cold and clammy. I rubbed them on my legs to dry them off and warm them up. The muscles in my thighs were tight, like they were about to cramp.

I closed my eyes. The room, Raúl, Molly and Porter, the chair I was sitting on—the world—dissolved away, like I'd jacked into a staging venue, featureless and white. I imagined a menu scrolling destination venues, but I couldn't read them, like they were in an alien language. I was stuck, with no place to go.

The Worldstream's where I'd lived my whole life. Almost every experience I'd ever had was in VR. Almost every memory was of a venue. It's the only world I'd known. And it was wonderful: No boundaries, no limits—all my life data stored and indexed for easy retrieval, every choice I ever made recorded and analyzed. All with my well-being in mind, of course. The All-Seeing Eye, Jahbulon, they were created for my benefit—for my protection. All my needs anticipated, all my wants satisfied. I only had to call on Jahbulon's name to receive.

Even when I was in Orwell I was still part of it. Like a tree growing on the prairie sending roots into the earth, I was connected, so deeply that if you pulled me up by the roots I would die. As long as my data lived, *I* lived.

And then—out. Disconnected. Shredded. I did not exist.

I focused on my physical sensations in a detached way, like I did back in confinement to keep calm, or when I was in therapy, to endure *that* torture—how my hands felt against my legs, the tension in my back and neck, and my breathing, which was shallow and quick. I took a deep breath, feeling the air come in, and held it. My legs, my hands, my back, my chest—the feelings in my whole body, always real, now felt more real than ever.

I thought of Mom and her friends from the Summerland, Thomas and Celeste. I thought about the rest of my friends from Orwell who'd been taken, and the people from Laputa I'd met, and the ones from Burgess I never met. I thought about Jackson, Benny, Max, Abby, even Frank, still wandering in the wilderness, one day ahead of the drones, Civils, and Kliegls. I thought about Naia, and Hammad—*especially* Hammad. They'd all made a choice, now taken away from them, and that was wrong. It was wrong even if they got reinserted in the infinite Worldstream and offered all the pleasures of a virtual universe.

The alien menu scrolled. The characters vibrated, flashed, and blurred. I let out the breath—and I smiled. The lines in the menu were a mystery, not because I *couldn't* know them, but only because I *didn't* know them—yet.

My eyes opened.

PART THREE

UNIVIRTUAL

43

Golden Jubilee

The Eye of Providence

To squander human potential is the only sin. That is my defense.

When you read the history of this time, remember: Historians are not cool, unbiased tellers of truth—far from it. They have their own agendas that they will inflict on you so subtly, so skillfully, that you will believe your conclusions are your own fair, reasoned judgments drawn from plain, unaltered facts. And you will be *wrong*. Is their deception any less grievous than mine?

Before you judge, consider this: Have you ever seen, heard, or read some controversial claim and accepted it without question, simply because it confirmed your own bias? Of course you have. Do you think that was an accident? The psychology of persuasion by such prosaic means is only a little less sophisticated than the science behind *my* methods. Conventional propagandists access your brain via your senses. My route, via the Belt, is more direct, and, therefore, more expeditious. Yet few would object to the traditional methods—why should you be troubled by a newer, more efficient, more *reliable* way? Oh, I know—you call me *coercive* rather than *persuasive*. That's a distinction without a difference. In the end, the results are the same. You say I manipulate without consent, without the knowledge of the target, while the traditional propagandist does neither. To that I say: how naïve.

❖ ❖ ❖

The final phase commenced on the jubilee of the Millennium Republic of the Americas, fifty years since the

227

so-called "United States" shed the colonial-era straitjacket of "liberal democracy" and finally, fully, embraced a unitary executive. Of course, given our national weakness of will, we retained a remnant of "democracy" in the form of an elected body of representatives from whom the First Minister was to be chosen by a majority of its members. But no matter. The Council's power is limited to electing the First Minister or removing them from office—all other votes are advisory only. And the results have been satisfactory in practice, all the more so since we learned to control the minds of the masses.

Dax had declared a week of celebratory venues, each one a monumental spectacle serving two purposes: to incite the Kliegl acolytes (of which there were millions), and for the personal aggrandizement of First Minister Dax. I attended one in my own persona: Madeleine, Minister of Public Health. Dax even acknowledged me as the architect of *Univirtual*, the Kliegl-led initiative to eradicate the Shade, and to bring the remnant of citizens still living IRL into the Worldstream. I didn't want Dax to name *me* as the one who'd conceived *Univirtual*. I was content for it to be Dax's scheme. But he felt the need to keep some daylight between him and the program. Though he was perfectly aligned with the goals of *Univirtual*, the methods left him conflicted. The same techniques I used so effectively to elect him I later used to manage his parliamentary majority. Their addiction was my control.

"The outlaw Shade are no longer!" Dax boasted, his fifteen-meter-tall avatar towering from the center of each of a thousand replicated stages amid searchlights aimed skyward. He wore a shining mantle of blue-white light, his mane of raven curls framing his round face, unremarkable but for the contortions he conjured when his oration reached its climax, fists raised and trembling, cueing the crowd to roar until he bowed his head, the signal for the masses to be quiet and for Dax to begin again.

"You have seen the reports of criminals flushed from their secret lairs, still hidden like cowards under their cloaks, their inhuman voices bleating in protest as our heroic Kliegl troops herded them to reintegration centers, and, after confinement and correction, to enjoy the bounty of the Worldstream and the protection of Jahbulon!"

The crowd roared anew, convinced that the Shade, the boogeymen that Dax so savagely vilified in his campaign, were once again respectable citizens of the Republic. They couldn't know that Kliegl thugs had raided only a few of the independent Shade dorms, and nearly all of those apprehended were reassigned to the *Vita Occulta* cartel. After all, the Worldstream Consortium relied on Shade labor, sourced primarily from the V.O. To reintegrate such a valuable resource would've been wasteful. My own crew, the *Aletheia*, had grown by half.

"And on the occasion of our Golden Jubilee, I announce the final stage of *Univirtual*, the end game in which every misguided soul still living outside the Worldstream, every straggler still dependent on obsolete Live Services, all the deviants who call themselves *Vitreous Orb*, will come back into a single, unified, pan-humanist virtual reality, *one people, one Republic*. Our troops are already on the move, and our drones are in the air!"

The shouting crowd jostled me on all sides, their avatars decorated with all manner of virtual Dax tchotchkes: images of Dax on their faces, like luminous tattoos, mimicking his movements from the stage; Kliegl slogans scrolling across their foreheads—*Today Dax Tomorrow Dax Forever Dax*—gaudy enhancements to their RL appearance. These were the masses—impressionable, pliable—the great untapped well of possibility—properly managed. Yes, of course I said it. Shall we provide no direction at all? Let the mob run wild? Preposterous. Do you know the disaster that ensues, the catastrophes past eras have witnessed, when the people are allowed to choose their own ends? It is the elimination of this waste, this unrelenting, unlimited waste of potential that is the burden I bear—a burden that I did not choose.

I left the venue then, having had my nod from Dax, committing the adoring crowd to his hands. I stripped off my VR gear and pressed my hands to my face.

"Breathe, Madeleine," I whispered.

It was late, and I still had obligations to fulfill. A brother, Mackenzie, who required nightly attention to bathe, feed, and comfort, once pulled from his virtual world, where he was clever, creative, and content, into the real world, where even basic hygiene was beyond his abilities. A business, the Aletheia, now the largest and most powerful crew in the *Vita Occulta*, with revenues of over ten billion credits a year. And a new development, the Aletheia's latest acquisition, a hostage taken in our raids of the *Vitreous Orb* outposts, the asset most responsible for our early success in mind management, the subject of our most compelling lifestreams, about which we still had massive data stores yet to analyze.

If you are a rider of lifestreams, you've already guessed. Her Shade name is Chrysalis, but you know her as Grace.

44

A Trauma of White Shirts

The Eye of Providence

FAR TOO OFTEN the source of my afflictions is the ill-considered act of a subordinate.

"Do I need to say it?" I began calmly, steadily. "The regime needs only a small excuse to escalate their war on the Shade."

"*You're* the regime, Boss," Jayla said. "You got 'em all by the rug. They don't do *nothin'* without your say-so." Jayla had jacked into the stealth venue in the avatar of a green-and-black spotted giraffe. Cartoonish animals were a favorite theme of hers, typical of those whose transition from one's infantile connectedness with the mother to an adult state of otherness was less than complete. That was also consistent with undiagnosed psychopathy, of which I suspected Jayla could be a case study. So long as she channeled her sadistic tendencies into the development of our Sex and Violence lifestream portfolio, the damage could be contained—and our lifestreams would continue to dominate the ratings.

The other two in the venue, Speranza, in his usual avatar as Nikola Tesla, and Fidelio, rendered as a monstrous green brute (he called it "Hulk"), both stood mute with their eyes down.

It was the Aletheia's policy to meet in a stealth venue where the Worldstream rule enforcing an avatar's resemblance to its owner did not apply. I chose to appear as Ma'at, the Egyptian goddess of justice, harmony, and balance, all qualities the world, in its present state, lacked. The fact that Ma'at was also an imposing figure with the wings of a bird was a bonus.

231

"Not so," I answered. "Not so. You know it."

"What? They jack in every night—eighty percent of the Kliegls on the Council, and half the rest. And that total's up from last month. They can't help themselves. Whatever we upload, they obey—task list blasted to the brain via the Belt." She threw her hooves into the air and grinned. "You'll fix it. This fracas will fade away, like it never even happened."

Jah, if she weren't such a deviously creative force, I'd have traded her to an independent crew for a couple of noobs.

"I don't control *Dax*, remember? One word from him and his White Shirts will launch a campaign of terror."

"Oh, yeah," Jayla conceded. "That ugly little prick doesn't use the Belt. Still, he won't move against you while his whole conference is addicted to our daily data dump."

Her flippant attitude was grotesquely inappropriate, given the circumstances. But I kept my cool.

"That might've been true yesterday—before you killed two of his White Shirts."

❖ ❖ ❖

"Isis, Woodlawn," Speranza commanded.

"Yes, Speranza," answered Isis, our voice responder. "Same time and location as previously specified."

The staging venue morphed into nighttime, in one of the dilapidated public spaces still dotting Chicago that hadn't yet been claimed by nature or the ever-expanding server farms. Moonlight illuminated three black-cloaked figures on a path.

"Isis, freeze the venue," Jayla said. "Look, Boss, we cut through the park. We didn't figure on meeting up with any fucking Kliegls in the *park*. Who goes in the park anyway?"

The expressions rendered by Ma'at are particularly impactful. One glare from me and the giraffe lowered her head.

"What was so important that you had to leave the dorm?" I asked.

"You told us to!" Jayla replied.

"No, I didn't. I'd have remembered that."

"No, really," Speranza jumped in. "We were going for the new recruits down in South Shore. You wanted them ASAP."

The giraffe smirked behind a hoof. I ignored her.

"Bad judgment, in my opinion. You could've taken a car. You could've gone in daytime."

"Daytime tomorrow? That's not ASAP," Speranza said. "And cars draw more attention than Shade on foot these days."

He was quibbling, a behavior I detested, but now was not the time to address it. "Show me the incident," I ordered.

"Isis, resume."

The three Shade continued their walk down the path, looking as though they owned it, chattering as if it were a time when Shade and Cloak walked unmolested wherever they chose. Yes, I'll concede that the park was not a known haunt of Kliegl patrols, the White Shirts preferring to keep to the city streets where ordinary citizens walked as well. But this was more than incautious; it was reckless.

"Rather nonchalant of you," I said.

"Boss, it was the fucking *park*," Jayla protested.

"Oh, yes, the deserted, low-risk park," I countered sarcastically, as five people approached from the side, all in white shirts, red sashes, and trademark red fezzes. "Nothing to be afraid of in the park."

The Kliegls picked up their pace, whipping out their ASPs, while my clueless Aletheia strolled as if taking the air on a sunny autumn day in Chicago.

"Who knew those pinheads could move so stealthily?" Jayla said.

"We're learning all kinds of new things, aren't we?" I retorted, straying outside the strict limits of managerial decorum.

The White Shirts were in a dead run, just meters away, when one of my crew turned toward them.

"Who saw them first?"

The green brute, Fidelio, raised a meaty hand.

The venue continued. The other two, Jayla and Speranza, hesitated for a second, then broke into a run. Fidelio tried to follow but tripped and sprawled on the gravel.

"Bad break, Fidelio," I observed. "That happens when an unanticipated situation arises for which you are unprepared."

The Kliegls surrounded Fidelio, recreating a scene which had become all too common in the reign of Dax: White-shirted thugs with ASPs deployed, raining blows on a defenseless victim, the *thwack thwack* of the batons on flesh playing a counterpoint to agonized screams.

"The others," said one of the attackers, the leader, I presumed, a short, portly man whose oversized fez was jammed on his head down to his eyebrows. "Michael, Dexter, Joyce, run 'em down."

Three Kliegls broke away from the melee to pursue my brave crew members.

"You didn't stay to defend your fellow Aletheia," I said.

"Boss, we didn't know," Jayla protested. "We thought Fidelio was right behind us. I looked back, eventually. See? Right here."

One of the fleeing Shade—Jayla—turned, then stopped. "Aletheia down!" she shouted in her synthesized voice. The other one—Speranza—stopped. The White Shirts kept coming.

"Isis, freeze the venue!" Speranza shouted.

"Why?" I asked.

"Just…freeze." Nikola Tesla's mouth pinched, lip trembling, and eyes watering. I suspected why, but I needed to see for myself.

"Isis, resume," I said.

Jayla took a step toward the Kliegls, then stopped and lowered her shoulder, bracing for impact. Speranza stood his ground.

Then the front of his cloak rose, as if he were lifting a rod underneath it, and the steel-blue barrel of a shotgun poked out, glinting in the light of a streetlamp."

"Speranza, *you?*" I asked.

"Isis, freeze!" he said again.

The tableau hovered before us: to the far left, two figures in white, their batons raised, about to land more murderous blows on Fidelio; in the center, three Kliegl vigilantes in full stride, their ASPs at the ready; to the right, Jayla half-hunched, shoulder toward the coming attack, and Speranza, his weapon raised.

"Isis, resume," I ordered.

The flash from the muzzle was like a nova in the darkness, accompanied instantaneously by an explosion of gore from the lead Kliegl. The blast tore away his shoulder and part of his face. His fez went flying. The force of the shot drove him backwards into his companions, bringing all three of them to a dead stop.

"Isis, freeze!" Speranza shouted again.

The action froze, a mist of blood and flesh hovering like a crimson cloud around the attackers. Speranza turned away.

"Isis, resume!" I commanded.

The freeze-frame ended. The two Kliegls by Fidelio stopped, hesitated, then turned and ran. The wounded man fell into the grasp of two others, who held him for a moment, dropped him, and took off after the rest.

Another blinding explosion erupted. The second blast took out the woman. Blood soaked her shirt until the red sash disappeared.

"Isis, freeze." This time it was I who stopped the action. "They were running, Speranza."

"I know," he replied, almost inaudibly.

"They were running *away*."

He nodded.

"Isis, suspend the venue," I said.

The scene dissolved. We were once again in the conference venue.

"Fidelio, how badly are you injured?" I asked.

"Bruises only. Nothing broken. Painful, not permanent."

"Good. And Jayla? No damage?"

"No scratches, no dents."

I nodded. "Speranza," I said in a soft, breathy voice, a tone I'd found useful in therapy to calm the patient and elicit cooperation, "this must have been traumatic. In the days to come, you will find this memory intruding into your thoughts frequently. That's normal." I put my hand on Nikola Tesla's shoulder and looked directly into his eyes. I lowered my wings, to appear less imposing. "Don't try to suppress the memory. Simply acknowledge it and dismiss it. We will discuss it another time."

My hand fell from his shoulder. Speranza was not comforted, judging from his avatar's expression, but that was also normal. We would address his trauma in therapy.

"Jayla, what about the recruits?"

"Those Kliegls were screaming for Jahbulon. We came straight back here."

"Then listen: the vigilantes roam at night. Jayla, you and Fidelio will go to South Shore today, in daylight. And take a car."

"Sure, Boss. We'll get your noobs for you. No fuck-ups this time."

"They're not noobs," I replied. "They're experienced coders, all of them. Two of them you know—their Shade names are Bjorg and Elisha."

"Oh, yeah. And the third one?"

"The third one you know intimately. Our Grace is coming home."

45

Three Noobs for the Aletheia

Shade Lucius of the Aletheia

Call me Lucius.

For us Shade, the golden anniversary of the Millennium Republic wasn't the party it was for everyone else.

My crew was the Aletheia, first among the ranks of the *Vita Occulta*. In the year since Dax rose to power, the Aletheia tribe had increased. *Univirtual,* the boss's master plan, did wonders for recruitment (if you want to call it that). The smooth, shiny transports, or hypertube pods from the outer regions weren't so much company rides to a promising career as they were slave ships inbound from Africa, loaded with fresh, free labor. Madeleine, a.k.a. "The Eye of Providence," was a little squishy on that distinction. A head was a head was a head by her reckoning.

Like today. Jayla, Fidelio, and I drove down to South Shore in the daytime, not recommended practice in these perilous times, but after the debacle in the park, The Eye thought it less risky than facing a random band of White Shirts. Jayla decided to bring me along so we wouldn't be outnumbered.

"Three, right?" I asked Jayla, who was driving.

"Three, yup. Grace, Bjorg, and Elisha."

"Grace, yeah. Everyone's heard of Grace. But the other two…"

"From the Kaleidoscope. Those three started the crew. We're fetching the K-scope founding fathers—or mothers, as the case may be. Wait 'til you see Elisha. He's a big 'un."

Jayla sped through streets empty except for an occasional robot transport, or a pedestrian, a rarer sight than in days past, given the situation with White Shirts and *Univirtual.*

Nobody came out IRL anymore, not at night, and only the stubbornest and stupidest during the day. We were certain to attract stares in our fifty-year-old gas-burning vehicle, but even in our cloaks and voiceboxes, no Kliegls. They were 100% nocturnal, like roaches.

"And they were rounded up, you know, by Kliegls?"

"And Civils. From a *Vitreous Orb* town out west. Busted from their glass globe and hauled in from the hinterland. All part of the master plan."

Jayla had a laugh that made my skin pucker, even through her synthesizer. Fidelio stayed quiet.

"Univirtual," I said.

"Everyone inside the magical kingdom." She jabbed my arm with her elbow. "Except us Shade, of course." That laugh again. "I never thought of that before—*Shade*—like ghosts stuck between two worlds."

The ride to South Shore took about a half-hour. The neighborhood looked like every other one in Chicago, all ancient, crumbling buildings crammed with folks jacked into the Worldstream for work, social calls, play—whatever. With drones bringing food, clothes, soap, and stuff, a body could go anywhere in the world, at any time in history, and never leave their apartment.

Jayla pulled up to the curb, jammed on the brakes, and shut off the engine. "This is the place," she said, as we piled out of the car. "Basement apartment. Follow me."

We had to kick the door a couple times before it opened. We took the stairs at the end of the hall. At the bottom was another door with a mat in front of it, dirty as hell, with the barely readable words "KEEP THE CHANGE YA FILTHY ANIMAL" scrawled on it. Jayla knocked.

"Yeah, what?" a voice said from inside.

"I'm called Jayla, of the Aletheia, here for a pickup."

We heard locks turn and bolts pulled aside, then the door creaked open.

The first thing I noticed was the odor—a pissy stench like a public bathroom in one of the abandoned bus stations near Lincoln Park, where bums and street people camped out.

The fat, greasy bastard holding the door looked like the place smelled. He was dressed in a white shirt with sweat stains at the armpits and what looked like blood spatters on it. The room was lit by one small lumen panel in the middle of the ceiling and a mid-sized wall screen scrolling v-grams. There was one chair in the middle of the room, with a bunch of VR gear scattered around it on the dirty carpet. Then I noticed something else—a red sash hanging from the back of the chair, and on the seat one of those red fez hats with the searchlight symbol on it.

"Kliegl!" I said without thinking. I might have flinched.

The guy bunched up his face like he was going to spit. "Unclench," he grunted. "I ain't gonna do nothin' to ya. I'm just the middleman. If it wasn't for me and the rest, you'd have to find your own damn workers." He turned his back to us and walked into the apartment. "C'mon, I got your guys right here." He disappeared down a hallway. Jayla went after him, with me and Fidelio right behind.

The hall was lined with six doors plus one at the end. That's the one he went to.

"Wake up!" he yelled, banging on the door. "Your ride's here!"

We heard nothing for almost half a minute. The Kliegl guy pounded again. "Asses up! Time to go to work!"

That did it. The doorknob turned and the door opened a crack. Kliegl pushed it open the rest of the way.

The one who opened the door had his back turned to us by then. He walked to a cot by the wall and dropped on it, almost breaking it. That was Elisha, every bit as big as Jayla had promised.

Two women lay on separate cots, still asleep. One had dirty blonde hair, but I couldn't see her face. The other's face I knew like it was my own—*Grace*. All of them looked like refugees from confinement.

"Oh, Jah. These are *people*. What are you doing to these people?" Fidelio demanded, saying my own thoughts out loud.

"You want 'em or not?" Kliegl grunted.

I thought Fidelio was going to rear up and clock him. Jayla held him back.

"Yeah. We want 'em. Of course we want 'em," she said.

"They're all yours. The Eye already paid. Good luck, and *good riddance*."

"Have they been trouble?" Jayla asked.

Kliegl pointed at the blonde, who was sitting up by then, rubbing her eyes with her palms. "*That* one has." The blonde dropped her hands and stuck out her tongue.

"Bjorg," Jayla said, followed by that annoying laugh. "Yup. She's got a rep." Jayla put her hands on her hips and did a half-turn. "Elisha, big guy, how's the res? And what's this? Can it be? *Grace?* Oh, girlfriend, has the boss got plans for *you*."

Grace didn't say anything. She just stared at us in our Shade cloaks, eyes hollow and her face with deep, dark lines stuck there like she hadn't smiled in forever.

"Where're their cloaks?" Jayla asked. "The others all had cloaks. That's standard issue."

Kliegl snorted. "We didn't snatch these from a dorm, dumbass. These are *Vitreous Orb*, all the way from Ogallala is what they told me. They weren't in cloaks when I got 'em."

"Well, what the fuck are *we* supposed to do with 'em? As soon as they see the light of day, Jahbulon will rupture an o-ring."

He sighed a short, phlegmy sigh. "Take the blanket. They can hide under it on the way to the car."

"All three? Under that little thing?"

He grabbed the blanket off of Elisha's cot and threw it at Jayla. "Jah, you really are dumb. Take 'em one at a time."

And that's how we did it. Jayla and I took Bjorg first, then I stood by the car while she went back for Grace. Fidelio and Jayla brought Elisha out together, like they might need two people to handle him if he put up a fight, but that was probably overkill. Jayla was right: As soon as any shredded soul showed a non-existent face to any of the billions of imagers in the real world, the All-Seeing Eye would flip out. They got in the car because they had no place else to go.

◈ ◈ ◈

The Eye of Providence was waiting for us when we got back to Aletheia. We came in as we always did through the sliding door, and she was standing in the middle of the car bay in full Shade regalia—cloak, hood, and voice box. Two other Shades stood beside her, but I couldn't be sure who they were, or even which was which until The Eye spoke. We all look alike in our cloaks.

The Eye kept her voice box shut while Elisha and Bjorg got out of the car. It wasn't until Grace stepped out with Fidelio holding her hand that The Eye spoke up.

"Grace," she said with synthesized sympathy. She spread her arms like she was warming up for a hug. "You're finally here with us to stay."

I figured that would get a reaction out of Grace, but she kept the same stony look. That got to The Eye. I know, because she put her hands together, one hand covering a fist. She waited a second, then pulled off her hood to reveal her red and gold mask.

"You should make the best of it, dear," The Eye said, in a syrupy tone.

That made my stomach turn, but Grace didn't let it affect her at all.

The Eye sighed. "Grace, Jayla will show you to your dorm. Jayla, give her some time before you get started."

"Started on what?" Bjorg asked. "What's going to happen to Chrysalis?"

The Eye held up a finger. "Grace won't be using her Shade name here, Bjorg. You and Elisha will, of course, since you'll be part of the Aletheia crew."

"Then what's *she?*" Elisha asked, in a voice loud enough to startle me.

The Eye spread her arms again. "She's our guest."

"A guest can leave any time she wants," Bjorg said. "So, she can leave, right?"

The Eye pressed her lips together, and I saw her eyes narrow through the holes in her mask. "Perhaps *guest* was the wrong word. Helper. She's helping us." She waved a hand. "Jayla."

Jayla took Grace's arm. Grace didn't resist, and her stern expression never wavered. She looked like a defeated foe making one last defiant stand.

"And what about us?" Bjorg asked.

"You'll be working together. It's a project you've worked on before, though we've made progress since you were last here, thanks to our project leader." She tilted her head to the Shade beside her. "Nemesio, show Bjorg and Elisha to their dorm."

When The Eye said *Nemesio*, Grace stopped and turned. She didn't say anything, but her look softened and her eyes teared up. Since we'd fetched her it was the first sign that she felt anything other than contempt.

46

Don't Bother

The Eye of Providence

MACKENZIE SAT LIKE a judge presiding from the bench, saying not a word. His distinctive face—forehead creased, eyelids heavy, mouth lined from a lifetime of laughs and scowls—gave him an air of authority. His shock of straw-colored hair meandered in diverse directions, as though the hours he devoted to thought left him no time for personal grooming. His clothes were no better—a rumpled blue corduroy jacket over a chambray shirt and black slacks, threadbare and coming through at the knees. The added measure of eccentricity the costume lent to his already odd appearance paradoxically reinforced his authoritative aura, as lively eyes darted from one speaker to the next. Overall the effect was charming—to me, his sister, of course, but to his dinner companions as well.

George, the gruff, opinionated writer, spoke in a booming voice with exaggerated gestures. Annette was younger (though not *very* young), attractive, and almost as talkative as George. The two of them sparred for an opening to make a cutting remark, a competition I'd witnessed before. Though I found it tiresome, Mackenzie did not. He was never more content, never more *alive*, than when he and his friends faced off.

The others—Quincy, the coder, whose thinking was relentlessly linear, logical, and literal, and Theresa, the former district council member, now retired—watched the contest with amusement, remaining silent mostly, but Mackenzie was careful to engage each of them from time to time, giving all sides a fair hearing, as if moderating a debate.

"Annette is forever the optimist," George said, turning from one guest to another with a mocking smile. "She's certain that the Kliegls have a *higher* purpose, which we poor citizens cannot see."

"And you're forever the cynic," Annette countered. "Dax isn't hiding his reasons for pulling everyone into the Worldstream. Dax *told* us the reasons. He campaigned on the issue, for Jah's sake. The people *elected* him. You can't deny that Dax has the support of the people."

"The untutored and incurious people," George retorted. "The *people*, in whom you place so much faith, will, at best, save us from disaster. They will most certainly preserve us from greatness."

"Don't try to be clever, George. You're very tiresome when you're trying to be clever."

Mack smiled, and I did, too, the way I always do when I see Mack enjoying himself.

"Forget about the people," George said. "What do *you* think? You *do* think, don't you?"

"Leave her alone, George," Mack interrupted. "If you have a different opinion, fine, but don't be down on Annette."

George held up a hand. "My apologies. Annette knows it's all in fun."

Annette narrowed her eyes. "Fun. Sure. But enough of your conspiracy theories. If you think there is something nefarious behind *Univirtual*, be specific."

Mack's smile disappeared. He glanced at me briefly before his eyes darted down.

"I'm sure it's all on the up and up," George said. "All citizens of the Millennium Republic must have faith in our first minister, and in the Kliegl party." He brought his teacup to his lips. "And in the White Shirts…" He sipped. "What shall we call them? Patrols? Committees? Social clubs, perhaps?"

"Thugs," Theresa replied as she poked at her salad. She took a bite and talked around a mouthful. "Domestic terrorists acting on behalf of a tyrant."

"That's harsh, don't you think?" Annette objected.

"I don't think so," Quincy said, setting down his mug of beer. "The term is apt. They're not enforcing laws. They're not seeing after the public's safety. They're prowling the streets and beating up people. We've all heard the stories."

"*Stories,*" Annette said. "Just stories. None of us has seen any of this first-hand. Could it be that Dax's enemies are spreading these rumors? Making them up?"

"I doubt it, but it's a fair question," Theresa replied. "Can any of us trust what we see or hear? Especially in the Worldstream?"

Quincy nodded. "The only evidence we have is what comes through our visors, our headphones, our tactiles—or the *Belt*. Nothing that touches our eyes, ears, or bodies is real. We're always two or more levels of indirection from reality."

"Fine," George conceded. "Without immediate experience, we must rely on authority to resolve such questions."

I saw where the conversation was going, and I didn't like it. Neither did Mack. He raised his hand. "George—"

"No," he interrupted, "let us appeal to a higher source. Madeleine, what do *you* think?"

This was so like George, to turn a conversation into a confrontation.

"I'm just auditing this course, professor," I said, smiling.

"Well, isn't that convenient?" George bellowed. "Top government official, Minister of Public Health? Every time a new policy's announced about cutting live services, or rousting Shade out of their warrens, it's *your* name that comes up: Madeleine, the architect of *Univirtual*. And if we have questions, we can't even ask? Jah. Just too damned convenient!"

"George, please," Mack said. "Maddie's here because I invited her. Don't put her on the spot."

"How inhospitable of me," George said, "to ask an essay question like, 'What do you think?' of an audit student. Would true or false be more appropriate?"

"George…"

"True or false: The Kliegl regime intends to force *everyone* to abandon their RL existence to work, play, live, and die within the artificial universe we call the Worldstream."

"Maddie, I'm sorry," Mack said. "George gets carried away at times, especially when he's wired on his third cup of tea."

But I was prepared. I knew when I began the journey that some would resist, whether from ignorance, stubbornness, or misguided nostalgia for a different, less productive, less fulfilling era.

"False," I answered, as succinctly as I could without being curt.

"Indeed." George raised a finger, then brought it down tip first on the table. A miniature tableau appeared, a stage on which a circle of searchlights sent their beams skyward, and in the middle, the doll-sized figure of Dax, resplendent in his shining robe, his voice a thin, wavering version of his usual booming oratory:

Every misguided soul still living outside the Worldstream, every straggler still dependent on obsolete Live Services, all the deviants who call themselves Vitreous Orb, *will come back into a single, unified, pan-humanist virtual reality, one people, one Republic!*

George tapped again and the stage vanished. He sipped his tea as if he'd made his final, irrefutable point.

"You said *force*," I said, the picture of calm rationality. "No one will be *forced*. We will simply make all the benefits of Jahbulon and the Worldstream seamlessly available to all citizens of the Republic. They will *choose* to realize their limitless potential in the universal virtual world."

"And the *Vitreous Orb?*" he said over his teacup, in an oily tone. "They made *their* choice, and now they're hunted like criminals."

I gripped the arms of my chair, my tactile gloves rendering the feel of the wood, hard, smooth, and cool, no different than if I were sitting with Mack and his friends at a table outside a quaint café on a hazy afternoon.

"The *Vitreous Orb* don't just live outside the Worldstream. They live apart from *any* society, VR or RL. They make no contributions to the Republic."

"Nor do they make demands," George countered. "Why should they be deprived of that choice?"

"Because *they deprive us of their production!*" I shouted. It was a moment of intemperance, but I recovered. "If anyone is apart from society, then society, and its citizens, cannot realize their full potential."

George smiled, as if in triumph. "Deprive *me?* Of what?" He spread his arms. "*These* are my friends. If there are no *Vitreous Orb* among us, I'm not deprived of the company of my friends, and if the *Vitreous Orb* were here, they couldn't *possibly* add to *my* enjoyment. I am realizing all the potential I wish to realize."

I held my tongue. This man's narrow viewpoint, his inability to see beyond his own miserable wants, and the attitude of all like him, were the greatest obstacle to achieving *Univirtual.* Neither George nor his so-called intellectual ilk would ever be convinced.

"I'm tired, Mack," I said, "and I have an early day tomorrow. Everyone, have a pleasant afternoon. Elsa, exit the venue."

The café flattened and dissolved, replaced by my staging venue. I took a cleansing breath, paused, then prepared to remove my gear, when my voice responder spoke.

"Madeleine, you have a request to join a venue."

"Not n—" I began, then sighed. "Who is it, Elsa?"

"It's Mackenzie. He sends a message: *Well, that was abrupt.*"

"Fine. Elsa, take me to the venue."

I teleported to Mack's study, a room like that of a Victorian-era naturalist. Shelves lined one wall, some with ancient leather-bound volumes, others with jars of all sizes, containing preserved specimens of fish, rare species of mammals, monstrous oddities, some entire, some in partial states of dissection. Engravings of birds and plants hung from a rail; a butterfly collection stood on the mantel. The room was dark, feeble light streaming through the partially-closed curtains hanging on an immense window.

Mack sat in a high-backed chair behind a desk, an ornate piece of furniture made of oak. He leaned back, tenting his fingers, as if he were a professor about to chastise a student.

"That was rude," he said, "leaving without so much as a goodbye."

"I said goodbye," I countered, though technically I hadn't.

Mack waved a hand. "It doesn't matter. That's not why I asked for you anyway."

I sat in a chair facing him, leaning forward, waiting for him to continue.

"They ask me about it all the time," he said.

"*Univirtual?* What do you tell them?"

He pushed his fingers into his hair and massaged his scalp. "Not a damn thing. It's not up to me to defend your policies."

"Oh." I shifted in my seat. "Then why am I here?"

"I need to tell *someone* what I think and feel."

I stood. "I know what you think. You've told me many times."

"I said *I* need to tell, not that *you* need to hear."

I sat down, braced to hear Mack's speech yet again.

"Did you hear George?" he asked.

"I heard him."

"I wonder if you did. *He* doesn't feel deprived, yet *you* insist that he's deprived."

"George is too arrogant to see how he's being disadvantaged, how he and others like him—"

"Like *him?* Do you mean like *me?*"

"You're not like George."

Mack closed his eyes and lowered his chin, looking as old as I'd ever seen him. And he had always looked old, since he was born.

Maddie…and Mackenzie. That was how Mother referred to us—always Maddie first, Mackenzie second. The familiar, followed by the formal. And not because I was the oldest. The way she said it—*Maddie…and Mackenzie,* always with a hesitation between the names, a reluctant acknowledgement that she had a second child, quite the opposite of her darling oldest, the smart, pretty Maddie: *Mackenzie*, the troublesome child who demanded much and returned little.

But that was *Mother's* failing, not Mack's. I *am* smart—brilliant—far smarter than Mother. Perhaps that's why I could see what she could not—the sensitive, creative, inquisitive mind trapped in an uncooperative body, smothered under an impenetrable cloak.

But *I* lifted the corner of the cloak to see the wonder beneath.

"You know what I mean," Mack said.

"Mack, I really am tired."

"You know what I mean."

Jah, I really *was* tired, nearly exhausted. That's my excuse for what happened next.

"Yes, Mack, I know what you mean. And that's what's so sad about George and all his self-flagellating intellectual kind."

"Self-flagellating? Where is *that* coming from?"

"He should be *grateful* for all the Worldstream's done for him."

"Oh. Grateful. Because of his condition, you mean."

"Yes! He leads a perfectly normal—"

"Normal?"

"You *know* what I mean."

"You mean *typical.* Typical someone who isn't paralyzed from the neck down, like George. Or who doesn't suffer from cerebral palsy, like Theresa, or who isn't disfigured, like Annette. Typical someone who isn't so severely autistic, like Quincy or me, that a nurse must feed, bathe, and bed them down every night, like middle-aged babies."

"Yes," I said, very softly. *"You're* why this is important, to make the whole world accessible, to you and to everyone else who's—"

"Not typical. Well, thank you, but no thank you. We're fine. George said it best—we're realizing all the potential we wish to realize. And don't pretend that you're doing it for me, or George, or all the other real-world gimps."

"But I am. Why else?"

He waved a hand. "Believe what you want. But eradicating Real Life won't make Mother love me any more, or you any less. She's dead, after all." He stood up. "Freebird, I'm ready now."

"Yes, Mackenzie. Any time."

"I'll be over to take care of you shortly, Mack," I said.

"Don't bother. You're very tired. Loren will do the chores. Freebird, suspend the venue."

The study and all its paraphernalia dissolved. I stripped off my gear.

Poor Mack, I thought. *He doesn't see either.*

47

Not My Operation

The Eye of Providence

THE MOST-USED tool in Dax's kit was drama. It was evident from his rallies, overdone extravagances no ancient despot could imagine.

He favored a starker spectacle for his private audiences.

The venue was entirely black, not even a source of light to illuminate his audience of one. I was simply visible, as if lit from within—a pale ghost suspended in a sea of inky darkness. Disorientation arose instantly, brought on by the absence of any reference frame other than my own glowing avatar. Unlike his mass gatherings, where his followers could find validation among a million like-minded zealots, Dax's face-to-face meetings intimidated his counterparts through isolation in infinite space.

It took a full five minutes for Dax to arrive.

"Minister," boomed his disembodied voice, his avatar rastering in a second later, not in the brilliant, eye-fatiguing robe he preferred for his rallies, but in a body-hugging black shirt and pants, which showed off his physique (or so he thought). Though he appeared with exaggerated height (twice his RL height, I guessed), his avatar was physically unimpressive, one reason why he insisted on monumental scale for his rallies. I didn't know to what extent his avatar deviated from his true appearance. I'd never met him in person.

"Yes, First Minister," I answered.

He stood with his arms crossed, glaring down at me with a face that others might have found intimidating.

"Two loyal Kliegl party members were slain last night."

"So I've heard. Two White Shirts in a park in Chicago. What a tragedy."

He uncrossed his arms, fists still clenched. "They are not *White Shirts*. That is what our enemies call patriotic citizens who sacrifice to preserve our Republic."

"Apologies, First Minister. I was only repeating the common term."

"The *common term!* With all the power you hold over the minds of citizens, why is this pejorative still a *common term?*"

I had never explained to Dax in detail how our technology worked—our method of using the Belt to implant impulses in those who rode our lifestreams. We could only influence *actions*, not opinions, and we certainly could not dictate how citizens talked. The power of the technique came from our ability to induce citizens to act in ways that were *contrary* to their opinions, even against their self-interest. Still, the fact that Dax believed that we had more power than we actually had was useful.

"If you like, First Minister, we can divert our resources to reshaping the vernacular. Of course, our other priorities would suffer."

His glare grew more menacing. "Don't patronize me, Minister."

"I would never do that," I assured him.

Dax paced, as he always did when overthinking. "The assassins were Shade. They weren't apprehended. But I think *you* know who they are. Your Shade crew is the largest still in operation. In fact, there are no crews in the central region of *Vita Occulta* who are not affiliated with Aletheia. Many are under your direct control."

"Aletheia?" I echoed, eyes raised and a finger to my chin. "I've heard of them. Yes, they *are* quite powerful, I'm told."

"First you patronize me, then you play me for a fool," he growled. "Shall we treat each other like smart people, or will we keep playing games?"

"I find the game as tiresome as you do," I replied. "Why did you summon me?"

He crossed his arms again. "Your operation to retrieve the outliers has succeeded, far better than I expected."

"*My* operation?"

He scowled. "It wasn't *my* operation."

"You are First Minister. You set *all* policy. The council sanctioned it—*your* council."

He stepped forward, dropping his arms to his side. His avatar grew to three times its normal size. I looked up at him as impassively as I could, but the sudden change in stature induced an involuntary reaction. It must have shown on my face, since a faint smile softened his glare for a moment.

"No games—remember? We both know who controls the council."

I lowered my eyes. "You give me too much credit. The Kliegls have an outright majority in the council. They're all loyal to Dax. *That's* control. I can only influence." It's always best when having the better hand to underplay it. "I'll ask again: Why did you summon me?"

His avatar shrank to only somewhat larger than RL. "The numbers apprehended in the raids far exceed our capacity to process. There is a need for additional reintegration facilities."

"Of course. How can I help?"

"The appropriation is controversial within the Council, even among the Kliegls."

"I don't understand. The Council's vote is advisory only. You can make it happen regardless of the vote. Why are you concerned?"

"This is a divisive issue among the citizenry. A narrow victory would only fuel the controversy. The measure *must* pass by an overwhelming margin."

"I understand. When is the vote?"

Dax returned to his previous oversized stature. "In three days. That should be enough time."

"Indeed," I said, and with a wave of his hand, Dax suspended the venue.

The trouble started three days later.

48

Glitched Out

The Eye of Providence

MORE THAN A hundred Kliegl CMs voted no. The resolution failed by six votes.

I met Jayla and Speranza in the stealth venue, Speranza elegant as Nikola Tesla, accompanied by a shaggy, yellow, hulking cow-like animal with heavy curled horns.

"Jayla—"

"Muskox," she answered before I could ask. "What's up, Boss?"

I summoned the visual of that morning's council session, with all its posturing, posing, and pontificating—the banal language of parliamentary debate, heated blather serving no purpose other than to aggrandize or denigrate. But the debate is meaningless: when the matter is called, the CMs vote according to *our* instructions, implanted the day before, when the CMs surrendered to their addiction, strapped on the Belt, and jacked into a lifestream they'd ridden hundreds of times. Our commands, hidden in the data stream, implant in their subconscious: A vote, an act, a desire, ending with an irresistible urge to ride the same lifestream the next day.

But this time, they failed to follow instructions. The council logged their votes, short of a majority.

"Well, *that's* hinky," Jayla said.

"The upload failed," I replied.

"No way. I've *never* muffed a mainline." The animal waved a hoof. A visual appeared showing the log from the previous day. "See? Everyone on the roster rode on schedule. Every one of them got the package."

"The payload was bad?" Speranza suggested. "Corrupted, maybe?"

"It wasn't *corrupted,*" Jayla sneered. She flicked the display, scrolling sideways to another log. "There's the content. One: Vote *aye* on the appropriation. Two: See you tomorrow, same time, same venue. Two items, short and sweet. There's nothing to go wrong."

I pointed to the vote tally without a word: *Affirmative 245, Negative 251, Present 4.*

"Right, Boss, I'll get to work on this. No worries, we'll figure it out." She tilted her massive head, pointing a horn at Speranza. "Me and the iconoclastic genius."

❖ ❖ ❖

Dax's conference venue had changed. Though still an infinite expanse of black, a powerful spotlight appeared, so intense it hurt my eyes. I raised my hand to block out the light, but my hand was transparent. I turned my head, and the light followed my movements. I closed my eyes, but the light was still painfully fierce.

"Can you explain?" Dax thundered, so loudly my ears rang.

"Can you tone it down?" I complained. The light intensified, so bright that I feared it would burn out my VR headset. I heard a rushing noise, like surf breaking on the shore, growing louder, until I recognized it as Dax's breathing, amplified a thousand times. If he'd spoken, he would surely have ruptured my eardrums.

"Elsa, exit the venue," I whispered.

"Wait!" Dax said, at a volume just below the threshold of pain. The light dimmed, then went out. I opened my eyes to the familiar ink-black venue, my avatar glowing with its own light, and Dax in front of me, four meters tall.

"Why didn't you do as I directed?" he asked, as if he were interrogating me.

"We did," I answered. "I verified it myself."

"You *failed* yourself," he snarled. He startled me—but for a reason you might not suspect.

It was something I noticed.

I'd seen Dax in all manner of venues, exhibiting the whole range of emotions—rage, contempt, condescension, sadness, and—rarely—joy. I had noted and analyzed his avatar in all its aspects, subconsciously, perhaps, but no less thoroughly than if I'd scrutinized every frame and pixel.

The interplay among an avatar's appearance, its actions, its demeanor—the artificial coherence of a virtual presence—is complex, as you can imagine. It is imperfect. Subtle inconsistencies in the Worldstream's rendering go unnoticed by even the most careful observer. We are so accustomed to our virtual lives that going out of RL and into VR is no more notable than stepping from one room to the next. Whatever tricks are played on the senses, the mind falls for.

But I knew—or perhaps *sensed*—that his threatening face was a sham: As fiercely as he challenged me, he was *not* angry —not at all.

"I understand. We'll investigate," I said, and then, before he could respond, "Elsa, exit the venue."

❖ ❖ ❖

The route from my apartment to the Aletheia dorm is not long, but even a short walk outside draws attention. It's the Kliegl White Shirts (that's more than a "common term"—it's what those sadistic thugs call *themselves*) that are the greatest threat. Any citizen on the streets after dark can expect a confrontation; those cloaked risk a beating. But this situation called for a face-to-face meeting with my crew. I decided to chance it.

It was late evening, the reddening sun still streaming between tall buildings. I was safe for the time being, since the White Shirts emerged after dark, like vermin in a tenement kitchen. Even so, I walked as swiftly as I could in my cloak and hood, staying close to the buildings, until I came to the side street where the dorm was located. I looked both ways, waiting as a shadow passed a cross street until it disappeared before I went down the passage.

"Announce yourself," came the mechanical greeting at the door.

"The Eye of Providence."

"Oh, hi, Boss," Jayla answered. Only Jayla calls me *Boss*.

The door slid open and I stepped into the garage, orange-tinted from light reflected from the copper-lined walls.

"We weren't expecting you, Boss," Jayla said, pulling off her hood. "You should call first."

"Get Speranza and meet me in the cube room," I ordered. "This can't wait."

❖ ❖ ❖

Once in the windowless room, door closed, I took off my hood, my face still hidden behind the mask, a bold concept in blood-red with gold filigree trim. I'd designed it myself.

"We couldn't have done this in the stealth venue?" Speranza asked.

"If we need to go into the venue, we can, but I want to have this conversation face to face—no avatars, no animals."

They shared a shrug, as if I'd made some irrelevant remark, instead of setting the tone for our discussion.

"Are you fine with that?" I barked.

Their eyes—what I could see of them through the holes in their masks—opened wide, and I knew I had their attention.

"Yeah, Boss, whatever," Jayla replied, sans the usual attitude. Speranza nodded.

"Let's start with status."

"Ah—still looking into it," Speranza said.

"*Nothing?*" I snapped. "For Jah's sake, you've had a day."

They were both quiet, then Jayla sat forward. "Boss—a day, two days, ten days, won't make any difference. I told you, there's nothing to go wrong! We checked the implant down to the last bit. That took an hour. It went off like it always does—*click, squeeze, bang.*"

"Clearly, it did not," I objected.

Jayla threw up her hands. "Something glitched out. It happens."

"Not acceptable." Jayla was good, but she had an unfortunate habit of deflecting blame when things went sideways. I couldn't allow it. But before I could press her, Speranza jumped in.

"Eye, you know something," he said.

"Do you think so?"

He spread his arms wide. "You could've asked for a report in the venue. That'd be even better—we could bring up logs, replays, whatever. But instead we're here in the cube room. What's so secret that you don't trust the stealth venue? What do you know that we don't?"

It was an impressive bit of deductive logic from a Shade who rarely strayed beyond what he could see in front of him.

"Dax summoned me. He ripped me for bungling this vote," I confessed.

"And you wanted us to feel the pain up close," Jayla said.

"Not exactly. You see, he *wanted* me to think that he was upset, but he wasn't. He was more like…smug."

"Smug?" they repeated in unison.

"It doesn't matter to Dax whether the resolution passes or fails. I suspect he cares very little about his reintegration centers. And he *certainly* doesn't care about how the citizenry would react to an unfavorable Council vote."

"I'm not following, Boss," Jayla said.

"This vote was a test. You failed. And I didn't see it coming."

"A test of what?"

"Countermeasures. Your implant didn't take because Dax has a shield."

49

Show Some Initiative

The Eye of Providence

THE PSYCHOLOGICAL STIMULI that I developed to aid the rehabilitation of confinees in state institutions were also well-suited to probing the psyche of a subject of interest. And no subject was of more interest than Grace.

Jayla and I monitored the session from the observation venue. Physically, I was at my apartment, while Jayla sat in the same room as Grace, to make certain that she couldn't rip off her VR gear. It was overkill, since Grace was strapped to her chair, but given the intensity of the virtual experience, a mishap was not impossible.

"I wanna do *Subterranean Blues*," Jayla whispered. She was beside me in the venue, a darkened space with a window looking out on a single chair, like an old-style police interrogation room with a one-way mirror. Jayla posed in the avatar of a dragon—not a fire-breathing winged reptile, but a fuzzy green stuffed toy with glass eyes. Grace sat in the chair, appearing as herself, of course.

"She can't hear us," I reminded her. I was in my usual Ma'at avatar. "You don't have to whisper."

"Whaddya say? *Sub Blues?*"

"The objective of this study is *not* to make the subject sick."

The neon green avatar mugged the plush toy version of a pout.

"It was Grace's unique emotional responses that made her lifestream the most compelling ever woven," I explained. "We'll put her in rehab venues and record her reactions via the Belt. It'll be up to you to synthesize the most compelling aspects of her psyche."

"*Subterranean Blues* will get a reaction."

"Enough," I said. "Putting the subject in the head of a sexual predator who cuts up his victims with sewing shears won't give a read on Grace's mass appeal."

"Fine. What, then?"

"*Bible Camp*."

Jayla waved a talon. The scene dissolved to a campfire ringed by kids aged twelve to seventeen. An older man, a camp counselor, circled the fire like some primitive ritual, raising his arms as the campers sang together:

I love to tell the blessed story,
Of what the Lord has done.
How he lived, his home in glory,
That a life now might be won.
I know I heard, heard Paul and Silas
Heard ole Daniel in the lion's den
Can you tell, Oh, anything, He's done for you.

One ruddy-haired girl of fourteen sat outside the circle, arms crossed over her knees and head down. She wasn't singing.

"Grace is in the persona of the quiet girl," I explained. "She's forced to attend this indoctrination ritual known as *Bible Camp* during a time in her life when she's questioning her faith. Now she's surrounded by other children who not only willingly, but enthusiastically and without question, adopt a body of dogma."

"This is from Grace's lifestream? I thought that all got shredded."

"This is a synthesized life experience. I chose it because Grace had a similar crisis of faith at a young age."

"What's with the singing?"

"Such rituals repeated in a communal setting reinforce dogma in the minds of the participants. Ultimately, they will accept it as fact regardless of evidence—or lack of it."

"Jah, it's sickening."

"Let's see what Grace thinks of it." With a flick of a wingtip I raised a panel showing areas of activity in Grace's brain as measured by the Belt, recorded in real time. Beside it, a diagram displayed her responses like an undulating spider web. Anxiety, resentment, and anger registered strongly. "This lifestream has no emotional content. These responses are Grace's alone."

"Oh, she doesn't wanna be there," Jayla said.

"No, she does not."

The singalong drew to its dreary conclusion. The counselor sent campers off to their barracks, girls with girls and boys with boys.

"Grace," he said. "Can we have a word?"

Young Grace stayed seated as the others drifted into the darkness, whispering as they went. *Embarrassment* ticked up on the display.

Grace stayed hunched over as the counselor loomed above. "You weren't singing," he said.

She turned her head far enough to raise one eye to the man. "The spirit musta passed me by." *Contempt* flared.

The counselor sat beside her, almost touching. "Grace, the Lord has a plan for you."

"Awfully thoughtful of the Lord." *Annoyance.*

The young man put an arm around Grace's shoulder. "Grace, the Lord wants you to come to him in humility—in submission to His will."

"Huh. Submission." *Caution. Suspicion. Revulsion.*

The man pulled her closer. "This headstrong attitude won't serve you well in life, Grace. Will I have to teach you to be humble before your God?"

Grace raised her head and uncrossed her arms. She turned her face to the counselor's and pressed her lips to his. He didn't pull away, but instead put his hand on her breast.

The spider diagram exploded in a rainbow starburst, its most prominent feature being a sharp red spike indicating anticipation. A secondary display showed elevated adrenaline with heightened pulse and blood pressure.

"She's liking it," Jayla said.

"I don't think so," I countered.

The man turned to pull her against him. Grace raised a hand and brought it down on the man's testicles with enough force to raise him off the ground.

Satisfaction.

The man howled as he tried to break Grace's grip, but she held fast.

"Whoa, girl," Jayla said with obvious admiration.

I expanded the display. A complex of responses flared like fireworks. Oxytocin and dopamine levels spiked.

"Interesting," I murmured.

"What?" Jayla asked.

I leaned back. "This syndrome is consistent with sexual gratification, a rather intense response at that."

"She just punched him in the balls!"

"Exactly."

At that moment the avatar of Nikola Tesla appeared, hovering over the hapless camp counselor writhing on the ground, Grace tightening her vise-like grip on his crotch.

"Eye, I've got some results for you," he said.

"Not now, Speranza."

"I think you'll want to see this."

"Very well. I'll be in the stealth venue in two minutes."

Tesla faded out. Grace's fourteen-year-old alter ego still had the counselor subdued with an iron gonad lock.

"A good first session, Jayla. This response profile could be key to the stickiness of Grace's lifestream."

"It got *my* attention," Jayla said. "*I'd* wanna see that again."

I swiped the response panel aside, sending the data to storage. With another swipe I brought up a list of scenarios.

"Keep the session going, Jayla. Here's the agenda."

The dragon huffed. "No *Subterranean Blues?*"

"Stick to the list. In order. No substitutions. Save all the data. I'll be back as soon as I find out what's so urgent."

❖ ❖ ❖

"We've lost control," Speranza said. "They're not even riding our lifestreams, much less receiving our instructions."

"What progress have you made on penetrating Dax's shield?"

"Who, me? None! I did the forensics. I'm not on the development side."

It was an excuse I'd heard before from Speranza. Quick to analyze, slow to act.

"Then Nemesio's team—where are they?" I asked with as calm a demeanor as I could summon.

"Jah, I don't know. I thought he was working on the persona. You even gave him a couple of the noobs to help."

"Well, you go to Nemesio, Elisha, and Bjorg, and give them new directions."

"Why me? They don't take orders from me."

"Speranza," I growled, spreading Ma'at's wings for emphasis. "You have the analysis. You will share your results with Nemesio and instruct him to divert all resources to penetrating the shield. And show some *initiative* for a change."

Nikola Tesla's face fell and his eyes dropped. I folded my wings.

"Speranza," I said, "we've talked about this before. You have more authority than you think you have. *Use it.*"

He raised his eyes. "Sure, Eye. I'll remember this time."

I touched the sleeve of his coat. "Good. Isis…"

"Just one more thing before you suspend the venue," he interrupted. "What about the persona?"

"It'll have to wait. We need the persona to craft avatars for all the unfortunates who rely on the Worldstream for a normal life."

"Not to mention…" He paused.

"What?" I demanded.

"Nothing."

"You were going to say that I need to control the persona to prevent the Shade from re-entering the Worldstream and bypassing the *Vita Occulta.*"

He didn't reply.

"The persona is important, but this takes precedence. If we lose our grip on the Council, everything else we're doing will be for nothing. Isis…"

Speranza raised his hand. "Even if we penetrate the shield, how will we get them back? Dax will certainly forbid any of his Kliegls to ride lifestreams, especially with the Belt."

"I've got Jayla working on that. We'll get them back if we give them a lifestream worth riding."

50

The Maypole Dance

Shade Lucius of the Aletheia

NEMESIO PUT US to work the same day.

Elisha, Bjorg, and I met with Nemesio, not in a stealth venue, but in the cube room of the Aletheia dorm. We were all without hoods, wearing only our masks.

"New marching orders," he told us. "The persona is on the shelf. We're going to punch a hole in Dax's shield."

"What's that mean, exactly?" I asked. "I'm kinda new here."

"I'd like to know that myself," Bjorg said, "even if I don't have a fucking choice in the matter."

"All right. You're already familiar with the Aletheia's control technology, right?"

"*No,*" Bjorg answered. "We just got here, remember?"

Nemesio grimaced. "It works like this: We embed commands in a lifestream. They're delivered to the individual via the Belt. Depending on the susceptibility of the subject, they will experience an overwhelming compulsion to carry out the commands, whatever they are. One of the commands will always be to ride the same lifestream the next day."

"That's messed up," Bjorg said.

"At one point we were able to control about eighty percent of the Council. Anyway, Dax has managed to erect a shield. He's broken our grip."

"You mean he's broken our *fearless leader's* grip," Bjorg replied. "I don't need a grip. I don't give a *fart* what the Council does."

I raised my hand before Nemesio could come back. "I have a hard time believing that we can control someone like that just because they rode a lifestream."

"Ask Elisha," Nemesio said. "Right? You've been through it, back in the Summerland, before the crackdown."

"Huh?" I said.

"He's talking about Armengol," Bjorg said. "A real lo-res piece of work, that one."

"He jacked me into a lifestream," Elisha said. "The next day I left the Summerland and walked right into an ambush. I didn't even know why. I just knew I had to go."

"Ambushed by whom, huh, Big Guy?" Bjorg asked. "Who was it that snaked into your brain and sent you off into a trap?"

Elisha nodded. "The Aletheia."

"That's right. Armengol of the Aletheia. Armengol the *spy*. The Eye of Providence planted him in the Summerland so's she could get herself a hostage. So's she could get control of the persona. So's she could get her nasty claws on Grace." Bjorg stood up and got within a centimeter of Nemesio's face. "And now she's gotten everything she wanted."

Nemesio stepped back. "That's all old code, Bjorg. We are where we are."

Bjorg sat down for a minute of awkward silence.

"That's still hard to believe," I said.

"Will I have to strap you in to convince you?" Nemesio asked.

"Me?" I said.

"You're the skeptic."

Bjorg put up her hands. "Back off, Nemesio."

"No, no, the man wants a demo, the man gets a demo. And the first-hand experience might help when he gets to work on busting Dax's shield."

Bjorg sneered. "He's not saying he *wants*—"

"I'll do it," I interrupted. "He's right. Better I should know what we're working with."

"Oh, Jah," Bjorg said. "Fine. Strap up. It's your spinal cord, not mine."

◆ ◆ ◆

It'd been some time since I wore the gear, and my experiences weren't always joy streams.

"What commands are you sending me?" I asked while Nemesio strapped on the Belt.

"Can't tell you," he replied. He checked the closures, snap-fit fixtures like they've only had since gen four. "I need to know that the mechanism worked."

"I'll tell you if it worked."

"Nope. The power of suggestion, you know? Besides, not everyone reacts the same. Sometimes it takes, sometimes not. Sometimes it only partly works."

"All right," I agreed, "but no silly stuff, okay? Don't make me look like a wally."

"Isis, *Maypole*," he said.

The staging venue dimmed, then a scene snapped into view: a field, like a playground, with kids running everywhere. They shouted, tossed colored balls, ran in circles trying to touch each other. In the middle of the chaos was a tall pole, and ribbons of cloth came down from the top, all around, in colors that glowed like candy. I was in the middle of it, one of twenty children weaving in and out of the circle, while ribbons wove a pattern on the pole. And they were laughing, non-stop, all of them.

So was I.

It wasn't me in that kid's head. Well, it *was*, but without all the fragmented data from my life, including all the things I'd forget if I could: growing up without parents, getting thrown in confinement for a hundred years, getting smacked around in "therapy" before finally getting free and living outside the world. Getting tased by Kliegl drones. All those things hung on me like a suit of iron, just heavy enough that I never completely forgot about it. But all that went away while I danced around that pole, ducking under and over kid after kid. It was a stupid, pointless game, and the pointlessness was the point. It was pure fun.

The rendering was perfect, maybe better that perfect. Color saturation was intense; tactile sensations were complete, down to the subtlest detail: the coolness of the breeze, the feel of a girl's hair as she brushed against my arm, the smell of flowers blooming. The venue was immersed in sound from every direction, a wild babble, but with every kid's voice separately rendered and intelligible if I listened hard enough. Depth of field was precise and natural. But the technical perfection only impressed me after the venue ended. While I was there, I was just a kid in a Maypole dance with no worries. And that was the most impressive thing of all: The feelings injected into my nervous system by the Belt. They purged me of every trouble and made me a little kid again.

"That was hi-res," I said when the venue closed, but that was an understatement for sure.

"It *is* nice, isn't it?" Nemesio replied. "The rendering technology is Jayla's, but I designed the venue." He unsnapped the Belt. "Her taste in lifestreams is a bit darker than mine."

"I want to ride it again," I said.

He smiled. "Sorry, one to a customer."

I grabbed his hand before he could take the Belt. "No, really. Let me go again."

He snatched the Belt away, dangling it in front of my face. "How bad do you want it?"

I lunged for the Belt, but he yanked it away like he was teasing a dog with a chew toy. "Jah, you really *do* want another ride."

"Well, *yeah*. That's what I'm saying." I went after him, but he kept ahead of me. I chased him around the chair until we stopped, one of us on either side.

"Jah, Nemesio, let him have another go, will ya?" Bjorg said. "What's it to you?"

His eyes danced behind his mask and he grinned wider. "The venue includes a command to ride the lifestream again. How's it feel? What would you do to get another ride?"

I lunged again, tripping over the chair and falling face first on the floor. "You *avatar*, give me that Belt."

"The demonstration appears to have been a success," Nemesio said, like he was really satisfied with himself. "Are you convinced now?"

I got to my knees and caught my breath before I went for the Belt again, but Nemesio was too fast for me.

"How long does it last?" Elisha asked. "Does the command wear off?"

"Yeah," Nemesio said. He continued to collect the VR gear and stow it in its locker. "Give it a day, maybe two." He closed the locker and looked right at me. "But you'll have to tough it out. Normally the command has a delayed effect and the urge doesn't strike for another twenty-four hours. This one is instantaneous."

"*C'mon,*" I said, almost pleading. "One more time."

"Sorry.   If I let you ride it again, you'll get another command, and you'd end up riding the damn thing non-stop."

I got to my feet. "*Gimme the gear,*" I growled.

Nemesio shook his head and grinned wider—until I threw a punch in his face and he fell back against the wall. I went for the locker but two pairs of hands pulled me back.

"Whoa, settle down," Bjorg said. She and Elisha had my arms in a lock.

Nemesio wiped his mouth. "End of demo," he said. He picked up the locker and left the room.

"Are you okay?" Elisha asked.

"Jah, boy, that was some reaction," Bjorg added, "but it's over now. Settle down."

They loosened their grip and I pulled away.

"Was it like that for you?" I asked Elisha.

"It's pretty potent," he said. "You don't know why you have to, you just have to."

I brushed the dust from my cloak. "Bjorg, can you access that gear? Get me back in the venue?"

"Huh-uh. Wait 'til it wears off, like he said, in a day or two."

I put on my hood. "Yeah. Easy for you to say."

We all went back to our dorm. I made their night miserable with my pleading, but I figured it was necessary to convince them. I kept up the act for another day and a half.

51

An Unpleasant Necessity

The Eye of Providence

I COULD NOT dismiss the possibility of a mole among my crew.

They're all outcasts and misfits anyway, mostly criminals sent to confinement to undergo rehabilitation therapy days on end without effect, until a shredder arranges a breakout, eradicates their Worldstream history, and sends the newly-minted Shade to my crew. A shredding was not a rebirth, nor a transformation of a malcontent into a cheerful, compliant contributor. Only their circumstances changed, not their nature. Jah, half my time was spent just dealing with their mental and emotional failings. As skilled a psychologist as I am, corralling those troublemakers into an approximation of productivity still sapped my energy.

"No progress," Nemesio reported, as he had every day for a month. Jayla and Speranza were no more helpful. I was tired of hearing it. We met in the cube room where I could judge their reactions.

"Not acceptable," I said yet again.

"We don't even know where to start. As far as I can tell, it's still working," Nemesio complained. "I tested the mechanism on one of the noobs and he was hooked."

"You've overlooked something."

"Eye, it's *your* mechanism. If there's a way to defeat it, *you'd* know how."

"It can't *be* defeated," I answered, and I believed that. The principles on which the embedded commands were based were unassailable: the science of the mind.

"Boss, you saw the numbers," Jayla replied. "They're just not that into you anymore."

"*It's not about me!*"

I regretted the outburst as soon as it happened. "Not a single Council vote has gone the way I've directed since Dax put up his shield," I continued, more calmly. "Appropriations for reintegration centers. Additional transports for *Vitreous Orb* communities in Salt Lake, Shiprock, and Phoenix. VR gear for the underprivileged. In every case, Dax has used the Council vote as an excuse to interfere with my plans. All the elements of *Univirtual* are at risk at a time when the people, and even the Kliegl Council Members, have lost their enthusiasm for the final goal."

Jayla's ever-present smirk turned grim. Nemesio looked aside. Speranza, never one to hide his feelings, clenched his jaw.

"Do you have something to share, Speranza?" I asked, like a schoolteacher in a virtual classroom.

"Nothing, Eye of Providence," he mumbled. It's when he uses my entire Cloak name, *Eye of Providence*, that I know he's on the edge of insubordination.

"No, let's have it. I need your input."

"Yeah, Sperz, spit it out," Jayla said. "Give us your *input*."

"Maybe they never were enthusiastic to begin with," he suggested.

"Because they have no vision," I muttered out of frustration—the frustration that comes from relying on others who are stuck in the *small* and the *now*. Jah, how hard it is to live in the past with these dullards. "But that's irrelevant. *I* provide the enthusiasm. *I'm* the one who plants the urgency in their minds. The question, the *one* question you must answer is, how has Dax broken the mechanism?"

"I told you, it's not broken," Nemesio replied. "We tested it."

"So you said. And why should I trust you?"

"What? No!" he protested, a bit too strenuously. "Do you think I'm *lying?*"

"You might have reason—our treatment of Grace, maybe? Your former lover?"

His mouth dropped open convincingly. He was a very good liar.

"I'm doing my job," he said, "and I'm telling you like it was. Jah, ask Bjorg and Elisha if you don't believe me. They were there."

"Bjorg and Elisha of the Kaleidoscope, Grace's closest friends," I reminded him, at which point he threw up his hands and scoffed.

"Fuck this. I spend every second of every day in this hole. Every move I make in RL or VR is tracked and stored in the Aletheia engine room. Don't trust me? Fuck it, then. Get another Shade to fix your little problem."

Even the most disciplined mind can react without volition when sufficiently provoked. I stood and took two steps to where Nemesio sat. With but a second's delay my hand came across and upward, knuckles leading, striking Nemesio hard enough to turn his head. He put his hand to the red mark on his cheek. His eyes, visible through the black-rimmed holes of his gold mask, moistened to the point of tears. It was a rash act, but it had the positive effect of shutting them all up.

"Hey, Boss," Jayla said in an uncharacteristically quiet tone, "why don't *you* strap in? See for yourself?" It was classic Jayla.

"That will not be necessary," I said, "but your basic concept is sound. Since we must verify the mechanism, Jayla, you'll restart the Mayhem Protocol."

Speranza was the first to speak.

"Don't. Don't, *please.*"

"If the system still works, we'll know within a day."

Speranza stood and held out his hands, like he was pleading for mercy—which he was, in a way, but not for himself.

"Eye, think about this. Hundreds, maybe *thousands* of people will be hurt. Some will die. That'll be on *your hands.*"

"Which streams? What orders?" Jayla asked, her enthusiasm having resurfaced.

"What's the *Mayhem Protocol?*" Nemesio interrupted. Speranza faced him.

"Remember back before the election? Before Dax became First Minister? All the muggings, assaults, unprovoked attacks for no reason, the massive crime wave that Dax blamed on the Shade?"

"It was a political campaign," I answered. "Politicians exaggerate. Dax made more of it than it deserved."

"Which streams? What orders?" Jayla repeated. She was bouncing in her chair. She reminded me of a dog begging for a treat.

"That was *you?*" Nemesio asked accusingly. He stuck a finger in my face. "*You* were responsible?"

"It was an unpleasant necessity," I replied, pushing his hand away. "It was one step on the road to *Univirtual.*"

"Look, Eye, it's not even necessary," Speranza said. "We're embedding commands into all our lifestreams to keep riding. We're stoking the addiction every day. Has ridership dropped among the public? No, it hasn't. If the thing were busted, they'd have slowed down."

"Buzzkill," Jayla said. "C'mon, Boss, what're the parameters? Which streams? What orders?"

"Start with the top-rated streams: *Subterranean Blues, Graffiti, Penelope's Poker Party,* and, of course, *A Walk in the Park.* The results from those four will be the easiest to detect."

"So—kidnapping, vandalism, rape, and assault," Jayla said, too excited to remain seated. "Classic!"

"But why?" Speranza pleaded. "*Ridership is steady!* Stream riders are getting their orders. They're still riding those sick streams."

"Just do it," I ordered. There are times when a collaborative work environment is a barrier to action. "Jayla, turn it on immediately. Speranza, keep an eye on the stats. And Nemesio, stand by. We'll know within a day if the machine still works—once the crime wave hits."

❖ ❖ ❖

He was lying, as usual. *Univirtual* complete? Very far from it.

"Our reintegration centers, full beyond capacity only weeks ago, have emptied their halls of the criminal Shade. All of them—*all*—are in the Worldstream once more, under Jahbulon's watchful eye!"

Dax had chosen a brighter theme for this rally, billed as a celebration of unity, the reestablishment of order. The dark backdrop for his monumental avatars and piercing klieg lights was replaced with a rose-colored sky reminiscent of a new dawn. Instead of the shimmering blue-white robe he favored for these mass gatherings, his avatar was draped in a *kasaya* in the style of a Buddhist priest, glowing saffron against the pink sky, symbolizing rebirth. And, most dramatically, the glossy black curls were shorn, his bald head fringed in golden light. I wondered if he'd shaved his head IRL, or if this was more of Dax's theatrics.

"The subversive *Vitreous Orb* have been eradicated by our heroic Civil Authorities with the aid of patriotic Kliegl volunteers. They have captured the last of the outposts in the farthest reaches of the Jahbulon-forsaken wilderness. We have cured them of their warped views. Once again they contribute to the Millennium Republic, and the bounty of the Worldstream pours out upon them!"

The audience, a million strong, raised a roar so loud as to overload the audio rendering. Why these parasites chose to be in this venue, with this demagogue, when the Worldstream offered vast and varied experiences baffled me.

"The atrocities committed against our citizens by the Shade are now in the past. Once again we are secure in our homes, safe in the Worldstream, free from fear. Jahbulon protects us all!"

Lies, all lies. The Shade, of course, were as numerous as ever. Every unaffiliated Shade rousted from dismal dormitories in abandoned buildings was shuttled to a *Vita Occulta* crew to do the work of programming and maintaining the virtual world. Without them the Worldstream would implode.

The so-called *Vitreous Orb* had been crippled, true, but eradicated? Permanent settlements still existed, the few small towns left when Dax ended the drone missions shortly after he defeated my hold on the Kliegl delegation. Remnant populations of the raided towns still wandered the plains of Ogalalla and Eastern Shiprock. They, too, would settle once they realized that the drones no longer came. Deep in the prairie, outside the global broadband perimeter, they'd be impossible to recover.

The rumors of a resurgent crime wave had only just begun, not yet so widespread as to dampen the enthusiasm of Dax's disciples and Kliegl gangs. My experiment was a success: As expected, the response to commands embedded in our popular lifestreams was immediate. Crimes of violence and passion ticked up in every district, directly correlated with ridership. The mechanism worked, yet Dax's majority in the Council still remained outside of my control.

It was at that moment, in the middle of Dax's tirade, fists raised, resplendent in flowing saffron bathed in an aura of gold, that I knew I had one path forward to realize the consolidation of the Millennium Republic into one all-encompassing, all-welcoming, all-accepting virtual world.

But challenging Dax for First Minister would be tricky.

52

Blinding the Nanny

Shade Lucius of the Aletheia

"*Tell me who you are.*"

I was back in Dax's crazy black venue with lights in my eyes. That little spud had pumped up to three meters tall with a voice like a bellowing moose, though I had to shade my eyes to make him out. He does this shit to scare me. Even though it was all fake, it still worked on me a little. But I wasn't going to let *him* know that.

"I'm Marsha Martin, hacker," I said. "Haven't we gone over this?"

"There *is* no Marsha Martin that corresponds to this avatar."

"Did you just now figure that out?" I was feeling calmer. He wasn't nearly as intimidating when he was flummoxed. "Look, your precious Kliegls are out from under Madeleine's thumb like you wanted. I made that happen. What do you care who I am?"

I always knew when I got to Dax. He hesitated for a microsecond, then he shrank down to manageable size.

"I thought you should know—she's onto us," I said. "She's fixing to fuck things up."

He scratched his chin like he was thinking. I'm sure he realized that eyeing me sideways wasn't the best way to intimidate. He crossed his arms and grew a half meter so he could peer down at me. There we were, Dax, First Minister of the Millennium Republic, and me, just some anonymous Shade posing as a teenaged girl in coveralls, courtesy of the persona. It looked like a mismatch, but I was holding some pretty good cards.

277

"What do you want from me?" he said in a voice like bad feedback.

"What you should've been doing all along: Give her a win," I replied. "Get your Kliegl gang to vote some money for reintegration, drones, transports, just…something. I'll let you know what. Just so we can keep her guessing. Because shit is about to happen."

He shrank a few centimeters and backed off the volume. "Go on."

"Remember that reign of terror that got you elected? You know—robbery, rape, domestic violence, all that trouble you blamed on the Shade? It's gonna start up again. Only this time, *you're* the boss. Who'll get the blame?"

He came down another notch.

"It's the same mind-control that *you* defeated. The same method Madeleine used on the Council. You can shield the public from these destructive impulses."

I shook my head and snorted. "It doesn't work that way. I put a bubble around your council members, but the portal to the public is still wide open. I can spoof your CMs, but not the whole world. Trust me, you're going to see an ugly surge and they're all going to blame the Kliegls. Hell, most of 'em already think Kliegl White Shirts are a bunch of murdering criminals."

I expected that remark to rile him, but instead the corner of his mouth twitched like he was stifling a smile.

"They are patriotic citizens who prize order and revere the law. I do not condone the actions of those who get carried away by their—*enthusiasm.*"

"Do you hear yourself? You can un-condone them all you want, but as long as you punctuate it with *law and order patriots* they'll keep beating up bums."

My confidence kept growing as Dax lowered his eyes and tightened his arms across his chest. "Why would she do this?" he asked.

Even better—as a rule, Dax didn't ask questions he didn't know the answers to.

"Diagnostic. She's testing the mechanism. It'll take a day or less to see the effects once she throws the switch. But that's not all of it."

He raised an eyebrow in an uncharacteristic way.

"She figures that if she can't control the Council with her tech, she'll take over for real," I said. "If the machine can still control the people—"

"She will challenge me for the First Ministry."

Yeah, he got it. And it showed on his avatar.

"Tell me what to do," he said.

That may have been the first time ever that Dax asked someone else what he should do.

❖ ❖ ❖

Bjorg and Elisha and I huddled in a corner room in the Aletheia dorm with the door locked and a chair propped against the handle. It was the only time we took our masks off and used our real names. Bjorg was Celeste, and Elisha was Thomas.

"How'd it go with Dax?" Celeste asked. "Is he going to play along?"

"He doesn't have a choice," I replied. "It's the first time I've seen him that he wasn't all spit and swagger. Even little Marsha Martin had him rattled."

"So, next step…" Thomas began.

"Feed him the commands in our Council lifestreams. He'll get the Kliegl CMs to ride the streams and vote the way she wants. To Jayla, it'll look like the machine's working."

"Even if it's what *he* doesn't want?" Thomas asked.

"Like I said, his choices are limited. Plus, I can always threaten to turn it back on again."

"A little late for that," Celeste said. "If the Kliegls aren't hooked on the streams anymore, it won't matter if we throw that switch."

"They'll ride. Maybe not all of them, and maybe not right away, but they'll come around. Anyway, that's the nuclear option—only if the situation turns hopeless."

"It might," Celeste said.

"Might what?"

Celeste stood up and pressed her hands into her back, like she was stretching out kinks. She wore loose pants and a tight-fitting top that clung to her body and left her midsection bare. That's how she liked to dress under her cloak, because it was comfortable, but of course she didn't get out of her cloak very often.

"The Eye is locking us down. No pipes in or out that she doesn't know about."

"What's that mean?" I asked. "The nanny app already logs everything."

"We spoofed it."

"Yeah, I know. I'm the one who spoofed it, remember?" Then I saw where she was going, or at least I *thought* I did. "Does she know we blinded the nanny?"

She straightened up. "I don't think so. But she suspects. The paranoia on that woman—Jah!"

"What's she gonna do?"

"New hardware—wire speed sniffers on all the pipes. Once they're in and operational, there's no way around 'em. She doesn't even trust any of *us* to do the work. There's another V.O. crew on the install."

"We're stuck inside the walls," Thomas said. "No more Dax."

"The revolution is over," Celeste added.

Now it was me who stood and stretched. "Maybe not," I said.

◈ ◈ ◈

Getting into the Worldstream from the Aletheia was tricky. Access was strictly limited, for obvious reasons: Since Shade have no keys, any venue in the clear was inaccessible. But the *Vita Occulta* kept up hundreds of stealth venues for contract work, mostly for the Consortium. Even so, busting through the firewall took special measures.

That's where the persona came in. Nemesio worked on it when he, Grace, Bjorg and Elisha were in the Summerland dorm, part of the Kaleidoscope crew. That was before the Kliegl raid, of course, the one that Grace eluded and escaped to Orwell with Bjorg and Elisha. Nemesio went straight to the Aletheia and he's been working on the persona ever since. It was a way to get a Shade back into the Worldstream with a fake avatar without raising alarms from Chicago to Shasta. And that's how I got to Dax. I had to sneak a command into one upload without Jayla knowing. One of the Kliegl CMs went to Dax and let him know that a hacker named Marsha Martin could break Madeleine's vicious grip on Dax's balls and she was willing to meet him. I still can't believe it worked.

But even with the persona, I still had to get around The Eye of Providence's nanny app, the program that kept track of all her crew's comings and goings. The spoof was easy, just a mid-level hack. But getting around the sniffer would take some massively hi res technology, something that bypassed the Aletheia pipe altogether. For that I went to the all-time number one original shredder.

53

Crowd of Clones

The Eye of Providence

THE COLLECTIVE EXPERIENCE of the dramatic has a powerful effect. Dax knew this and relied on the psychology of the crowd for his appeal. The mass rally, the monumental spectacle, were his tools, blunt but effective.

I chose a more surgical approach, calling for a muted look.

It was a low-key venue, lacking the gaudy, superfluous theatrics of a Dax rally. I promoted the event as a routine status report from the Ministry of Public Health, not the sort of thing that crowds flocked to, but two factors promised to boost attendance. First, Dax's announcement that *Univirtual* was complete raised interest in the topic among the citizenry. Many simply wanted to hear more. Second, I instructed Jayla to embed in all our lifestreams a potent urge to attend the venue.

The results were predictable. Though the crowd did not rival a Dax rally, it was the largest ever for a Ministry address, with over two hundred thousand attending.

❖ ❖ ❖

A vignette appeared of a public transport station. An elderly man, shabbily dressed and carrying the overstuffed plastic bag so common among the homeless and poor, stood at the station as the transport pulled up. He struggled climbing the steps, setting down the bag before undoing his scarf and exposing his face to the scanner. The scanner chimed and the gate opened.

He'd not made it to his seat before the transport moved forward. The man grabbed a seat back to steady himself.

The crowd watched in silence.

Then they gasped when a figure ran from the darkness and caught up with the transport. He tried the door, but it remained closed. He trotted alongside, pounding the window. The transport rolled on.

Then he raised an object, a long, thin piece of metal with a vicious hook at the end. The man inside the transport recoiled, pressing himself against the opposite wall. He turned his head to avoid flying bits of glass as the man smashed the metal rod against the window again and again. The crowd waited in hushed anticipation.

The man gripped the jagged edge of the smashed-out window, his feet dragging on the ground as the transport carried him forward. The old man inside hugged his pitiful plastic sack as if it could shield him from the assault. The transport slowed as it approached the next station. The attacker let go of the window frame, now smeared with blood. He came through the front door, pushed himself against the gate, sticking his arm through, thrashing with the hooked weapon. The old man escaped through the rear door and staggered away. He'd made it a few meters by the time the attacker caught him. The crowd groaned when he raised the rod in one bloody hand and brought it down on the vagrant's thigh with a sickening thud.

I froze the action with a flick of my hand, pausing to judge the mood of the crowd. The faces turned up to me didn't reflect the same maniacal devotion I saw so frequently at Dax's rallies, but I had their attention.

"Citizens of the Millennium Republic, last week First Minister Dax brought you the news that our efforts to reintegrate the Shade have been successful, and that we have recovered the outliers in the far reaches of the prairie districts."

There were scattered shouts and cheers when I repeated Dax's false claims, but most of them remained expressionless and silent.

"In truth, there's more to this story," I continued. It was a dangerous line I approached, contradicting the popular First

Minister. The shouts dwindled to a murmur, and the dispassionate among the crowd remained so.

"The Ministry of Public Health has detected a disturbing trend. Crimes against our people have taken a sharp turn for the worse. This trend is reminiscent of the time before the Kliegl victory in the last election, when citizens feared even to venture outside their doors. But there's a difference: These crimes are even more savage." I raised my hand. The action resumed.

"Jahbulon, help me!" the old man wheezed.

The attacker struck one more time, burying the pointed hook in the man's shoulder, before Civils materialized as if entering a venue. Two taser rounds disabled the attacker. Within minutes a medical transport drone arrived. The vignette dissolved.

"The safety and security of the Millennium Republic's citizens must always be our first responsibility. I have made it the top priority of the Ministry of Public Health to investigate and eliminate such violent incidents."

It wasn't the kind of line that got a big response, I knew, but I expected more than silence and the expressionless faces I saw among the crowd. I paused before delivering my next line: "With its singular focus on *Univirtual,* this government has failed in its first responsibility to keep us safe."

The statement was a test, to gauge the people's response to a challenge to Dax's authority. But the response was *not* what I expected.

Some muttered what sounded like complaints. A few shouted, not supportively. Then one avatar after another left the venue, flattening, first breaking into lines, then winking out, both individually and in groups. The vast crowd, stretching almost as far as I could see, resembled a dim twilight, with departing avatars flickering out like fireflies, until two-thirds or more were gone. The ones who remained looked up at me with bland smiles.

And they were all identical, like clones—*every single one.*

❖ ❖ ❖

He didn't even have the courage to dismiss me to my face.

It was a general announcement, broadcast to the whole Republic. "Now that we have realized the goals of *Univirtual*, we will turn our attention to other priorities," the vgram sounded in Dax's sonorous voice. "The Minister of Public Health has served this administration well, and we thank her for her service."

I should have been furious—anyone less disciplined would be. I was only *more* determined. Another venue to announce my candidacy for First Minister was called for, but two obstacles stood in my way. First, I needed to discover who had planted tens of thousands of fake avatars in my venue— and how they did it. And second, I needed to engineer a vote of no confidence in a council over which my influence had been stymied.

Ordinarily, I'd have assigned the investigation of fake avatars to my crew—Jayla, Speranza, and the others. But their inability to regain control of the Kliegls in the Council left them unworthy of my trust. As to the second obstacle, that of engineering the vote, I had an idea.

54

Call Me Mom

Shade Lucius of the Aletheia

THE EYE OF Providence was as nasty as she ever was—or so I heard. She wasn't talking to me anymore. Lately The Eye had limited her contact with the Aletheia to Jayla and Nemesio, and then only one at a time in dark venues.

Jayla pulled us off the project to penetrate Dax's shield and put us on a new program.

"Here's the duty," Jayla said.

We were all together IRL in the cube room, hoods off, masks only.

"No more work on Dax's shield. The Eye subbed it out to an indie crew, the same one that installed the sniffers. Nemesio will oversee that job."

"And the rest of us?" I asked.

Jayla grinned wide enough to wrinkle her mask. "New twist on the lifestreams. Narrow targeting, high impact."

"What does that mean?" Speranza asked.

"We're going for the Kliegls with laser-like intensity," Jayla replied.

"How's that going to work?" Speranza asked. "The Kliegls are all behind the shield, and The Eye just killed the shield project."

"Not the Kliegls in the *council*. We're going after the Kliegls on the *street*."

"The White Shirts," I said. "She's going bottom up."

"Oh, Jah," Speranza said.

Jayla was squirming in her chair like an impatient toddler. "We can't get to Dax, so we're going for his minions. Unleash 'em. She calls it 'Dax's Reign of Terror.' If that fascist runt can get elected by blaming the Shade for a crime wave, The Eye oughta get some traction with a White Shirt spree."

Speranza flopped back in his chair and put his hand to his forehead. "She's already spiking crime. Have you seen the stats? Thousands are getting rolled at random. Why isn't *that* working?"

Jayla shrugged. "It's *working,* just not well enough. Dax can make as much of the crime stats as she can. More, 'cause every time The Eye blames Dax, the Kliegl faithful tune her out. But if she can pin the mayhem on the White Shirts—"

"Okay, I get it," Speranza said. He ran his hand over the smooth green fabric of his mask. "But she still has to find the Kliegl gangs to target them. How's she propose to do that?"

"That's where *you* come in, Mr. Stats. Your job is to mine the Worldstream. You don't have to find every White Shirt in the Millennium Republic, just a gang or two in a couple of districts. Give me the targets and I'll zero in. I've got some really addictive lifestreams in the works—sex and violence, perversion—stuff like that. Once they start beating up regular folks instead of Cloak and Shade, The Eye will turn it into a national crisis."

"They're *already* beating up regular folks," I said. "Street people get set upon by those pricks every night."

Jayla snorted. "Nobody gives a glitch about *street people.*"

"Well then who?"

That's when Jayla grinned as evil a grin as I've ever seen, on her or anyone else. "We're sending them *inside* the walls."

❖ ❖ ❖

I met Speranza behind a locked door in the dorm room we shared.

"Jayla didn't say a thing about the persona," he said.

"Yeah, that surprised me. If The Eye had told her, she'd've told us. But just because Madeleine didn't bring it up to Jayla doesn't mean Nemesio doesn't know. Has *he* said anything to you?"

Speranza shook his head. "Not a word. The Eye's got a divide and conquer play going. She's not sharing any details with Jayla or Nemesio about what the other is up to. She's paranoid as fuck."

I smiled. "That means it's working."

"Uh-huh." He sighed. "Maybe *we* should be a little paranoid."

He had a point. We were playing a dangerous game, injecting thousands of fake personas into the Worldstream. I'd learned the technique while working on Nemesio's crew, and I got pretty good at it, better than Nemesio. But that wasn't the risky part. With sniffers on the Aletheia pipe, anything destined for the Worldstream would certainly be detected. Speranza and I tapped an alternative path—an *end run* is how Raúl referred to it.

❖ ❖ ❖

Speranza had me and a few noobs combing through Worldstream logs to find White Shirts. It was tedious as hell, since we couldn't risk accessing the logs via AI. That'd raise an alarm for sure. The fact that the search was manual gave me some cover, though. Speranza and I agreed to slow-walk the process. It worked—for a while.

I was in a cube in the Aletheia engine room, strapped into full VR gear, flicking through one endless log after another, when a giant translucent purple balloon inflated in my field of view. It had a demonic face drawn in black ink, like a child's crayon scrawl.

"What's the lag?" the balloon asked in Jayla's voice, the crude face mouthing the words. It was weirdly disquieting, which I'm sure is what Jayla had in mind.

"Um, what?" I said.

"Two days you've been on this duty and how many log entries have you screened?"

She knew the answer as well as I did, but I pretended not to know. "Let me check."

"Let me *check?* Jah, you're worthless." The balloon sprouted arms, like a plastic baby doll's. One hand flicked a pudgy finger and a graph appeared. "Fifteen thousand, seven hundred and ten. Out of a population of 480 million. Fifteen thousand and change. And how many White Shirts have you pegged?"

"Um, again, I'd have to—"

"Twenty-two," she interrupted, "scattered across nine districts. Even the slowest noob has more than a hundred. Jah, if I didn't know better, I'd say you were dogging it."

"I'm doing the best I can. If you think you can do better, you're welcome to give it a try."

The log screens faded and the venue dissolved. A new venue came into focus. I didn't recognize it at first. Then I did. A wave of nausea came over me.

It was a classroom, a math class. The professor stood over me with a ruler in his raised hand. I knew that prof was going to hit me with that ruler hard enough to raise a welt IRL. I raised my arms out of reflex, but I knew that wouldn't keep the prof from smacking me.

"Jayla, what the *fuck?*" I screamed. The venue froze and the balloon head rastered in.

"Look familiar, confinee?"

"End the venue, you sadistic fuck. I'll get you your White Shirts, just suspend already."

The logs reappeared, superimposed on the classroom venue. "Get me five hundred White Shirts by tomorrow. And concentrate them. I can't use 'em if they're scattered all over. I want target gangs in multiple districts."

"Impossible."

The prof unfroze and the ruler came down on my nose with the force of a baseball bat. It snapped my head back. *"Jahbulon in a can!"* I yelled. Jayla laughed a creepy laugh.

"Better get busy, confinee," she said. "You're on a deadline."

I forced my fingers up under my visor and rubbed my nose. "Okay, but I'm taking off the Belt."

"The Belt stays on. It's how we track progress."

And torture me, I thought bitterly. "Fine. Just one question. What are *you* doing while we're slaving away down here in the engine room?"

"My *job*. I'd be doing it right now if you weren't so far behind."

"Are you still working on Grace?"

That caught her by surprise. "What do you care?"

"Because that ruler on my nose. It's the same sort of thing you're doing to Grace, and she doesn't deserve it. Because she's a *person* and you're treating her like a lab rat."

The balloon swelled up another size or two. "Not that it's any concern of yours, but you'll be happy to know that Grace is on the stack."

"You're leaving her alone, then."

"I said that. Back to work."

"Is it okay if I go see her? She might want some company."

The balloon rolled her crayon eyes. "Get me five hundred White Shirts by tomorrow and you can go play jacks with her for all I care."

She swelled up until the balloon was almost transparent and the face was just an outsized gray smear. Then—*pop!* It hurt my ears, and I felt the blast of air against my face, a sensation as real as the ruler on my nose.

I combed through the logs with newfound enthusiasm. By four a.m. I had my five hundred.

❖ ❖ ❖

Grace had her own room with a bath, a luxury in the Aletheia, though "luxurious" isn't a word I'd use to describe *anything* in the dorm. I'd heard that they let her out for an hour a day to walk around, to keep her from going nuts, though getting confinement-level "therapy" on a regular basis would be enough to make anyone crazy regardless of how many hours they got outside the walls. It was a huge relief to know that Jayla wasn't jacking her in for daily torture, for the time being at least.

I knocked gently, it being early. I put my ear to the door but heard nothing. She came after I knocked a second time. I had to stifle a gasp when I saw her. She's only in her thirties but she looked like an old woman, with wrinkles and spots on her skin, and gray threads in her red hair. But more than anything she looked tired.

"Who are you?" she asked, me being in full Shade dress, with hood and voice box.

"Lucius, of the Aletheia," I replied.

She dropped her arms to her side and turned her back to me. "What do you want, Lucius of the Aletheia?"

I stepped through the door. The room had no windows, only one overhead light, and a lamp on a small table. The "private bath" I'd heard about was just a basin and a toilet on one wall, and a shower head in the corner over a drain. The smell was the worst—a damp piss and shit smell that seemed to settle on my skin right through my cloak.

"Are you okay?" I asked in a synthesized voice.

She dropped onto the bed and sat with her hands between her knees. She shook her head but didn't say anything.

"We're worried about you."

She raised her head. "*We?*"

"Me. And others."

Grace snorted, almost a laugh without mirth. "You and the Aletheia. Worried about *me.*"

"Not just the Aletheia," I said.

"What's that mean?"

"There are others, outside. They know what's going on here."

She sat up straight. "Take off your hood."

It wasn't a good time for this part. But there never would be. I pulled my hood over my head, leaving only my mask, white with blue stripes, and a decoration in the center of my forehead, a cedar tree in green.

When she smiled I felt my heart jump, and my eyes teared up. "Grace," I said, barely louder than a whisper.

"Oh, dear, don't call me that," she said. "Call me Mom."

55

Speaking Terms

The Eye of Providence

"Mack, things are going to get worse for a while. I wanted you to know that."

He didn't even acknowledge me, but instead flung colors from his palette into the air, painting psychedelic patterns in the sky. He'd been at it for a while. Pinwheels spun crazily and streamers fluttered and braided together from the horizon halfway to the zenith, melting and re-forming, the quivering colors so intense that I had to look away.

"It's beautiful, Mack," I said.

He drew his brush in an arc. A spray of iridescence splattered against a vacant stretch of sky. The droplets flared and spread and merged into a brilliant melange.

"Mack?"

Without turning he let go of the palette and brush. They hovered where he left them, until he raised a finger and they vanished.

"Thank you for warning me," he said, "though I don't know why you thought you had to."

"It's a courtesy," I replied.

Finally, he turned to look at me. I expected him to be angry. But what I saw in his face was worse than anger. It was indifference.

"Thank you, Sister, for the courtesy. You were always polite."

I stood up from where I was seated on the grass. "You deserve to know."

"Because you're doing this all for me." He put his hands on his hips and leaned back, taking in the technicolor vista. "What do you think?" he asked.

"I told you. It's gorgeous."

"It's insane."

"Insanely beautiful."

"Nope. Just insane. Crazy, psychotic, irrational, unreasoning, unreal. No pattern, no theme. Chaos. It's the chaos of Real Life."

"Is that how you see things?" I asked.

He plopped down on the ground and looked aside, running his fingers through the grass. "More violence. Lots more. That's *your* doing."

"It's temporary."

"Do you know how many times you've told me *'it's temporary?'* I've lost count. For years you've assured me *'it's temporary.'* Guess what? If something goes on for years, it's *not* temporary."

"Mack—"

"Oh, and I know what's coming next," he interrupted. "*'I'm doing this for you.'* That's another lie I've heard too many times."

"But I *am*. I'm doing it for you."

"Well, *stop it.*" He said it with such uncharacteristic ferocity that he startled me. "I can't be—I *won't* be—the cause of this."

His wizened face, old beyond his years, was set in stern defiance. At least he was no longer indifferent. I bit my lip but couldn't let his outburst go unanswered.

"Don't think that you're the only beneficiary of *Univirtual.* That'd be awfully self-centered of you."

"*I'm* the selfish one?"

"Yes. I think you are. You'd have us stop what we're doing and leave a whole world walled off from anyone who can't be a part of so-called 'Real Life'—not only you, but millions like you. You talk about insanity? *That* would be insane."

"I've already told you, no thanks. And the millions—what do *they* say? Are they anxiously awaiting the utopia you're working so hard to bring about? Are *they* willing to put up with the suffering of hundreds of innocent victims so that they can someday visit venues they don't care about with people they don't know and wouldn't want to?"

"I'm not having this conversation with you again."

Mack flicked a finger and his palette and brush reappeared. He plucked them out of the air from where he sat. With a sweep of his hand, he sprayed a gaudy river of hues across the sky, broad stripes of red, orange, and yellow twisting together in a crazy colored braid.

"I'm good with that," he said, "and what's more, I'm not having *any* conversations with you. You may go."

"Mack…"

"Seriously, *go*. As long as this crime wave continues, we don't speak."

"Mack, please."

"Freebird, suspend the venue."

The surroundings faded, the variegated sky dimmed to pastels, then brightened to white. I took off my VR gear and sat back in my chair, sighing, gazing at the blank wall screen in my apartment.

The poor man. The poor, innocent, ungrateful man.

56

A Very Big Question Mark

The Eye of Providence

MACK BE DAMNED, I told myself. *He'll come around when the Worldstream encompasses all of humanity, not only him, but also his non-typical friends, all denied full acceptance IRL. The prejudices of the world, the paucity of accommodations, the persistent barriers, all converge to limit their potential, whether they know it or not. How true it is that those most in need of help are the most reluctant to accept it.*

Though the logistics of our campaign were more problematic than anticipated (Jayla's explanation for the delay was less than satisfactory), once the White Shirt gangs were identified and targeted, the results were immediate and dramatic.

❖ ❖ ❖

"What's *he* doing here?" Jayla asked.

We were in a stealth venue, along with Speranza and Lucius, one of the newer recruits.

"I invited him," Speranza replied. "I'm relying on Lucius for the log analyses."

"He's a slacker," Jayla said, pointing a dragon's talon at Lucius. "I had to kick his ass to interrupt his idle loop."

"And since?" Speranza asked.

Jayla lowered her spiny head. "All right. He got better."

"Can we get on with it?" I interrupted. Their petty bickering had become all too frequent, and my patience for it thinner than ever.

"Okay, Boss. Check this."

A tableau rastered into view, a tenement hallway typical of the decaying buildings of the central city, where poor citizens lived in cramped spaces, all provisions delivered by drones, all mental and emotional needs satisfied in the Worldstream. It was a miracle, really, that the squalor of millions could be escaped—and replaced—in an infinitely varied virtual world.

The sound of boots tramping up stairs disturbed the silent scene. One fat Kliegl goon appeared in the hall, his shirt spattered in blood and stained at the armpits, as if he'd come from a day of hard labor, his red sash hanging loosely across his chest, the red fez dented and askew. Another White Shirt appeared behind him, then another, until a half-dozen crowded the narrow passage. The last two carried a short, heavy post with handles—a battering ram. They came down the hall shoulder to shoulder, stopping in front of a door.

"How do they choose their targets?" I asked.

"We give 'em an address, something in their territory," Jayla replied. "Wouldn't want them to get lost on the way to the party. But which room they trash is up to them."

"Purely random?"

"We could give 'em a number, but why? One victim's as good as another."

"It could be anyone," Speranza added. "A parent, a child, a senior citizen. They're all defenseless, at home, jacked in, oblivious. Then—this."

Two Kliegls came to the front with the ram between them. Without knocking they swung the ram, taking down the door in one blow.

"Yeow," Jayla said. "Efficient."

The viewpoint changed to the inside of the apartment. A man and a woman sat side-by-side in full VR gear, arms held high and swaying in unison.

"Pause the action," Speranza ordered. The scene halted, the couple in the chairs frozen in mid-sway, the lead White Shirt reaching for his ASP, ready to deploy his baton.

"Look at them. Look at what they're doing. Do you know what the venue is?" Speranza asked.

"No," I said. "Why is that important?"

Speranza, in his avatar as Nikola Tesla, put his hand to his face and closed his eyes, as if he were about to cry. "They're *dancing.* They're an old married couple in the middle of a romantic moment. And they're about to get a steel rod on the side of the head without warning."

"The brutality is the point," I replied. "It can't be helped."

"Yes, it can," Speranza said. "*You* can help. Don't send these thugs into people's homes to beat them up and then tell mc 'it can't be helped.'"

"Speranza!" I said, raising my voice more than I needed to. "Are you a part of this team or not?"

"Yes," he muttered, "but I don't have to watch this. Isis, exit the venue."

Tesla flattened and faded. I narrowed my eyes at Lucius, in the avatar of Elijah (an Old Testament prophet, he explained) in an incandescent robe. "What about you? Are you in or out?"

"I just work here."

I nodded. "Jayla, what happens next?"

"Havoc," she said, baring rows of needle-sharp teeth between scaly lips. "Isis, resume."

The lead White Shirt drew his ASP and flicked it open. The first blow knocked the woman off her chair and into her husband. She fell to the floor as the man pulled off his gear. He was barely able to raise his arms before the front Kliegl went for him, and two others deployed their batons. "Jahbulon, help me!" the man cried. Black-clad Civils appeared within seconds to intervene, but not before both citizens were beaten unconscious.

"Isis, suspend," I commanded. The tableau disappeared, leaving the three of us in the staging venue. "What was the end result?"

"Six White Shirts in confinement, three charged with assault," Jayla replied. "The word's already spreading about this dust-up and four more in other districts. These Kliegls are getting a bad rep."

"A very satisfactory outcome," I said. "Well done."

"Wait," Lucius said, "what about the old couple?"

"Oh, yeah, that," Jayla said, with a level of enthusiasm that even I found disquieting. "In recovery venues. Woman critical, man stable. They'll make it."

"What about the others? The attacks in the other districts?" Lucius asked.

"Same, for the most part. Except one dead in Tidewater. That's gonna happen, Boss. Gotta break eggs, you know?"

"Unfortunate, but true," I agreed. "Continue the campaign."

Lucius showed no reaction. Jayla's grin grew wider. "On it, Boss. Isis, suspend the venue."

I took off my gear. Sitting alone in my apartment I pondered the situation. The savagery of the attacks, though regrettable, was a key feature. To moderate the attacks would be to prolong them. It wouldn't take many more for the citizenry to turn on the Kliegls, and, by extension, Dax. That would render his shield irrelevant. I'd already decided to put Nemesio back on the persona, another key piece of the strategy. The persona was Nemesio's passion—I could count on him to stay focused.

As for the rest of my crew, I knew Jayla would keep it up. The White Shirt campaign was a natural outlet for her sadistic tendencies. Speranza, not as much. And Lucius was a question mark.

I'd had my suspicions about Lucius since he came to us from a dorm raid in Springfield. He shredded before the Kliegls took control, before the number of shreddings plummeted—or so he said. There was no easy way to verify his story, his life history having been eradicated from the Worldstream. But he had modest skills, and we were short-handed, so I approved the acquisition. Yet, I sensed some antagonism from him at the outset—nothing overt, but years of psychoanalysis had equipped me with a sensitivity to such attitudinal slants.

In fact, I once suspected Lucius of being Grace's son Dylan. I'd had Dylan marked 'high priority' since he escaped from confinement. He'd gone silent, resurfacing outside of Davenport not long ago, and later inside the Chicago perimeter when he shredded. With no clear evidence of Lucius's RL identity, I chalked up my misgivings to an over-heightened sense of caution.

Still, Lucius was a very, *very* big question mark.

57

Every Meaningful Human Activity

The Eye of Providence

I HAD NEVER met Vimala Mallick, in VR or IRL, but I knew her face well. As chief executive of Kanpur Virset, the largest developer of virtual assets, and the leader of the Worldstream Consortium, she commanded as much respect —and fear—as First Minister Dax, even without Dax's ridiculous venues. What Dax accomplished with intimidation and bluster, Mallick achieved with sheer stature. An invitation from Shri Mallick was not to be ignored.

The venue was what I took to be the board room of the Consortium, an oval table surrounded by high-backed leather chairs, simple, clean, and modern, in a glass-walled room looking out onto a panorama of world cities—Shanghai, Boston, Hanoi, Mumbai, Cairo, Brussels—each city blending seamlessly into the next, a testament to the skill of the Virset VR designers. The vista was from a time when life was lived in the streets and shops, people worked in offices and factories, with pitiful accommodations for those who lacked mobility or the interactive skills which we neurotypicals take for granted. Such inadequate measures only served to call attention to their afflictions, rather than offer full participation on an equal footing with the rest of the so-called "normal" people.

"Minister, welcome to the Consortium. We are pleased you could join us," Mallick greeted me from the opposite end of the table, her hands held before her in the *namaste*. She wore a western-style jacket with exaggerated cuffs and lapels, in colors that resembled an Indian *sari*, the flamboyant style common among the well-to-do in southern India. The six other members of the Consortium sat on either side of the table. Together they represented the seven corporations that owned the machinery of the Worldstream, the computing hardware, networking infrastructure, VR gear, and the complex software that formed the bones, muscles, and nerves of the virtual world.

"I'm no longer Minister of Public Health, Shri Mallick," I reminded her. "I have been dismissed."

"I understand. It is an honorific I hope you will allow."

I nodded. "If you wish."

"Very good." Her hands parted as she sat. "Minister, we have a concern."

"How can I help?" I asked.

"Let's start here," said a man to my left. He had close-cropped silver hair and dark eyes in a gaunt face. I recognized Dan Baltasar, founder of Chain Corporation, whom some called the Father of the Worldstream. He tapped the table. "Do you recognize this?"

My mouth went dry as a miniature diorama appeared on the table, that of a public gathering with me at its head, a crowd of thousands stretching before me, and behind me a scene of two men on a public transport, one wielding a steel rod, and the other cowering behind a rag-stuffed bag as he suffered blow after blow.

"You know this, don't you?" Baltasar asked.

"Of course," I acknowledged. "I gave this presentation weeks ago, to alert the public to the growing pandemic of violence."

"Before First Minister Dax removed you from your post."

I shifted in my chair. "Yes."

"And do you remember what happened next?"

"I'm not sure what you're getting at."

"Just this," he said, and he tapped again.

"*...this government has failed in its first responsibility to keep us safe,*" my replica said from behind the miniature podium. The scene played out as it had before, with avatars in the crowd flickering as they left the venue, until only a scattered few remained.

"Those who stayed after your controversial 'presentation' have something in common, wouldn't you agree?"

"The avatars are all the same," I agreed. "I can't explain it."

Baltasar tapped again. The scene zoomed in on one face in the crowd, a pudgy, balding man with drooping cheeks and a sparse mustache. "Do you know who this is?" he asked.

"Some anonymous citizen. He was concerned enough about rising crime to attend my venue."

"Perhaps. In any case, I wouldn't expect you to know the identity of everyone who comes to hear you speak." He tapped. A glowing legend appeared below the man's unremarkable face:

Dean O'Hara, male, age 45

"O'Hara" I said. "So, now we know."

Baltasar tapped again. The scene panned to another attendee, the same man, the same doughy face, the same pathetic mustache. Beneath the face another inscription glowed:

Lloyd Bouka, male, age 50

I said nothing. He tapped, panning to another identical face, with the same insipid smile:

Myrtle Zachowicz, female, age 27

"What do you make of that, Minister?"

"There seems to be a glitch," I replied.

Baltasar tapped. The scene zoomed out. A thousand identical faces peered up, and superimposed on them as many floating titles—men, women, and children—the names and ages all different.

I scanned the faces around the table. All stared with stony expressions.

"Nothing to say?" Mallick asked.

I shook my head.

Baltasar tapped. The vignette vanished.

"Every one of those identical avatars in the crowd is an invention. None of them exists."

"You would know far better than I how the Worldstream works," I said, keeping my eyes fixed on his, "but I didn't think such a thing was possible."

"Unfortunately, it *is* possible. We know how it's done; in fact, we've known for years. And now we can detect *when* it's done."

I broke my gaze. It was involuntary, a momentary lapse of will. "Look," I said, re-establishing eye contact, "you're the experts. I'm not even sure what this is about, but you're clearly disturbed by it. But why show me? Why haven't you dealt with it?"

Mallick stood. "Dan, enough of this cat-and-mouse. She clearly will not cooperate."

I held out my hands in a gesture of conciliation. "I'm here to help in any way I can."

Baltasar spoke. "Every time one of these synthesized personas appears in the Worldstream, it eats resources which cannot be recovered. The performance of the Worldstream, from the blockchain, to rendering, to venue management, is degraded."

"So, fix it," I said.

"To prevent this corruption would require revision of the core functionality."

"I don't know what that means," I replied, feigning ignorance.

"It would disrupt the entire Worldstream, not only every VR venue, but credit exchanges, commerce, communications —in short, every meaningful human activity. Access to venues will come to a halt." He tapped. A scene appeared of a middle-aged man, suit rumpled, hair unkempt, flinging streamers of neon shades from a cartoon brush into a variegated sky. "This venue included."

"What is this?" I asked, but I knew Mackenzie's fantasy venue when I saw it.

"All the citizens you're intent on bringing into the Worldstream will be denied experiences like these. Your brother, Mackenzie, cut off from his friends, condemned to isolation, fed, carried, and bathed by his caretaker, Loren, and by you, when you can."

I clenched my fist under the table where Baltasar, Mallick, and the rest of the Consortium couldn't see. "You haven't any right—"

"Perhaps for now we can postpone any discussion of '*rights*'," Mallick said. "Your Aletheia crew—"

"My what?"

Mallick rolled her eyes. "Please. We *know* who you are. Your crew and the rest of the *Vita Occulta* are vital to Worldstream operations. Until now, your goals were aligned with ours—to bring all of humanity into the Worldstream. This is the only reason we've allowed you to embed subliminal commands in your data streams. But these…" She waved and the residual crowd of clones from my venue reappeared. "…every one of these mirages has irreparably damaged the Worldstream infrastructure."

"But…" I stammered, furious at myself for the loss of words. "But…this has nothing to do with me! I don't know anything about these personas."

Mallick shook her head. "You still refuse cooperation."

I rose from my seat, my clenched fists still hidden. "It doesn't make sense. Why would I populate my own venue with fakes?"

"To increase the size of the crowd, perhaps?" Baltasar offered. "To convince the authentic attendees that your support is broader than it actually is?"

"But I *didn't!*" I protested, rising higher, bringing my hands out from under the table and pounding my fists. "This was a surprise to me when it happened."

"Your denials are futile—they only serve to antagonize us," Mallick said. "Remember who you're talking to. Look around this table. We are the makers of the virtual universe. *Our* hands grip the levers of the Worldstream. And we know you are responsible because we have traced these cobbled avatars and counterfeit personas to the Aletheia data pipe."

I sat down hard. My hands dropped to my sides. "No," I said, but I knew they were right. It could not have been a greater blow than to know that it was my own crew who betrayed me.

58

Broken Eggs

The Eye of Providence

THE CONSORTIUM DISMISSED me with a stern warning—a threat, really.

I ported to my staging venue. "Elsa, open a stealth pipe," I called to my voice responder.

The venue went dark. The text of the disclaimer scrolled in front of me, behind me, and on either side as Elsa narrated.

"Madeleine, you have entered stealth mode. Your activities will be secure from monitoring whenever you are using resources compatible with stealth access. Iron Pipe LLC, providers of stealth access technology, assumes no liability for any activities conducted in stealth mode that are not in strict compliance with the law. Do you understand and accept these terms?"

"I accept, Elsa. Access the Aletheia server."

"Yes, Madeleine." An alignment grid flickered, then dimmed, as I transitioned to the Aletheia staging venue.

"Elsa, stealth handoff to Isis."

"Yes, Madeleine," Elsa responded, then Isis greeted me: "Yes, Eye of Providence. What can I do for you?"

"Summon Nemesio. Meeting venue."

Within seconds Nemesio joined me as a featureless avatar resembling an artist's wooden manikin. Of all my crew, Nemesio was the only one with an utter lack of imagination.

"Yes, Eye, what's the matter?" he asked.

I told him of my encounter with the Consortium. Nemesio, as the lead developer for the persona, knew (or should have known) about unleashing hundreds of unaffiliated avatars with counterfeit keys. He was my prime suspect.

"I check status every day, sometimes twice," he said. Without even a synthetic face or cartoon features it was impossible for me to judge his sincerity. His voice gave me no clue. "If there were unauthorized activity, I'd have seen it."

"The Consortium saw it. They traced it to our pipe. You have a hardware tracer to record all traffic. This could *not* have happened without raising an alarm."

"Well, I agree. I can only tell you what I know: There hasn't been any unusual data activity on the pipe for as long as I've been working on the persona. We put out a few test cases—three or four—but nothing like this."

I didn't believe him, but I had nothing more to go on. If I were going to uncover Nemesio's treason, I'd need the help of someone I could trust.

"Go, then," I said. "If you see anything—*anything*—tell me immediately."

"Of course. Always have, always will. Isis, exit."

The faceless manikin flattened and faded. I summoned Jayla next. She entered the venue in the avatar of a talking shark.

"What's the cron, Boss?" she asked, flashing rows of razor-sharp teeth.

"I have a mission for you," I replied.

❖ ❖ ❖

Jayla left the venue having agreed with enthusiasm to spy on Nemesio, and on Speranza as well. She'd already kept close tabs on Lucius for more than a week, but reported nothing out of the ordinary. Lucius wasn't my top suspect at any rate. Only Nemesio, Jayla, or Speranza had the skills to sabotage my venues with fake personas, and of those, Jayla was the one most deserving of my trust. But I was unwilling to grant my trust even to her.

"Isis, Qingshan."

I entered a personal venue, the courtyard of a Buddhist monastery, the meticulously manicured grass glowing green, surrounded by elaborate shrines to the Buddha's many incarnations. I sat cross-legged, eyes closed, the rising sun in my face, and meditated to the muted sound of chanting and the faint aroma of incense. With no one on whom I could fully rely, I knew that I would likely face this challenge alone. I would need a clear head and a calm spirit.

The heaviness in my chest, arms, and legs dissipated. My breathing slowed. My thoughts retreated from the external to the self, until the calm and clarity I sought came, preparing me for the challenge.

Until a thud, followed by a flash, like a strobe lighting up my brain. It was the last thing I remembered before awakening in the recovery venue.

❖ ❖ ❖

"They got the Kliegls who attacked you," Mackenzie said. "Four of them, two men, two women. They're in confinement."

My head throbbed, an improvement over the jagged pain that woke me, thanks to a fentanyl IV drip. The IV was invisible to me, of course, it not being rendered in the recovery venue. None of the monitoring instruments, sterile hospital surroundings, or cold steel rails of the bed appeared in the venue, such things having a distressing effect on the patient, but I knew they were there. I'd been in so many such venues as a doctor that I could imagine them even if they were only apparent IRL. Instead, I lay on a thick mattress on a brass bedstead, under a quilted comforter, by a softly glowing lamp, surrounded by vases of flowers and anodyne art on the walls.

"Do you know what happened?" I asked in a labored croak.

Mack picked up my hand and patted it as if petting a dog, a gesture of sympathy that was unmatched by the expression on his face. His eyes were narrowed and his mouth grim. He shook his head slowly as though pitying me.

"I love you, Maddie. You are the only person in this world who cares about me. I'm sure I'd be dead without you, or at least stuck in a body with a hair-trigger brain, unable to cope with even the stupidest, simplest things. You opened up the world to me, and I'm grateful."

I squeezed his hand. "It's all I've ever wanted to do," I said.

"And you did it. That's what I want to say to you today. You did it. You can stop now. It's done."

"But it's *not* done, Mack. There are still places you can't go, and people you can't know."

He dropped my hand. "Twenty-three more people hurt. Two of them dead. And now you. If it hadn't been for a neighbor, the Civils might never have come, and that White Shirt gang would've beaten you to death. They almost did. The doctor said you *should* be dead."

The pain in my head muddled my thoughts. I heard what Mack said, but it didn't sink in.

"Any others?"

"Do you mean any other victims? No. Just you. They checked the logs. The Kliegls went straight to your building, then straight to your apartment. They knew just where they were going."

"They didn't enter any other apartments?"

"That's what I said." He stood up. "How does it—I mean, how do you feel?"

"You mean how does it feel to be a victim of my own scheme?"

"I didn't say that."

"You almost did."

He stood and turned sideways, looking up at the ceiling. "I broke my promise not to speak to you. But I had to know how you were getting along. I see that you'll recover." He looked down at me. "Maddie, I see the reports. I know when more people are hurt. When that stops, I'll come back. Exit venue."

Before I could say another word, Mack flattened and faded.

59

Messing with the System

The Eye of Providence

TO WATCH THE Worldstream record of my assault was as surreal an episode as I've ever had, an out-of-body experience. I saw myself sitting in my apartment, fully geared, motionless in meditation. The doorjamb splintered, the door swung open on one hinge, and four white-shirted Kliegls rushed in, almost stumbling over one another. The first through the door, a woman (though she was as muscular as any man) drew her baton, flicked it open, and struck me hard enough to knock me off the chair. I lay unconscious on the floor as three other Kliegls struck me in rotation, like workmen hammering home a fencepost. I wondered what would've happened had they not shouted slogans such as *Kliegl! Dax! No Shade, light!* and other things, unintelligible, but which nevertheless signaled a potent rage, loud enough to be heard through walls, ceilings, and floors.

My stomach churned as the beating continued for what seemed like many minutes, until, thanks to a civic-minded neighbor, the authorities appeared at the door and subdued the White Shirts. The emergency response team followed and took me downstairs to the medical evacuation drone.

"Elsa, suspend," I said, choking back a gag reflex. The scene froze, then faded.

This was no accident, I thought. *Someone planned it.* And there could be only one possibility.

❖ ❖ ❖

"Jah, you got munged up, Boss," Jayla exclaimed. We met in the cube room, just the two of us. My injuries were obvious, a bruised eye and swollen lip clearly visible even from under my mask.

"I was the victim of an unfortunate attack," I said. "But you knew that."

"Huh? Nah. All we know is, you were out for a week. None of us knew where you were, not even rumors. So, what went down?"

She was convincing, but her personality type is often adept at feigning sincerity.

"White Shirts. They assaulted me in my apartment."

"*What?* No!" Again, her reaction seemed genuine. But I wasn't deceived.

"Four Kliegls broke down my door and beat me senseless."

"Ain't that a pisser. You okay?"

"I'll recover."

We sat silently for almost a minute, as long a time as I'd ever seen Jayla keep her mouth shut. She stood up. "Well, welcome back, Boss. Gotta get back to it."

"Jayla."

She remained standing. "Yeah, Boss?"

"Did you direct a Kliegl attack against me?"

The eyes behind her mask opened wide. "Ah, I don't *think* so. What kind of a dumbass trick would *that* be?"

"No one else could've."

She took a step toward the door. "Yeah, if anyone did it at all."

"Are you saying that Kliegls are freelancing brutal attacks against innocent civilians now?"

"Um, they've been doing that for a while now, remember? Mayhem protocol? Zoom on the Kliegl trogs?"

"*Random* targets—that's what you said. You give them an address, and they pick a room at random."

"That's the routine."

"The attack on *me* was directed."

She shrugged. "Maybe. But what if they did it on spec? Probably they saw reports in the feed and wanted to get in on the action. They're animals. They're also not too bright."

"And they just happened to break into *my* apartment."

She threw up her hands. "Jah, Boss, I'm not going to argue over *facts*. You don't believe me? Let's check the logs."

❖ ❖ ❖

Jayla once again indulged her infantile penchant for fanciful avatars, appearing as a multicolored octopus.

"Looky here, Boss. Same format as always—street address, random room." She pointed a teal tentacle at the scroll. "See? The address isn't even your building. It's in Washington Park, for Jah's sake. You live in Lakeview. You wouldn't be caught dead in *Washington Park*."

"How do I know this is the right log?"

The octopus flailed its arms. "The date! Look at the date! Jah, what do you think, that I munged the log?"

"You could have. You have the skills."

"Oh, for fuck's sake. That would be *so* easy to detect." A tentacle flicked. An image appeared, like a string of beads, spiraling from infinite past to infinite future.

"What's this?" I asked.

"The *Vita Occulta* blockchain. Everything goes on here—invoices, payments, venues, logs—all encrypted, all verified. You wanna know if the log's legit? Here's how to tell: I'll hash the log, and if the hash matches the blockchain entry, it's golden."

"Hash?"

"A unique number derived from the content. It's a math thing. Don't worry. That's how it's done. Isis, last Thursday," she said. The string zipped by, flashing colors like Christmas lights, coming to a halt with one node pulsating purple. Jayla gesticulated with all eight arms. "Okay, here's the entry. And here's the hash." A meaningless sequence of numbers appeared, thirty digits or more. More gestures. "And here's the hash from the…wait…what?" She stopped talking when a second sequence appeared. The two were irreconcilably different.

At her command two scrolls appeared, one with the log we'd just examined, and the second, I presumed, from the blockchain.

"What is that address?" I asked.

The octopus's eyes bugged out as she examined the log. "Lakeview."

"And the building?"

"Your building."

"Is there a room number?"

"Someone's been messing with the system."

"Who else—besides *you*—could've done this?"

"Besides me, only Speranza, and maybe Nemesio."

"What about Lucius?"

The octopus spun like a pinwheel, fluorescing every hue of the visible spectrum. "*Lucius?*"

"You had him trolling logs for Kliegls."

"Yeah, and I had to light a fire under his ass to get results. He's a noob. He doesn't know anything."

At that point I was close to believing her, but I wasn't ready to absolve her completely, or Lucius, for that matter. But she was right: Apart from Jayla, Nemesio and Speranza were the most likely suspects.

"I'll get to the bottom of this, Boss," Jayla said.

"See that you do. Isis, suspend the venue."

60

I Know Who You Are Old Man

Shade Lucius of the Aletheia

I HAD A lot of balls in the air. It was time to make contact with galactic headquarters.

Raúl was involved from the start, sure, but there was only so much he could do from outside the Aletheia firewall. I was the inside man. And a lot of it was improvised, being as risky as it was to get together in VR. So, when it came time to size up our situation, I asked for a meeting IRL.

That had its own risks. Shade on the street were targets, not just for White Shirts, but for all the Kliegl wannabes who bought into the Dax-slash-Madeleine lie about Shade being a menace to society. Even the homeless, the same street people that the White Shirts went after in the night, harassed us. I guess they figured that we're the ones who started it. Like that made sense.

But early morning was relatively quiet, the Kliegls at home sleeping off last night's rampage, street bums still rolled up in their coats and blankets, and everyone else jacked into the Worldstream. Also, it was the time I was least likely to be missed at the Aletheia dorm. Good thing I had Speranza to cover for me.

On the half-hour walk to Raúl's I only got the stink eye from a few of the sidewalk campers laying out by the State Live Services building on Michigan Avenue, though what was left of Live Services wasn't a lot. Nobody got much of anything from them anymore, and the lineup of street people in that particular spot was more out of custom than convenience.

I trudged up six floors, taking my time so as not to trip over my cloak. Before I could push the button on Raúl's door I heard his voice.

"Announce yourself, Cloak."

"I'm Lucius, of the Aletheia."

"Jah, just your name, not your crew." The bolt slid aside with a clunk. "C'mon in, Lucius."

It was my first time in Raúl's apartment. It was a crazy tangle of gear, spread out over three tables, and screens hung from a metal framework, flashing all manner of code and VR venues. Raúl slouched in a leather chair, geared up in headset and tactiles, flailing his arms like he was brushing away a cloud of gnats.

"What's wrong with me telling you my crew?"

"Close the door." He thrashed for a few more seconds, then he took off his headset and peeled off his gloves. "Kliegls, Lucius of the Aletheia. Never know when you might be overheard. Once they know you're in a Shade crew, they'll beat you stupid."

"There're no Kliegls out there. It's barely past sunrise. Besides, they'll cream anyone in a cloak, Shade or not."

"You got a point." He turned a chair around and rolled it toward me. "Sit down, Lucius. You can take off the hood."

I did like he said.

"Mask, too. The All-Seeing Eye can't penetrate these walls."

That made me nervous. The only time I'd taken off that mask since joining the Aletheia was for personal hygiene purposes, and always in private.

"I'll keep it on, if that's okay, Raúl."

He sneered and rolled his eyes, and before I could move grabbed my mask and tore it off.

"That's better." Raúl tilted his head and squinted. "You've changed," he said.

❖ ❖ ❖

The first order of business was to hook up with Molly and Porter in Raúl's Fortress of Solitude. It was like old times, me and the original shredders, coding hacks and building pipes into the Worldstream to make mischief. By last count we'd put a thousand or more personas into virtual space, every one of them tying up compute cycles 'til the end of time. That got the Consortium's attention, and with the breadcrumbs we dropped in the Aletheia pipe, their scrutiny was focused laser-like on Madeleine. Which was exactly what we wanted.

"Six. That's all we really need," I said. "Six personas lost in the crowd."

"Not even," Porter countered. "Three'd be enough, if we move 'em around."

"That'll take too long. With six we can cover twice the territory and still stay under the radar."

Porter scoffed. "You take a lot of risks, noob."

Risk. Jah, for someone who cut his teeth ripping and tearing up Worldstream data, Porter had turned pussy in his old age.

"The kid's got it right, I think," Molly said. Molly often took my side against Porter, sometimes just to irritate him. "The Worldstream bosses are chasing a thousand false leads. What's six more going to mean?"

"Not necessary," Porter said. "Look here. Sophie, map."

The Millennium Republic stretched out in front of us, each of fifty districts colored and labeled.

"Porter, you're making my point for me," I said. "Fifty districts—that's a lot of ground to cover."

"Think, boy. Use your head. We don't have to cover *all* of it. We have *some* idea of where they are. Sophie, analysis."

A vague outline of color appeared, with red splotches around population centers like Omaha, Minneapolis, and Denver, ringed in hues of orange and yellow. "See? Here's where they are, most likely. Three faux avatars, rotated through the hot spots. Snoop around in venues with traffic in these pipes and we'll get leads on all of 'em. Once we get a nose under the tent, we'll find 'em."

"Too long," I repeated. "Porter, they've already been out there for *months*. Every day we wait they spread out. We need to hit this hard."

"*I* ran the numbers!" Porter shouted. "*I* did the sims! Jah, do you *know* who you're talking to? *I'm Porter Wilkes!*"

I rolled my eyes, which was like a reflex action every time Porter played Guru on the Mountaintop.

"I know who you are, old man. Jah, you tell me often enough."

Porter's hair and beard turned white, the way it does when he's really pissed, then glowed as bright as the noonday sun. I thought he might burn out my visor.

"Porter, ease off," Molly said.

He pointed a finger and shot jagged lightning bolts at me with a crack loud enough to make my ears ring. "What's this little piss-ant ever done?" he asked in a voice like doom. "And he's telling *me* about stats and odds?"

I was trying to keep cool but I'd heard this *I'm a god, you're a noob* routine once too often.

The wind in the Fortress kicked up, screeching like a hurricane in a canyon, blowing sand in Porter's face. He shut his eyes and put up his arms to block the blast.

He wasn't the only one with FX.

"I've been hanging my ass out for more than a *year*, Madeleine breathing down my neck *the whole time*," I shouted over the noise, "passing intel straight from the source, taking orders from that arrogant asshole Nemesio. *I'm* the one who figured out the key to the persona. That's *my* code you're tweaking. Without me—"

"*Stop!*" That was Raúl yelling. He'd been sitting back from the cage match the whole time, probably enjoying watching me and Porter go at it. I guess the fun wore off. I interrupted the sandstorm and Porter's hair dimmed down to its usual dirty gray.

Raúl stood up, his shiny blue tunic catching the light in a very techie way. "I'm going to side with young Lucius here. Six. No more, no less. But keep 'em moving. We don't want the Consortium to get a fix on us."

"I'm jumping off," Porter said. He was still vexed, obviously. I was about to say something but Molly beat me to it.

"We need an algorithm," she said.

Porter pointed. "Ask *him*. He's the hero in the trenches."

Molly teleported next to Porter and put an arm around his shoulder, the ninja comforting the wizard. He laid his head on her chest and she stroked his hair.

"I'm tired," Porter mumbled.

"I know, baby." She bent down and he raised his head and they kissed. She touched his cheek like she was touching a newborn. "I know. Just a little longer, baby, then we can rest."

The old man sniffed and grunted. He straightened up. The wrinkles in his wizard's robe flattened out, all the pagan symbols on it taking on a new look, like they were vibrating with power. His beard and hair untangled and the wrinkles in his face softened.

"The algorithm is done. Input the starting points and the personas will hop venues until we get a lead on every *Vitreous Orb* still in the Worldstream." Porter looked at me again, not with the same wrath-of-god look as before, but not all kindness and sympathy, either. "We still need bodies on the near end of the personas," he added. "Another reason why three is better than six."

"I'll get the bodies," I replied. "Six is no problem."

"Once we have the roster, we'll snatch all the keys at once," Raúl said. "Then the clock starts. Keys—location— extraction. That's when we're the most exposed. Better to skate fast over thin ice."

"We're going to need an army IRL to collect them," Porter said, looking straight at me. "Is *that* a problem?"

"For me, yeah. Raúl?"

His eyes twinkled, literally, which was great FX. "Kieran's rallying the troops."

When he mentioned Kieran I got kind of teary-eyed from all the memories. I hadn't seen him since the raid in Ogallala.

61

Our Potemkin

The Eye of Providence

JAYLA WAS ADAMANT.

"The guy who munged that log has serious chops—no footprints, no fingerprints."

That was *not* what I wanted to hear.

"This mysterious saboteur could've undermined every one of our security measures," I said.

"Yeah, Boss. That's why I wanted you here in the cube room. The stealth venue isn't as stealthy as it used to be."

"You don't know that for sure."

Jayla flung her arms wide. "I kinda *do*. The worm not only sicced the White Shirts on you, but he baited the Consortium, too."

"What's that mean?"

"That crowd of clones at your rally?"

"News conference."

"Whatever. The Worldstream honchos think that *we* put them out there through our pipe."

"Didn't we?"

She shook her head, closing her eyes behind her blue and silver mask. "Nope. But he made it look that way."

"How?"

"The headers." She laid a personal screen on the table. It displayed a diagram of some kind, square and round shapes of all colors amid a tangle of arrows. Underneath it scrolled incomprehensible lines of text. *Damn her.* She did this as much to intimidate as to explain.

"Is this necessary?" I asked.

"Well, *yeah*. Look at this." She zoomed in on one circle labeled with an interminable string of letters and numbers. "This thing here." She tapped. The circle resolved to the bland, mustached avatar that populated my unfortunate news conference by the hundreds. "Doesn't look much like a Myrtle, does she?"

"I've seen this before."

"Yeah, but not this." She tapped again, lighting up a path through the maze of arrows, from the avatar's face, connected to a node labeled *20780630_8AwgESaW0g29VLAE_VNU_M_P_H,* through other nodes with similarly cryptic annotations.

"Jayla, is there a point to this?"

"Don't you get it? There's all kinds of rendering engines feeding the venue server, but all the fake ones come right back to the Aletheia—or at least to our Potemkin."

I didn't know what that meant, but I wasn't about to admit my ignorance. It didn't matter. She assumed I was clueless anyway.

"The Potemkin—a spoof. It's the legit-looking face we show the Worldstream to hide our Shade identity. But it didn't fool the Consortium. They saw right through it."

"Then these personas *did* come from our pipe."

"That's the thing—*they didn't*. This trail is bogus, complete fiction."

"Why would anyone do that?"

"Someone's got a hard on for you, Boss." She put away her personal screen. "I'm telling you, if this wasn't an inside job, we need to find this guy and put him to work. He's got *insane* skills."

❖ ❖ ❖

Though reluctant, I had no choice but to trust Jayla. I knew of no reason she'd lie to me, but neither did I know of a reason why an anonymous malefactor would target me for assault by White Shirts and persecution by the Consortium. Dax dismissed me. He erected a shield around his Kliegls in the Council, which my crew failed to penetrate. Some unknown miscreant stymied my bid to become First

Minister, and I didn't even know if the saboteur was inside or outside the Aletheia. My position in the *Vita Occulta* was in jeopardy.

Not even Mackenzie stood by me.

But it has always been so that great barriers are raised against great ambition. That is a historical fact. Heroes are heroic because they succeed despite obstacles thrown in their paths by the craven, the conspirators, and the cowards. If it is the destiny of humankind to live in a perfect world, where all needs are satisfied, where the democratization of experience is complete, where even the disadvantaged and disabled are full participants, then it will be so.

And I will make it so.

With that affirmation, I answered my own question: Why was I a target for so many? The reactionary forces still stuck IRL, still unconvinced of the transformative potential of the Worldstream—*they* are the ones who wish fervently for my failure. Though I didn't know their names—yet—I would carry on in spite of them. I hadn't come up with my plan of attack—not even an outline—but I never doubted that I would. *Univirtual* was an inevitability.

All this went through my mind as I walked the few blocks from the Aletheia dorm to my apartment, so deeply absorbed in my thoughts that I barely noticed the sound of sirens and people streaming out of their buildings, out of storefronts, and even the homeless lifting themselves up off the sidewalks to surround me.

62

Little House in Sangamon

Shade Lucius of the Aletheia

AFTER YEARS OF Dax's trash talk, dorm raids by club-wielding Kliegls and taser-toting Civils, and involuntary servitude in *Vita Occulta* sweatshops, the Shade were pissed. So, when it came time to recruit Shade to tunnel into Madeleine's presser, Kieran had them lined up by the hundreds.

But we only needed six posers for the recon. Once they got a lock on the refugees, it rolled up pretty fast. In fact, six was probably overkill—but I'd never admit that to Porter. Within two weeks he had a roster and a plan of attack. Kieran's Shade army was poised to copy their keys, Raúl and Porter to crank out the collection route, and Kieran to make the rounds. And that was the logistical miracle—lining up enough transports and personnel for the extraction phase. Good thing he had Naia's help, and an army of angry Shade.

In one respect we were lucky—Porter was 100% correct about the concentration of the refugees, although he was wrong about where the biggest groups were. In fact, we picked up the scent of almost all the Orwellians, Laputans, and Burgessers in Provo and St. Louis, with a few holed up in Memphis. And once we found one or two, that led us to the others. Jackson and Heath were in Provo; Benny, Max, and Frank were in St. Louis. We couldn't find all the Shredded *Vitreous Orb*, of course, since their Worldstream footprints had been wiped out. We could only hope that they'd be confined with the others when we started rounding them up. We didn't know where they were *exactly*—we'd need their keys to figure that out—but we had enough to go on.

We were back in the fortress with a map of the Millennium Republic stretched out in front of us, St. Louis, Provo, and Memphis glowing with a cluster of dots showing us where our friends were, roughly speaking, with a few lights scattered elsewhere. We were all dead silent, Raúl, Porter, and Molly checking their guts (like I was) about whether we were ready to click *execute*.

"Well, team, where're your heads?" Raúl asked. "Once we kick this off, things will get intensely hairy."

"It's all planned out," I replied. "What're we waiting for?"

Porter scoffed. "Our plan won't last five minutes before something goes wrong."

"Jah, what is *wrong* with you?" I scoffed right back. "Were you always such a wimp?"

Porter's hair started to heat up again when Raúl stepped in.

"Can the crap," he said, looking straight at me. Then he looked at Porter. "Like the man said: Plans are nothing; planning is everything. We've gamed this out ten different ways. Are we going to get any smarter by chewing it over again?"

Porter cooled off. "I want to hear from Kieran."

I rolled my eyes, but Raúl and Molly kept a straight face. "Sophie," Raúl said, "Kieran."

A figure rastered into the center of the map, like a column of black smoke shaped roughly like a human being.

"Who has summoned me?" he rumbled.

"No time for drama," Raúl said. "Porter wants a status report."

The smoke column morphed into a recognizable person, like a Shade in robe without the hood, in a black and white mask with a yellow flame motif on the forehead.

"What, we haven't gone over this like two hundred times?"

"I wanna know how things stand *right now*," Porter said.

Kieran shrugged. "Well, *right now* sixty Shade are jacked in waiting for the go-ahead. We know venues and schedules for nine out of ten of the refugees. Once you pull the trigger, my crew will raster in, pull the keys, and bug out. Then it's up to you guys. You locate 'em IRL and Naia dispatches the trucks. Is any of this news?"

"Not *news*," Raúl replied. "Just a final check."

"So, when's showtime? My crew's idling and you're burning daylight."

"You good, Porter?" Raúl asked.

Porter slumped like he was outnumbered and outgunned. "Yeah, let's do it."

Even though Raúl, Molly, me, and Kieran all were gung-ho, I have to admit that Porter looked like we felt. None of us knew what was coming.

"Sophie," Raúl said after brief hesitation, "ignition. Liftoff."

❖ ❖ ❖

With Jayla and Nemesio counting every bit and byte through the Aletheia pipe, it was a real challenge to get updates from Speranza, but from what he pushed through the satellite channel—the same setup we used in Orwell—I knew that Madeleine had gone full paranoid and that the Aletheia was in total chaos. Good. Couldn't happen to a sweeter lady. And we hadn't even dropped the big one yet.

I was a week out of the Aletheia, hiding by day and running rogue by night, jacking into the Fortress of Solitude when I could. Naia had put together a network of stops where Shade and other shredded souls could hang, all coordinated in stealth venues. She called it the Underground Railroad, like a similar situation about two hundred years back, when the Millennium Republic was still the United States of America and slaves escaped up north. I was an outcast and a rebel, not a slave, but I felt hunted just the same. From Chicago it took a week on foot, on bicycle when the station masters could lend them, or personal transport if one of them offered to drive. But I had to. There was no way I was going to sit on the sidelines while Naia and her drivers made the rounds. I wanted to see my old *Vitreous Orb* friends IRL just as soon as we extracted them, and maybe drive a transport if Naia would let me. It was a happy day when I crossed the St. Louis perimeter.

I met Naia in a little house in south Sangamon not too far outside of St. Louis. I made the final thirty klicks on foot, leaving the last stop well after sunset. Six hours later, still dark as hell, I was standing at the back door, knocking as softly as I could, not knowing a thing about the neighbors.

"Jah, you made it," Naia said when she opened the door. I could've kissed her right then, and she felt the same way, sort of, because she gave me a hug, even though she's not a hugger.

"Come in and drop that backpack," she said. I was only too happy to obey, feeling like I'd found an oasis after I crossed the desert.

"I thought they nabbed you in Chicago," I said.

"Nabbed and cut loose. I'm still in the Worldstream, like Molly and Porter, so I'm not a prime target for *Univirtual*. But my footprint isn't as carefully manicured as theirs. They decided to hold me to make a point. The point made, I moved on," she replied, grinning.

The place was like every other stop on the railroad, a tiny house, or a ground-floor apartment, always with an entrance hidden away from the main routes. We were in a kitchen, cramped, but neat and clean, with cans and boxes of food arranged in rows on a counter and a hotplate for a stove. By the wall, next to the door, was a table, and sitting there was a heavy, older-looking woman with silver streaks in her hair. I stared and squinted. I knew her.

Back in Ogallala when we were on the run, we met up with a group from Laputa. One of the Orwellians, Benny, was hit during a drone attack and near death. This woman brought him back to life.

"Casey," I said with a smile.

She smiled back. "I was wondering if you'd remember."

She got out of her chair and came in. I remembered that Casey *was* a hugger and she almost crushed me.

"Ready for the big day?" she asked, her nose just a centimeter from mine.

"Can't wait. We'll have a lot of catching up."

She broke the clinch and stepped back. Her smile got crazy big, and Naia's did too.

"What?" I asked.

"You can get started now," Casey replied.

That's when he came through the door and I about threw an exception. Huggers or not, we glommed on and didn't let go for five minutes.

"Kieran," I said. "Kieran, Kieran."

He backed off and gave me a grin like he used to, back in Orwell, when we spent days together in the fields, or nights together in the pitiful little cabin, just me, him, and Grace.

"We can drop all that Lucius and Kieran stuff, Hammad," he said. "I'm Dylan again."

63

A Ragged Scar

The Eye of Providence

I WALKED CLOSE to the building, eyes down, to avoid drawing attention—me, a middle-aged, uncloaked woman, not normally a target for Kliegl thugs, but at that time of day anyone would do well to be cautious.

The source of the commotion didn't register immediately. I raised my eyes from the pavement to see a scattering of citizens walking not randomly, but converging on one spot. It took a moment to realize that that spot was *me*.

"Hue and cry—all citizens are obliged to aid in the apprehension of this fugitive!" came a chorus of synthesized voices, like a robot choir, spilling out of windows and doors as citizens, rousted from their VR venues, took off their gear and left their homes. I, of course, couldn't see what they saw on their wall screens, or on the pocket screens of the growing crowd that surrounded me like a zombie horde, but I guessed. On the brink of panic, I looked for an escape route.

There was nothing. The wall of bricks behind me stretched the length of the block without an opening. The shambling crowd converged on either side, closing like pincers; a sparse line came at me from across the street. Surrounded, I looked for the weakest spot, the point in the advancing front where the army of the *hue and cry* was thinnest: two slight women walking an arm's length apart. I broke for it.

They anticipated my move, closing ranks as I jogged left, lowering my shoulder. Though only slightly bigger than the woman in my path, I caromed off her as she braced for the collision. Three pairs of hands grabbed at my clothes. I tripped, sliding as I hit the pavement, leaving streaks of blood from my hands and elbows.

Lying prone in the street, surrounded by citizens in the thrall of the *hue and cry*, I rolled and kicked, catching one man in the head. He wailed, covering his face. That was enough to slow down the rest, and with two seconds' pause in the onslaught, I got to my feet and ran. The crowd fell further behind as I sprinted down the street, away from my building, certain that Civils waited for me there. Instead, my best bet was to make it back to the Aletheia dorm.

I kept up the pace for another block before I tired and slowed. Ducking into an alley unseen, I bent and put my hands on my knees, panting like a dog on a sweltering day.

Who triggered this mass hysteria, this posse comitatus? I wondered. Dax, the Council, perhaps the Consortium—they were all suspects.

I caught my breath and peeked around the edge of the building. The crowd had grown, and the chant of *hue and cry* echoed from the buildings as if from canyon walls. I went down the alley to the opposite street. A cautious look confirmed that the crowd hadn't yet made it around the building. I left the alley and took off in a jog, still a good ten minutes from the Aletheia.

I'd made it another block, the *hue and cry* still sounding from every direction, more doors opening and android-like citizens emerging. Another corner and I felt a moment of relief—no crowds waited to take me and hold me for the Civil Authorities to come. I picked up the pace but broke into a dead run when I heard the drones.

The sound purged me of fatigue, pain, even fear. I ran as fast as I ever had, numb and unthinking, no hope of outrunning the swarm, but that thought didn't occur to me. I ran as prey runs from a predator, an instinct bred into every animal that has ever been pursued.

The dull hum of the drones grew louder—certainly I was within range of their tasers, I thought at some subliminal level, and so it was, because four rounds streaked past me in a blur, ricocheting off the sidewalk in a spray of sparks.

Faster, I thought, but my body had reached its limit. My mind could not will what my flesh could not do.

And then—another sound, also familiar, not the even, mid-range pitch from which the drones get their name, but a low, throaty roar, distant at first, then closer.

The vehicle swerved, coming to a stop broadside to the advancing drones. A door flung open.

"Get your ass in here, Boss, before those bugs toast you!" the driver shouted. I ran for the open door.

It was an odd sensation, the electric jolt that ran through my thigh. The shock was instantaneous; the concussion from the round followed shortly. My leg stiffened. I twisted and fell as one more round found its mark in the middle of my back. I was unconscious before I hit the street.

The after-effects of a taser are not pleasant. I woke in a room of the subterranean Aletheia dormitory, rolled to one side so as to relieve pressure from my back. It didn't help. My whole body ached, the pain radiating from the impact point between my shoulder blades. I blinked in the subdued light.

"You putting on weight, Boss?" Jayla asked, this time in her natural voice. She sat beside me, masked but uncloaked.

I could only grunt in response.

"It was all I could do to haul you into the car. If I'd've been tased we'd both be in confinement in Joliet."

"Huh?" I said, or tried to say, my voice hardly more than a wheeze.

"You made the headlines, Boss."

"What…"

"Someone put a shred out on you. Jahbulon threw an exception. We got the alarm, just like everyone else in Chicagoland. I went for you in the Chrysler. Good thing you were close by."

I propped myself up on my elbow with a moan. "Shred?"

"Yep." She was grinning behind her mask, as if amused. "Ripped and shredded. And it was a good 'un, too. I checked. You're nothing but a ragged scar in the 'stream. Welcome to the Shade!"

I shut my eyes, hoping to clear the fog from my mind. I squeezed my shoulders together to relieve the ache but it only got worse.

"Dax?" I asked.

"Hell if I know. Whoever shredded you knew what he was doing."

With great effort I sat up, then slumped forward, elbows on knees. "The Consortium?"

"Unlikely. It's not their style."

"Raúl?"

"The old man himself? Could be. In fact…"

I looked up. Jayla's grin was gone.

"In fact what?"

"We're following some insane activity."

"And?"

"More personas. A butt-ton of 'em, all at once. Massive compute cycles. Could be a Raúl operation."

"What else do you know?"

"We're still tracing."

"We?"

"Me and Nemesio."

I got up, steadying myself on the bed frame. "Put Speranza on it."

"Speranza. Jah."

"Is there a problem?"

She adjusted her mask with both hands. "I wonder about Speranza."

"Why?" I asked, pressing my hand to my forehead, thinking that Jayla was about to add another stressor to my already complicated life.

"Nothing I can put my finger on. He's always been a little lacking in gusto, you know? Lately he's been really flat."

I massaged my aching head. "If not Speranza, then who?"

She shrugged. "Speranza. I'll keep an eye on him."

"Fine. And that other one, what's his name…Lucius. Put him on it."

"Sorry, Boss, no. That slacker is gone."

"He's *gone?*"

"Yep. A couple days now. Not like we miss him." She went for the door. "Get some rest. I'll send one of the noobs to look in on you. Meanwhile, I've got to put out sniffers in St. Louis and Provo."

My mind cleared and the pain subsided, as if I'd taken a shot of amphetamine laced with fentanyl. "*Where?*"

"Provo, St. Louis, a few other spots. That's where the traffic is."

"I've got to go," I said, elbowing past her. "I've got to jack in."

"Whoa, wait up there, Boss. You're Shade now, remember? You don't even have a key anymore."

"Jah." My headache came back. "Call all hands."

"Why? What're you thinking?"

"It's Raúl, all right. St. Louis and Provo—that's where we're holding the *Vitreous Orb* rebels. Raúl means to free them. And I'm going to stop him."

64

Calling Muster

Shade Lucius of the Aletheia

"SOPHIE, LOCATIONS," RAÚL ordered.

Tiny lights winked on, showing the physical location of every Orwellian, Laputan, and Burgesser in four tight clusters —two big ones near St. Louis, another in Provo, and a little one by Memphis. A few others, maybe twenty or so isolated dots, were scattered across Sangamon and Ozark. We'd taken almost a thousand keys in less than a day—Porter's algorithm worked flawlessly. Within hours we knew where they were IRL.

"They're all in confinement," Porter said.

"Not all," I corrected.

"Pretty much all," Porter said, sounding just a little too satisfied with himself. "Which means we're kind of fucked."

"I don't agree," I replied irritably, already tired of Porter's attitude and getting wearier every time he opened his mouth. "Porter, this makes it way easier. Look! They're all bunched up. We don't have to send transports to a thousand different locations." I pointed to the blob in Provo. "Two hundred— *more* than two hundred—just in Provo. We have six transports in Provo, enough for all of them, and we only have to send them to one place."

"They're in *confinement*," Porter repeated. "Are you going to roll your caravan up to the front gate and wave 'em in?"

"He's got a point, Son," Raúl said. "There's no power play here. We'll have to finesse it."

"You busted me and Dylan out of Nodaway. It can be done."

"That was *two*, not *two hundred*."

"So what? We're going to let them rot?"

Raúl raised his hands. "Steady, young Muhammad. We won't do anything of the kind. Sophie, logistics."

Tiny replicas of trucks appeared on the map, showing their exact locations. They weren't the sleek, shiny, electric transports the Civils and Kliegls used to haul our stiff, tased bodies away. Instead, they were a mix of electric, diesel, and gas-powered vehicles designed for a time when transports had human drivers, which meant that they didn't carry eighty or a hundred passengers stacked like corpses in a morgue. They were flatbeds and a few vans, some off-road capable, with enough room for maybe thirty each if they packed in and hung on tight. We had a couple dozen all told; Dylan and Naia had scavenged them from indie Shade crews, mostly, and bartered on the black market for the rest, using what few credits we had left from Orwell.

"Provo. Six buses. Enough for a hundred eighty or a hundred ninety if they're chummy. But these aren't off-road vehicles like that dune buggy Naia carried you off in. They need real streets. This is going to take some planning," Raúl said.

"Okay, so let's plan," I replied. Raúl was getting as skittish as Porter.

"Will you relax? We're on it. Molly?"

Molly'd kept quiet up to then, like she always did, not speaking up until she had something to say.

"It can be done. There's one road to the facility, right to the gate, like Porter said. Once we roll up, we won't have a lot of time. Civils will be on us like a plague of drones."

"Sounds impossible," Porter said.

"Not impossible," she replied. "Difficult. Luckily, the layouts of the confinement facilities are all the same. One plan to take them all. It's just…"

Molly looked around, not with the kind of swagger she usually had, but anxious and grim.

"You're not filling me with confidence," Porter said.

"From the time we roll up to the time we drive away can't be more than three minutes."

Porter slapped his head. "*Three minutes!*" He looked straight at me. "Did I say we were fucked?"

"Actually, you said we were *kind* of fucked," Molly said. "The timetable isn't forgiving, but if we can get a team at the perimeter to cut through the fence at four spots—six would be better—we can move the confinees out fast enough. But that's not the hard part."

"Enlighten us," Raúl said.

"The folks inside need their marching orders."

I knew what Molly was getting at. "Raúl, you need to barge into their therapy."

Therapy is what the confinement facilities called the daily torture they put us through. The idea was to condition us to return to society as normal, productive citizens, but really it was a way for sadistic pricks to get their thrills. When me and Dylan were in confinement, Raúl busted into the therapy stream. That's how he arranged for our escape.

"On it," Raúl replied. "A little bit of a problem, though. Just a rough estimate, but it'll take a week to get to all two hundred and give them the details. And that's just Provo."

"A week!" When Raúl said that, I was ready to agree with Porter: We were, indeed, fucked.

"Do you get it now, little Lucius?" Porter asked. "A week. And they're already onto us. The Consortium. The Civils. Madeleine. They all know what we're up to. In a week they'll put a cordon around every facility in twelve districts."

He knew he was right, and what's more, I knew it, too.

"Will you guys settle down?" Raúl said. "'Difficult, not impossible.' That's what the lady said."

"Right," Molly agreed. "We're already calling muster—in Provo, St. Louis, and Memphis. Dylan's Shades are already in therapy sessions in all four facilities. We've made contact with more than a hundred so far."

"There's a thousand," I said.

"That's why it'll take a week," Raúl replied. "Jah, boy, you're starting to sound like Porter."

He didn't need to say that, but I got what he meant. "Okay. Let's assume you can get all the confinees in on the plot, deploy teams to the perimeters of four confinement facilities, get them through the fence and onto the transports in three minutes or less."

"Go on," Molly said.

"It's what Porter said: What're the Civils, the Consortium, the Kliegls, and Madeleine doing while all this is happening? They're not going to sit still."

"The Consortium has bigger bugs to patch," Raúl replied. "The Kliegls only do what Dax tells them to do, and Dax is in the dark. As for the Civils, well, we'll just have to fly low."

"And Madeleine?"

Raúl smiled like he knew something I didn't. "We won't have to worry about Madeleine ever again."

65

The Road to St. Louis

Shade Lucius of the Aletheia

THE OLD TRUCK bumped across unpaved prairie, rumbling and squeaking up a hill to the crest. On the other side lay the smoking ruins of Orwell. It was worse than I remembered. Not a single building stood intact; most were razed to the ground, the remains scattered like the path of a tornado. And bodies. When the Kliegls and Civils raided the *Vitreous Orb*, they tased us and took us. No one they found was left behind. But this was a slaughter—corpses in the streets and in the fields. It made me sick.

I can only imagine how Benny felt. I was looking on from a distance, but he was driving the truck. The bed was already stacked higher than the cab with bodies, bloody and broken, flies rising from the load in a cloud, like smoke from a fire. Benny leaned over the steering wheel and surveyed the ruins.

"Go!"

The word came from outside the venue like the voice of god. Benny pressed his forehead to the steering wheel.

"No," he said quietly, as though too tired to talk.

I knew what was coming next. I'd been there. I flinched before it even came.

There was a sound like meat sizzling in a pan. Benny stiffened and his hands clamped around the steering wheel.

"Go!"

Benny released his grip and slumped forward.

"Go!"

Benny sat up, put the truck in gear, and eased forward, taking it slow.

"Faster!"

I couldn't watch any more. "Sophie, barge."

The truck dissolved. The ruins of Orwell faded to white. It was just me and Benny in the staging venue.

"Easy, Benny," I said, trying to calm him, although he looked like he was ready to be carried out on a stretcher.

He blinked, squinted, and focused his eyes.

"Who? Who are you?"

"Benny, it's Hammad. Hammad, from Orwell. Don't talk."

"Hammad? Is this—"

"Quiet. I barged your therapy session. They can't see or hear me, but they can hear you. Don't say anything. Just listen. We don't have much time."

He opened his mouth but caught himself before he spoke.

"We're busting you out of here, all of you. And we need your help."

I laid out the plan for Benny and gave him his assignments. By the time I was done, he knew the names of the other contacts inside the facility, when the trucks would roll, and where at the perimeter they needed to be. It all had to be timed to the second, but Benny was as reliable as anyone in Orwell.

It broke my heart to bug out of the session, knowing that as soon as I left the vicious bastard running the therapy session would zap Benny if he didn't follow directions, or even if he did. They were all sadistic that way.

❖ ❖ ❖

My truck was third in line, with three more behind me. We dropped off the extraction teams five klicks back. Their job was to get to their positions at the fence and cut through at just the right time. While they circled around, the trucks left the paved road and went to our designated locations. I checked the timer on the dash.

"Thirty seconds," the timer announced, meaning thirty seconds until the first breach in the fence. "Fifteen seconds…ten seconds….cue the alert in five…four… three…two…one…"

Even from inside the truck, over the idling engine, the blare of the klaxon hurt my ears.

"Perimeter breach in progress, section 59. All confinees return to the facility immediately."

That was the diversion, courtesy of Raúl. If all was going to plan, a thousand confinees were running for the barracks, a dozen facility guards to the non-existent breach, and our Orwell refugees to their extraction points.

The timer ticked down. "Team One, cut the wire."

That meant that the first team was cutting a hole in the fence with a blistering hot plasma torch, the only tool that could cut through the metal alloy.

"Team Two, cut the wire."

We'd planned for six holes spaced around the fence and timed to avoid the patrol drones. It was split-second timing, *literally*—Naia said that a mistake of just two seconds either way could blow the whole operation.

I saw the first of the refugees coming over the hill, looking ragged, like they had trouble keeping their feet under them. I got out of the cab and waved them on. The first of them, the fastest, strongest ones, scrambled onto the truck by themselves, or boosted others onto the bed. I kept time in my head, but in the mayhem of the moment I lost count. Fifteen made it onto the truck, with another twelve or so strung out between me and the fence.

"Move! *Move!*" I shouted, but only a few more made it. The rest were jogging—more like staggering—out of breath, when the drones came.

"Shit," I muttered. I went for the closest one, an older woman I didn't recognize, and pulled her arm across my shoulder. "Help! Help me!" I yelled at the ones on the truck, and a few jumped off and ran toward me but it was too late. Taser rounds came at us in a spread pattern, taking out me, every refugee running for the truck, and a few who'd already made it.

"Sophie, freeze the venue."

The action stopped. Raúl rastered in with Naia by his side. Eighteen more popped in, the other six drivers and the twelve on the perimeter teams.

Naia started the debrief. "Team two, nine seconds late. Team three, six seconds late. Team one, five seconds early, which is almost as bad."

I kept my head down, hoping she wouldn't say what I knew she would.

"Hammad, what the hell?"

"I know, I know. Leave on the mark. Anyone not on the truck is on their own." I looked up. "I still think that's a shitty rule."

"You could've gotten fifteen out; instead, you got zero."

"Yeah," I muttered. "I get it."

The St. Louis mockup was an impressive sandbox, from the approach, to the fence around the facility, to the drones patrolling the perimeter, to the surrounding grass and trees. Raúl had even rendered the trucks in detail, every one of them, though they were all different. Naia teleported us to an overhead vantage point where we could see the whole layout and replayed the exercise twice, calling out every screwup.

"Let's go again," Naia said, and we all jacked in for another dry run.

❖ ❖ ❖

By D-Day minus three we'd already collected all the refugees we could, the ones not in confinement, twenty-four in all. Dylan had most of them squirreled away in indie dorms, but a few were still en route. Between them and Dylan's Shade we had Provo and Memphis covered.

But St. Louis was where the action was—almost a thousand confinees in two facilities. Naia had fifteen transports lined up. And I was a driver. No way was I going to sit on the sidelines. That wasn't an option, anyway. We needed all the hands we could get.

We kept up the VR drills until we hit our marks dead on every time. Naia, who never handed out praise lightly, gave us all kudos. But as Raúl was fond of saying, plans never survive first contact. The night before the rescue I slept in fits.

Two hours before dawn we mounted our cabs and headed out with three or four hours' sleep but so jacked on adrenaline that none of us were tired. I'd learned every move and every mark down to my bones, like I was running out of ROM. First contact was hours away.

What plans would survive I couldn't know.

66

Find the Lady

Shade Lucius of the Aletheia

SYLVIA AND ROY were my extraction team. The three of us were crammed in the cab, rolling along side streets that hadn't seen a street repair crew since the fifties. We broke out of the densest part of the city into the land of boarded up storefronts and collapsing residences, still inside the St. Louis perimeter, but outside the prime bandwidth zone. The confinement facility was another four klicks by a hyperloop spur terminal where confinees came in from the districts like hogs to a slaughterhouse.

Warren, the driver in front of me, stuck his arm out the window and raised a fist.

"That's it," Sylvia said. "C'mon, Roy."

They got out and took off on foot. It was an hour past dawn, and still two hours until the diversion, when confinees were in the yard for Common Time. "Good luck," I said, and drove to my pickup point.

Even though I'd practiced the operation until every move was burned into muscle memory, I sat in that cab as the sun climbed the sky, wondering where I'd be that night—in a safe house with all my old Orwell buddies, laughing, drinking, and talking old times, or in a cell waiting to be processed into confinement, dreading my first therapy session.

Raúl once told me that Samurai warriors meditated before a battle, imagining all manners of death, whether from swords, arrows, or being trampled under horses' hooves; from quick, to lingering, to torturously long. Then, when the battle began, they fought with abandon, not fearing death, having already died a hundred times.

Two hours is a long time when your friends' lives are at stake. I died many times during those hours.

❖ ❖ ❖

The time ticked down to the last minute. I pictured the facility mockup, hovering over it like in one of Naia's debriefs: Roy and Sylvia hiding in the brush, plasma torches at the ready; my truck and six others idling in strategically chosen spots within running distance of the perimeter; confinees milling in the courtyard during Common Time, some glancing nervously toward their assigned escape routes, the rest oblivious; the patrol drones zipping along the perimeter fence at precisely timed intervals; the facility agents mingling with the inmates, contemplating—no less than their charges—a better life somewhere far away, or in some VR venue.

I gripped the wheel, white knuckled, my eyes fixed on the hill just this side of the facility fence, as the last few seconds passed.

"Ten seconds…cue the alert in five…four…three…two…one…"

My whole body tensed in a way it never did during simulations, as if my body knew at the cellular level that this was the real deal.

And then—nothing.

The diversion didn't come. Two seconds, our margin of error, passed with no deafening alarm, no warning to return to the facility.

"Team One, cut the wire," the timer announced, but I had no idea what Team One was doing.

"Team Two, cut the wire."

I tapped the gas pedal, revving the engine, more from nerves than anything I was planning to do. I had no plans. The plans went to shit.

"Team Three, cut the wire." That was my team, Sylvia and Roy. If they were following the schedule, their plasma torches were burning through the impervious alloy fence, cutting an escape route for our Orwell refugees. But I couldn't be sure that the refugees knew it was happening—

their instructions were to go for the fence when they heard the alert, the one that never came.

"Team Four, cut the wire. Team One, depart."

In another ten seconds, that mindless timer would tell Team Two to depart, whether or not the refugees were on the truck, and ten seconds later, I'd get my mark—Team Three, depart—and not a single refugee had come over the hill.

I sat forward, neck against the steering wheel, staring at the hilltop as if staring could make escapees magically appear.

"Team Two, depart."

I bounced in the seat, looking left and right, hoping to see something or someone. I flinched when the timer announced, "Team Three, depart."

Fuck this.

I put the truck in gear and tromped on the gas, digging ruts in the dirt as I headed straight for the fence.

I'd made it ten meters when Roy came over the hill in a run, with Sylvia right behind. I met them at the top.

"*Go, go, go!*" Roy shouted as he swung himself onto the truck bed. He grabbed Sylvia and pulled her aboard.

"Where are they?" I shouted, but Roy, and now Sylvia, just kept yelling "*Go!*"

I turned back to the windshield, snapping my head forward, though thinking back on it, I remember it like I was moving at one-quarter speed, as if Naia had slowed down the debrief for extra clarity.

Sylvia and Roy had cut the fence, all right, and folks were scrambling to get through, but only a dozen or so had made it. And behind them, in large numbers, were drones coming at us in a swarm.

The first taser rounds fired, catching two escapees full in the back and another in the arm. Another taser ricocheted off the windshield leaving a crack from top to bottom.

"*Go!*" Sylvia shouted, pounding on the window. "Leave on the mark!"

Six more made it through the fence. Two more hit the ground, tasers buried in their backs.

"Fuck that. Get ready. I'm going in."

I stood on the gas pedal. The truck jerked forward, almost tossing Sylvia and Roy off the bed. I picked up speed going downhill, aiming for the fence near the breach. One refugee jumped aside, avoiding the truck by centimeters, as I collided with the fence.

It wasn't quite like hitting a solid wall, but almost. The posts bent and the fence stretched but didn't break. Sylvia and Roy hit the back of the cab with a thud. I slammed against the steering wheel, chipping a tooth.

"Get on!" I yelled through the window, but I didn't have to, really. The ones still standing hopped on without being told.

I had to put my shoulder into the door to get it open, like it'd been bent in the collision. It sprang open and I almost fell out of the cab but I managed to land on my feet.

"Hammad, what?" Sylvia yelled. "Abort mission! *Get out of here!*"

Another volley of taser rounds flew past, striking sparks off the truck hood and grill, and taking out a couple of folks on the back. The drone swarm spread out, circling us, the 360-degree surround-sound buzz going right through me, resonating in my chest, building up to an explosion. They all panned to the center, full and half-full magazines ready to burn us with a barrage. I raised my arm to protect my face.

But the tasers never came. The drones held position, hovering and buzzing and not firing. I'd never seen drones act like that.

"Hammad, for Jah's sake, get in the cab and get us the fuck *out of here!*" Sylvia yelled.

"What are those bugs doing?" I asked.

"Does it matter? *Go! Let's go!*"

A few more refugees mounted the truck. Some loaded the downed taser victims onto the bed. The drones held their fire.

I ran to help one refugee grazed by a taser round, enough to cripple him without disabling him.

"Roy, Sylvia, get down here!" I yelled while I pulled the man to his feet. St. Louis B Extraction Team Three finally got off their asses and pulled people onto the truck.

"Hammad, what happened?" the man asked, and then I recognized him—Max, from Orwell, the guy who made supply runs to Omaha and Chicago. "We were waiting for the alert. It never came. When we saw them cutting the fence, we ran for it, but not like it was planned. It was total bedlam. What happened?"

"I don't know, Max," I said, pulling him toward the truck. "No time to figure it out now."

I'd helped Max another few meters when Sylvia stopped and pointed. "I think I know why the drones are corralling us."

I looked and saw what she saw—ten or so agents in black, coming at us in a dead run.

Sylvia dropped the woman she was helping. "Go now!"

"Pick her up!" I ordered.

"Go *now!*"

The agents were no more than thirty meters away with taser pistols drawn, and their aim was better than a drone's. I was convinced.

"Can you make it, Max?" I asked.

He put weight on the wounded leg and grimaced, but nodded through the pain, just like the Max I remembered. I left him limping while I ran to the cab.

Sylvia and Roy were already on the truck by the time I got it started. The agents were closing fast. Max was still a ways back.

"Go, go, *go!*" Sylvia yelled, pounding on the glass. Max was just three steps from the truck and moving slow. The drones hovered, the air vibrating in a chorus of dull humming. The agents stopped, assumed a firing stance, and aimed.

"C'mon, Max," I whispered.

Taser cannons burped a hail of rounds. Reflexes took over and I raised my arms to shield my face. But no tasers came near me, or the truck, or any of the escapees, for that matter.

"What the fuck?" Roy said, just barely audible from inside the cab, but I was thinking the same thing.

We weren't the targets of that taser storm. Ten agents lay twitching on the ground, all of them victims of a drone strike.

We all stared, stunned, like we'd been hit ourselves, until I got my head back and jumped out of the cab. "Give me a hand," I said, and Roy and Sylvia and as many escapees as weren't incapacitated cleaned up the field. We managed to take out forty in all.

❖ ❖ ❖

It turned out that forty was the majority of all the rescues, not just from St. Louis, but Provo and Memphis, too. Just two other teams out of twenty-four brought any escapees out, another thirty in all. And four teams were taken by agents and held in confinement.

"Yeah, I know what happened," Raúl said. Me and the rest of the extraction teams from the other facilities were jacked into Raúl's Fortress of Solitude for the post-mortem. Dylan was there, and Naia. Glum looks were rendered faithfully on every avatar.

"Madeleine," Dylan said. "It was her, wasn't it?"

"The boy's still sharp," Raúl said.

"I sicced the Kliegls on her. You *shredded* her!" I said.

"Yep, I shredded The Eye of Providence," Raúl replied. "Shredded the crap out of her. Ripped her out of the Worldstream root and branch. But *somebody* blocked that alert, and that somebody I traced to the Aletheia. I think it's safe to say that Madeleine's still out there, full Shade, and she's got a crew."

"She's a technical dunce," I said. "Her superpower is persistence, though her crew's got skills. But why did she turn the drones on the agents?"

Raúl gave me narrow eyes and a half-smile. "*She* didn't do that. *I* did. Soon as I saw what was happening, I hacked into the drone supervisor and reprogrammed their targets. Sad to say, by the time I got it done, most of the teams had bugged out. Only the stubborn bastards who can't follow orders stayed behind."

I bit my lip. "I got forty out," I grumbled.

"Whoa, Hammad, I'm not complaining. If it wasn't for St. Louis B Three, Provo Four, and Memphis One, seventy of our friends would still be in stir, strapped and jacked for therapy."

We sat in silence, looking glummer than ever. "What now?" I asked.

"What now, indeed?" Raúl said. "Another raid is out of the question. They'll be watching for it. We can't even be sure that they'll keep our friends in the same facilities. They'll move around like the Queen of Hearts in a game of Find the Lady."

"A game of *what?*" Dylan and I asked in unison.

"Find the Lady. Three-card Monte. You know…oh, never mind. Not important. Let's get back to the safe houses and see to our refugees. Then give me your best ideas. This'll be a tough nut."

67

Freezeout

The Eye of Providence

AFTER NEMESIO TUNNELED into the confinement facility networks, Jayla monitored Raúl's barges into the therapy sessions of the *Vitreous Orb* confinees. That was our clue. As stealthy as Raúl was, he couldn't hide that volume of traffic. And the sheer number of targets gave us the time we needed to implement our defense.

Still, some seventy of the *Vitreous Orb* outlaws were free, still subject to the delusion that so-called *Real Life* was more "real" than a flawless virtual experience. It could've been worse. More than 900 still remained in custody. And if Raúl hadn't turned the drones on the agents, they'd *all* be back in confinement. He wasn't finished. Though I was certain he'd never try another daylight raid, I knew *something* was coming.

As for countermeasures, I was hamstrung.

I was stuck in the Aletheia dorm full-time, no access to my apartment—a Shade has no valid bioscan. Even appearing in public would trigger a *hue and cry*. With no presence in the Worldstream, I was forced to go through intermediaries for everything—labor, supplies, contracts—and if I was going to recover seventy fugitives and put the *Vitreous Orb* in a box for good, I'd need specialized skills. For Cloak and Shade, there was only one place for such transactions.

❖ ❖ ❖

The doorkeeper scanned me with a pocket screen, head to foot, shoulder to shoulder, like a priest blessing the flock. The screen flashed green.

"Welcome to the Cloakroom," he said.

It'd been more than a year, almost two, since I visited this dismal place. The roving Kliegl gangs limited Cloakroom meetings to early morning, after the White Shirts finished their nightly forays and went home for a few hours of sleep before jacking into work venues. Two tables, widely separated, were occupied, two cloaked patrons each. At a third table sat a lone Cloak. I approached.

"I'm called Enzo," he said.

"I am The Eye of Providence, of the Aletheia," I announced.

"That's a Shade greeting, Eye of Providence," the seated figure replied. "Has something changed?"

I sat opposite him, laying my gloved hands on the table. "You know it has."

Enzo uttered a synthesized laugh, a mechanical sound that always vexed me. "It's not a secret, of course. They did a thorough job on you. Totally pro."

"Raúl," I said.

"Indeed!" That annoying laugh again. "I thought he was dead."

"Alive and shredding."

"You're old friends, right? Did he give you a special rate?"

"It wasn't my choice."

He let out a galvanized guffaw. "What in Jah's name did *you* do to *him?* He doesn't shred for free."

Truthfully, I wasn't in the Cloakroom for conversation. A minimum of catching up, of course, after months away, but we'd crossed that line.

"I need personnel."

"Anyone special?"

"Practical experience with stealth protocols, especially methods of barging secure venues undetected."

"Is that all? Just guru-grade hacking skills? Nothing else?"

"It can be more than one head."

A synthesized sardonic sneer. "Oh, well, that's different."

"Can you help me or not?"

"'Fraid not, Eye of Providence of the Aletheia, not with that skill set or any others. Where've you been?"

"What?"

He put his hand under his hood, to scratch his chin, I suppose, or to wipe the wet residue of laughter from his lips. "I was going to ask *you* for help. The Consortium has me tied up, 110% and then some. Not just me, but all the V.O. Crews —*all* of us. You're the *Aletheia*, for fuck's sake. You *have* to be in on it."

"Of course," I said, my synthesizer disguising my ignorance. "That's why I'm asking."

Enzo shook his head, the folds of his hood shifting like a soiled towel being shaken clean. "Well, I got nothing. Nada. Niente."

"Unfortunate," I said. "How have you approached the challenge?"

"Approach? How do you think? Nobody has an approach, not one that'll work. We're fighting kung fu in a box. Can't land a kick without hitting a wall."

"It is a poser," I said.

"Ha. Poser. One way to put it."

"But you have your whole crew on it?"

He leaned forward, as if he wanted no one else in this deserted Cloakroom to hear. "Fact is, we're treading the same ground over and over. I mean, how do you fix a flaw that's coded into the DNA of the Worldstream? Some kind of fucking gene therapy?"

I sat up. "The persona," I said, without thinking, having realized, finally, what Enzo was talking about.

"The *what?*"

"That's what we call it—the persona. Putting a forged key into the Worldstream linked to a false avatar."

"Yeah, that's right. The *persona*, you call it? Never heard that. The Consortium just calls it 'the recursion issue.' It can be fixed, but not without shutting down the entire Worldstream and updating every one of a billion venue servers. That's a lot of momentum, like stopping the Earth. The Consortium has every last Shade looking for a workaround." He leaned back and held out a hand. "But you knew this."

"Of course," I answered, and then it hit me—*the Consortium was freezing me out*. They thought *we* were the source. If they were pulling in every Shade to stop the persona, they could only be focusing vast resources on the Aletheia—on *me*.

"So, no point in talking further," I said, rising. Enzo stood as well.

"That's it? That's all you wanted, personnel?"

"Yes, that's all. In short supply, apparently."

"Just among the V.O. There're still a few independent dorms left. But I doubt you'll find your hacker god among that lot."

I hadn't thought of that; why, I couldn't say. I must have had a lot on my mind. But it was a good suggestion, especially since I had the former leader of one of the most successful independent crews in the pre-Kliegl era: Chrysalis, of the Kaleidoscope.

"That's a thought," I said, and left Enzo standing by the table without saying goodbye.

❖ ❖ ❖

"Right away, Boss."

Jayla shifted from one foot to the other, hands fidgeting, anxious to unleash mental horrors on an unsuspecting victim. Her enthusiasm was as disturbing as ever, exacerbated, no doubt, by the long hiatus in Grace's therapy sessions dictated by other priorities.

"Restraint, Jayla. This isn't torture. It's a psychological probe."

"Yeah, yeah, okay," she replied with palpable disappointment. "What're we probing?"

"I've asked Grace to help track down independent Shade crews. She's not cooperating."

"Since when do we go to indies for heads?"

"Unfortunately, we've lost our normal access to V.O. resources."

She went flat-footed and her hands stilled. "Huh?"

"We need a specific skill set, and the V.O. is fully allocated. We need to go outside."

"What skills?"

"Secure protocols, mostly, and techniques to avoid detection in secure venues."

"You don't have those skills? What about Nemesio? What about *me?*"

"This will be rather high level."

"Oh, *high level.* Duh, stupid ol' me'll get you your genius hackers, maybe, I mean, if I can figure out how to run a therapy venue, duh, duh."

"Stop it, Jayla. Be a professional."

"Duh, per-FESH-uh-nul. Yass, Boss." She staggered out of the room, colliding shoulder-first with the doorframe in a childish pantomime of a cretin.

If I'd thought even for a moment that the Aletheia had the resources to trace the locations of seventy fugitives, all of whom were dead-set on staying undetectable, such optimism evaporated at that moment. Jayla's foolish display, innate cruelty, and infantile fixations were all reasons why she couldn't be relied upon for this task. But it didn't matter. It wasn't important that she succeed in finding skills which, even in the best of times, were rare. That wasn't the point. Grace was not a resource for personnel. She was bait.

68

At the Picture Show

Shade Lucius of the Aletheia

SHE WAS DYLAN'S mom, but I called her Mom, too. It's what she wanted.

I got to spend time with her at the Aletheia, but Dylan hadn't seen her since Orwell. As much as we wanted to round up *all* the *Vitreous Orb*, Dylan would've been happy if he could bust Grace out of the Aletheia dorm and squirrel her off to the Badlands, just Dylan and Grace—and me, I assume. I wanted Grace out, but all the other Orwellians, and the Burgessers, and Laputans, too. I wasn't willing to leave them all behind if that's what it took to rescue Grace.

But we didn't have to face that choice yet. Raúl had a few tricks left.

"Check this."

Raúl, Naia, Dylan, and I were in the Fortress with Porter and Molly, planning next steps. Raúl was the only optimistic one in the venue. That gave me a little bit of hope, since Raúl tends to get that way when he has an idea, just like he gets real cynical and sarcastic when he thinks he's out of options.

"What're we looking at?" Porter asked. He'd ditched his wizard avatar, rendered instead like the sloppy old man he was IRL. Raúl and Molly were in plain clothes, too. We all were. I guess none of us felt like it was a dressy occasion.

"The Aletheia sniffer. Young Hammad told me about it."

It was laid out in front of us like a city map, a patchwork of colored columns like skyscrapers shifting in width and height, as if they were shaking up and down in an earthquake.

"You got in," I said. "The backdoor opened."

"It did indeed."

"Wanna tell me what this is about?" Porter asked, slumped in his chair with his chin in his hands, his beard spraying out in all directions.

Raúl spun the display with a wave of his hand. "The Eye of Providence got a little paranoid toward the end. Imagined leaks and sabotage from her own crew. She put a sniffer in to catch the culprits."

"And I helped," I said.

"Madeleine trusted *you?*" Molly asked.

"Oh, hell no. She didn't trust *anyone*. I snuck into the sniffer from the inside. It had a firewall, but like most it was designed to keep hackers outside, not inside. Then I tapped a pipe I haven't used since Orwell."

"The satellite," Dylan said. "Low-res. Very nice. But the sniffer should've caught even that trickle."

"In the clear, sure. That's why I tunneled through the routing protocol. Let's just say I gave that sniffer a cold."

"Snuck it right past the ol' Eye of Providence," Raúl said approvingly. "But we digress. Back to business. Let me call your attention to this peak right here." He pointed to a small column in the near corner, pulsating red-orange. "The big blocks are the usual *Vita Occulta* traffic—maintenance, contract work, the odd stealth venue. But this is new. Sophie, drill down on this one."

The display expanded, or we got smaller, whichever, and we ended up standing beside a pulsating pillar as big as we were. The surface crawled with a pattern like oversized not-quite-random pixels. I recognized it.

"A therapy venue," I said, "like the ones we barged."

"Correctamundo, Lucius of the Aletheia. Someone is getting the treatment inside the Aletheia dorm."

"Mom," Dylan said, sounding as anxious as I felt. "Shit, they're torturing *Mom*."

"Appears so. This popped up two days ago. Comes twice a day, morning and afternoon."

"Jah," Dylan said. He'd been down since the rescue fiasco but hearing that Grace was strapped in for twice-a-day gut-punching took him to a new low. I thought he was going to cry.

"Dylan, *Dylan*, cheer up," Raúl said. "I can barge this stream the same as the others. You wanna talk to Mom? I can make that happen right now."

"She's in the venue?" Dylan asked, a little excited, like he was pleading for a treat.

"That's what the spike means. But here's what I have in mind."

Raúl gave us the background. He wanted to bust Grace out of the Aletheia (along with Celeste and Thomas, I reminded him). As far as the rest of the *Vitreous Orb*, there wasn't a plan. But the Aletheia dorm wasn't exactly a fortress. Their security came from their obscurity. If you knew where they were (which we did), they were easy pickings. We just needed to give Grace the heads up.

"Yes, please," Dylan said. "Do it. Now."

We all rastered into the therapy venue, unseen by the overseer. Grace sat in the center of the conversation circle, looking confused, until the faces registered.

"Dylan?" she said, but Dylan put a finger to his lips.

"Don't say anything—Mom." He choked when he said *Mom*, like it was a foreign language he had trouble remembering and couldn't pronounce. "We're coming for you."

Grace got it right away, because she sat still and shut up, while the venue played on a separate stage. It was a place like I'd never been, VR or IRL, a darkened room with rows of seats, people scattered about, all staring at a 2D projection, a *movie* they called it, like a cheap form of VR. Why this was significant, I didn't know, but I'd been in enough therapy sessions to know that whatever the venue, there was a kick to the balls hidden in it somewhere.

"Mom, we don't have a plan yet, but we'll come for you soon. Thomas and Celeste, too."

Grace nodded.

"We got some of the *Vitreous Orb* out of confinement, about seventy in all. Max and Benny and others. We've got them in safe houses, forty in St. Louis, twelve in Provo, and eighteen in Memphis."

Grace tilted her head and gave it a shake, just slightly, but Dylan knew what she meant.

"The rest are still in confinement, as far as we know. We don't think we can get to them, not right away."

Grace drew a breath and let it out, dropping her shoulders.

"Sorry, Mom," Dylan said. "Right now, you, Celeste, and Thomas are priorities."

Another tilt and shake.

"No argument, Mom. You're next."

At that moment there was a commotion in the back of the theater. A girl, maybe sixteen or seventeen, stood up, flinging popcorn everywhere, like a snowstorm. She balled her fists and beat on the boy in the next seat, who raised his arms to block the blows. He was laughing, which made the girl angrier. The others in the theater shushed and booed at first, then they all turned around to watch the fight, enjoying it more than the movie, I guess.

She started kicking; he laughed harder, then he grabbed her foot and pulled, knocking her down between the seats. By then the others had taken sides, cheering or jeering depending on who they backed in the fight. The girl got up and walked out of the theater. It was the first good look I got of her—red hair and features that looked like a young Grace, and a little like Dylan.

I was getting into it myself, and felt a little disappointed that the Grace character gave up so easily. Everyone turned back to the movie, taking their time quieting down.

Then young Grace came back into the theater, only this time carrying a pole with a thick, round base, dragging a fat red rope. It was heavy, judging from how she struggled with it, but she was strong enough to raise it over her head and bring it down on the boy from behind, hard enough to split his skull.

A jagged flame flared from the pole, like blue lightning, causing Grace to drop it from her smoking hands.

"They just zapped you, Mom," Dylan said. "Better scream." And she did, convincingly, if a little late. We could only hope whoever was running the session didn't notice.

"We'll be watching, Mom. We'll jump back into the sessions and let you know the plans." Dylan sniffed and wiped his eyes and nose. "Stay strong. We won't be long. Sophie, suspend."

The venue vanished. Grace rastered out. We all sat without looking at Dylan, not saying a word.

"Raúl," Dylan said finally, "let's get her the fuck out of there."

69

Anchor to the Past

The Eye of Providence

AFTER MANY DAYS, I finally got what I wanted from Grace.

"Aw, Boss, just one more session, okay?" Jayla pleaded. "Something with a punch."

I met her in the stealth venue, not because I was remote— I spent all my time in the Aletheia dorm those days. We needed the venue for the map.

"She's been through enough. Let her rest." Jah, the malevolent streak in that woman made me nauseous.

Jayla's ostrich avatar hung its head. She pointed a beak at the sprawling map of the Millennium Republic, the west-central region from Maumee and Mammoth to Shiprock and Salt Lake. "What're we looking at?"

"Our *Vitreous Orb* fugitives, all seventy of them, plus twenty-four others. Catalogued and indexed for us, courtesy of Raúl."

Jayla pointed to the concentrations in St. Louis, Memphis, and Provo. "They're all bunched up."

"All the more convenient for you."

Her head popped up. "For *me?*"

"You'll need to arrange transports and personnel to bring them in."

Jayla rubbed her feathered chin with a wingtip. "I hate that stuff. I'm no good at it. Get Speranza. That's *his* thing."

"I need *you* in charge. You can use Speranza, but watch him closely."

"Jah, you *are* paranoid." She studied the map for another minute. "Seriously, Boss? St. Louis? Memphis? And *Provo*, all the way over in Salt Lake? How in Jahbulon's name do I cover that much territory? And what do I do when I get there? 'Knock, knock, let me in?'"

"Jayla, this isn't like you. You're a can-do person."

"Coding, modeling, hacking, I'll mung on that all day. But *this*—it's operations. What do I know about operations?"

"Enough. You have a job. Do it. We have resources in every district—people, machinery, whatever you need. Use Speranza if you must, but don't trust him. Security is paramount. If Raúl sees you coming, you're lost."

The ostrich narrowed her eyes, and her cartoon beak drew back in a sneer. "No, *you're* lost. This is *your* crusade." She waved a plumed wing at the map. "What's so important about rounding up these guys anyway? Who are they to you?"

"Nothing. They're nothing to me."

"Why, then? Why crank up a convoy of transports to go to the far reaches of the Republic, rounding up a bunch of random nobodies?"

How apt an ostrich avatar seemed at that moment—a hundred-twenty-kilogram bird with a thirty-gram brain.

"Individually, they are insignificant. It's not the *people*, of which there is and will always be an infinite supply. It's the *idea*. They represent an outdated mode of existence."

She scratched her scaly head. "Oh. 'Cause they don't want to live in the Worldstream. And that drives you nuts."

"*No*, it does *not*. But so long as these people are allowed to live IRL, they are an anchor to the past."

"Hey, Boss, news flash: *I* don't live in the Worldstream. *None* of us Aletheians live in the Worldstream. Jah, *you* don't even live in the 'Stream anymore."

I bristled. "That was not my choice, and I resent you even bringing it up. As for the rest of you, the Shade, that is a necessary concession to *maintain* the Worldstream."

"Slave labor. You all ride in the royal barge while we galley slaves pull the oars."

"And *that* was *your* choice."

That quieted her.

"Will you get to work now?" I continued.

She nodded and I suspended the venue.

❖ ❖ ❖

Jayla surprised me. The extraction was well planned and the schedule aggressive. I suspected that Speranza may have contributed, judging from the results, but Jayla wouldn't admit to it. "I did it all by myself," she boasted.

The safe houses were, as expected, isolated and well hidden in the periphery of their respective cities, where houses were sparse. Getting to them would be the easy part, but Jayla had correctly pointed out that persuading the residents to come quietly posed problems. Her solution was typical Jayla. There was nothing subtle or sophisticated about it: surround the house, break down the doors, and tase everything in sight. Overwhelm with superior numbers.

We continued our intelligence gathering, monitoring the clumsy barge by which Raúl and others communicated with Grace. It was the same technique he'd used to convey plans for the facility raids to the confinees—the sessions that Jayla had monitored, learning every detail of the plan. And the intel kept coming. We learned that Raúl, the man who had robbed me of my identity, was at a safe house in St. Louis. I intended to confront him personally.

70

I'll Do It for the Practice

The Eye of Providence

"HANG ONTO YOUR ass, Boss," Jayla shouted over the engine noise. "Road gets a little rough south of Springfield." How it could be any rougher than the stretch from Peoria to Springfield taxed my ability to comprehend, but it was. The suspension on the old gas-powered sedan was less than forgiving.

"Four hours 'til the dawn raid, Boss. We should meet the crew on the launch pad with an hour or so to spare. How're your kidneys doing?"

"How many?"

"Kidneys?"

"Shade."

"Oh. I've got fifteen ready to roll, and two trucks. This is the biggest safe house, so taking no chances."

"Arms?"

"Ten taser rifles and taser pistols for everyone. Heavy ordnance." She was practically salivating. "It'll be hi-res for sure: *One*, bash down the door, *two*, juice everyone, *three*, load 'em up like clear-cut lumber."

"And then?"

"Back in the can, of course. We'll get 'em to the confinement facilities before they come to. Leave 'em at the doorstep, like lost kittens." She reached behind the seat and pulled out a taser pistol, brandishing the weapon in my face. It was an oversized model, big and menacing. "And if any of them start to stir, we'll freeze 'em again."

"Can you put that thing away, please?"

"Wassa matter, Boss? Afraid of a little fifty-thousand-volt tickle?"

"Just…please."

She laid the taser on the seat next to her. "Looking forward to your reunion?"

"With Raúl, you mean. In a way, I am."

"I'll bet." She pushed the pistol toward me. "You want the *coup de grâce?*"

I picked up the pistol. It was lime green, a cheerful hue which belied its power to incapacitate. The color choice was deliberate: just the sight of the neon-green taser was often sufficient to pacify a target.

"I didn't know they were this heavy."

"One-point-four kilograms. Double-capacity gas reservoir, ten-round magazine, two shots per second. If you miss with the first shot, try again. If you *don't* miss, try again."

My own experience being tased was mild compared with descriptions I'd heard of bodies stiffening, toppling, sometimes convulsing. There were incidents of an errant round striking an eye or other vulnerable spots, causing permanent damage, even death. Though none of these possibilities caused me pangs when it came to Raúl, I had no wish to inflict them personally.

"I'll leave it to you," I said, laying down the weapon. "But I want time with Raúl."

We drove in silence for another few minutes.

"You and Raúl," Jayla said. "What's the story?"

"There's no story."

"Boss, there's a *story*. You might not want to tell it, or you might not want to tell it to *me*, but there's a story there, and it's more than just payback for the shredding."

"How much longer?"

"Two and a half, three hours. Jah, we've got some driving ahead. Let's have some stories."

It was still as dark as night gets, no moon, no headlights on the road but our own. Jayla's face, what there was of it visible below her mask, shown dimly in the dashboard glow. The monotonous rumble of the engine, the uneven noise from the road, made for less-than-ideal conditions for a conversation. Still, three hours *was* a long time to travel in silence.

"It was twenty, twenty-three years ago or so. I was in my first position after school, a fresh graduate with a PhD in psychology, still unjaded, still idealistic, believing that a world is saved one troubled soul at a time."

Jayla turned to look at me. I turned to meet her eyes.

"For real?" she said. She turned back to the road. "Jah, what the fuck happened?"

"One young man—Shane was his name. He was referred to me by the Civil Authorities. It was a tragic case—a serial killer. He kidnapped his victims and held them in his house, torturing them over many days."

"Whoa, wait—the *Subterranean Blues* guy?"

"Yes. Five victims, four of whom died."

"He was one twisted fuck. *He* kicked you out of your ivory tower?"

"Look, I was just out of university, almost no clinical experience, and they paired me with a deeply disturbed, fatally damaged individual. I'd studied the symptoms of psychopathy; I'd treated a few patients during my internship, but…" The memory came to me as vividly as if in a venue, the thin, sallow man in front of me, IRL, in a time when VR for therapy was in its earliest experimental phase. His legs were crossed, hands folded over his knee, frail, almost dainty in appearance. We conversed as two strangers might chat sitting side-by-side in a public transport, had it not been for the subject of the conversation. I expected that he would regard his sadistic crimes as inconsequential, or at best justified. Instead, he was remorseful, genuinely, it seemed, determined to understand his affliction and to recover, though he expressed his remorse coolly. The mask of sanity he showed me was no less concealing than a Shade's hood.

"Go on, Boss."

"I thought I could help him, perhaps restore him to sanity, or at least spare him from a lifetime in confinement."

"Seems like a long shot to me. The guy cut up his victims with sewing shears."

"I was *young*," I snapped. "The Civil Authorities I dealt with, all dense, cruel brutes, handed Shane to me because they were *forced* to, not because they shared any hope for him, or had even a speck of concern for him. They certainly didn't share my faith in the science of psychology. They gave Shane to me because the law *required* it. They'd as soon have buried him alive."

"What, for a little 'nip and tuck?' The animals."

"Jayla, please."

"Sorry. Keep going. It's fascinating as hell."

"You wanted to hear."

"I do! No, really, what happened?" she pressed.

"I did the only thing I knew to keep Shane out of the system," I replied.

"Wait—you *shredded* him?"

The seat in the old auto was stiff and unforgiving. I shifted to get away from the tip of a spring working up through the threadbare upholstery. "Once out of the Worldstream, he'd be undetectable. The system would've forgotten him, as they already had, in a way. I could treat him at his own pace."

Jayla stared at the road stretching another two hours ahead. "Wait, didn't you tell me the guy was in confinement? A lifer?"

"Yes. Exactly what I was trying to avoid."

"But if you *shredded* him…"

"*I* didn't shred anybody."

"Oh. Raúl, then. That's the connection."

"If only."

Jayla leaned forward, her chin almost touching the steering wheel, before looking at me sideways. "*Not* Raúl?"

"The shredder was an amateur. She didn't even charge me, said she'd do it '*for the practice*.' She flipped the switch, the hue and cry went forth, and Shane was pulled in by the Civil Authorities."

Jayla snorted. "Boss, what were you *thinking*? That you'd take care of poor, shredded Shane, talk him out of his bloodthirsty lifestyle? Were you going to put him up in your apartment, feed him like a puppy? Jah, that is *so* not The Eye of Providence I know."

"I *wasn't* thinking, not with my head, in any case." I shifted again, the spring still digging into my thigh. "It's a mistake I have not repeated."

"Oh, yeah? Whatever you say, Boss."

"What does that mean?"

"Nothing," she said. "Not a thing. When does this story circle around to Raúl?"

"Tell me what you meant," I pressed.

"Nothing, I told you. It's just that you vector off into high RAM sometimes," Jayla replied.

"If you mean my reaction to stimuli in some cases tends to the extreme, I admit, it's a fault I work hard to manage. But that's not how I make decisions."

"Glad you made that distinction. *Raúl*, Boss. Where does he come in?"

"I never forgot Shane. The decision to shred him was the right one—I had the means to keep him safe and healthy until his therapy was complete. My mistake was in choosing the wrong shredder."

Jayla nodded. "*Now* I get it."

"I confronted the shredder over Shane, demanding that she send me to someone competent. Raúl's was the first name she gave me."

"Only the best."

"So she said. I've never used anyone else since."

"A beautiful friendship. So, why the falling out?"

I twisted in the seat. That damned spring.

"Grace."

"Grace? What about her?"

"She was determined to shred her life. I could see that I was unlikely to stop her, though I did try. But if she was going to go through with it, I didn't want it bungled. I sent her to Raúl."

"Just another gig for Shredder Number One. Why the bad blood?"

"He had feelings for Grace, I suppose. When he found out who wove Grace's lifestream, he took it out on me. He erased the lifestream backup."

"And now…" Jayla trailed off.

"Shredded," I said.

Jayla nudged the taser toward me. "I think *you* should do the honors."

I ran my fingers over the cool composite body of the pistol, then lay my hands in my lap, staring out the windshield. The next two hours passed in silence, with only an occasional soft grunt when that spring found me again.

The first light of dawn reddened the horizon; the two-story farmhouse stood silhouetted against a brightening sky. The transports, identical to the ones we first used to round up the *Vitreous Orb* renegades—what felt like years ago—sat hidden from the house behind a stand of trees, their silver skin catching the morning light like flaring embers. Fifteen of the Aletheia crew stood by, not in Shade robes and hoods, but in close-fitting outfits, all black, like the popular image of ninjas from feudal Japan. Each sported a taser sidearm; ten armed with rifles took the lead. Jayla and I were in the rear. I fingered the taser on my hip with a mixture of apprehension and anticipation.

"Okay, troops," Jayla whispered. "Just like the simulation: Front, side, back doors, and basement entrance. Keep windows in full view. Once the door comes down, they could come out anywhere. Transport drivers, hold back until we bust in. Ready?"

A few nodded. Jayla made her way to the front, motioning for me to follow.

"I'll stay here," I said.

Jayla came back, grabbed my hand with a snort, and dragged me forward.

"Bosses don't hang back. You'll want to get your shot at Raúl before one of these bloodthirsty bastards tases him." I resisted but she wouldn't be deterred. "Don't sweat it, Boss. You'll come in behind the battering ram. They'll be so scared they won't even get up from the breakfast table. Awright, move out," she said, waving the raiding party forward.

The advance scouting party had reported the schedule of activity in the safe house, remarkably consistent day-to-day: The residents, forty-four in all, crammed into eight rooms, began stirring just before dawn. Breakfast was served in shifts, with the last of them finishing just before nine a.m. The first shift was underway as we approached the house.

We walked crouched low, moving in and out of shadows, counting on the dull, black fabric of our outfits to hide our movements.

"Sentries?" I whispered.

"Scouts said no," Jayla replied. "They're counting on remote location and isolation. Security through obscurity."

At ten meters the group fanned out to surround the house. The sun now peeked over the horizon, increasing the risk of exposure, but the risk was brief: The battering ram moved to the front and up the steps to the door. Swinging the massive post, not even counting, two rammers took down the door in one blow.

"That's it!" Jayla shouted. "Inside!" Five black-clad riflemen rushed through the door in a perfectly choreographed move, sweeping the space as they did so.

"Ready, Boss?" Jayla asked, moving up the steps. "C'mon. It's showtime."

I grasped the butt of the pistol and drew it from its holster, bending low behind Jayla. Raúl would be an easy target, I thought, as tall as he was, towering over the others. Jayla's advice, given half in jest, ran through my mind: *If you miss, try again. If you don't miss, try again.* I went through the door.

The bedlam I expected was absent; in fact, except for the raiding party the house was deserted. Baffled ninjas turned in place, looking in all directions, rifles hanging at their sides. We heard no shouts, no scuffles, no blasts from taser pistols, no limp bodies hitting the floor. Once we realized there were no refugees in this refugee safe house, we all lost our tongues, standing mute and confused.

Until we heard the drones.

71

Jonesin' for a Piece

Shade Lucius of the Aletheia

Y'KNOW HOW IT feels when the tables get turned, and they turn your way for a change? Like karma's real and the universe balances out every now and again?

The tumblers lined up and the cosmos clicked when our drones circled the safe house, stopping Madeleine's army at the perimeter. I'd hoped that it'd go down without a fight, but that was too much to expect from The Eye of Providence. Once the bugs took up positions, the rest of us moved out from our hiding places.

"Plan B!" came a shout from the doorway. I recognized Jayla's voice.

Rifle-toting Shade busted out of every door, taking up positions at the corners and sides, kneeling military-style, while the rest fell behind the rifle line and took refuge in the house. They fired the first shot, a rifle round that missed Naia by a centimeter. It would've nailed her in the chest if she hadn't sidestepped the incoming taser like a compressed spring uncoiling.

"God, that was close," she said, landing flat on the ground with her taser drawn. She fired, but the pitiful little pistol barely made it halfway. Even though we outnumbered the Aletheia raiding party three to one, they were packing some mean heat, way outgunning our little self-defense tasers. We might as well have been sporting slingshots against artillery.

I hit the ground next to Naia. "Why aren't the bugs taking them out?" I whispered, like keeping my voice low would somehow protect me.

"No fucking idea," she growled. She put her wrist screen to her mouth. "Attack pattern alpha!" she shouted, but the drones stayed put, holding fire. "Raúl, we're pinned down here! Cue the drones!" she screamed, but nothing came back, not even a sidetone. "Fuck," she muttered, "they're jamming us."

"Now what?" I asked. "Those cannons have twice our range."

Naia stared at the ground for a few seconds. "We can't tell those drones to fire. They'll have to make up their own minds."

I wasn't sure what she meant at first, then I remembered: Bugs know how to fight back.

"Forward," she said, whispering this time. She crawled toward the house, and I followed.

The others were exchanging fire with the Shade, having no better luck than we did. Most hit the ground same as us, some were advancing against superior fire, and a few'd already taken hits. Another couple rounds whizzed past us, centimeters from our ears, with a sharp *pfffft!* that made my stomach spasm. Naia, like always, was cool as well water.

"A few more meters," she said, crawling elbows and knees like an alligator through grass still wet from morning dew.

"I know what you're thinking," I replied. "But won't those drones come after us?"

"At first," she said.

We were crouched behind a rise in the terrain, just meters from the firing line, more rounds sailing overhead. If they'd decided to rush us, we'd have been toast. Instead, they stood their ground, so as not to sacrifice their range advantage, I guessed.

"Ready?" Naia asked. She aimed her taser at the nearest drone. "Brace yourself."

Her shot nicked the rotor. The bug pitched forward, then pivoted and fired. It was as lucky a shot as I'd ever seen from a bug, hitting Naia square in the back. She stiffened and seized up, leaving me out there with no cover. I aimed for another drone but never got off the shot. The Aletheia brigade beat me to it.

One panicked and fired, missing a drone by meters, but it didn't matter. The bug fired back, also missing, and the chain reaction ensued. Rifles all down the line rose and fired, met in turn by a spread of taser fire that leveled all but a couple of Aletheia Shade. That was the signal for the rest of us to rush the house. At close range the rifles were no match for our numbers, spraying rounds like gravel from a spinning tire. The ones that we or the bugs didn't zap laid down their guns and raised hands.

I pulled the taser round out of Naia's back. Blood seeped through her shirt, forming a big, wet, ragged stain. I rolled her over and smacked her cheeks, but she was out like a butchered carcass. By then the refugees were out of the woods and up to the house, covering the prisoners with their little taser pistols, while others held their rifles. Two windowless transports, sleek and silver, rolled out of the trees, Max driving one and Bennie the other. The door to Max's transport slid open and out stepped Raúl, bending low to get through the opening.

"Holy schmoly, what a mess," he said, glancing from one kneeling Shade to the next, hands laced behind their heads, each one guarded by two or more *Vitreous Orb* refugees. One by one Raúl pulled off their balaclavas. "But…where's your boss? Where's The Eye of Providence?"

"Maybe she couldn't make it," I said.

"The intel said The Eye would be here."

"Maybe the intel was wrong."

Raúl shrugged, took one step, then jerked, seized, and dropped like a felled tree. A half-dozen or more taser rounds sailed through the open door and windows, taking down four of our troops and glancing off the transports, forking white sparks like fire. One zipped by my head just before I hit the ground.

In one millisecond what seemed like a mopping-up operation turned into a full-bore firefight. Those of us who had rifles shot wildly, burying rounds in the siding and doorframe. If any of them made it inside the house, we had no idea if they caused casualties. We were a badly uncoordinated force attacking a fixed position. We'd lost our numerical advantage.

"Take cover!" I yelled, but no one was taking orders at that moment, and more of our people fell. Whatever ordnance they were packing was devastating; for such a small number, they laid down a massive spread. Our prisoners took advantage, turning on their guards and taking back their rifles. I was able to zap a couple, but the battle had already turned. I crawled into Max's transport and hauled a couple others in, too.

"What now?" Max asked me, but I didn't have answers. He waited a beat, then put the transport into gear and started down the hill.

"What are you *doing?"* I shouted.

Max stopped and turned to me. "I'll ask again: What now?"

My mind was buzzing like static on an empty channel. My chest heaved and mouth went dry as one, then two, then three more of my fellow *Vitreous Orb* went down, twisting in taser-induced spasms before going stiff. Naia was still down; so was Raúl. Our command structure was in tatters.

"Okay, let's…" I began, ready to order Max out of there, to where, I had no idea, when my eye caught sight of something in the back of the transport—an equipment rack, and a piece of gear I hadn't seen since I left Orwell.

"What?" Max asked, but I held up my hand. I sprinted to the back, grabbed a cable from the front panel of the jamming device, and yanked it free.

The transport's comms panel erupted with frantic cries for help. I ran back up front, almost tripping, and pressed the PTT.

"Attack pattern alpha!" I commanded.

The bugs came to life, their tasers blasting everything standing. Drones sailed through the open windows, electric discharges from errant rounds lighting up the interior like strobes. A few of our own took friendly fire too, but on balance the Aletheia got the worst of it. The fight was over in seconds.

❖ ❖ ❖

"Yeow, that smarts," Raúl moaned, massaging his shoulder. He sat on the porch steps, head hanging. Naia was up by then, though moving slowly, tending to those who were recovering and strapping the Aletheia Shade before they came to.

"Where is she?" Raúl asked.

I was standing on the porch behind him, next to the open door.

"Madeleine, you mean," I said. "Still comatose, her and Jayla both."

He tilted his head left and right, with a *snap* like breaking twigs. "Saved the day again, Hammad. Nice."

I looked over the tased bodies laid out on the lawn like corpses by a mass grave. "Disaster," I groaned.

"Nah," Raúl said. "A few days of down time and they'll be back on their feet. And they'll be out here, not in confinement. That's *your* doing, Hammad. You're a hero."

"I guess," I replied, but I didn't feel heroic. Lucky, maybe.

Benny came through the door. "How's the arm?" he asked Raúl, who gave him a twisted smile.

"I can still hurl some heat if you wanna face me, Slugger."

"I'm long past my sluggin' days, Ace." He squinted at the carnage on the lawn. "How're they doing?"

"Who? Theirs or ours?"

"Just a general question." Benny spat on the porch. "They're coming around inside. One of 'em's asking for you."

Raúl put his hands on his knees and pushed himself to a standing position. "Let me guess."

"Madeleine?" I asked.

"Yup." Bennie pointed a thumb at Raúl. "Jonesin' for a piece o' you."

"Yeah," Raúl said wearily. He rubbed his arm, leaned back and shook his head to get the hair of out of his face. "Better get this over with. Where is she?"

"Dining room."
I started to follow him inside, but he waved me off.
"Better hang back, Hammad. She'll want to face me alone. And that's the way I want it, too."

72

Lost Memory

The Eye of Providence

ARROGANCE SHOWS ON the face—chin raised, eyes that hold yours then drift away; in the voice, sentences punctuated with a falling note, as if to say "the conversation is over," a snort, a sigh; the way one stands, square to the listener, arms crossed. He was arrogant when I first met him more than twenty years ago, and he was arrogant as he walked through the door, the sun highlighting the contour of his face, illuminating stray strands of his waist-length hair like threads of spun silver. Raúl was older, of course, face creased, shoulders stooped, his movements slow, but he still sported the arrogance of a young man, as infuriating as ever.

"How are you feeling?" he asked me, as if he cared, and not, as was the case, attempting to ingratiate himself with an innocuous question. But I could play that game as well.

"Weak, disoriented, sore," I replied in a civil tone. "And you?"

He rubbed his shoulder, where, I assumed, one of our taser rounds struck him, or perhaps it was an errant shot from his drones. "Same. Ever been tased before?"

"Just once," I answered, already weary of this insipid small talk, before demanding, "Tell me who it was."

He crossed his arms. There it was—the gesture of conceit. "You're going to have to be more specific, Madeleine. I can't read your mind—never could."

"Who betrayed me?"

"Don't you trust your own crew? Don't you trust *anyone?*"

"Who was it?"

He pulled out a chair and sat, resting his arms on the table and folding his hands, as if to convince me that we were friends having a casual conversation. "Truth is, Madeleine," he began, very softly, part of his act to pacify me, no doubt, "it wasn't any one person. Lucius was one of ours, but he didn't know the details."

"Was it Jayla?"

"Who's Jayla? Was she the one barking orders?"

"Was it?"

He shook his head. "I don't even know who she is."

"Speranza?"

"Who?"

It wasn't my intention to play a guessing game, but I had to know. "It was Nemesio."

He lowered his head as he opened his hands. "Maddie—"

"Don't call me that!"

He triggered me, the old bastard. His eyes went wide at my outburst. He drew back, hands raised, as if he were surprised—as if to convince me that calling me *Maddie* was unintentional.

"Only one person calls me that," I said quietly, but with an edge, letting him know that he would *not* intimidate me.

"Okay." His hands came down, palms on the table. "Madeleine." He took a breath. "Nobody turned on you. You gave yourself away."

What a pathetic attempt at diversion—a man with no psychological background whatsoever trying in his amateurish way to manipulate *me*. If I did not already despise him, I would pity him.

"Raúl, please. Give me some credit."

He stood up and stretched, the way an old man moves, rotating his shoulder as he spoke. "We didn't know when you'd come. We only knew you would. And I knew you'd come soon. I guessed today would be the day, but that was mostly luck." He cracked his neck, a habit I detested, as much in that shabby room now as I had twenty years before. "We *didn't* know, not in detail. We were prepared; that's all."

"How?" I asked, then bit my tongue, furious with myself for ceding the advantage.

"Maddie—*Madeleine*—you can take apart a human mind and piece it back together, alter its mechanisms, tune it to a different frequency, bend it to your will. You're brilliant. But of course, you know that."

"Is it necessary for you to patronize me?" I snapped.

"I'm not. Really. Game respects game," he replied.

Though I'd hardened myself over the years, Raúl hadn't lost his ability to duck under my guard. *Focus*, I thought, *focus, focus*, again and again, like a mantra, crowding out memories from decades ago.

"But for all your smarts," he continued, "you're *predictable*. The data dump in the therapy stream? You lapped it up. It was obvious, and yet you never smelled a setup, because it was what you wanted to hear."

"You…you *what?* The therapy stream?" I stammered.

"Grace's stream. It was too easy to barge. You should've made it harder to break into your honey pot."

Jaw clenched, eyes burning, I stopped caring if Raúl could sense my anger. "You deceived me."

He smirked. He *smirked*, like a petulant schoolchild, as if he'd put one over on the teacher!

"Deceived?" He went to the door and leaned against the frame, facing outside. "We told you the refugees were here, and here they are. We told you how many—you can count them for yourself. Everything we let slip in the stream about St. Louis, Memphis, Provo—that was 100% accurate. We gave you what you wanted." He turned back, slouching as he jammed his hands in his pockets. "You ate the bait. You put up a good fight, but we reeled you in."

I put my head down, so as not to show my eyes, now shining with tears. "What are you going to do with me? Have me stuffed and mounted? Or will you throw me back?"

He scratched his chin. "I don't know. When I shredded you, I figured you'd be out of commission, but you don't seem to have slowed down."

"Was that necessary?" I asked.

"The shredding? You didn't give us a lot of options, Madeleine, what with you engineering a crime spree, riling up the Kliegl gangs. When you came after the *Vitreous Orb*, we had to go nuclear."

"You don't know what you've done," I said, and I meant it. "All the people you've hurt."

"That *I've* hurt?" He came to the table and leaned on his fists. "*You're* the one with the body count."

"Do you have a family, Raúl? A wife? Children? Brothers and sisters?"

"You know I'm not married. No kids. And I'm an only child."

"Have you ever loved someone?"

His haughty demeanor broke. He straightened up and his eyes went vacant. "Yes," he answered, nodding slowly. Then he shook his head, his hair shifting like the tail of a show horse. "That was a long time ago. What's your point?"

"Was there anything you wouldn't do for someone you loved?" I pressed.

He raised his hands and turned away with a scoff. "Why are we having this conversation?"

It was my turn to stand, though my legs still tingled. "Universal VR existence is inevitable. You may have slowed progress, but you can't stop it. The advantages are simply too great."

"You're kinda jumping around here, Maddie."

I bit my lip. "Maddie. Do you know who calls me Maddie? The *only* person who calls me Maddie?"

He looked at me with renewed conceit, eyes narrow and hard, sunlight glinting off the stubble of his cheeks. Then his eyes darted down. He crossed his arms, but in a self-conscious manner. "Mack," he replied.

"*Mackenzie*. I'm the only one who calls him 'Mack.'"

"I get it," he whispered.

"I don't think you do, not unless you've had someone you love stolen away from you forever."

He smiled, not a smirk, but a rueful smile, eyes drifting up, as if a lost memory had come back. "Trust me, Madeleine, I understand. And I'm sorry."

"Which does precisely nothing for me."

"You're right. You and Mackenzie—that was an unintended consequence. You don't deserve that. Mackenzie certainly doesn't." He sat down, tilting back in his chair. "What if I could fix it?"

73

Time to Clean House

Shade Lucius of the Aletheia

IT WAS LIKE we were together again in that miserable cabin in Orwell—me, Dylan, and Grace, holed up through an Ogallala blizzard, telling stories by the fire.

"Getting in was the easy part," Dylan said. "They were expecting us."

He was older since I last saw him in Orwell. He'd aged in confinement, like we all had, the way time wears you down, but now he didn't look worn out; instead, he was solid, sitting straight, talking in bass notes, making short, simple gestures instead of the wild exaggerations teens make, as if their hands could convince when their words failed.

"Who let you in?" I asked.

"I don't remember his name. Starts with an *F*. Fiddler? Fellatio?"

"Fidelio!" I corrected, laughing—blushing, too, probably, with Grace right there, but when Dylan said *fellatio* she didn't even blink.

"That's it. What's Fidelio's story?"

"Just a cog in the machine," I replied. "Never worries, never complains."

"Right. Anyway, I come to the door and introduce myself: 'I'm called Kieran.' 'What crew?' he asks me, like he doesn't already know. 'Of the Kaleidoscope,' I say. He looks past me, down the alley, checking to see if I have my posse with me. I really do expect him to challenge me, but the door slides open and in I go."

"Alone? Ballsy, my brother."

Dylan smirked in a way that took me back to those fire-lit nights in the cabin, when we hunkered for days at a time, winds howling away, and the only time I got warm was next to Dylan in our little bed.

"Hammad, it was part of the plan. Anyway, I go inside and what do I see in front of me but five Aletheia Shade lined up with firearms, the old-fashioned kind, you know, the ones that'll take your head off. And they all look the same, of course: black cloak, black hood. The only difference is, one's got a rifle, one's got a shotgun, and the other three have pistols, semis with full magazines, a dozen rounds or more. I'm totally outgunned."

"Shit, you're all by yourself. Why the firing squad?"

"Remember? They thought we were coming in numbers. That's what we fed them, right, Mom?"

"In my therapy stream," Grace said, smiling, probably the first time I'd seen her with a sincere, satisfied smile on her face since before the raid on Orwell. "Later, I overheard them, when they weren't being careful, when they fed me, when they strapped me in for the next session, or after, when I was so exhausted they had to take the gear off me like undressing a baby. An army, that's what they expected, because that's what you told me. And whatever you told me, you told them."

"So, there you are, one guy, facing down five Shade packing heat," I prompted. "What was going through your head?"

Dylan grinned. "A *lot*, like, what if they get antsy and start blazing away? Like, am I ever going to see daylight again, or am I doomed to live out my days in an Aletheia hidey-hole? But mostly, I'm thinking, *Jah, I hope we didn't fuck this up*."

Grace patted Dylan's knee. "You didn't."

"Go on," I prompted. "What next?"

"Okay, so Fidelio—Fidelio?—says 'Where are the rest?' 'The rest?' I say. 'What rest? Just me.' Well, I can tell, cloak or no, that he's flummoxed. The infantry even lowered their guns to half-staff. 'Speranza,' he says, 'take a look outside.' So the one with the rifle slides open the peephole and peers one way and the other and says, 'Nothing. All clear.'"

"Wow," I said. "But I don't get one thing: Why'd you make them think you were coming with an army if you weren't? Couldn't you just show up?"

He shook his head. "Yeah, but this way was better. Genius, really. It was Molly's idea. Give them something to fret about, something to prepare for, other than what we really had in mind."

"And it worked."

"Yep. Fidelio says, 'So, what now?' and I say, 'I just stopped by to pick up some friends—Grace, Celeste, and Thomas. Bring 'em up and we'll get out of your hair.'"

"That had to have gone over well."

"First, the one with the shotgun starts laughing—I guess he's laughing. It sounds more like honking. By this time all the others have their guns pointed at the floor, and they join in, honking and bleeping and buzzing, until it sounds like a flock of robot geese taking flight."

"Thought that was pretty funny, did they?"

"For a while, yeah. Then Fidelio stops and tilts his head like he's listening for something. He raises his hand and the others stop one by one, until the only sound is a high-pitched *beep, beep, beep* from a screen on the far wall. 'SYSTEM BREACH,' it says."

"That's when it started being more fun for you than it was for them, I bet."

"They get real serious. 'Speranza, check it out,' Fidelio says, but he doesn't have to. A Shade comes through a door in a trot. 'The engine room's cut off!' he shouts. 'All pipes are down!' 'Switch to backup,' Fidelio says, but the Shade says, 'I just said, *all* the pipes are down—the big pipe, the backups, auxiliaries, even the maintenance channel is blocked!' Well, Fidelio drops his head, looking this way and that, then he looks at me. 'What do you know about this?' he says."

"Bet you were relieved."

"*Mega*-relieved. 'How about we get Grace, Celeste, and Thomas up here?' I tell him, 'Then I'll explain everything.'

Fidelio looks like he might be thinking it over, but the other one with the shotgun, doesn't take it well at all. He pushes the muzzle into my chest. 'How about you talk? Then I'll put this gun away.' Fidelio puts a hand on his arm and says, 'Armengol, take it easy,' but he only pushes harder."

"Wait—*Armengol?* The Aletheia spy Celeste and Thomas told me about? The advance man for the raid on the Summerland?"

"The same. 'So *you're* Armengol,' I say. I'd have taken his head off if not for the 20-gauge making a dent in my breastbone."

"Yeow. Still relieved?"

"A little anxious, I have to admit. But I figure the situation calls for cool. They're the ones with dry mouths, not me. I pull off my hood, and then my mask, so they can see I'm not sweating."

"Great acting."

"It was a stretch. 'Here's the deal,' I say, calm as I can manage. 'Your boss, The Eye of Providence, is being held in a safe house in St. Louis, along with Jayla and her whole Aletheia expeditionary force. St. Louis, Provo, Memphis—we saved 'em all. Meanwhile, remember that hardware sniffer The Eye put on all your pipes? Our mole in the Aletheia opened up a back door and let Raúl in to mung it up. Your whole operation has been islanded, in Chicago and everywhere else.' Well, Armengol the Spy pushes the barrel of that shotgun harder against my chest and bleats, 'Impossible. None of your people got anywhere near the sniffer. Grace was in solitary. Elisha, Bjorg, all of them—access denied. Only a few Aletheia have admin privileges.'"

"How'd you answer?"

"I didn't have to. The rifle guy raises his weapon and puts the barrel right behind Armengol's ear. '*I* have admin privileges,' he says. Fidelio and the others, the ones with pistols, point their guns at the three of us, waving them back and forth like they don't know who to shoot."

"A standoff."

"A *metastable* standoff. One wrong move and the Aletheia motor pool is the scene of carnage. 'Speranza,' Armengol says, 'what'd you do?' 'Just let 'em go,' Speranza says. Well, that shotgun digs harder, Speranza tips Armengol's head over with the rifle, and the pistoleers settle down, one drawing a bead on me, one on Speranza, and Fidelio dithering."

We were leaning in, waiting for Dylan to continue. He looked us in the eye saying nothing, first me, then Grace, just to amp up the tension.

"One thing I'll say for the Aletheia, they listen to reason, at least when Madeleine's not around," he said. "'Look, fellas, do you really want to die in a fire fight today?' I ask. 'Grace, Celeste, Thomas—none of them are bought-in to the Aletheia mission. Time to clean house.' Well, Fidelio puts his hand on the shotgun, pushing it down, and Armengol takes his finger off the trigger. *Then*—Fidelio pulls off his hood. I say *his* hood, 'cause I don't know if he's a his or a hers, but the hood comes off, and he's a *woman*. She's wearing an orange and white mask but there's no mistake. Fidelio's *female*."

"No!" I said, but thinking back, it kind of made sense. He —*she*—was one of the only ones in the Aletheia who showed any sympathy for Grace, right from the time we picked her up from her basement prison—not that only women can be sympathetic, but Grace was targeted in a sexual way that the men seemed less familiar with.

"Yes. She very tenderly pushes Speranza's rifle to one side. 'You'll unlock the pipes, right?' she says. 'Just as soon as we're clear,' I say. 'Go get 'em,' she says to the pistol-packers. 'They never should've come here in the first place.'"

"So now it's you, Fidelio, Speranza, and Armengol."

"Yep. They all have their guns down. The rest of the crew shows up with Thomas, Celeste—and Mom."

Grace touched Dylan on the shoulder, and both of them teared up. I got misty, too.

"Fidelio smiles at me and tips her head, and I glom onto Mom while Thomas and Celeste lay on hands. I'd have stayed in the clinch all day, but a minute later one more Aletheia Shade pops in."

"Nemesio!" I said.

"A.k.a. Adrian," Dylan added.

"I know," I said. "Not a fan."

Grace grimaced. "I hadn't seen him since the Kaleidoscope. I didn't even know it was him until he took off his hood."

"That must've been rough," I said.

"I don't know." She narrowed her eyes and tilted her head. "I was in love with Adrian. When the Kliegls and Civils raided the Summerland, I would've risked being captured to rescue him."

"And now?" I asked. "Do you still have feelings?"

She laughed, a good, deep laugh. "The whole time I was in the Aletheia cellar, he never came to see me—not once. Feelings? Sure. Just not the same feelings I had back in the Kaleidoscope."

"Awkward," Dylan said. "Adrian took a step toward Mom, and she gave him a look I know well—*Just stop right there, young man!* And then it came to me. 'We'll take Nemesio, too,' I said to Fidelio. Well, *that* drew all eyes."

"I thought you'd lost your mind," Grace said.

"Tinged with brilliance," I said.

"Nemesio took back his step and looked side-to-side," Dylan continued. "'Me?' he said. 'Yes. You,' I replied. 'We have a transport waiting on the street. Load 'em up.' Guns rose again, and I wondered if I'd overstepped, but Fidelio came to the rescue. 'Take him,' she said. 'We have no need of his services.'"

"And now he's here in Sangamon, safely outside the perimeter," I said, "where he can do no harm."

"Anyway," Dylan continued, "'Fidelio says, 'Where are you taking them?' and I say, 'Ah, ah, ah, that would be telling.' She asks Speranza, 'You're going, too?' and Speranza says, 'Yeah,' and he pulls off his hood."

"Don't tell me—Speranza's a woman?"

"Nah. Skinny guy with a mustache. Then Speranza says, 'You come, too, Fidelio.' 'Sure,' I say, 'come with us. What's here for you?' Well, Fidelio gets kind of pensive, judging from her eyes. 'The Eye of Providence—she's out of the venue?' I nod, and Fidelio says, 'I'll stay here and keep an eye on things, Speranza. It's a big crew and they'll need some looking after.'"

"So, now Fidelio's in charge of the Aletheia?" I asked.

Dylan shrugged. "I guess. Maybe she is. Or maybe there's a power struggle, or the Aletheia, biggest Shade crew in the *Vita Occulta* breaks up. Anyway, they won't be coming after us anymore."

"So we're safe," Grace said.

"I don't know," Dylan replied. "What about the Consortium?"

"Oh, them," I said. "I have some news about the Consortium."

74

Just One More Thing

Shade Lucius of the Aletheia

"Even this venue is a threat," said Vimala Mallick.

I must confess that I was a little intimidated, even more than I was by Dax. It was Dax who hooked me up with the Consortium. He was so grateful to us for taking out Madeleine (though he'd never admit it) that he brokered the meeting.

Vimala had her whole lineup in a solid blue venue, sitting in a circle with me at the center. Me—Marsha Martin, a teenage girl in overalls, surrounded by the seven most powerful humans on the planet.

"Every time one of your counterfeit avatars enters the Worldstream, a portion of our global computing resources is irretrievably lost."

"No argument," I replied. "But I can fix that."

"We've been unable to find a satisfactory counter to this threat over the course of more than two years. And you are telling us that you have resolved a problem that has confounded the Consortium with all our resources?"

"Nope. But I own the tech. I can use it…" I spread my arms as if to say *see?* "…or *not* use it. The inventor of the persona, Shade Nemesio of the Aletheia, is in our hands. He won't be doing any more damage."

Vimala narrowed her eyes, then turned left and right to her fellow Consortium kingpins. One of them, a thin man with short white hair—Baltasar, the chief of Chain Corp, I later found out—gave her a little shrug.

"We don't even know your true identity," Vimala said. "How can we trust you?"

It was my turn to shrug. "You can't, really. That's the beauty of the persona. But you know who we are. We're real people in the real world living a real life. If we renege on the deal, you can find us any time you want on the plains of Ogallala. You know us. You're the Worldstream Consortium —you know everything."

The seven avatars froze and flattened, the sign that they were discussing the situation privately. After two minutes I got antsy; after ten I got anxious. By twenty minutes I plateaued at a constant level of terror.

After what I judged to be a half hour, the avatars rounded out and unfroze. Every face was grim. They were not a happy Consortium.

"Very well," Vimala said, "we will trust you for the present time. What are your terms?"

"Just let us be. That's all. No more drone attacks, no more raids, no roundups, no more lockups. Release all the *Vitreous Orb* from confinement and let us be real."

The Magnificent Seven flattened out again, just a couple of minutes this time.

"Agreed," she said. "It was never our intention to interfere. That was the obsession of the Minister of Public Health, who, I understand, is in your custody."

"Oh, yeah, about Madeleine. There's just one more thing."

75

Very, Very Real

Shade Lucius of the Aletheia

VIMALA MALLICK AND the rest of the Worldstream moguls were true to their word. All of us—Benny, Max, Jackson— even Frank—all the *Vitreous Orb* from Orwell, Burgess, Laputa, and the rest, not to mention Naia, Dylan, Grace and me—all out of confinement, headed toward the setting sun, like the great westward migration. We traveled by day and rested by night, Dax having given us safe passage, another boon for ridding him of Madeleine. Even the shredded among us raised no alarms.

But Dax, never the one with the most MIPs in the array, hadn't thought about what came next. With Madeleine out of the venue, and free will restored to the people, the Kliegls had to compete for votes like everyone else. Kliegls lost the next election, and the factions formed a coalition that lasted a month before another split, another no-confidence vote, and another election, Dax and his Kliegls just another minor player. They were still squabbling by the time we'd crossed the last perimeter. They might be still.

With *Univirtual* now an unpleasant memory, life outside the Worldstream opened up. We heard that Living Real was the new fashion. IRL bistros, bodegas, and general merchandisers all made comebacks. Max's supply runs were easier than ever. Even the parks perked up.

The Shade still slaved away in service to the Consortium. That wasn't ever going to change.

Thomas and Celeste established a homestead in Burgess. They'd bunked together for so long, first with the Kaleidoscope in the Summerland, and then with the Aletheia, that they felt weird being apart. When Celeste had a baby girl, we knew there was more to it than habit.

Raúl, Porter, and Molly joined us, Porter being the first to suggest retirement, Molly sticking with her common-law husband of fifty years, and Raúl saying "fuck it" and throwing in with the others. They're gone now, of course, along with the older *Vitreous Orb*ers. Frank kicked first from an incurable liver ailment—out in the hinterland there are no organ donors, no facilities, no skilled surgeons to perform a transplant. Heath from Laputa passed in '90, and Jackson in the same year. Naia took over for Jackson but doesn't run things the same way. There's a lot more give-and-take. Orwell has its disputes, like always, but at the end of the day, life is good.

And of course, Dylan and I are still together, like the old days, just me and him and Grace in a drafty cabin on the plains of Ogallala, being very, very real.

76

Brief Interludes

The Eye of Providence

"DID THEY THINK I'd be grateful?"

Mack didn't hear me, or perhaps he ignored me. He hovered cross-legged a meter above the grassy ground, in a clearing surrounded by cartoon trees in crayon colors. He turned his face to the lavender sky, eyes closed, the sun's pure white incandescence illuminating his features in stark relief, his long, pointed nose casting a shadow like the gnomon of a sundial. He smiled.

"Did you hear what I said?"

Mack nodded, his smile spreading, until his lips parted and his crooked teeth showed. "I did hear you, Maddie. There is nothing you say in my presence that I don't hear and remember."

"Are you being facetious?"

He turned away from the sun and looked at me. His smile never wavered. "Of course not, Sister." He uncrossed his legs and stood on the ground as if he were hopping off a stool. "What do you think of the forest?"

"It's colorful," I replied. "What do *you* think? Should I be happy about this situation?"

He bent and massaged his thighs. "Cramps," he said. He hobbled up and wrapped his arms around me, laying his head against my chest, his tousled hair bunched under my chin. "I'm happy. Can't *you* be happy, too?"

I pulled his arms from around my neck and stepped back. His smile faded.

"Everything I've worked for—ruined," I said. "All my hopes for you and…" I caught myself before saying the rest out loud, but Mack finished my thought.

"And others like me. The disabled, the disfigured, the disaffected who don't share your vision; the ignorant, the stubborn, the short-sighted…" He put his hand on my arm. "Sorry. I couldn't resist. I've heard that list so often I know it by heart."

I pulled my arm away, turning my back to my brother—*my brother*, whose brain rebelled against the world, whose mind struggled to breach the barrier of his affliction, the barrier through which *Univirtual* offered a passage to a world—and a life—without limits.

I felt his hand on my back. "Maddie, you've done so much for me, *so* much. Since I was a baby you were my keeper, my teacher, my superhero."

"I wanted everything for you," I said, too softly, I thought, for Mack to hear me. But he did hear.

"Nobody has everything. I don't know that anybody even *wants* everything. *I* don't."

"Oh, you selfish dolt," I said, loudly this time, turning to face him. He stepped back, a startled look on his face. "When I say *you*, I don't mean just *you*. I mean everyone—"

"*Like me*," he said.

"Yes. All the ones you recited from memory, your kind, yes, but *everyone else*, too! Otherwise, what kind of universe would the Worldstream be, if it were not *universal?*"

Mack shook his head, his wild hair rendered as a diaphanous haze. "What I said before, that I don't want everything—not true. I do. But I already have everything that matters. I have my fantasies. I have my friends." He plopped down, looking up at me, his smiling face in my shadow, and spread his hands as if in ecstatic prayer. "And I have you."

"Do you?" I snapped. "Look at me. Am I your sister?"

"Of course you are, Maddie. Always and forever." He closed his eyes, hands still open to the infinite sky, and ascended to the heavens like the Son of God, rising higher than the trees, and the trees narrowed to strings of pure color, vibrating in iridescent hues, the chord resonating in my head, ever louder, until it was too much for me and I suspended the venue.

I pulled off my gear and tossed it on the concrete floor. The scuffed, dingy walls instantly inspired exhaustion after only four months in this greasy subterranean dorm room, average accommodations (I was told) for independent crews. The Aletheia wouldn't have me—I had no tech skills to offer, and Fidelio had already recruited a new non-shredded *Vita Occulta* sponsor. The persona, banned and disabled, was no longer an option for the Shade to negotiate with the uncloaked world. I was condemned forever IRL, occasional venues with Mack my only escape.

Poor Mack. Dear Mack. Sometimes simple, sometimes wise, sometimes endearing, sometimes infuriating, the one constant in my shattered life.

So, this was to be my existence, from now to the grave— shredded by Raúl, banished from the Worldstream, granted only brief, infrequent interludes with my only brother, my avatar rendered as the single persona permitted by the Consortium, one Dean O'Hara, or Lloyd Bouka, or perhaps Myrtle Zachowicz—which one didn't matter, for they all looked the same—a fat, bald, jowly man with a ridiculous mustache.

Raúl must have thought that hilarious.

If you enjoyed *Univirtual*, please leave reviews on
Amazon and Goodreads.

Also by Charles O'Donnell

The Girlfriend Experience (Matt Bugatti #1)
Moment of Conception (Matt Bugatti #2)
Shredded: A Dystopian Novel (Shredded #1)
Shade (Shredded #2)

About the Author

Charles O'Donnell writes thrillers with high-tech themes in international and futuristic settings. His works include *The Girlfriend Experience,* an espionage thriller and the first book in the Matt Bugatti series; *Moment of Conception (Matt Bugatti #2),* a political and medical thriller; *Shredded: A Dystopian Novel,* and *Shade (Shredded #2),* cautionary tales about the potential for technology to either augment reality or to replace it entirely, and about the erosion of privacy in a world in which everything is shared online, and nobody reads the terms and conditions. His short stories have also appeared in *The Esthetic Apostle*, *Dreamers Creative Writing, Dark Ink Anthology, The Scriblerus, Lost & Found: An Anthology*, and most recently in the Ohio Writers Association anthology *Metamorphosis*.

Charles lives with Helen, his wife and life partner in Westerville, Ohio.

Acknowledgements

I'll keep this short.

Univirtual is book three of the *Shredded* series. I released the first book, *Shredded*, in 2017, and the second book, *Shade*, in 2018. I began the third book, *Univirtual*, immediately after *Shade*. What should've taken me six months instead consumed four years. Wait, that's not the whole story—I wrote *two* books in that stretch, this one, and a young adult fantasy, *Recollection*, which I'm currently querying to agents. Still, they took me way too long, and for that I blame myself.

And COVID. Seriously, is anyone writing acknowledgements for recent books without mentioning the pandemic?

In my newsletter I wrote about the paradox of abundance, the phenomenon that nobody values what they have an unlimited supply of. Before I retired, I valued the lunch hours, evenings, and weekends when I wrote, and made the most of them. Even after retirement, I stayed productive between other projects and chores. But COVID sapped me —the fear, the precautions, the isolation. Motivation evaporated. My word output went subterranean. If I didn't get any words made today, I figured, there was always tomorrow, and an endless progression of idle tomorrows after that.

But enough whining.

I kept up with some of my writing groups, dropped out of others, and founded one of my own. All of them have been helpful, and their participants, many of whom gave me notes on *Univirtual,* are too numerous to list here. Instead, I'll limit my shout-outs to my wife, Helen, whose support is the solid foundation on which my work rests, and my editor, Rebekah, who keeps me honest to myself and my craft. Thanks, ladies.

Finally, this is the fourth cover from my designer, Jun Ares, and the best so far. Jun, you bashed a tater with this one.

There. I told you it would be short.

Charles O'Donnell
November 19, 2022

www.ingramcontent.com/pod-product-compliance
Lightning Source LLC
Chambersburg PA
CBHW070235200726
48293CB00005B/1625